transcendent
Destiny's Children: Book 3

STEPHEN BAXTER

Copyright © Stephen Baxter 2005
All rights reserved

The right of Stephen Baxter to be identified as the author
of this work has been asserted by him in accordance
with the Copyright, Designs and Patents Act 1988.

First published in Great Britain in 2005 by
Gollancz
An imprint of the Orion Publishing Group
Orion House, 5 Upper St Martin's Lane, London WC2H 9EA

This edition published in Great Britain in 2006 by Gollancz

1 3 5 7 9 10 8 6 4 2

A CIP catalogue record for this book is available
from the British Library

ISBN 13 9 780 57507 814 7
ISBN 10 0 57507 814 6

Typeset by Deltatype Ltd, Birkenhead, Wirral
Printed in Great Britain by
Mackays of Chatham plc, Chatham, Kent

www.orionbooks.co.uk

The Orion Publishing Group's policy is to use papers that are
natural, renewable and recyclable products and made from
wood grown in sustainable forests. The logging and
manufacturing processes are expected to conform to the
environmental regulations of the country of origin.

For Sir Arthur C. Clarke

One

Chapter 1

The girl from the future told me that the sky is full of dying worlds.

You can spot them from far off, if you know what you're looking for. When a star gets old it heats up, and its planets' oceans evaporate, and you can see the clouds of hydrogen and oxygen, slowly dispersing. Dying worlds cloaked in the remains of their oceans, hanging in the Galaxy's spiral arms like rotten fruit: this is what people will find, when they move out from the Earth in the future. Ruins, museums, mausoleums.

How strange. How wistful.

My name is Michael Poole.

I have come home to Florida. Although not to my mother's house, which is in increasing peril of slipping into the sea.

I live in a small apartment in Miami. I like having people around, the sound of voices. Sometimes I miss the roar of traffic, the sharp scrapings of planes across the sky, the sounds of my past. But the laughter of children makes up for that.

The water continues to rise. There is a lot of misery in Florida, a lot of displacement. I understand that. But I kind of like the water, the gentle disintegration of the state into an archipelago. The slow rise, different every day, every week, reminds me that nothing stays the same, that the future is coming whether we like it or not.

The future, and the past, began to complicate my life in the spring of 2047, when I got an irate call from my older brother, John. He was here, in our Miami Beach house. I should 'come home', as he put it, to help him 'sort out Mom'. I went, of course. In 2047 I was fifty-two years old.

I had been happy in Florida, my parents' house, when I was a kid. Of course I had my nose in a book or a game most of the time, or I played at being an 'engineer', endlessly tinkering with my bike or my in-line roller skates. I was barely aware of the world outside my own head. Maybe that's still true.

But I particularly loved the beach out back of the house. You understand this was the 1990s or early 2000s, when there still *was* a beach in that part of Florida. I remember I would walk from our porch with its big roof-mounted swing chairs, and go down the gravel path to the low dunes, and then on to the sandy beach beyond. Sitting there you could watch space shuttles and other marvels of rocketry from Cape Canaveral, rising into the sky like ascending souls.

Mostly I'd watch those launches alone. I was out of step with my family over that one. But once, I believe around 2005, my Uncle George, my mother's brother visiting from England, walked out with me to watch a night launch. He seemed so stiff and old, barely able to make it down to sit on the scrubby dune grass. But I guess he was only in his forties then. George was an engineer, of sorts, in information technology, and so a kindred spirit.

Of course that's all gone now, the venerable Moon-shot launch pads abandoned, thanks to the Warming, the rising sea levels, the endless Atlantic storms; Canaveral is a theme park behind a sea wall. I guess I was lucky to be ten years old and able to watch such things. It was like the future folding down into the present.

I wonder what ten-year-old Michael Poole would have thought if he could have known what the girl from the future told me, about all those old and dying worlds out there waiting for us in space.

And I wonder what he would have thought about the Transcendence.

I think over those strange events, my contact with the Transcendence, one way or another, all the time. It's like an addiction, something you're aware of constantly, bubbling beneath the surface level of your mind, no matter how you try to distract yourself.

4

And yet I can remember so little of it. It's like chasing a dream after waking; the more you focus on it, the more it melts away.

Here's what I make of it now.

The Transcendence is our future – or a future, anyhow. A far future. The Transcendents had made (or will make) themselves into something unimaginably powerful. And now they were on the cusp, the cusp of a step change into something new altogether. After this point they would transcend to what we would think of as godhood – or they would subside to defeat, at the hands of a foe I barely glimpsed. Either way they would no longer be human.

But at this point, on this side of the cusp, they were still human. And they were tortured by a very human regret, a regret that had to be resolved now, before they shed their humanity for good. This was what I was drawn into, this strange inner conflict.

Everybody knows about my work on the climate disaster. Nobody knows about my involvement in something much larger: the agonies of a nascent superhuman mind of the far future, the culminating logic of all our destinies.

The future folding down into the present. That ten-year-old on the beach would probably have loved it, if he'd known. It still scares me to death in retrospect, even now.

But I guess even then I had my mind on other things. For the most remarkable thing I saw on that beach wasn't a spaceship being launched.

The woman who sometimes came to the beach was slim and tall, with long, strawberry-blonde hair. She would wave and smile to me, and sometimes call, though I could never make out what she said for the noise of the waves and the gulls. She always seemed to stand at the edge of the sea, and the sun was always low, so the sea was dappled with sunlight like burning oil, and I had to squint to make her out – or she would show up in some other equally difficult place, hidden by the light.

When I was a kid she visited occasionally, not regularly, maybe once a month. I was never frightened of her. She always seemed friendly. Sometimes when she called I would wave back, or yell, but the crashing waves were always too loud. I would run after her, but running in soft wet sand is hard work even when you're ten. I never seemed to get any closer, no matter how hard I ran. And she would shrug, and step back, and if I looked away she was gone.

It was only much later that I worked out who she was, how important she would become to me.

Uncle George never saw her, not during his one and only viewing of a spaceship launch from the beach. I wish he had. I'd have appreciated talking it over with him. I didn't know much about ghosts when I was ten; I know only a little more now. George knew a lot of things, and he had an open mind. Maybe he could have answered a simple question: can you be haunted by spirits, not from the past, but from the future?

For, you see, the mysterious woman on the beach, who visited me intermittently all my young life, was my first visitor from the future. She was Morag, my dead wife.

The future folding down into the present.

Chapter 2

The girl from the future was called Alia.

She was born on a starship, fifteen thousand light years from Earth. She lived half a million years after Michael Poole died. And yet she grew up knowing Poole as intimately as any of his family.

She had Witnessed his life almost since her mother and father had first brought her home from the birthing pods, when her hands and feet could grasp nothing but the fur on her mother's chest, and the world was an undifferentiated place of bright glowing shapes and smiling faces. Michael Poole had been there for her even then, right from the beginning.

But she was thirty-five years old now, almost old enough to be considered an adult. Michael Poole was a relic from childhood, his little life like a favourite story she listened to over and over. She would always turn to him when she needed comfort. But he was a small, sentimental part of her world, his story tucked away in the Witnessing tank, unconsidered for days on end.

What really mattered to Alia nowadays was Skimming.

She met her sister in the Engine Room, the deepest bowel of the *Nord*, where hulking, anonymous machinery loomed in steel-grey light. The sisters faced each other, and laughed at the delicious prospect of what was to come.

Like Alia, Drea was naked, the best way to Skim. Drea's body, coated with golden hair, was neatly proportioned, with her arms only a little shorter than her legs, and she had long toes, not as long as her fingers but capable of grasping and manipulation. It was a body built for zero gravity, of course, and for hard vacuum, the natural environment of mankind, but it was believed that this body plan was pretty much the same as that of the original human stock of old Earth. Drea was ten years older than Alia. The sisters were very alike, but there was more gravity to Drea, a little more levity to Alia. As the light shifted multiple lids slid across Drea's eyes.

Drea leaned close, and Alia could smell the sweetness of her breath. 'Ready?'

'Ready.'

Drea grasped Alia's hands. 'Three, two, one—'

Suddenly they were in the *Nord*'s Farm deck.

This was a high, misty hall, where immense ducts and pipes snaked down through the ceiling, lamps shed a cool blue-white glow, and green plants burgeoned in clear-walled hydroponic tanks. The *Nord* was a starship, a closed ecology. The big pipes delivered sewage and stale air from the human levels above, and carried back food, air and clean water.

Alia breathed deep. After the cold, static austerity of the Engine Room she was suddenly immersed in the Farm's vibrant warmth, and the deck plates thrummed in response to the huge volumes of liquid and air being pumped to and fro. Even the quality of the gravity felt subtly different here. Alia had felt nothing of the Skimming: no time passed during a Skim, so there was no time for sensation. But the transition itself was delicious, a rush of newness, like plunging from cold air into a hot pool.

And this was just the start.

Drea's eyes were bright. 'Jump this time. Three, two, one—' Flexing their long toes the sisters sailed up into the air, and at the apex of their coordinated leap they popped out of existence.

On the sisters fled, to all the *Nord*'s many decks, shimmering into existence in parks, schools, museums, gymnasiums, theatres. In each place they stayed only a few seconds, just long enough to lock eyes, agree the next move, and jump or pirouette or somersault into it. It was really a kind of dance, the challenge being to control the accuracy of each Skim and the mirror-image precision of their positions and movements at each emergence.

Skimming, voluntary teleporting, was so easy small children learned to do it long before they walked. Alia's body

8

was made up of atoms bound into molecules, of fields of electricity and quantum uncertainty. Alia's body was *her*. But one atom of carbon, say, was identical to another – absolutely identical in its quantum description – and so it could be replaced without her even knowing. She was just an expression of a temporary assemblage of matter and energy, as music is an expression of its score regardless of the medium in which it is written. It made no difference to *her*.

And once you knew that, it was easy to see that she, Alia, could just as easily be expressed by a heap of atoms over *there* as one over *here*. It was just a question of will, really, of choice, along with a little help from the nanomachines in her bones and blood. And very little Alia willed was denied her.

Most children Skimmed as soon as they found out they could. Adults found it harder, or gave it up as they gave up running and climbing. But few of any age Skimmed as skilfully as Alia and Drea. As the sisters passed, scattering startled birds, young people watched them with envy, and older folk smiled indulgently, trying to mask their regret that they could never dance so gracefully again.

And at each step, in the instant after the girls had vanished, two clouds of silvery dust could be seen suspended in the air, pale and transparent, still showing the forms of the two sisters. But in the ship's artificial breezes these chimeras of abandoned matter quickly dispersed.

In one last mighty Skim the girls leapt all the way out of the *Nord* itself.

Alia felt the tautness of the vacuum in her chest, the sting of hard radiation on her face as delicious as a shower of ice water on bare skin. With her lungs locked tight, and the Mist of biomolecules and nanomachinery that suffused her body eagerly scouring for damage, she was in no danger.

There were stars all around the sisters, above, below, to all sides; they were suspended in three-dimensional space. In one direction a harder, richer light came pushing through the thick veil of stars. That was the Core, the centre of the Galaxy. The *Nord* was some fifteen thousand light years from the centre, about half the distance of Sol, Earth's sun. Only ragged clouds of dust and gas lay before that bulging mass of light, and if you looked carefully you could make out shadows a thousand light years long.

Alia looked down at the *Nord*, her home.

The ship beneath her feet was a complex sculpture of ice and metal and ceramic, turning slowly in pale Galaxy light. You could just make out the vessel's original design, a fat torus about a kilometre across. But that basic frame had been built on, gouged into, spun out, until its lines were masked by a forest of dish antennae, manipulator arms and peering sensor pods. A cloud of semi-autonomous dwellings, glowing green and blue, swam languidly around the ship: they were the homes of the rich and powerful, trailing the *Nord* like a school of fish.

Their hands locked, the sisters spun slowly around each other, their residual momentum expressing itself as a slow orbit. Complex starlight played on Drea's smiling face, but her eyes were masked by the multiple membranes that slid protectively over their moist surfaces. Alia savoured the moment. When they were younger the sisters had been the most important people on the *Nord* for each other. But Alia was growing up. This was a cusp of her life, a time of change – and the thought that there might not be too many more moments like this made it all the sweeter.

But Alia was distracted by a gentle voice, a whisper in her ear.

Her mother was calling her. *Come home. You have a visitor...*

A visitor? Alia frowned. Who would visit *her* that could be important enough for her mother to call? None of her friends; any of them could wait. But there had been a gravity about her mother's tone. Something had changed, Alia thought, even as she had danced through the *Nord*. Drea clung to Alia's hands. Drea's expression was complex, concerned. She knew something, Alia realised. Alia felt a surge of love for this sister, companion of her childhood. But there was suddenly a subtle barrier between them.

They swam towards each other, and they Skimmed one last time. Like a clash of cymbals their bodies overlapped, the atoms and electrons, fields and quantum blurrings blending. Of course this merging was frowned on; it was a dangerous stunt. But for Alia it was delicious to be immersed in her sister's essence, to become heavy with her, everything about the two of them joined into a single cloudy mass, everything but some relic trace of separateness in their souls. It was closer even than sex.

But it only lasted a second. With a gasp they Skimmed apart, and drifted side by side. And with that moment of oceanic closeness over, Alia's niggling worry returned.

Let's go home, Drea said.

The sisters spiralled down towards the *Nord*'s bright, complicated lights.

Chapter 3

When I flew into Miami, in response to my brother's call, all I seemed to see from the air was water. It was everywhere, the encroaching sea at the coast, and shining ribbons inland that sliced the landscape to pieces. Much of the downtown was protected, of course, but outlying districts, even just blocks away, were flooded. I was mildly shocked.

But the place still worked. Impressive causeways linked up the islands, and I saw pod buses in chains like shining beads, navigating around the new archipelago much as in my childhood you could drive down the Keys from Largo to West.

A dutiful if reluctant son, I was returning to Florida. I hadn't been back here for, shame to say it, over ten years. That's a long time these days. It's a changing world, and over such an interval change heaps up like a head of water behind a sandbank, and then bursts over you.

Out of the airport, I took a pod bus down to Calle Ocho, 8th Street, and then a ferry. It was a smart, agile air boat, not much more than a sheet of plastic driven by an immense fan. My pilot was a girl, maybe twenty, with not a word of English. She made that little boat skim like a skateboard; it was a fun ride.

We headed into Little Havana. We squirmed through swarms of boats and yachts. There were people on jet-skis and old Everglades swamp buggies and even battered tourist pedalos, many of them laden with stuff. Along Calle Ocho the boats and junks had been ganged together to make huge, ragtag floating markets: there were cafés and *tabaqueros*, and floating stores selling cheap clothes, even bridal wear. Bugs and flies rose everywhere, great clouds of them, far more than I remembered from my childhood. But there were still old men playing dominoes in the Maximo Gomez Park, and in Memorial Boulevard, heavily sandbagged, the Eternal Torch still burned in honour of the Bay of Pigs counter-revolutionaries. All this took place at the feet of the old buildings, many of which were still occupied, in their higher floors anyhow. The ageing building stock gleamed silver, coated in smart Paint, as if they had been wrapped in foil. Beneath the tide marks you could see how the water was working away at the stone and the concrete. Barnacles on skyscrapers, for God's sake. In places there were cleared-out swathes, great lanes of rubble over which kids and scavengers swarmed. The tracks of hurricanes, probably, gaps in the urban landscape that would never be filled in. A coast is a place of erosion, Uncle George used to say to me, a place where two inimical elements, the land and the sea, war it out relentlessly, and in the end the sea is always going to win. One day all these grand old buildings were going to just subside into the ocean, their contents spilling into great mounds of garbage in the patient water.

In the meantime, life went on. My pilot waved at rivals or friends, cheerfully yelling what sounded like obscenities. Everybody had some place to go, just like always. Despite the dirty water everywhere it was still the Little Havana I remembered, a place I had always found exciting.

When we reached the coast I had the boat drop me at a small ferry stop a couple of kilometres from my mother's house. I had decided to walk the rest of the way, my pack on my back.

It was the middle of the afternoon. The road, a north-west drag following the line of the coast, was good enough and had been resurfaced recently with a bright central stripe of self-maintaining silvertop. But you could see that the sea sometimes came up this far: there were bits of dried-up seaweed in the gutters, tide marks around the bases of the telegraph poles. The housing stock had changed from my memory. The timber-frame houses I remembered, each nestling in its half-acre of lawn, were mostly abandoned, boarded up and in various states of decay, or they had gone altogether, leaving vacant lots behind, as if they had been spirited up into the sky. A few had been replaced by squat poured-concrete blocks with narrow windows: the modern style, fortresses against hurricanes, each an integral block, seamless from its roof to its deep foundations. There wasn't a single car to be seen, not one, and the silence in which I walked was dense. That was another jarring discontinuity with my memories of childhood: on a comparable Tuesday afternoon in 2005, say, the cars would have been purring past, an endless flow.

The air was bright and hazy, and the wet heat settled on me like a blanket. I was soon sweating, and regretting my decision to walk. There was an unpleasant smell in the air too, a stink of salty decay, as if some immense sea animal was rotting on the beach. But it couldn't be that, of course; there were no animals in the sea.

At last I bore down on my mother's house, my childhood home. It was one of the few of the old stock still standing. But it was surrounded by heaps of sandbags, all slowly decaying. Big electric screens shimmered around the yard, designed to keep the mosquitoes at bay, and on the roof a wagon-wheel home turbine languidly turned, barely stirred by the breeze.

And here came my big brother, around the corner of the house, large as life, paint brush in hand. 'Michael! So you showed your face.' Instant criticism, but what could you expect? John wiped his palm ostentatiously on his coveralls, leaving a silvery streak, and held his big hand out to shake mine.

I shook back, cautiously. John is a big man, built like a football player. He always towered over me. A couple of years older than me, he's balding, and his brown eyes are hard, set in a broad face. My features come from my mother's side, but where she was always tall, pretty, with grey eyes like smoke, I'm small, round-shouldered, dark. Intense, people sometimes say. I'm more like my Uncle George, in fact. My mother always said I reminded her of England. I got her grey eyes, though, which looked good in the fleeting years when I was almost handsome.

John takes after our father. As always, he intimidated me.

'I flew in,' I said lamely. 'Quite a journey these days.'

'Isn't it just? Kind of hot, too. Not good weather to work.' He clapped me on the back, spreading more Paint and sweat over my shirt, thus messing up my laundry *and* my conscience. He led me round back of the house. 'Mom's indoors. Making lemonade, I think. Though it's sometimes hard to tell exactly what she's doing,' he said with conspiratorial gloom. 'Say hello to the kids. Sven? Claudia?'

They came running around the side of the house. They'd being playing soccer in the yard; their ball rolled plaintively along the ground after them, chiming softly for attention. They faced me and smiled, their eyes blank. 'Uncle Michael, hi.' 'Hello.'

Sven and Claudia, in their early teens, were tall, handsome, well-fed kids with matching shocks of blond hair. They were the products of John's marriage to a German called Inge, now ended by divorce. They had their mother's colouring, though both had something of their father's heavy-set massiveness. I always thought they looked like Cro Magnon hunters.

For a couple of minutes I tried to make small talk with the kids about soccer. It turned out Claudia was the keenest, and even had a trial lined up for her local pro club. But as usual the talk was strained, polite, a formality, as if I was a school inspector.

We were all wary. I'd committed a faux pas a couple of Christmases back when I'd sent them packages addressed to Sven and Claudia *Poole*. After my parents' divorce my mother had taken to using her maiden name, as had I. But when he left home John switched back to my father's name, Bazalget – I'd never known why, some row with my mother - and so these two were officially Bazalgets. John had a way of blowing up at me about such things at family occasions, spoiling the day and upsetting everybody.

I'd learned to tread carefully. We are an unusual family. Then again, maybe not.

I remembered how, when Uncle George had come visiting, I would go running to him. But then George always brought us gifts. Smart man. Of course it wasn't my insensitivity as an uncle that made these kids so bland. They were Happy kids, and this was the way Happy kids turned out. I'd never even dared challenge John about his choices over *that*.

John waggled his paintbrush. 'I ought to get on. And you ought to go see Mom,' he said, as if I'd been putting it off.

So I walked back round the front of the house, picked up my bag, and knocked on the door.

The front door was faded by the relentless sun, and in places the clapboards were peeling back, the nails rusting and coming loose. The place wasn't in bad shape, however. The coat of Paint which John was busily applying was a silvery scraping over layers of creamy old gloss.

My mother opened the screen door. 'It's you,' she said. She stepped back, holding the door to let me pass, with eyes averted to the floor. I stepped over rotting sandbags and dutifully delivered the kiss she expected; her skin was crumpled, leathery, warm as melted butter.

She said she would make me a cup of tea, and she led me through the hall. We passed the old grandfather clock that had come with her from England. It still ticked away with imperial resolve, even though the world in which it had been manufactured had all but vanished.

My mother was a stick-thin figure, upright and stiff and animated by a fragile sort of energy. She was still beautiful, if any ninety-year-old can be said to be beautiful. She had never dyed her hair, and it had slowly faded to white, but even now, tied back, her hair looked lustrous, soft and full of light.

In the kitchen she had ingredients for fresh lemonade laid out over the working surfaces. She made me tea, hot and strong and laced with milk, English style, and she sat with me at the breakfast table. We sipped our tea in cautious silence. I enjoyed the tea, of course, though I rarely drank it myself; it brought back my childhood.

I hadn't neglected my mother. But I'd mostly seen her when she'd made her occasional, loudly self-sacrificing pilgrimages to come visit me in my home with Morag, or later after Morag's death in my small apartment in New Jersey, or at holiday times at John's brownstone apartment behind the Manhattan sea walls. But those trips had got more rare as the years passed; mother would say she wasn't sure if it was her getting old, or the world, or both.

She opened hostilities. 'I suppose John called you in.'

'He was concerned.'

'You didn't need to come here,' she sniffed. 'Either of you. I'm ninety. But I'm not *old*. I'm not helpless. I'm not gaga. And I'm *not* moving out.'

I pulled a face. 'You always did get straight to the point, Mom.'

She was neither annoyed nor flattered, and she wasn't about to be deflected. 'You can explain that to your brother. He's just like your father. And there's nothing wrong with this house.'

'Needs a coat of Paint, though. You'll be able to make back the cost by selling solar power to the microgrid. And you have to comply with the sentience laws; a house of this age needs a minimal IQ-equivalent of—'

'I know the damn laws,' she snapped. 'Just so we understand each other. *I'm not moving out.*'

I spread my hands. 'Fine by me.'

She leaned forward and inspected me. I stared right back. Her face was hard, all nose and cheekbones and sunken mouth. It was as if everything else had melted away but this inner core, leaving nothing but her one dominant central characteristic.

But what was that character? Energy, yes, determination, but all fuelled by a kind of resentment, I thought. She'd come out of England, heavily resenting her own flawed family and whatever had happened to her there. She certainly resented my dad, and the way their marriage had broken down, and even the fact that he had died leaving her with various complications to sort out, not least her two sons. She resented the slow drift of the climate, which had left her under pressure here in the family home in which she had hoped to die. She was one against the world, in her head.

Her eyes, though, her beautiful eyes belied the harshness of her expression. They were clear and still that startling pale grey. And they revealed a surprising vulnerability. My mother had built a kind of shell around herself all her life, but her eyes were a crack in that shell, letting me see inside.

Not that she was about to let up on me. 'Look at you.

17

You're round-shouldered, your hair's a mess, you're over-weight. You look like shit.'

I had to laugh. 'Thanks, Mom.'

'I know what's wrong with you,' she said. 'You're still moping.' That was the only word she ever used to mean grief. 'It's been, what, seventeen years? Morag died, and your baby son died, and it was terrible. But it was all those years ago. It wasn't the end of your life. How's Tom? How old is he now?'

'Twenty-five. He's in Siberia, working on a genetic sampling of—'

'Siberia!' She laughed. 'Could he get any further away? You see, by mourning your dead son, you've pushed away the living.'

I stood up, shoving back my chair. 'And your amateur psychoanalysis is a crock, as it always was, Mom.'

She closed her eyes for a moment. 'All right, all right. Your old room is made up for you.'

'Thanks.'

'You might fill a few sandbags. The tide's out.' She pointed to the cupboard where she stored empty sacks.

'OK.'

'It isn't so bad here. Even now. We still have doctors and dentists and police. So-Be isn't a ghost town yet, Michael.' She said absently, 'Not to say we haven't had our problems. You know what the most awful thing was that happened here? In one place the water table rose so high a cemetery broke open. Boxes and bones just came bubbling out of the ground. It was the most grotesque thing you ever saw. They had to bulldoze it all out of sight. And I miss the birdsong. Everywhere you go the birds seem to be missing.'

I shrugged. Birds were bellwethers of the Die-back. In 2047, their vanishing was banal. I said carefully, 'Mom, maybe you should think about moving away.'

She eyed me with a bit of humour in her expression. 'You're claiming it's any better anywhere else?'

'Not really, no.'

'Then stop wasting time.' She sipped her tea, dismissing me.

*

18

My old room was small, but it looked out to sea, and I'd always loved it.

Of course it wasn't really mine any more, and yet there had never been a precise date when it had ceased to be mine. I just slept in here less and less frequently, and at some point my parents had had to make decisions about sorting it out without consulting me.

Well, they had stripped it. Now, replacing my turn-of-the-century gadget-age décor, it was done out in the faux-naturalistic style that had been so popular in the 2020s, with a bamboo-effect wall covering and a green carpet of soft-bladed artificial grass. In those days, before I had started to work on the commercial development of Higgs energy, I was a consulting engineer for the nuclear-energy industry, and I had stayed in a *lot* of hotels. This style of decoration had been everywhere, endless lengths of tropical-parrot wallpaper and crocodile-skin-effect floor covering, adorning anonymous concrete blocks in Warsaw or Vancouver or Sydney. It was as if we were mourning the loss of the green stuff, even while the real thing was imploding into the Die-back all around us.

I dumped my bag on the bed and opened the wall cupboards, looking for somewhere to hang my few shirts. But the cupboards were piled high, mostly with my mother's clothing. The materials felt brittle to the touch, the clothes very old and rarely worn.

But there was still a relic of my own old stuff stored here. No clothes: no doubt they had disappeared into the maw of charity, and my old T-shirts and trousers might even now be adorning some refugee child from flooded Bangladesh or parched Egypt; it was an age of refugees, plenty needing to be clothed. But there were computer games, books, and a few of my classier-looking models, such as the huge mobile of the International Space Station that had once hung over my bed, now neatly disassembled and swathed in bubble-wrap. Some toys had survived, mostly tie-in figurines and die-cast models, carefully stored inside their boxes.

It was, to my eyes, an eclectic mix; parents sorting out their children's middens are a random filter. It seemed my mother had selected objects not of sentimental value but that might be worth money some day: a toy survived the cull only so long as it was in good condition and if she could find its packaging. But those mint-condition auction candidates, of course, were precisely the toys I had spent least time with. Still, her eye for value had been good. A lot of the computer games could have raised some cash; there was a whole industry of silicon-chip archaeology turning out readers for such things, gizmos several electronic generations old and yet still precious to sentimental old fools like me.

I did come across one chance fossil that had escaped the cull, despite having no discernible value. It was a small tin, slotted so it served as a money box. Here I found newspaper cuttings and collector cards and internet printouts, mostly to do with the space programme, and a little leather pouch full of pennies dated the year 2000, and loose postage stamps, and fast-food stickers and button badges from TV-show promotions, and a tiny travel chess-set on which I had taught my brother to play, late at night when we were supposed to be asleep. All of this junk had been handled and pored over endlessly. That little box was a screen grab of my mind aged ten or eleven, the stuff so small and worked-over it was almost like scrimshaw. But it was also a little off-putting, grimy with the handling. I probably ought to have got out more, I thought. I closed the box and put it back on its shelf.

But as I did so I was suddenly overwhelmed with sadness. It hit me like a physical blow, a punch in the neck, and I had to sit down. It was just that the kid who had filled that box had gone as if he never existed, the whole rich complicated texture of his life unravelled. Life was so rich, but so transient: that was what made me sad.

But moping over this junk wasn't filling any sandbags. I closed the cupboard, changed into T-shirt and shorts, threw on some fresh sun cream and bug repellent, and headed down the stairs.

The porch with the swings was intact, though it would benefit from some TLC. I walked across the backyard, where John's kids were still playing. It used to be a lawn; now it was just a concrete slab. The kids gave me polite Happy smiles, and

I waved back and walked on, with an armful of empty bags for the sand.

From the back gate the old gravel path led down towards the coast, as it always had. But before I got to the dunes I found myself walking across dykes and culverts and drainage ditches, and the rotting remains of many, many sandbags. I imagined my mother labouring here, determined, stubborn. But all her hydrological systems had failed, and when I looked back I could see the lines of sandbags retreating ever further up towards the house. You couldn't drain away an ocean through a five-centimetre culvert.

I walked through the dunes and came to the shore. There was still a beach here, of sorts, but it sloped sharply away, soon disappearing under the restless sea. The erosion here had been relentless. Even the dunes seemed to have been eaten away. Here and there I saw patches of a greyer mud, like a stretch of sea-bottom, not a beach at all. Driftwood and scattered bits of plastic garbage littered the shore, and I passed great reefs of dead seaweed, dug out by storms and stranded. The reefs were the source of that salty smell of decay I'd detected earlier. Bugs swarmed everywhere, not just mosquitoes but tiny little bastards that threw themselves at my exposed flesh. Insects, the great winners of the years of the Die-back.

The sea looked beautiful, as it always did, even if, stirred up by the endless storms, it was not quite so blue as it used to be. It was hard to believe the sea had done so much damage.

I found a dune that was resisting the ravages of time with the help of some toughly bound grass. In its shelter the sand was clean and even reasonably dry. I squatted down and began to scoop sand into my sacks. It was late afternoon by now. I was looking into the sun, which was declining to the south-west, to my front right.

That was when I saw her.

It was just something in the corner of my eye, a bit of motion that distracted me. I thought it might be a rare sighting of a sea bird, or maybe it was the sun playing on the lapping water. I stood up to see better. It was a woman. She was a long way down the beach, and the light reflected from the sea behind her was bright and sent dazzling highlights stabbing into my eyes.

Morag?

I was never frightened by these encounters, or visitations. But they were always characterised by ambiguity, muddle, uncertainty. It might have been Morag, my long-dead wife, or it might not.

I also felt a certain irritation, believe it or not. I'd had such visitations all my life, and was used to them. But in recent months the frequency had increased. I'd been plagued by these visions, apparitions – whatever. Their incompleteness hurt me; I wanted resolution. But I didn't want them to stop.

I took a step forward, trying to see better. But I was holding a three-quarters-full sandbag, and it started to spill. So I bent down to set it on the ground. And then I had to step over the hole I had dug. One thing after another, in my way. When I looked up again she was still there, bathed in light, though she seemed a bit further away.

She waved at me, a big hearty wave, her arm right over her head. My heart melted. There was more warmth in that simple gesture than in any of the responses I had had from John and his Happified kids. It was Morag, dead seventeen years; it could only be her. Now she cupped her hands around her mouth and shouted. But the waves crashed, echoes of some remote Atlantic storm, and only a splinter of sound reached my ears. *John*, she said. Or it might have been *bomb*. Or *Tom*.

'What did you say? Something about Tom? Morag, wait—' I blundered forward. But away from the line of the dunes the sand quickly got muddy, and soon my feet and lower legs were coated in great heavy boots of sticky sea-bottom ooze. Then I came to one of those big reefs of seaweed, piled high and deliquescing to a stinking mush. I cast back and forth, looking for a way through.

When I looked beyond the heaps of rotting weed she had already gone.

Back at the house, the kids had gone inside to join in an immersive virtual drama on Grandma's huge wall-mounted softscreen. The rising tide had caused water to bubble out of the ground around the house and lap over the yard; even their smart soccer ball had been defeated.

As the sun went down, I joined John at his patient Paint-work.

We applied the Paint laboriously. It was heavy, sticky stuff, full of lumps, kind of like Artex, and difficult to work to an even coat. Silver in colour, it looked odd on my mother's clapboard walls, making the house look like a mocked-up stage set. And as we scraped on the Paint it started to thank us, in a whispery voice that wafted from the wall: *Thank you, thank you for complying with all local sentience ordinances, thank you...*

'Oh, screw you,' said John.

The dubious colour scheme was one reason my mother hated this stuff. But it was silver to deflect much of the sunlight, so cutting down on air-conditioning costs, and it was laden with photovoltaic cells to make the whole house a solar-power sink.

And the Paint was dense in processors, billions of tiny nanofabricated computers each the size of a dust speck and about as smart as an ant. As we applied it the little brains linked up with each other through the conducting medium of the Paint itself, and burrowed their electronic way into the house's systems, seeking connectivity with power points and actuator controls. Artificial intelligence in a can: when I was a kid it would have seemed a miracle. Now sentience was a commodity, and this was just a chore.

For a while we worked together in stolid silence, my brother and me. The light leaked out of the sky, and my mother's porch lanterns, big cool bulbs, popped into life. Mosquitoes buzzed and swarmed.

John made small-talk. 'So how about the digital millennium, huh? You're the engineer; tell me if I need to worry.'

I shrugged. 'We'll survive. Just like Y2K. It won't be so bad. They've done a few trial system excavations to check.'

John laughed at my choice of word. *Excavation.*

It was the latest scare-story to sweep the planet. Next year's date, 2048, was an exact power of two, in fact two to the power eleven, and so it would require an extra binary digit to represent it in the memory of the world's interlinked computer systems. Nobody quite knew what that was going to do to the 'legacy suites', some many decades old, crusted over with enhancements and embellishments, that still lay at the heart of many major systems, grisly old code rotting in computer memory like the seaweed on my mother's beach.

'So,' John said, 'just another scare?'

'We live in a time of fear and wonder.'

'It's not a rational age.' As the Paint continued to thank him for applying it, John sighed. 'Listen to this damn stuff. Lethe, maybe it's rational *not* to be rational.'

Intrigued, I asked, 'What do your kids think of the millennium?'

'Nothing, as far as I know. I try to get them to watch the news, but it's a losing battle. But then nobody watches the news nowadays, do they, Michael?'

'If you say so,' I snapped back.

This conversation, tense, on the edge of fencing, was typical of us. It was the thin surface of an antagonism that went back to our late teens, when we had started to become aware of the world, and we had begun to shape our attitudes to the future.

I had aimed to become an engineer; I wanted to build things. And I was fascinated by space. After all, when I was ten years old they discovered the Kuiper Anomaly: an honest-to-God alien artefact sitting at the edge of the solar system. For those of us who cared about such things, our whole perspective in the universe had been changed. But we were in the minority, and the world continued to turn, and I was out of step.

John, though, became a lawyer, specialising in environmental-damage compensation suits. I thought he was cynical, but in the wake of the vast political and economic restructuring that had followed the Stewardship programme he was undoubtedly successful. By tapping into the vast rivers of money that sloshed to and fro in a destabilised world he had become hideously rich, and was now aiming for greater ambitions – while I, an engineer who built things, could barely pay the bills. That probably tells you all you need to know about the state of the world in those days.

We really got on remarkably badly, for brothers. Or maybe not. But still, this was my brother, the only sane person left who had known me all my life, with due respect to my mother.

And I longed to tell him about Morag on the beach.

I'd never told anybody. Now I felt I should. Who else to tell but my brother? Who else should know about it? He would mock, of course, but it was his job to mock. Standing there working with him, as the lights grew brighter in the gathering gloom, I plucked up my courage, and opened my mouth.

Then the lights fizzed to a silver-grey nothingness. Suddenly John was a silhouette against a darkling sky, holding a useless paintbrush. We heard cries of disappointment from the kids inside the house.

'Damn it,' John snapped.

The house, or anyhow the Paint, was apologising. *Sorry, sorry for the inconvenience.*

It was a cooperative brown-out, as the sentiences dispersed in the neighbourhood houses and bars and shops and streetlamps, and in the water pumps and buses and boats, responded to symptoms of alarm coming from the local power microgrid – usually a glitching in the mains supply frequency – and shut themselves off. It was better this way, better than the bad old days of stupid systems and massive blackouts, everybody said. But it was a royal pain in the butt even so.

My mother stuck her head out of the window. 'And that's another reason I don't like that silver stuff.'

John laughed. 'We'll have to finish tomorrow, Ma. Sorry.'

'You'd better come in; the mosquitoes will be at you in minutes now the electric fences are down. I've got no-brain-chicken slices, and cookies, and a pack of cards to keep the kids quiet.' She shut the window with a bang.

I glanced at John. I couldn't see his face, but glimpsed the whiteness of his teeth. 'Gin rummy,' he said. 'I always hated fucking gin rummy.'

'Me too.' It was one thing we had in common, at least.

He clapped me on the back, a bit more friendly than before. Side by side we walked into the house.

That was when I got an alarm call in my ear so loud it hurt. There had been some kind of explosion in Siberia. Tom, my son, was out of touch, maybe hurt.

Chapter 4

As she had grown up and become aware of her world, Alia had always known that the *Nord* was a ship, an artefact, everything about it *made*. And that implied it had an origin, of course, a time before which it hadn't existed. She had never really thought about it. The present was the thing, not some discontinuity in remote history; wherever you grew up you always assumed, deep inside, your world had existed for ever.

Nevertheless, it was true. This ship had once been built, and named, and launched, by human hands.

The *Nord* had once been a generation starship. Crawling along at sublight, it was designed to journey for many centuries, after which the remote grandchildren of its builders would spill onto the ground of some new world. It was believed it had been launched from Sol system itself, built of the ice of a remote moon, perhaps of Port Sol itself – and perhaps even by the legendary engineer Michael Poole, descended from the subject of Alia's Witnessing, an earlier Michael Poole who had been doomed to live in a much drabber time.

But that was probably just a story. The truth was the *Nord*'s port of origin was long forgotten, its intended destination unknown. Nobody even knew who its builders were or what they had wanted. Were they visionaries, refugees – even, it was whispered deliciously, criminals? Even the ship's name was a subject of intellectual debate. It might have derived from *nautilus*, a word from old Earth referring to an animal that lived its life in a shell. Or perhaps it derived from *North* or *Northern*, an earthworm's word for a direction on a planet's surface.

But whatever its target had been, the *Nord* had never

reached it. Long before it completed its voyage it had been overtaken by a wave of faster-than-light ships, a new generation of humans washing out from Earth and rediscovering this relic of their own past. It must have been a huge conceptual shock for the crew on that day when the first FTL flitters had come alongside.

But when that generation had died off, the crew had accepted their place aboard a bit of bypassed history. They had begun to trade with the passing ships – at first with the *Nord*'s reaction-mass ice, billions of tonnes of which still remained, and later with hospitality, cultural artefacts, theatre shows, music, elegant prostitution. The *Nord* was no longer a vessel, really; it was an artificial island, drifting between the stars, locked into a complex interstellar trading economy. Nowadays nobody aboard had any ambition for the voyage to end.

Of course if you lived on a spaceship there were constraints. The *Nord*'s inner space was always going to be finite, and the population could never grow too far. But two children were enough for most people: indeed most had fewer. Alia knew that she was fortunate to have a sister in Drea; siblings were rare. Her parents, though, had never made any secret of the deep and unusual joy they had derived from their children.

And anyhow if you didn't like it here in this small floating village you could always escape. You could pay for passage aboard one of the *Nord*'s endless stream of FTL visitors, and head for any of the worlds of a proliferating human Galaxy. And likewise some of those visitors, charmed by the *Nord*'s antiquity and peace, chose to stay.

Thus the *Nord* had sailed on, its crew rebuilding their ship over and over, until it had passed through the dense molecular clouds that shielded the Galaxy's Core from eyes on Earth, and had broken into a new cold light.

And half a million years had worn away.

The sisters' home was a cluster of bubble-chambers lodged just underneath the *Nord*'s ceramic hull. Windows had been cut into that ancient surface, so that from Alia's own room you could see out into space. The room was small, but it was a pleasant retreat she had always cherished.

But today there was a visitor here. An intruder.

It was a man, a stranger. He stood quietly in the centre of the floor, hands behind his back. Her mother, Bel, stood beside the visitor, her hands twisting together.

The stranger was *tall*, so tall he had to duck to avoid the ceiling. He was dressed in a drab pale grey robe that swept to the ground, despite his angular height. His face was long, a thing of planes and hard edges of bone, as if there wasn't a morsel of spare fat under his flesh. His arms were short, too stiff for climbing; he was a planet-dweller. He kept subtly away from the furniture, Alia's bed and chairs and table and Witnessing tank, all heaped with clutter and clothes. His expression was kindly, almost amused as he looked at her. But Alia thought he had an air of detachment, as if she was some kind of specimen.

She didn't like this judgemental stranger in her room, looking at her stuff. Resentment flared.

Her mother's face was flushed, and she seemed tense, agitated. It took a lot to get a bicentenarian so visibly excited. 'Alia, this is Reath. He's come to see you, all this way. *He's from the Commonwealth.*'

The man, Reath, stepped forward, arms outspread. 'I'm sorry to intrude on you like this, Alia. It's terribly ill-mannered. And I know this will come as a shock to you. But I've come to offer you an opportunity.'

She couldn't tell how old he was. But then, you couldn't tell how old anybody was past the age of thirty or so. He was different, however, she thought. There was a stillness about him, as if he had weightier concerns than those around him.

She said suspiciously, 'What kind of opportunity? Are you offering me some sort of job?'

'In a sense—'

'I don't want a job. Nobody *works*.'

'Some do. A very few,' he said. 'Perhaps you will be one of them.' His voice was deep, compelling, his whole manner mesmeric. She felt he was drawing her down some path she might not want to follow.

Her mother had gone, she noticed, slipped out of the room while Reath distracted her.

Reath turned away and walked around the room, his hands still folded behind his back. 'You have windows. Most people would prefer to be hidden away, buried in the human world, forget that they are on a starship at all. But not you, Alia.'

'My parents chose the apartment,' she said. 'Not me.'

'Well, perhaps.' With an elegant finger he traced faint shadows on the wall, a cross-hatching of rectangles, hexagons, ovals and circles. As the occupancy patterns of the *Nord* had changed, windows had been cut here, then filled in and cut again, each repair leaving a ghostly mark. 'And these usage scars? They don't bother you?'

'Why should they?' In fact she liked the sense of history the faint scarring gave her, the idea that she wasn't the first to live here, to breathe this air.

He nodded. 'You don't mind. Even though these overlaid scars must give you a sense of transience, of the evanescence of all things – of youth, of love, even of your own identity. I don't mean to patronise you, Alia. But I suspect you're still too young to understand how rare that is. Just as they would prefer to forget where they are in space, most people would rather not think about their position in time. They would certainly prefer not to think about death!'

She felt increasingly uncomfortable. 'And that's why you've come here? Because I think too much?'

'Nobody thinks too much. Anyhow you can't help it, can you?' He approached her Witnessing tank. It was a silvered cube half his height. 'May I?'

She shrugged.

He tapped the tank's surface.

It turned clear to reveal a softly translucent interior, filled with light that underlit the planes of Reath's face. And through the light snaked a pale pink rope, looping and turning back on itself. If you looked closely you could see that the line wasn't a simple cable, but had small protuberances and ridges. And if you looked closer still you could just see that it was actually a kind of chain, with its links tiny human figures, one fading seamlessly into the next: there was a baby at one end, fingers and toes pink, and at the other end of the sequence an old man, bent and gaunt.

Reath said, 'Your subject is Michael Poole, isn't it? I envy you. Though it's no coincidence you've been assigned such a significant figure, historically.'

'It isn't?'

'Oh, no. We – I mean, the councils of the Commonwealth – have had our eye on you for a long time, Alia.'

That chilled her. And she still didn't know what he wanted.

'I am certainly pleased to see you keep up your Witnessing.'

'Doesn't everybody?'

'Sadly, no. Even though we all have our duty: to Witness is to participate in the Redemption, which has been mandated by the Transcendence.' When he said the name, Reath bowed his head.

Alia knew it was true that others skimped their Witnessing. She had always been fascinated by her assigned Witnessing subject; others, even her own sister, thought she was a bit too earnest, and in the interests of popularity she'd learned not to talk about it.

Reath reached into the tank and touched the flesh-coloured chain, close to one end. That 'link' was cut out, magnified and became animate, and the tank filled up with the light of a distant sun, a vanished beach. A boy played, throwing brightly coloured discs to and fro through the air. There was a contrail traced by a spark of light climbing in the sky, maybe a rocket; the boy quit his playing to watch, his hand peaked over his eyes.

Reath murmured, 'My history's a little rusty. Didn't this Poole grow up in Baikonur? Or was it Florida? One of those palaeological spaceports ... '

'I like watching him as a kid,' Alia blurted. 'He's so full of life. Full of ideas. Always tinkering with things. Like those toys. He would cut and shape them, trying to make them fly better.'

'Yes. The shapeless dreams of youth, so soon replaced by the complexities and compromises of adulthood. But his life was so short. By the time he was your age Poole's life was probably half over. Most of them could only follow one career, make one significant contribution before—' Reath snapped his fingers. 'Imagine that! But we, who have so much time by comparison, often choose to do nothing at all.'

He was trying to recruit her, Alia remembered. But for what? '*Why* would I want to work, for you or anyone else?'

'It's a valid point,' Reath said. 'In our society of limitless material wealth, what rewards can there be? Have you ever heard of money, child?'

'Only historically.'

'Ah, yes.' He turned to her Witnessing tank. 'They still had money in Poole's time, didn't they?'

'Yes.'

'And Poole himself worked.'

'He was involved in one of the big geoengineering projects.'

'Yes,' Reath said. 'The struggles to get past the great Bottleneck of his day. But what motivated Poole, do you think? I'm sure he was *paid*. But was it just money he wanted?'

'No.'

'Then what?'

She frowned, thinking. 'His world was in trouble. Duty, I suppose.'

'Duty, yes. Of course everything is different now. But even though money has vanished, duty remains – don't you think? And I already know *you* do your duty, Alia, with your Witnessing. Tell me what you think of Poole.'

'His legacy—'

'Never mind his place in history. What do you think of *him*?'

She studied the playing boy. To her, Poole was a stunted creature, living in a cramped, dark time. Why, he was barely conscious most of the time. His mind was only half formed, his speech a drawl. It was if he walked around in a dream, a robot driven by unconscious and atavistic impulses. And when tragedy hit, when his wife died, he was overwhelmed, unable even to comprehend the powerful emotions that tore him apart.

Yet this flawed animal was a citizen of a civilisation that was already reaching out beyond the planet of its birth, and Michael Poole himself had a grave, history-shaping responsibility. Yet this man, in a way, would save his world.

Uncertainly she tried to express some of this to Reath.

Reath said, 'Just think how you would look to *him*. Why, you're a different category of creature altogether. If Poole was standing before you now, I wonder if you'd even be able to talk to each other! You and Poole are as different as two humans could ever be. And yet you have always watched him. Do you think, Alia, that you could ever *love* him?'

'Love? What are you talking about? What do you want, Reath?'

His eyes were a deep, watery gold. 'I have to be sure, you see.'

'About what?'

'If you really are what I'm looking for.' He turned in response to a faint sound. 'I think your father is home.'

Alia was happy to run from the room, fleeing from this strange man and his intense scrutiny, seeking her father's reassurance. But in the end reassurance was the last thing she found.

In the apartment's living room, her mother and father stood side by side. Her sister Drea was here too. Reath followed Alia, and stood discreetly to one side.

Alia's attention was distracted by the Witnessing tanks stacked up in one corner of the room, her parents' and Drea's. It struck her that she couldn't remember when the others had last done any Witnessing. Maybe Reath was right, she was unusual.

Her family was staring at her.

And then, as if noticing it for the first time, she saw that Ansec hadn't come home alone. In her father's arms, fresh from the birthing tanks, was a baby.

Alia found it difficult to speak. 'Well,' she said. 'Quite a family gathering.'

Her mother was anguished. 'Oh, Alia, I'm sorry.'

Ansec, her father, was calmer, though distress showed in his face. 'It's not a crisis,' he said. 'At least it doesn't have to be. An opportunity – that's what we have.'

Alia turned on her sister. 'And you – did you know?'

Drea snapped back, sibling rivalry briefly flaring, 'Don't

take it out on me.' She waved at Reath. 'It's you the Commonwealth wants, not me!'

And all the time, in her father's arms, there was the mute, incontrovertible existence of the baby. Bel's eyes were shining now. 'It's a boy, Alia, a baby boy!'

Ansec said, 'You know how happy this will make us, don't you? You know how we love children – how we've loved having you as you've grown.' He cradled the baby. 'This is *us*, Alia. The two of us, Bel and me. Having children. It's what makes us what we are.'

'And what about me?' Alia said. 'It takes two years for a gestation in the tank. So you've known this day would come for that long. And you've known what would happen then...' It was the *Nord*'s one iron rule. In its limited spaces, you were allowed two children; if you wanted a third, one of the others had to leave to make room, leave the ship altogether. 'You kept it secret from me. You went to the tank. You planned it all—'

Her mother took her hands. 'It's not like that, Alia, not at all. We weren't supposed to tell you the Commonwealth was interested in you.'

'Why?'

'In case the Commonwealth didn't want you after all,' Reath said gently. 'You might feel rejected, you see. It is thought to be kinder this way.'

'But we had to plan,' Bel said. 'You see that, don't you? We thought we would lose you. We had to plan for what would follow.'

And Alia saw it all now. 'So that's it. The Commonwealth wants to take me away, and that's an excuse for you to get rid of me and have a new child. You just assume I'm going to go with Reath. With this *stranger*. So you can stay home with this baby.'

'But it's a marvellous opportunity,' her father said. 'An honour. Anybody would want to go.'

'You will go,' her mother said. But she glanced at the baby, and there was an edge of panic in her voice. 'Won't you?'

Reath stood beside Alia, a tall, calm presence. Suddenly she felt closer to him than she did to her own family.

He said, 'Don't worry, Alia. It wasn't supposed to be so

difficult. We are all to blame. But I've seen enough of you to know that if you come with me you won't regret it. I'll take you to places you can't imagine. The centre of the Galaxy – worlds beyond number. You will be trained, your full potential brought out. Your mind will open up like a flower!'

'But what *for*?'

'Why, haven't you worked that out yet?' He smiled. 'I want you to become a Transcendent, child.'

She gaped. 'Me?'

'You're just the type.'

To be a Transcendent – it was unimaginable. Her heart was tugged by curiosity, pride – and, yes, by awe. But she was afraid too. 'Can I choose to stay?'

'Of course,' said her father. But her mother cast increasingly desperate looks at the baby, and Alia knew there was really no choice, none at all.

Chapter 5

The news of the disaster had come to me third hand, through a friend of a friend of Tom's. Arriving out of nowhere, it was a punch in the head.

John acted compassionate and concerned. What a jerk. I always thought that at times of difficulty like this my brother never really got it; he never really felt the deep emotions swirling around, and was never quite capable of understanding what *you* were feeling. He had a role to play in putting things right, a role he fulfilled well. But he didn't get it.

And nor did his two Happified kids. With their blank, pretty eyes they watched me to see what I would do, as if I was an animal that had been poked with a stick.

My mother was a more complex case altogether. She fussed around making hot drinks for everybody, her self-control absolutely rigid. But she was hollow inside, and fragile, a china doll that had somehow survived nearly a century. John didn't feel it at all; my mother felt it, but fought it. So who was more screwed up?

Anyhow I had things to do. I escaped to my room.

I sat on my bed, the bed I'd slept in as a child, the bed Tom had used a few times when he stayed here, and spoke into mid-air, trying to contact my son.

I couldn't place a call to Tom's implants, or to the office he worked out of. The local communications in Siberia were down, and the networks as a whole seemed to be suffering. I imagined a great gouge torn roughly out of the world's electronic nervous system, waves of pain and shock rippling out, and flocks of counsellors, artificial and human, swooping down to help the wounded artificial minds cope with their trauma. Sentience comes as a piece: if you want the smarts you have to accept the self-reflection, the angst.

And it didn't help that right now, as was patiently explained to me, all available bandwidth was being gobbled up by the news networks. The Siberian disaster, caused by a detonation of something called 'gas hydrate deposits' about which I knew nothing, seemed to have all the right hooks for the news: lots of gore, some kind of link to the Warming and so a grave if-this-goes-on angle, and, last but not least, the aid workers who had been caught up in the blast, a set of photogenic young western casualties.

But none of that was any use to me. I left my systems trying to make the call to Tom, while I set off more search agents to book a flight.

The cost of a plane ticket to Siberia, even one way, was frightening. In 2047 nobody flew, nobody but the very rich and very important, or if you *really* had to. It was cheaper to orbit the Earth in a tourist-bucket spaceplane than to fly the Atlantic. Tom, working for his genetic-legacy agency, had travelled out by cruise ship, taking weeks to crawl around the polar ocean, a way of travelling with a much smaller environmental footprint, which was important to him. But that would be too slow for me. I had to be there now, and I would have to pay. The flight to Florida had already cleaned me out, but what else could I do?

Of course booking the ticket was only half the battle. Actually being deemed worthy of a seat came next. The booking system referred me to the airline's counselling service, a man's voice sounding older than me, fatherly, stern. 'Michael, let's work out why you *really* want to fly.'

'My son is hurt!'

'Flying is a generational aspiration, you know. In your youth you probably flew many times, as did your parents. But then you indulged in many unhealthy pursuits in those days. That doesn't mean you should carry on now.'

'I don't *want* to fly. I just want to get there.'

'Is it possible that what you really want is a flight, not to Siberia, but to your past? Is it possible it is not a destination you seek but an *escape*, a release from the responsibilities of the present?...' And so on.

37

My phone was implanted; you couldn't muffle over the handset and say what you really thought. So I let off steam by pacing around the room as this virtual Freud lectured me about the necessity for the 'hidden extras' I would be paying for, in terms of environmental-damage costs, and compensation for communities I would disrupt with the noise of the plane, and even clean-up taxes relating to the disposal of the aircraft itself a few years down the line. It was all part of the social-responsibility package the airlines had had to accept years before, to keep flying at all. But it was difficult to wade through.

'I don't have to justify anything about my relationship with my son to you,' I snapped.

'Not to me,' the empathist said. 'Not to the airline, or even your son. To yourself, Michael.'

'No,' I insisted. 'There are times when we need to *be* with people. It's a deep primate thing.' I was having trouble keeping my voice steady. 'It's part of my programming, I guess. You ought to understand that.'

'But your son has stated, on record, that he doesn't need to be with *you*.'

Tom had said that, and it wasn't helping my application. 'A child's whole life after about the age of ten is devoted to establishing his independence from his parents. And in our case our relationship has been particularly strained ever since the death of his mother, in childbirth. Even you must have figured that out.'

'Yes, I—'

You don't interrupt airline psychoanalytical machines, but I interrupted. 'But we need each other. We're all we've got. Tom's words are only the surface. It's what we feel underneath that counts. And if you aren't a complete waste of memory you'll understand that... ' You aren't supposed to insult the shrink machines either. But I meant everything I said.

I had been with Morag when she died, on that grisly hospital table. And at that instant I had wanted nothing else in the world, nothing, but to be with Tom; it had been as if a steel cable had been lodged in my gut and connecting me to him. But of course everything quickly became complicated.

Tom was only eight; he was too young to deal with his own grief, let alone my own. And in the months that followed, as he watched me sinking into myself, some particle of his mixed-up feelings transmuted into resentment. That awful time had shaped our relationship ever since.

'But that deep feeling remains,' I told the airline machine. 'The steel cable. And I believe that's true for Tom too, even if he doesn't want to admit it. To every action there's an equal and opposite reaction. Newton's third law.'

'But, you see, Mr Poole, that over-academic remark merely illustrates what I have been saying...'

John came to the door. He leaned against the frame, hands in pockets, watching me. 'I wouldn't do that,' he said. 'The pacing. The counsellor can probably detect your motion. A dissonance between your body posture and your words is a giveaway.'

'I feel like I'm wading through cotton wool.'

He shrugged. 'That's the modern world. Energy-deprived. Constrained.' He stepped forward. 'Let me help.' He reached out his finger towards my ear, my implant.

I flinched; I couldn't help it.

For once John seemed to understand. 'What's more important, sibling rivalry, or getting through to Tom? Let me win this one.'

I nodded. He touched my face, just before my ear, and I felt a slight electric shock as his systems interfaced with mine. He took over my calls, and with a few soft words transferred them to his company in New York.

It took only five minutes or so for his company's systems to come back with a reply. John, standing easily in the corner of my bedroom, turned to me regretfully. Not even John's powerful reach could cut through the mush into which a sector of the global communications net had melted, so he couldn't put me in touch with Tom, and he hadn't had much more joy with the flights. 'No availability until the middle of next week.'

'*Next week*? Jesus. But—'

He held up his hand. 'I can get you a VR projection in twenty-four hours. I think it's the best we can do, Michael.'

I thought that over. 'OK. How much?'

'Let me cover it.'

'No,' I snapped reflexively.

He seemed to suppress a sigh. 'Come on, Michael. He's my nephew as well as your son. Lethe, I can afford it. And you don't know what you might need your money for in the future.'

I conceded this second defeat. 'OK,' I said. 'But, John, I still don't know if he's alive or dead. I don't even know that much.' I hated to ask him for more help like this. But he was right. Better to let him win; what did it matter?

He nodded. 'I'll keep trying to get through. Leave it with me.' He walked out to his own room, talking quietly to his own implant.

It was still only ten p.m., too early to try to sleep. I wandered downstairs, where my mother was sitting with the children, watching VR images of a mountainous landscape. 'Non-immersive, you'll notice,' my mother said to me. 'Immersion's bad for them so close to bedtime.'

I told them the news, or non-news, about Tom. When my mother heard that John was helping me out, she wrapped her thin bird's-talons fingers around her cup of tea, and raised it to her lips for a cautious sip. She looked satisfied, though she was too smart to say so openly. After we left home she had always tried to encourage her sons to have a close relationship, to keep in touch; she had even tried to engineer ways for that to happen. And even now, even in this awful time when it was possible that her grandson lay dying somewhere, she was calculating how to exploit this latest shift in our relationship.

I watched the VR images with the kids for a while. They were holiday pictures, of a trip the kids had taken with their father up into the Rockies. It was a beautiful place where whitewater rapids tumbled into limpid pools, and doll-like VR manifestations of the kids clambered past sheer rocky walls. I remembered some spectacular vacations we had had as kids, when my parents had taken us to the Galapagos Islands, Australia, the African game parks – places full of exotic life forms that had astounded and excited me. But nobody went in search of wildlife any more, because it

40

wasn't there to be found. There were still beautiful places in the world, where rich people went to vacation, but they were inanimate, like this, landscapes of rock and water. But even dead landscapes had changed. You could see how the faces of the rocks had been fenced off and wired over. Rising temperatures were destabilising high-altitude rock faces by thawing the deep permafrost beneath them. Climbers were another endangered species nowadays.

I had got lost in thought. Both the children were looking at me, calm concern marking their perfectly smooth faces. They looked as if they had been coached to sit like that. I got out of the room.

I rattled around the house. Maybe I could call a water cab and go into town for a while. Find a bar, preferably non-floating. Or maybe just walk the shore. But I didn't want to stray too far from John and his calls. Even then, even at such a dreadful time in my life, I was in his power, and my mother's. I was in a kind of prison, I thought, trapped into immobility by all the unspoken rules and treaties that had been laid down in my fifty-two years of life with my family.

Defeated, I trailed back upstairs to John's room.

He was sitting on his bed, glancing at headlines on a soft-screen. 'No news.'

'You've checked with your office?'

'No need. Feliz is a good guy; he will keep trying until he gets through, and he will call the minute he does. Take it easy. Do you want something? A drink – I brought some beer.'

'No. Thanks.'

Hands in pockets, I mooched around the room. There seemed to be even less of John in here than there had been of me in my room, although John being John would have systematically stripped the place of anything valuable long ago. But in one shadowed corner I found a small bookcase. 'Hey. Here are my old science fiction novels.'

'Really?' He came across to see. We bent down side by side, brothers, two thick-necked middle-aged men, straining to see the titles on cracked and yellowing spines.

I said, 'I imagined they had been thrown out. I guess

41

mother moved them in here in one of her clear-outs.' Which would have been typical of her, I thought sourly; this stuff had been unbelievably important to me as a kid, but she didn't even know whether it had belonged to me or John.

John ran his fingers over the titles. Some of these books went back to the 1960s or even earlier. They had mostly been gifts from Uncle George, who had collected books that had been old when he was a kid. 'These might be worth something.'

'They were mine, you know,' I said, too hastily.

He held his hands up, a faintly mocking smile on his face. 'I don't dispute it.' He pulled a couple of copies off the shelves, took them out of their protective Mylar bags, and leafed through them. 'Not in great condition,' he said. 'See how this is yellowed – too long in the sun.'

I straightened up. 'Yeah. But I wouldn't want to sell them. And anyhow the collectors' market for this stuff isn't what it was.'

'It isn't?'

'Too far in the past. We're all too old. For every collectable there is a demographic. You're at your peak as a collector at thirty, forty – old enough to be nostalgic, rich enough to have disposable income, young enough to be foolish about spending it. But science fiction is older than that, long over.'

'It was over even when we were kids,' he said. 'I never understood what you saw in the stuff.'

'I know you didn't,' I said testily. 'Which is the difference between us.' I glanced along the shelf and pulled out a novel. 'Nobody reads the literature, but there's still a scholarly tradition around it. And there's a fascination to it, you know, John. All those lost futures.' When I was a kid the future was still a bright, welcoming place, a place I wanted to live. We might all have been kidding ourselves even then – the Die-back was already underway – but that was how it felt to me. Now, if you thought about the future at all, it was as a black place that would erase you, like a hospital, a place you went to die. I put the frail old book back on the shelf. 'It's an anti-progressive viewpoint, almost medieval. We're regressing, philosophically.'

'But this stuff – fantastic dreams of rocket-ships and aliens – it always repelled me. It never seemed real.'

'But the future *is* real,' I said. 'To ignore it is absurd. It's as if we decided we don't believe in Mount Everest, or the Pacific Ocean. They are still *there*, even if we close our eyes. The future is coming whether we like it or not. The world is changing, and so are we. The future *must* be different from the past.'

'But nobody cares any more,' John said brutally. 'And what bothers you is that the future turns out not to have a place for people like you. Engineers. People who want to build things. People who want to fly in space! Well, we're too busy fixing what we broke before to build anything new.'

He was right. The space programme had been a big disappointment to me, all my life. Nearly eighty years after Neil Armstrong, still nobody had been to Mars, nobody had left Earth's orbit since the Moonwalkers. We hadn't even sent a probe out to the Kuiper Anomaly. The Warming had absorbed all our energies, and the great shock of the Happy Anniversary flash-bombing in 2033 had jolted us even more. We were too busy coping with one set of destructive changes after another, spending our civilisation's resources just to maintain stasis, to dream of interplanetary adventure.

I think John probably knew that I was, in fact, working on a design study for a new generation of spacecraft. But the work paid peanuts, and would most probably never fly – it was a hobby, a paper model as I had once made models of the Space Station of plastic and paint and decals. Maybe that proved his point.

John sat on his bed and leaned against the wall, his big football player's hands locked behind his head. 'You know, if you were to write a science fiction novel now, I'd be the hero.'

That was outrageous enough to make me laugh. 'How so?'

'Because I'm dealing with the future as it exists. And I'm helping people.'

Basically he dealt with compensation for environmental impacts. He had started out representing individuals, people who lost their homes or their health through avoidable toxic spills and the like. He had moved on to advise legislators on adjustments to the tax system concerning such things as polluting fuels, heat sources or greenhouse-emission processes.

It was all about a striving for balance, John said; you had to balance the drive for economic development with a need for environmental stability, you had to balance economic efficiency with equity for those impacted. He had even worked on the notion of 'intergenerational equity', in which, rather than ignoring future generations altogether or at best using them as garbage handlers for your waste, you actually paid a 'future tax' for any impact you might have on them. John had made something of a name for himself; indeed, to my chagrin, he'd appeared on TV a few times as a talking head on the issues.

His first love, though, had always been adversarial law, and in his fifties he had been drawn back to it – but now to much larger cases. 'Rather than defending the little old lady against the company who is poisoning her drinking water, I'm now, for instance, advising the Administration on a massive suit against China.' While the US had become a leader in global environmental management in the 2020s, China, in a relentless drive for economic growth, had continued to pollute, even to the present day. 'And then there are redistribution charges...' It was a rule of thumb of the Warming that hot areas lost out while cooler areas won. So, for instance, an Iowan farmer afflicted by increasing aridity lost, while a Minnesota farmer with a longer growing season won. 'Simple equity is the philosophical guide,' John said. 'The guy in Minnesota uses his bounty to subsidise his colleague in Iowa. And if things change around in the future, the flow of funds can always go the other way. People accept this, I think; it's manifestly fair.' He even said you could extend this on a planetary scale – not through lawsuits, like the US v. China, but through 'planetary bargaining'. Canada, a winner, could bail out India, a loser, and so on.

A lot of work came John's way through the various Stewardship agencies. The whole notion of the Stewardship was based on taking responsibility for your actions, on accepting the true cost of what you did, or sharing any benefit.

Of course you'd always put 'winning' and 'losing' in quotes; really it was all simply change, which hit everybody to varying degrees.

But all this equity and balancing and taxing and fairness was just a way of sharing out the impact of the Warming, I thought, not of reducing that impact in the first place. It occurred to me there was a narrow assumption hidden here, that things would carry on much the same as they had for a while – falling apart, maybe, but doing so slowly, staying more or less bearable, manageable, soothed by a little money flow. But what if not?...

John started to tell me about a book he was working on.

'Back up,' I said. 'A *book*?'

He grinned smugly. 'It's about the future of money.'

He was developing an idea that dated back to John Maynard Keynes, an economist who worked in the middle of the twentieth century. 'You'd run international trade in a whole new currency which would earn *negative* interest. So you would naturally spend your diminishing wealth as quickly as possible, which would boost trade and the exports of other nations. It's a new paradigm,' he said. 'A way to avoid the debt mountains of the past, and to boost the global trade on which we rely. Why not? Money is just a mental construct. We can make up its rules any way we want. I have some contacts in the Administration through the China case, and I think I can garner some support...'

And so on. I listened to this with a sickening feeling. Whereas I, the engineer, was a nineteenth-century relic, a sad Jules Verne character, perhaps my smart-ass brother really was an archetype of our times, a modern hero. 'So you're going to become more prominent than ever,' I said. 'I'll never be able to get away from your face.'

He laughed. There was a grain of sincere bitterness in my harangue; of course he detected it. 'I'll invite you to the launch of the book,' he said.

I managed to sleep that night, but only a little. I got up early and left the house.

I went down to the coast, and walked and walked. I wasn't going anywhere; I was just trying to escape the contents of my own head, as my airline therapist had so wisely inferred.

Everywhere I walked, the angry sea had risen. The water had washed away fences, waves had lapped over lawns, and palm trees sagged over the water, undercut, surely doomed. One guy had built a chicken shack right at the edge of his land, not metres from the sea. When the wind blew the chickens must have got soaked, terrified; I wondered what kind of eggs he got out of them.

It was all depressingly predictable. Florida was always flat and soggy. Human efforts over centuries had pushed the water out of there, and reclaimed much of the land. But now the ocean was coming back. Even the Florida aquifer was contaminated with salt, as well as with industrial spill-off. It wasn't good news for the flora and fauna, either. The salt water that now pushed inland with every tide had played havoc with freshwater ecologies. The Everglades weren't a place the tourists went to nowadays; the rotting vegetable matter that clogged the dead swamps stunk to high heaven. It was said the alligators still survived though, living off the rotting detritus around them, surviving this extinction event as they had survived so many others.

The wind changed, to blow off the sea. That ocean breeze smelled foul, a choking smell like rubber burning some-where. It was a cocktail of toxins that might have blown all the way from the sprawling industrial wastelands of central Europe and Africa or even Asia: some of that crud got very high up, and could even circle the Earth.

I wondered how I would be feeling right now if I were Happified, like John's kids. I had once discussed this with John, the only time I dared, the only time I was drunk enough, with his wife out of the way.

'The pursuit of happiness is our inalienable right, Michael,' he had said. 'Every parent wants their child to be happy, above all. You try to care for them, you give them education, money, to maximise their opportunities to get on in life – but in the end happiness is the final goal. That's an argument that goes back to Aristotle, actually; he argued that every other good is a means to an end, but happiness *is* the end.'

'Smart guy.'

'And now we know that at least fifty per cent of the likelihood of your happiness is inherited, even without modification. But we can modify. We're the first generation that can *guarantee* their kids happiness.'

So you plied your kids with drugs and therapy. Or you spliced their genomes, as John had, to make them happy come what may.

I thought I saw something slithering through scrubby dune grass. It might have been a tree snake, which had come into Florida and other parts of the continental US from Guam, via Hawaii. Poisonous as hell, and a vicious predator of birds. On the other hand, tree snake meat recipes were spicing up the menus in Miami restaurants.

Tree snakes could grow three metres long. Looking at it sliding through the grass made me shudder. I turned back, heading for home.

By the time I got back to the house it was around eight in the morning.

My mother was already out, working on a row of potted plants at the top of the yard, in the lee of the house. She was on her knees on a raised pad, an old lady's gardening aid. But her bare fingers were crusted with dirt, and she dug away with a will.

I remembered how she had always loved her garden. When we were kids I used to think she loved it more than us. Now, watching her, I wasn't so sure I had been wrong.

She glanced up irritably as my shadow fell over her. 'You missed your breakfast,' she said.

'I wasn't hungry.'

'I'll fix you something.' She sniffed. 'Better yet, do it yourself.'

'Really, I'm fine.'

'There's no news. About Tom, I mean.'

'I know.'

'I'm sure everything will be fine. You'd have heard by now if not.'

'You're probably right.' I sat down on the wooden floor of the porch. She had a jug of lemonade beside her; I accepted a glass.

'I don't suppose you want to help me with this,' she said.

'Not especially.'

'Where did you walk to?'

'Nowhere particular.'

'Oh, you're always so vague, Michael, you're maddening.'

'Mom, the breeze off the sea—'

'I know. The air used to be so clean here. One reason I always loved it. Now it's like Manchester.'

'Yeah.' I watched her doggedly digging away at the roots of her plants. 'It can't be good for you.'

'My lungs are made of leather. Don't trouble yourself.'

'They're evacuating Miami Beach, aren't they?'

She snorted. 'No, they aren't. Nobody uses that word. There is a programme of transfer. Of migration, if you want to put it like that. *Evacuation* is what refugees do,' she said sternly. 'It's not as if we'll be underwater tomorrow.'

I knew how painful this was. Since the automobile had vanished from America, this had become an age when you stayed home rather than travelled, an age of villages, of local stuff. And for a close community to be broken up was difficult.

'We have a programme of agreements with other population centres,' she said. 'In Minnesota, for instance. John has helped negotiate the settlements.' I hadn't known that. 'Seventy-five here, a hundred there. Always family groups, of course.' It had to be planned, she said. You couldn't let the community left behind just fall into decay. So there were incentive schemes to keep teachers, doctors, civil servants working here, even though there was no future career for them. 'It's a long-term programme. A cultural achievement, in its way.'

'But Minnesota is a long way from the sea,' I said.

'Well, I know that, but it can't be helped. What's worse is that everything is being...' She waved her trowel vaguely. 'Dispersed. All the history here. The culture.'

'History? Mom, you're a newcomer here. You're from England!'

'Yes, but so is everybody a newcomer but the Tequesta Indians. That's part of the charm of the place. I think it's important that we stay, you know. We old ones. Isn't that what old people are, symbols of the past, of continuity? If we go then the place will just die. And what will happen to people then?... It does feel very strange to live in a place which has no future, I admit that.'

'Mom—'

'You know, it's odd. In my lifetime they've taken away so many of the things that used to kill you when I was young. Cancer, diabetes, Alzheimer's, heart disease, even schizophrenia – *all* of those chronic diseases turned out to be caused by infection, all of them preventable once we targeted the right virus or retrovirus. Who'd have thought it? So with nothing left to kill you, you just live on, and on. But then they took away the world instead.'

She wasn't really talking to me, I saw. She continued with her patient gardening, digging and digging.

I found John out back. He was sweeping windblown sand off the porch.

He had a distracted expression. I wondered if he was getting news about Tom. But it turned out he was listening to his personal therapist. He grinned, touched my ear, and I heard a gentle male voice: 'John, you're overly perturbed about a situation you can't control. You know you have to accept what can't be changed. Take an hour off, then let me read you some stuff on cognitive feedback which...'

I pulled away.

'You should try one of these things,' John said. 'Spin-off from the space programme, in fact. It can even prescribe pharmaceuticals. Would you like me to set you up?'

'No, thanks.'

He stepped towards me. Our closeness of last night had dissipated back into the usual rivalry; his blocky face, in the slanting morning light, looked ugly, coarse. 'You never did accept any drug therapy after Morag, did you? You know, it is possible to block the formation of traumatic memories altogether. You just take the right pill in the hours immediately after the event – you target the formation of proteins, or some such – I guess that's too late for you now with Morag, but—'

'I suppose you started feeding pills to your kids after Inge left, did you?'

He flinched at that, but he snapped back, 'They didn't need it. You, on the other hand—'

My anger, frustration, helplessness came boiling out. 'You know the trouble with you, John, your whole fucking life? You deal with symptoms, not causes. You fix your kids so they'll never be sad. You listen to a tin voice in your ear and you pop your damn pills so you don't carry scars from anything bad, even from your wife dumping you. And your work is all about symptoms too. The coasts are flooded? Fine, spread what's left of the wealth around a little more. The Atlantic coast is hammered by a dozen hurricanes a season? Add a couple of zeroes to your law suit against the Chinese. You don't do squat about the root cause of it all, do you?'

'It's not my job,' he said. His voice was mild, as if I was no more than an irate client, which maddened me even more. 'Michael, I understand how you are feeling—'

'Oh, fuck off.' I turned on my heel and stalked off.

He called after me, 'If I hear anything about Tom I'll let you know. Keep your implant switched on...'

I wasn't even gracious enough to acknowledge that. It was not one of my finer moments. I stomped around the house, trying to calm down.

In the yard, the kids were playing with their smart football again. Both of them wore masks, flimsy transparent things, presumably to guard them against the foul breeze from China. They welcomed me, and I joined in their game, volleying and heading. I was always lousy at soccer, and I always will be, but they were gallingly kind.

So I was spending time with them, with Sven and Claudia, John's beautiful kids, my niece and nephew. But I felt uncomfortable.

At one point the ball rolled off the yard's bare concrete floor and ended up in long scrubby dune grass. You could see it roll back and forth, trying to find its way back to the game, but its rudimentary sensorium was confused by the blades of grass that towered around it. After a time it started to sound its little alarm chime.

Sven and Claudia stooped over the thing as it rolled about. 'Look,' Sven said. 'When it sees us it comes towards us.'

'Get out of its sight,' said Claudia. 'Let's see what it does.' They both stepped back out of the way.

The ball resumed its rolling, utterly baffled. There was a fragment of sentience in there, of genuine awareness. The ball could feel pain, the way a simple animal can, perhaps. Why, even the plaintive way it rang its stupid alarm chime was enough to break your heart. But those kids just stepped backward and forward, experimenting with it.

When I looked at Claudia, especially, I always felt a chill. It wasn't so much what she did but what she *didn't* do. There was nothing behind that pretty face, I thought, nothing but emptiness, like the endless black abyssal emptiness that lay between worlds. She made me feel cold, just looking at her.

In the end I picked up the ball myself and threw it back into the yard.

And John came running around the corner, wheezing. His assistant Feliz had called. It was news of Tom. My son was injured but alive.

Chapter 6

On this planet the clouds were tall, rising in soft mounds around the equator and gathering in immense creamy swirls towards the poles.

To Alia this was a pretty view, but meaningless. She knew nothing about planets. She had never even visited one before. The only planet she had ever studied in detail was Earth, the root of all mankind, with its layers of archaic planetary defences, its skim of ocean, its clustering city-covered continents.

But there were no continents here. When the flitter dipped into the atmosphere of *this* world there was nothing but an ocean, a crumpled silver-grey sheet that spread to the horizon. Above, the clouds were heaped up in a vast three-dimensional array of sculpture. This whole world was water, she thought, nothing but water, water below, water in the air. And under the clouds the prospect was oppressive, gloomy, illuminated only by shafts of sunlight cast through breaks in the cover.

She was here, under this dismal sky, because the Transcendence had willed it.

The Transcendence: the god-like assemblage of immortals at the heart of human society, from whom all political authority flowed. Truthfully, Alia knew little about it, save that it was, so the creepy scuttlebutt had it, a project of ancients, of *undying*. But what was the Transcendence itself? In her head she vaguely imagined something titanic, superhuman, beyond comprehension, perhaps like the muddled light of the Galaxy Core occluded by its interstellar clouds. Nobody talked about it much.

But now, it seemed, the Transcendence had taken an interest in her own small life. And it had already brought her far from home.

With Reath, agent of the Commonwealth, she had already travelled thousands of light years. This water-world's sun was on the fringe of a giant stellar nursery, a huge glowing cloud of roiling dust and ice that was spawning one hot young star after another. The nursery was on the inner edge of the Sagittarius Arm, one of the Galactic disc's principal star-birthing regions, and the water-world itself was a moon of a massive gas giant. So the sky here was crowded and spectacular – but right now, through those clouds, she couldn't see a trace of it, not even the primary giant.

'Ah – look at that.' Reath pointed to the horizon, where a column of darkness, writhing visibly, connected the ocean to the sky. 'Do you know what that is?'

'Is it *weather*?'

'Alia, that is a hurricane. A kind of storm, a vortex of air. It is fuelled by heat from the upper levels of the sea. It twists and moves, you see – chaotically, but not unpredictably.'

'Is it a phenomenon of a water-world?'

'Not just water-worlds. Any planet with extensive seas and a respectable atmosphere can spawn such twisters. Even Earth!'

Alia had grown up in a bubble of air less than two kilometres wide, every molecule of which was climate-controlled and cleansed by the *Nord*'s antique, patient machines. She tried to imagine such a monstrous storm slamming into a town or a city on Earth. Her imagination was unformed, filled with images of catastrophic breakdowns of environment-control systems. 'How terrible,' she said.

'Oh, humans mastered hurricanes long ago. All you have to do is cut off their energy supply before they do any damage. And of course by tracking onto land they detach themselves from the ocean that feeds them, and die of their own accord.'

'But not here, for there is no land.'

'Not here, no. Here a twister can live on and on, sucking up energy, spinning off daughters, tracking around the world. One twister system here – I'm not sure if it is *that* one – reaches right up to the top of the atmosphere. You can see it from space, like a glowering eye. And it has persisted for thousands of years.'

This was terribly disturbing for a ship-born girl like Alia. She was relieved when the storm receded from sight behind the horizon.

It was a month since she had agreed to follow Reath, to leave her home and begin the programme of training which might, ultimately, remarkably, lead to her becoming that unknowable entity a Transcendent, to become one of the host of god-like post-humans who governed mankind. A month since she had placed herself in the care of an agent of the Commonwealth.

The Commonwealth! Before she had left the *Nord* it had been little more than a name to her, a shadowy authority which arched over human civilisation. Now she was beginning to get a sense of the reality of it – and it was much more than she had ever imagined.

The Commonwealth was based at the most logical place for a Galactic capital: on a cluster of worlds that drifted amid the millions of crowded suns of the Core, where mankind had always anchored its Galactic empires.

The most visible sign of the Commonwealth's presence was the Clock of Humanity. Lodged in the Core, this was a machine the size of a star. It used the decay of certain types of subatomic particles, called W and Z bosons, to produce pulses of neutrinos. These were the fastest known physical processes; no conceivable clock could be more precise. And as neutrinos passed like ghosts through all normal forms of matter the pulses washed through the stars and dust of the Galaxy, never occluded or dispersed, so you could pick up the Clock's chiming wherever you were. Once, it was said, human clocks had been devised to fit the natural rhythms of Earth, its days and years. Now humans had scattered over millions of disparate worlds, and so the Clock was calibrated to a standard human pulse rate. Thus a civilisation that encompassed the Galaxy marched in step to the rhythms of a human heart.

'And all of it,' Reath told her, 'is driven by the Transcendence – a Commonwealth within the Commonwealth, a centre within the centre, the innermost heart of everything.'

The Transcendence was the source of all authority. As far

as she could make out, it was a meshing of minds, a titanic superhuman mass around which human affairs pivoted, much as the Galaxy itself wheeled about the unmovable black hole at its very centre. But the Transcendence needed agencies to carry out its will in the human world: it was a god embedded in bureaucracy.

The Commonwealth was more than a collection of dusty agencies, though, Reath said. The Commonwealth itself was an aspiration. As it worked on a Galactic scale, bit by bit, humans were drawn closer together, knit more integrally into the whole – to be brought, ultimately, into the great confluence of the Transcendence itself. Reath liked to say that whether you knew about it or not, if you were of human descent you were a citizen of the Commonwealth already. 'And one day, it is hoped,' Reath said, 'we will *all* be drawn in, not just into the Commonwealth, but even into the Transcendence itself – and then a new kind of human history will begin.'

But if it was to achieve such aspirations, the Transcendence had to grow. It had to recruit. Astonishing as it seemed, the Transcendence needed people like Alia.

If her ultimate goal was barely imaginable, Reath reassured her that the training would come in easy chunks. There were three formal stages, which he called Implications: the Implication of Indefinite Longevity, of Unmediated Communication, and of Emergent Consciousness. Needless to say she had little idea what any of these terms might actually mean, though they all sounded scary. But as well as the formal steps they would enjoy some 'fun' together, Reath said: notably, travel to exotic worlds like this one.

She wasn't happy.

It wasn't the distances that troubled her. To a Skimmer distance was supposed to be meaningless anyhow. No, it wasn't the distance but the company she had to keep: her only companion, in his austere, joyless tube of a ship, was the silent and watchful Reath.

Reath wasn't *bad* company, really. He was attentive to her needs, and tolerated her moods, and much of what he had to say was even interesting. But his face was blank, expressionless, as immobile as if the nerve ends had been cut. He was a walking, talking emblem of the great severance she had undergone, her separation from the *Nord*, her whole world, and her rejection by her parents in favour of a baby brother she did her level best not to hate.

Reath had done her one great favour, though. He had allowed her to bring along her Witnessing tank.

She could watch Michael Poole any way she pleased. The basic worm-like chain of images, from Poole's birth to death, was a simple four-dimensional representation, an index. She could allow a scene from his life to unfold inside the tank, with Poole, his family and friends, enemies and strangers like tiny actors. Or she could magnify it and immerse herself in the scene, an unseen witness. All of this was utterly authentic, so she understood, though she knew nothing of the technology involved: this wasn't a reconstruction, this really was the life of Michael Poole as he had lived it, five thousand centuries ago, all of it from birth to death embedded deep in the irrevocable past, and locked up inside her tank for her benefit.

Reath reminded her it was the obligation of every citizen to keep up her programme of Witnessing, as ordained by mysterious bodies at the heart of the Commonwealth which he called 'the Colleges of Redemption'. So he allowed her to believe she wasn't after all being helplessly sentimental in clinging to Michael Poole, her childhood companion; it was her duty. Perhaps he was sparing her feelings, and if so she was grateful for his indulgence. But he did take the Witnessing very seriously indeed, for he said that it, and the greater programme of Redemption of which it was part, was at the heart of the loftiest ambitions of the Transcendence.

And so, in the bowels of Reath's unstimulating ship, she had spent long hours immersed in the bright Florida light of Poole's long-ago childhood. She wished she could be there now, gazing not on this dismal water-world but on the sparkling seas of Earth.

Hundreds of kilometres of featureless ocean passed under the flitter's prow.

'Reath, what is this world *called*?'

'Names are relative,' Reath said. 'They depend on your viewpoint.'

Any world had a multiplicity of names, he said. The Commonwealth maintained formal catalogues, numbering every star and planet, comet and asteroid, every object of any significant size in the Galaxy. Some of these catalogues were based on antecedents that went back hundreds of millennia, to the days when the whole Galaxy had been an arena of war. There were other viewpoints too. Those near enough to see this world's star in their sky would give it a more formal name, as part of some constellation, say; they might even name the world itself if they could see it. Thus the world might have a dozen, a hundred such names, assigned from different interstellar viewpoints. But a world's primal name (or names) was that given it by those who lived there.

Alia gazed down at the endless seascape. 'So what do the locals call this world? *Wet*?'

'You'll see,' he said evasively.

'And *why* is there no land here?'

He smiled. 'Because the ocean is too deep...'

There was no world quite like this one in Sol system. This world was bigger than Earth, six times as massive. It had first formed far from its sun, so far out that water and other volatiles had not been driven off by its sun's heat as it coalesced. As it cooled it was left with a rocky core about the size of the Earth, but that inner core was swathed in a blanket of water ice.

After its formation was completed, this world had been gathered in as the moon of a gas giant. Thus things might have remained, if not for the fact that the parent Jovian, its orbit impeded by the remnant dust cloud from which it had formed, migrated steadily in towards its sun. And the ice moon began to melt.

'At last almost all the ice went – there's just a couple of islands of it at the poles now – leaving an ocean more than a hundred kilometres thick, over a remnant ice mantle. That's, oh, ten times as thick as the oceans on Earth. And then a little outgassing created the atmosphere. Weather started, and—'

'And that's why there is no land?'

'How could there be dry land, Alia? Even if the seabed was rock, you'd need a mountain a hundred kilometres tall

57

to poke above the ocean surface to make an island. No such mountains are possible on Earth, let alone here, where the gravity is about fifty per cent above standard. And besides the seabed is ice, not rock.

'Because of the lack of land, it was difficult for life to get started. There *is* life here, though: life that kick-started on other, more hospitable worlds of the system, and drifted here as spores.'

'Panspermia.'

'Yes.' He nodded approvingly. 'And then, of course, people came.'

People? But, she wondered, how could they live here?

Reath pointed. 'There it is at last. Our destination.'

Adrift in the middle of the endless ocean was a scrap of bright orange – a rectangle, a manmade thing. Alia felt unreasonable relief to see this bit of human engineering in the immense emptiness of the sea.

At first glance the platform seemed to be resting on a narrow stalk that protruded out of the ocean. But it turned out that the platform was studded with antigravity lifters, and the 'stalk' was actually a cable anchored in the deep ice, under tension as the lifters endlessly tried to pull the platform into the sky. It struck Alia as a cheap and quick solution to the problem of stability on a watery world.

The flitter slowed, and dipped towards the platform. Alia felt reluctant to Skim; she hadn't done so since leaving the *Nord*. So she and Reath climbed down out of the flitter the old-fashioned way, through a door.

The wind was strong and buffeting, and cold on her face, only a little above freezing. Reath seemed unperturbed, though he was so tall and skinny he looked as if he might blow away.

The air was mostly nitrogen and carbon dioxide – scarcely a trace of oxygen; life was rare here. But of course there was Mist in the air, the invisible population of nanomachines and engineered bugs that infested the atmosphere and oceans of every human planet. Alia stood still to let the Mist rebuild her. Her bones and muscles tingled as they were strengthened to cope with the heavy gravity, and the air she drew into her lungs fizzed with oxygenation. The cold was kept out of her body, but she could taste the salt-laden air in her mouth, the sharp, heavily salted tang of the global sea.

Though the platform was high above the waves it rocked and tipped subtly, its anchoring cable creaking noisily. The motion was slight, but very unsettling.

'Don't worry,' Reath shouted over the wind, 'we're quite safe. It's just that there's a cable a hundred kilometres long beneath us! No matter how strong the tension in it is, you're going to get vibration, resonances. The cable is a string plucked by the ocean! Why, if the worst came to the worst and the cable snapped altogether, the antigravity lifters would just take us flying up through the clouds into space.'

'I think I'd prefer it if it did snap,' she said. She made her way cautiously to the edge of the platform. There was no rail, no barrier between her and the abyssal ocean. Near the edge the wind grew stronger, and on the water below waves growled back and forth. 'I'm glad we're out of reach of those waves.'

'So we are – most of the time. Remember there's no land here, Alia, nothing to make the waves break. A wave system can just keep on travelling, gathering up more and more energy—'

'Like the hurricanes.'

'But we should be safe from being washed away for today.'

She looked around the platform. Aside from the sleek form of their flitter, glistening with spray, there was only a huddle of automated sensors. 'Reath, why have we come here?'

'For the people,' he said. 'Because people are here, *we* must come here. The Commonwealth, I mean. That is the mandate of the Transcendence.'

'How will they even know we are here? We can't integrate them if we can't find them!'

He held a hand to one ear. 'Can't you hear?'

She frowned, concentrating, expanding her hearing. She made out a deep thrumming, far below the standard human range.

'It is a beacon,' he said. 'Audible for hundreds of kilometres underwater.'

'They live *underwater*?'

'Where else, on a world like this? They will come.'

'How? Will they swim here?'

He grinned, his face gleaming with the spray.

She stepped closer to the edge, peering out at the churning sea. But there was no sign of the swimming citizens.

Chapter 7

Suddenly I was standing in the open air.

I was on a plain. The ground was scrubby and pocked by pits, some like the holes you leave when you dig out a tree stump, some bigger than that. The sky was a lid of cloud, a washed-out grey-white that seemed to suck all the colour out of the landscape. There was a breeze on my face, and I could taste and smell salt, overlaid with a fouler stench of bad eggs, marsh gas maybe. But your senses are always dull in a VR; nobody wants to pay good money for a bad smell, no matter how authentic.

Before me was some kind of industrial plant. It was a collection of squat concrete blocks crenellated by aluminium ducts and fans. A rusting pipeline stalked away on spindly trestles across the landscape. The whole set-up was surrounded by a chain-link fence at least twice my height; it looked to be backed up by an electrical barrier. There was no activity, nobody about; the concrete was stained, the buildings looked abandoned. Standing there, a ghost in the landscape, the buildings made me queasy just to look at them, though at first I couldn't figure why.

This was Siberia, the tundra, and it was spring. The landscape stretched to my left and right, and I had a sense of space, of immensity. This strip of tundra, between the sea to the north and the forests to the south, stretched a third of the way around the pole of the planet. But it was a petro-landscape, littered by oily lakes, pipelines, and rusting derricks.

Because of that breeze, I thought I must be near the sea. Looking away from the factory, I could see a line of iron grey, an ocean horizon. It made sense. This was the Yamal Peninsula, in the north-west of Siberia, maybe five hundred kilometres north-east of the Urals. Here, I had checked, the Arctic Ocean was known as the Kara Sea. Or I could be looking at the vast gulf at the mouth of the Ob river, a huge waterway that drained a continent. There was some kind of activity nearer the shore, low structures I couldn't make out, people moving urgently around. Was that where Tom had been working? I was ashamed that I didn't know.

In a VR projection you are stuck near the presence of your transceiver drone, which the service provider drops in the destination you ask for. Possibly this industrial plant was the nearest location logged in the provider's database. It had been the time taken to fly my drone from Moscow that accounted for the delay before the link was established. But I saw no activity within the site. There was nobody here, nobody to ask about Tom.

I hadn't approved of him coming to as unstable a part of the world as this, and had hoped that my frosty silence would have deterred him from going. It didn't. And now the result of my stubbornness was that he was hurt, somewhere in this depressing, worn-out landscape, and I had no idea how he had been injured or how badly, or even where he was.

Then I saw that one of those big concrete cubes was *leaning*. That immense building was tilted maybe ten degrees out of true, and one towering wall was cracked from top to bottom, yielding to the strain. The ground at the base of the tipping building looked as if it had melted, and was piled up in big static ripples, like warm chocolate. Further out, I saw, that pipeline dipped out of its line too. That was why I felt faintly nauseous. The vast tilting had disturbed my sense of the vertical, already tenuous in my VR state. It was a strange sight, a surreal drunkenness. I imagined the whole plant slowly sinking out of sight, those immense concrete walls cracking and spilling their toxic contents, until the brown earth closed over the ruined buildings like a welcoming sea.

A helicopter flapped overhead, painted bright blue, UN colours. It flew so low it came on me suddenly, making me duck. It was heading towards that township near the coast. I turned away from the plant and began to walk that way.

As I walked the system glitched. The view around me

would freeze and shatter into blocks, before reforming again, and I suffered a few strange smells and sounds, a bell-like ringing and sharp smells of cinnamon or almond: VR synaesthesia, bugs in the works. It was a sharp reminder that I wasn't really here; this was only a phone call with special effects.

I didn't grow up with immersive VRs. I could never get used to the pale washed-out sensation of the immersion, or the slight mismatch between the impulse to move and the motion itself, and I always imagined I could feel an itch at the top of my spine where data was pouring into my nervous system. I was restricted to walking pace, for such were the health and safety rules of the service. In theory you could fly around like Superman, and some people did, but nine out of ten threw up in the process. Cautious, I followed the rules of the game, but it seemed to take me an inordinately long time to tramp across that wounded landscape in search of my son.

My anxiety built. I felt like I was trapped in a dream, unable to hurry, unable to run. I didn't want to be here, dealing with this, a faulty VR projection in this awful, desolate, dream-like place where buildings melted into the ground.

It was at that low moment that I saw her: a slim figure, a pale dot of a face, a flash of strawberry-blonde hair.

She was standing in my path, but ahead of me, perhaps as much as half a kilometre away. She was calling something, and pointing towards the coastal village. I couldn't hear what she was saying. I tried to focus on her, but when I stared straight at her she seemed to disappear, to melt into shadows and clouds; I saw her clearly only when I wasn't looking at her.

Phantoms weren't so unusual in VR worlds. Often the system would wipe over something it was not expecting to see, editing it out of its reality altogether. Or, other times, the system would show you something that wasn't really there, a construct of badly imaged shadows and highlights, an interpretation of objects it couldn't recognise. She could be an artefact of the visual processing system.

She wasn't an artefact, though, I knew that deep in my gut. This was Morag. Even in here, in VR reality, she wouldn't let me alone. But I didn't have time for this, not now.

I continued to stalk across the landscape. Morag didn't come any closer, but nor did she walk away from me. She just retreated, her movement subtle, mysterious. 'Go away!' I shouted. 'I'm here for Tom, not you!' I dropped my head and stared at my VR feet as they padded across the broken ground.

When I looked up again, she had gone.

At last I approached the little township. The place was small, maybe a dozen buildings in all, set out in a rough grid pattern. A few cars were parked on the rutted tracks, big battered four-wheel-drives with minuscule engine compartments that looked like early hydrogen burners, 2020s vintage. No pod-bus service here, I thought.

There were plenty of people around. Some of them moved purposefully between the buildings, talking rapidly in a language I didn't understand. Others were gathered in little huddles, some of them weeping. They all seemed squat, small, round, and were dressed in heavy coats and boots – bright Day-Glo artificial fabrics, not the seal fur or whatever that I had been expecting. They looked to be a mix of races, some round-faced Asiatic, others more obviously European, even blond and blue-eyed. I vaguely knew that Siberia had been used as a vast slave labour camp by the Soviets in the last century; perhaps some of this mixed population were descended from prisoners or exiles.

They were hard-faced, weary-looking. And they were all spattered with mud. Though I was cast an occasional glance, there was no curiosity, no welcome. I walked on through the town.

Most of the buildings were wooden-walled huts. But I saw a few rounded tents made of what looked like leather: maybe they were yurts, I wondered, as the Mongols had once erected in another part of this great ocean of land. And there were buildings something like teepees, tented poles tied off at the top, walled not with skin but with brush and dried earth. Ribbons dangled from poles: prayer ribbons, I learned later, put up by people who still practiced shamanism and animism, people only a generation or so removed from a

64

hunter-gatherer lifestyle, and the idea that the very land is crowded with spirits. If that was so, the spirits weren't being too propitious that day. The strange melted-ground subsidence had affected some of the more solid buildings. One little shack adorned with a cross, perhaps a Christian church, was leaning at a spectacular angle. The yurts and teepee structures looked more or less upright, though. I supposed that if the ground started to give way you could just roll up your home and move to somewhere a bit more stable.

Everything was plastered by that grey-black mud. It clung to the walls and roofs in big dollops as if it had been sprayed out of a vast hose. Even on the ground, trampled bare between the buildings, there were splashes and craters, the grey of the mud mixing with the earth's dark brown.

I soon walked right through the township and out the other side, and found myself facing the sea. Perhaps this was a fishing village, but I saw no boats, no harbour. A few hundred metres away the coastline rose up in low sandy cliffs that looked as if they were melting into the sea. I saw no sign of that chopper; perhaps it had passed on along the coast. The sea itself was solid grey, and looked bitterly cold. And it seemed perilously close; I could see tide marks on doorsteps and around the bases of the houses. It looked to be eating into the shoreline here, the way it was in Florida.

There was one building obviously not owned by the locals. It was a tent in camouflage green, with a Red Cross painted brightly on the canvas. Familiar from too many disaster-zone news reports, it was an ominous sight.

Somebody screamed, so loud it hurt my ears before muffling filters cut in.

A little girl was standing before me. She was just a bundle, almost lost in an oversized parka. Her face was a round, ruddy ball, streaked with tears, and she was staring at my feet. A woman came and scooped her up, glaring at me.

And as I watched the woman walk away I noticed a row of body bags on the ground, all neatly zipped up.

'Hey, you!' It was a crisp summons in an American accent, West Coast perhaps.

A woman walked towards me in a spacesuit – or anyhow that's what it looked like, a bright blue coverall marked with

UN relief agency logos. But she had her masked hood open and pushed back from her head. She was black, late twenties maybe, a severe expression on her small face. 'You shouldn't be out here with so much exposed flesh,' she snapped at me now. 'Haven't you *heard* of tick-borne encephalitis? And how did you get here anyhow?'

'I'm not really here,' I said. I reached out as if to shake her hand. She responded automatically, offering me her own gloved hand; my hand passed through hers, briefly breaking up into a cloud of boxy pixels, and a protocol-violation warning pinged in my ear.

'Oh, a VR,' she said, her urgency morphing smoothly to contempt. 'What are you, some kind of Bottlenecker? A ghoul, come to see the dead people?'

Her words chilled me. 'I'm no disaster tourist—'

'Then show some consideration.' She pointed to my feet.

Looking down I realised what had upset the little girl so much. I was hovering a few centimetres above the ground surface; no wonder the kid was spooked. I hastily issued system commands, and I sank down to the ground.

The soldier turned to go. Evidently she didn't have time to waste on the likes of me.

I hurried after her. I wished I could grab her arm to get her attention. 'Please,' I said. 'I'm looking for my son.'

She slowed, and looked at me again. Her name was Sonia Dameyer, I read from a tag on her chest, Major Sonia Dameyer of the US Army. She was a familiar sight, an American soldier dressed in a spacesuit in some Godforsaken corner of the planet, like most of her kind nowadays devoted to rescue work and peacekeeping rather than war-fighting. 'Your son was here in person, through the burp?'

'The what?... Yes, he was here. I heard he was alive, but maybe hurt, I don't know anything else. His name is Tom Poole.'

Her eyes widened. 'Tom. The hero.'

She said this gently, but it was *not* what you want to hear about your missing child. I was dimly aware of my body, my real body, immersed in a body-temperature fluid and mildly anaesthetised, churning in the dark, as if I was having a bad dream. 'Do you know where he is?'

'This way.' She turned towards that big hospital tent.

I followed. My VR steps felt very heavy.

We walked into the tent. We had to pass through a kind of bubble airlock, inflated from clear plastic. Of course I could just walk through the walls, but Dameyer lifted the flaps for me, and I followed protocol. Inside it was dark; my vision blinked and juddered. But my VR eyes responded to the changed light levels as fast as a camera aperture dilating open.

When I could see, I looked around wildly at rows of fold-out canvas beds. Med robots, clumsy gear-laden trolleys, whirred self-importantly. Most of the patients wore oxygen masks, and drips snaked into arms. I couldn't see too many signs of traumatic injuries, no broken legs or crushed ribs. They looked like victims of a poisoning, or a gas attack, like the London underground incident in the 2020s. Not that I'm an expert on medical emergencies. The patients were all adults – and obviously not locals; this whole set-up was sent in by the western powers to tend for their own.

My vision shattered again. I shook my head, as if that was going to help. 'Damn it.'

'The trouble,' came a weak voice, 'is the tent. Partial Faraday cage woven into the fabric. It might be the UN but this is a military operation, Dad...'

I whirled. It was Tom, that familiar face staring up at me from a green military-issue pillow. I could barely even see him.

It was a tough moment. As a VR you can't cry, not with the cheap software John had hired for me anyway. But *I* was crying, that overweight, out-of-condition body floating in a tank in downtown Miami like a baby in a womb crying its embryonic heart out. Not only that, my comms link kept crashing, so that Tom's image would break up into planes and shadows, as if it was him who wasn't really there, rather than me. I tried to hug him. I closed my arms on empty air while protocol warnings pinged. How sad is that?

Tom was bound to disapprove of the way I'd come running out here after him. The logic of our father-son relationship would allow nothing less. But in the gloom of that hospital tent, as I fumbled to make contact with him, his expression was soft – not welcoming, but at least forgiving. In his way, I thought, he was glad to see me.

After a few minutes of this farce, the doctor attending Tom ordered me out of there as I was distracting the other patients. But he took pity on us. Tom's 'dose' had been light, he said, and though Tom still needed bed rest he could leave the field hospital.

So Tom swung his legs out of his bed, and a med-bot helped him pull on his trousers and jacket. Carrying only a light oxygen pack, with the mask loose around his neck, he limped slowly out of the tent. I longed to support him, but of course I couldn't. Instead he allowed Major Sonia Dameyer to take his arm.

She walked him all the way to one of those mud-covered teepee-like buildings, and helped him through the low door-way with its leathery flap. Inside, a dirt floor was covered by rugs of some kind of animal skin, very old and worn with use. There were three grass-stuffed pallets, and a stack of cooking pots. The only significant piece of furniture was a big old trunk, firmly padlocked: the family treasure of a nomadic people. My systems brought me a stink of stale cooking fat.

The teepee had one occupant, a local, a boy in a cut-down military-looking parka jacket. Aged maybe twelve, thirteen, he was forking his way through an open tin of baby carrots. When we came in – injured Tom with his oxygen mask, Sonia in her spacesuit, and me, a VR ghost – the kid, wide-eyed, tried to push past Sonia and run. Tom spoke to the kid softly. The kid answered before running out, though not without another spooked stare at Sonia and me.

Tom eased his way painfully down onto one of the pallets. He clutched his chest as if it hurt. Somewhat to my surprise, Sonia settled down on a pallet near Tom.

I asked, 'You two know each other?'

'Not before the burp,' Tom said.

Sonia said, 'It's advisable for Tom to have some protection. Some of the locals take it out on the westerners. Even aid workers like Tom.'

'Well, you can understand it,' Tom said. He wheezed slightly, as if he'd suddenly turned into a turn-of-the-century heavy smoker; it was a lung rattle you didn't hear any more. 'The locals have a difficult time of it, Dad. Even before the Warming the industries in the area made a mess of everything. You must have seen the plant a couple of klicks away. Even in the last century you had oil spills, the rivers killed by waste, the ground melting around the factories—'

I wanted to scream at him. 'Just for once,' I said, 'can't we talk about you and not the state of the damn planet?'

Tom stiffened. 'It's why I'm here in the first place.'

Sonia Dameyer watched this exchange, an amused expression on her face.

I backed up and tried again. 'Tell me what happened.'

He took a deep, rattling breath. 'I got a lungful of gas.'

'Gas? Poison gas, nerve gas? What are we talking about here?'

'Dad, take it easy—'

'Not an artificial agent,' Sonia said quickly. 'You don't have to worry about that, Mr Poole. It wasn't terrorism, not intentional. The event was natural. The gas was mostly methane laced with carbon dioxide.' She raised her eyebrows at Tom. 'But your son got rather more than a lungful. He wouldn't have got that if he hadn't gone running into the worst of it to pull the children out.'

So this was his heroism. Tom looked away, embarrassed even by this laconic description, suddenly very child-like.

'Who was that kid?'

'His name is Yuri. He's in one of my classes, Dad. His parents are, were, putting me up.'

'I didn't know you spoke Russian.'

He rolled his eyes; Sonia kept a neutral expression. Tom said, 'Dad, neither does Yuri. That wasn't Russian. This is a big country. Most of my students here are locals. Well, it is their ecosystem.'

I said, 'Ecosystem? You're teaching them ecology?'

'Teaching them to save it. It's a crash programme, Dad,' he said. 'The ecosystem in this place is falling apart. The permafrost is melting.'

In this place, on the northern edge of the world, the deep soil had never thawed out since the Ice Age: there had been a great cap of permafrost, in some places more than a kilometre thick, and the thin skim of soil on top of the permafrost had been the basis of an ecology – always impoverished, but unique. You had lichen and fast-growing grasses and herbs, and trees that could never grow tall because their roots couldn't dig into the frozen ground, and so on. There was a unique community of birds and animals here, lemmings and foxes, rare migrant birds; there had been reindeer that fed on the lichen, and humans that followed the reindeer herds.

'And now,' I guessed, 'it's all dying back.' The usual story.

'The permafrost is thawing,' he said. 'Dad, you're an engineer; you can imagine the consequences. It's as if the bedrock is melting.'

I thought of the buildings sinking into the ground, the pits in the landscape. Maybe the rapid coastal erosion was a consequence too, I mused, if the permafrost had actually been holding the dry land together.

'Even the lichen is dying off,' Tom said. 'Without lichen, no reindeer, and without them the people are screwed. Even fifty years ago they were still hunter-gatherers. But now – you must have seen how old the skins they use are, reused and scraped until they are paper-thin, and then used again. And even the land is crumbling away from under their feet.'

I had switched off long ago from thinking about the parlous state of the world. But now, sitting there as a VR projection in that scrappy mud-walled hut, I thought about what lay north of here. I remembered the year it had been reported that the last of the Arctic ice had finally gone, how the night of extinction had come at last for the polar bears and walruses, the seals and belugas. Now, beyond this coast, there was nothing but ocean all the way to the roof of the world, and the naked oceanic North Pole viewed from space was an alien, eerie image.

And that was why Tom was here supervising genomic grabs.

He had a pack under his pallet; he pulled out a little white-box gizmo the size of his palm. 'You like gadgets, don't you, Dad? Have you seen one of these before? Sonia, do you mind?' He pressed the edge of his gadget against the back of her hand. There was a small flash; she yelped and flinched a little. 'Sorry,' Tom said. 'Burned off a little body hair. Just give it a minute ... There it is.' He showed me the back of the box. I could make out nothing of the diagram it presented – it was cladistic, I learned later, a tree-of-life representation – but I could understand the words below: *Homo sapiens sapiens.* 'Dad, this is a DNA sequencer,' Tom said. 'Sequences a genome in seconds.' –

I marvelled briefly. I was a kid when the human genome was first sequenced, and that only at summary level, around the turn of the century; it had been a vast multinational effort. Now you could do it in seconds, with a gadget which probably cost less than this VR trip of mine. We're all used to progress, but every so often something like this hits you in the eye.

Tom was a trained teacher. But teaching had changed a lot since I was young. For any academic subject there were fully interactive VR tutors, available for free to every kid on the planet. Meanwhile flesh-and-blood teachers like Tom had been 'released back into the wild', as he put it. He taught kids by setting up hands-on schemes and letting them learn by doing it for real, rather than lecturing at them. This was the modern way. Tom trained at a college in Massachusetts, and he once proudly shown me its motto: 'The only source of knowledge is experience' – an Einstein quote.

That was the philosophy behind Tom's work here. He had been working for an international programme, sponsored by the Stewardship agencies, under the umbrella title the Library of Life. He had been training local kids to DNA-sequence as many living creatures as they could: the people of their community, the plants, animals, fish of their environment, even insects and bugs. All these genomic grabs, instantly analysed, were fed back into a massive central archive.

Conservationists had long been trying to preserve threatened species intact, or in frozen store as embryos or seeds or spores, or at least to save a drop of blood or a bit of leaf or bark that would allow analysis in the future. They still did all that, but there had been growing despair at the sheer size of a biosphere that was disappearing faster than it could be mapped, and the impossibility of preserving more than a fraction of it.

The rapid advance of genetic-sequencing technology had offered one solution. With the new kits, as a gene sample was collated with the massive central data stores, linked to a great phylogenetic tree of life, and given a provisional name within minutes, even an untrained child could 'discover' a new species. And once the information was extracted there was no need any more to worry about storing the long, fragile molecular strings of DNA itself. I'd heard that even fossils barely mattered nowadays, compared to the great flood of data and interpretation now flowing directly from the genes.

It was an eerie thought that even as the real-world ecology died back, a ghostly logical copy was being assembled in the abstraction of cyberspace. In a very real sense Tom and his kids, and similar volunteers all over the planet, really were saving the ecology for the future.

But none of that mattered to me, not in those awful minutes.

'OK,' I said to Tom carefully. 'It's a worthy goal. But it almost cost you your life.'

He found the incident painful to talk about, I think; maybe he was in some kind of mild shock. 'We were at the coast. Me and a dozen kids. I was actually fifty metres or so back, cross-checking their data streams as they sampled away. Then there was a water spout.'

'A spout?'

'Like an underwater explosion. It was like something from a cartoon, dad. It must have been a hundred metres tall.'

'Nearer two hundred,' Sonia said dryly.

'At first the kids stood and stared. I screamed at them to come away from the ocean. Some ran, others hesitated. Maybe they were too busy watching the spout. I was worried about waves. I didn't know what was happening; I imagined some kind of tsunami. Then the mud started coming down. Dad, it came in big handfuls, and when it hit you it *hurt*. All the kids started screaming, and came running from the sea with their hands over their heads.

'That was when I saw them falling, the ones closest to

the water. Just falling down as if they'd decided to go to sleep.'

'And you ran towards them,' I said.

'I was responsible for them. What else could I do? I'd only run a few paces before I could smell that rotten-egg stink—'

'Methane?'

'Yes. And then I understood what had happened.'

It had been a 'methane burp'. He told me that deep under the Arctic seafloor there are vast reservoirs of trapped gas. Molecules of carbon dioxide, hydrogen sulphide and methane can be trapped within cages of water-ice crystals – ice formed under extreme conditions of pressure, under the weight of the sea. You can find such stuff in sediments all the way around both poles, immense banks of ice and compressed gas. There is thought to be as much carbon locked up in these reservoirs as in all the world's fossil fuel stores. Until that dreadful day in Siberia, I had never even heard of them.

And it's very compressed, at more than a hundred times atmospheric pressure. Any engineer would recognise that's not too stable a situation. When the 'lid' is taken off that pressure vessel – for instance when the permafrost starts to melt, the containing pressure relieved – the eruption can be severe.

I thought it through. 'So a pocket of these gas hydrates gave away. The carbon dioxide and methane came gushing up. Carbon dioxide is heavier than air, so it would settle back to the surface of the sea and start spreading out...' Choking anything in its path.

Everybody understood the consequences of a carbon-dioxide flood. There had been an incident on Cephalonia ten years earlier that had killed thousands, an industrial accident, a carbon-sequestration scheme gone wrong.

All of a sudden Tom broke down. He buried his face in his hands. 'I couldn't get them all out. The stink of the methane drove me back. And I was *scared*, scared of the cee-oh-two. I couldn't help them.'

I had to sit and watch, frozen, as the competent soldier put her arms around his shoulders. 'You couldn't have done any more,' Sonia said. 'Believe me, I saw your medical charts. You went as far as you could.'

'Well, one thing's for sure,' I said. 'You can't stay here any more.'

Tom looked up, and anger flared on his tear-streaked face. 'You always said I was a quitter, didn't you, Dad? I'm not going anywhere.'

As I tried to work out what to say, Sonia butted in. 'Actually Mr Poole's correct. The aid agencies won't support any more work in this area, Tom. You're going to have to leave. We can't get you directly back to the States. But we can chopper you to Moscow, then to a military base near Berlin, and then by civilian charter to London.'

I kept my mouth shut, knowing from long experience that while he might listen to Sonia, he certainly wouldn't listen to *me*.

At length Tom said miserably, 'All right. But the sequencing project—'

'That will go on,' Sonia said brightly. 'They have robots to do this sort of thing now.' She stood up. 'I'll make the arrangements. I'll, um, I'll leave you to it.'

She pushed her way out of the tent, and Tom and I were left together, inarticulate, joined by electronics, separated by more than distance. We started to make plans. I would fly to England to meet him in person, if I could.

But even as we talked it through I was thinking over what had happened here, and in a corner of my mind I wondered what would happen if *all* those icy methane deposits, all around the poles of the planet, decided to yield up their treasures in one mighty global burp.

Chapter 8

On the ocean world, in the shelter of the flitter, Reath continued Alia's education.

'Have you thought any more about what I've told you?'

'You haven't told me anything,' she said sourly. 'Nothing but that list of names. The Implications of This and That.'

He laughed. 'Of Indefinite Longevity. Of Unmediated Communication. Of Emergent Consciousness.'

'What am I supposed to think? They're just names!'

'Isn't that enough? Alia, do you imagine I have a set of textbooks for you? To become a Transcendent is a process of discovery about yourself.'

'You mean I have to figure it all out?'

'You may discover more wisdom in yourself than you imagine. Let's start with the first stage, for instance—'

'Indefinite Longevity.'

'What do you imagine that means?'

She thought about it. 'Not dying.'

'Why is this important?'

'Because the Transcendence was created by immortals.' Every child knew that, even though it sounded like nothing but a scary story.

'Do you think extreme longevity is possible?'

She shrugged. 'On the *Nord* we expect to live to five hundred or so, barring accidents. In Michael Poole's day, it was rare to live much beyond one hundred. Surely it would be possible to come up with a treatment to stop the ageing process altogether.'

'An immortality pill?'

'Yes.'

'And if I had such a pill, and gave it to you, you would expect to live for ever?'

'Not *for ever*. There will always be accidents. This stupid plat-form might fly up and tip me off into the sea any second.'

He laughed. 'Yes. Undying, then, if not immortal. But, statistically, with luck, you could expect a much longer lifespan. An indefinite lifespan, in fact.'

'Indefinite Longevity.'

He smiled. 'You see, we don't just pluck these terms out of the air. And how would *that* make you feel?'

'It would be a wonderful gift. So much extra life—'

'Don't spout clichés, child,' he said.

She was taken aback; he rarely snapped at her.

'Think it through,' he said. 'Suppose it were true. How would you *feel*?'

To know you would certainly die one day was one thing. To know that there was at least a chance that you might live on and on and on, without limit, would change everything. How would she feel? 'Different.'

'How? What about other people? You've just had an almighty row with your family. Would you feel differently about that if you thought that you might face millennia more of life?'

'I wouldn't have had the row at all,' she said immediately. If her mother was to die before they could be reconciled, Alia would always regret it. And if she lived for tens of millennia or more, that regret would burn away at her soul, irresolv-able. 'It would drive me crazy, in the end. If I knew I was not going to die I'd try not to do anything I might have to regret for ever.'

'You'd become cautious.'

'I wouldn't make enemies. And I wouldn't hurt my friends.' But I might not even *make* friends, she thought, if I knew I might be stuck with them for ever – or, worse still, outlive them.

Reath was watching her, as if trying to follow her thoughts. 'What else? I know you are a Skimmer. I envy you that! But the real excitement of Skimming comes from the risk, doesn't it? Now, as things stand, if you were to have an accident, if you managed to kill yourself, you would be giving up a few centuries of life. But what if you were risking millennia – an indefinite future?'

She snorted. 'I'd have so much more to lose. You don't think about that consciously when you Skim, but – if I took your pill I'd never leave my room!'

'Suppose your sister was here with us now, and she fell into the sea. Would you try to rescue her?'

'Yes.'

'You'd risk your own life to save hers?'

'Yes!'

'Even at the cost of a hundred thousand years of existence?'

'I...' She shook her head.

'How do you think other people would feel about you?'

'They would hate me,' she said immediately. 'They would envy me – turn against me.'

'For your long life? Even if they knew that your longevity was for a purpose, for their own betterment?'

'Even so. Nobody would see past the fact that I would live on when they were dust. *I* would think like that. I would have to hide...' She shook her head. 'Some gift it would be! I'd be paralysed by the thought of all that future. I'd have to hide away.'

'I think you're beginning to understand,' he said. 'To be given Indefinite Longevity, to be released from a finite lifespan, is a step change, like ice turning to water, a total transformation. And you would have to find a way to *act*, to contribute to the human world, to make a difference, even though this great weight of time was hanging over you.'

'Why must I act?'

'Because in an ancient universe longevity is necessary for the greatest projects of all. A human life is just too short to accrue true wisdom. By the time you've figured out how things work, you're ageing, losing your faculties, dying.'

'But Michael Poole lived less than a century.'

'True. It's amazing those poor archaics achieved as much as they did!'

'Reath, if I were to become a Transcendent, what about my family?'

'They couldn't follow you,' he said gently.

She would be alone, she thought, left stranded by time. One by one her family and friends would turn to dust – even

Drea, even her new kid brother. Could she live with that? Only by shutting herself off, by closing down her heart. How could she possibly choose such a path?

'Reath, you said I might discover wisdom within me. I'm not wise at all. I haven't lived long enough. Ask my mother how wise I am!'

'Your age isn't the point. If you know you are undying, it's not your past that gives you wisdom. *It is your future* – or your awareness of it. And I think you are already starting to acquire some of that awareness. You don't have to choose now,' he said gently. 'We're only at the beginning, you and I, of our exploration.'

'Reath—' She hesitated. 'Are *you* a Transcendent?'

'Me?' He laughed, brusquely, but he turned away.

An alarm chimed. 'Oh!' Reath said. 'They're arriving at last.'

They hurried from the flitter.

At first she could see nothing but the clamour of the waves as they swelled and subsided. But then she saw a sleek shape, pale white, passing just under the surface of the water. Another followed, coming up from the darker depths, and a third, skimming like the first around the platform.

Soon there were a dozen of the creatures, perhaps more. Some of them were smaller – children, perhaps, calves with their parents. They were streamlined and coated with a thick fur; they moved with grace and startling speed. And they swarmed past and over each other, moving with an awareness of each other that seemed uncanny.

Reath peered down, smiling. He was clearly enjoying the sight.

But Alia was ship-born; living things didn't interest her much. 'Very pretty,' she said. 'So what? Where are the people?'

He looked at her, raising his eyebrows. 'You must learn to *see*, Alia.'

One of the creatures broke away from the pack and came swimming towards the surface. Now she could see that it had four stubby limbs – four limbs as she had, though these were fins. At the end of each fin was a kind of paddle, webbed with five extensions, perhaps the relics of fingers and toes.

She got the point. That there were four limbs, not two or six or eight, was a clue. A tetrapodal body plan was a hallmark of Earth life, an accidental arrangement that had been settled on early in the development of animals there – including the ancestors of humans – and had been stuck to ever since, even as most of those animals either went extinct or scattered across the Galaxy. But it didn't have to be that way; six or eight or twelve limbs would have been just as effective. A four-limbed body was a signature: *I am from Earth.*

The creature broke the surface and lifted its head out of the water. It had a face, with a smoothed-over nose, and a mouth that gulped at the air. And though its brain pan was flat it had a smooth forehead, a distinct brow – and two eyes, sharp blue, that met her gaze. She felt a powerful shock of recognition, something deep and ancient that joined her to this animal. But those eyes were blank, empty.

The creature broke the brief contact, and dived back beneath the waves and out of sight.

'Remarkable,' Reath murmured. 'But now you see why I was evasive about this world's name...'

'They are human,' she said.

'Well, their ancestors were – and so are these, their remote children, in the terms the Commonwealth recognises.

'Their ancestors came here, long ago, at the time of the Bifurcation. They tried to settle. They built rafts, ganged together. They trained their children to fish for the native life forms – they must have engineered their digestive systems to enable them to eat the fish and crab and eel analogues to be found here.' He shook his head. 'But the children and grandchildren took to the water, more and more. The rafts couldn't be maintained, not in the very long run, for there was no raw material to fix them, and no will to do so either. Soon the ocean closed over the rafts' last remnants. But the people remained, and their children.'

'And they lost their minds.'

'Well, why not? Alia, big brains are expensive to maintain. If you have an unchanging environment, like this endless ocean, you don't *need* to do much thinking. Far better to spend your energy on swimming faster, or diving deeper. A big head would be good for nothing but creating drag! And the adaptation worked.' He stared out. 'This ocean could drown ten Earths. There's no limit to how many of these critters there might be out there. There is room for billions, trillions! Perhaps some of them have adapted further – to go without air, to reach greater depths, greater pressures, even to reach the ice of the seabed. Down there they could become exotic, I suppose, and the overlap between the world as they see it and yours would diminish, until you could no longer recognise each other at all.'

'I never heard of anything like this.'

'You will learn this is a common pattern. Over time humans have been projected into all sorts of environments, and they have adapted. And anywhere the living is stable you find the same phenomenon, an enthusiastic discarding of the burden of thinking.'

She frowned. 'The *Nord* is half a million years old. We were isolated. *We* could have lost our minds.'

'But *you* remained a people in transition – never settling, taking your little world with you, rebuilding it all the time. Why, the stroke of genius was to have even your breeding cycle dependent on technology!'

'The birthing pods.'

'Yes. Of course it is possible to retain a technological capability without consciousness – think of the Shipbuilders – but you couldn't afford to become dumb, for your lives depend on the mechanisms that keep the *Nord* habitable. For your kind, the trick worked.'

Your kind. It was a chilling phrase – and an insulting one.

Alia's people were proud of their pedigree, proud of what they had become. It was a very long time since her remote ancestors had left the home planet, and her physiology, her frame and musculature, were built for low-gravity climbing as much as walking. And after half a million years of selection and purposeful enhancement, in Michael Poole's terms she was an intuitive genius. But to Reath, it seemed, she was just one of another *kind*, her people on the *Nord* and all their rich history just another type of post-human, no better than the mindless creatures swimming in this monstrous sea.

Alia felt resentful, and wanted to have nothing in common with these creatures. 'All they do is swim around chasing fish. They are sub-human – aren't they? If their brains have shrivelled, if they have no mind—'

'I always prefer the term "post-human", regardless of encephalisation. Best to avoid value judgements.'

'I can give this world a name,' she said. '*They* can't.'

'But what need have they of names? Alia, names or not, *they were once human*. They may have no advanced consciousness now, but they have feelings, sensations, a sensorium probably unlike any other type. They are a thread in mankind's history, Alia, that must be drawn back into the tapestry. This is why I brought you here. You must learn to see mankind as the Transcendence sees it, without prejudice—'

She hazarded, 'And with love?'

'Love, yes! And though we have talked of long lives, time is short – at least, in the longer view of the Transcendence. For we are all diverging from each other, we different sorts of humans. Just as these watery folk are swimming away from our world of air and stars, there may come a point when we can no longer talk to each other, even recognise our commonality. We have to find our way back together again before we lose each other completely…'

The post-humans, swimming beneath the platform, were baffled. They had responded to the subsonic beacon that drew them here, but there was nothing for them, no food, no mates. Disappointed, in pairs and family groups, they drifted away.

Chapter 9

Once I'd surfaced from VR I tried to get down to some work, which I figured was the best way to waste the days I had to endure before I could get in that plane seat. With a fat mug of coffee I went to my mother's study, which had the best connection and display facilities in the house, and closed the door.

The first thing I did was bring up a VR of the current design-freeze of our paper-study space probe. The bulky main body unfolded, bejewelled with lacy antennae and instrument booms, hanging in the air before me like a beautiful toy. I inspected the liquid-lead coolant tanks and the neutron shield and the instrument buses, and the suite of tiny probes we planned to drop off on the way out of the solar system, and the Higgs-field power plant at its very core. Just looking at the thing was calming. This was my pet starship.

It was called the Kuiper Probe, in the requests-for-tender documents from NASA and the USAF that defined it. If it ever actually got built it would no doubt be given some more sonorous name. Strictly speaking it wasn't really a starship, of course. For one thing it was unmanned, and for another it wouldn't go to the stars. But it was an 'interstellar precursor mission', in the jargon.

Our probe was designed to sail a thousand astronomical units from the sun – that is, a thousand times as far as Earth is from the central star. By comparison the furthest planet, Pluto, is a mere forty AU out, but the nearest star, in the Alpha Centauri system, is more than a quarter of a *million* AUs away. But our probe's ten-year, thousand-AU mission would be a first step, a preliminary sail out of the cosy harbour of the inner system. Nothing had travelled further from Earth save the long-derelict Voyagers and Pioneers, planetary probes from the 1970s. And where the Voyagers had had to rely on gravitational slingshots to hurl them so far, *we* would be going under our own steam, fuelled by cosmic might.

It would be a proving flight for the key technologies that might one day take our machines, or even us, very much further. And there was even good science to do on the way. We would be able to explore the outer solar system, far beyond Pluto, where ice moons, the Kuiper objects, flocks in the frozen dark. Our trajectory would give precise measurements of such huge numbers as the total mass of the solar system. We would pass through the heliopause, where the wind from the sun disperses into the wider interstellar medium, and study whatever strange cosmic particles and radiations from deeper space are blocked from Earth's view.

And, most significant of all, we could visit the Kuiper Anomaly. That glimmering tetrahedron had continued its own long, aloof orbit around the sun ever since its discovery in the first decade of the century. Now it was time to go confront that strange visitor.

That, in fact, was the reason the US Air Force was involved. In our little design community there was even a rumour that in among the reserve payload weight, set aside for contingencies and late additions, was an allowance of fifty kilogrammes or so for a bomb.

I tried to focus. I had plenty of challenging work to get done; I was in the middle of involved structural analyses of the Probe's propulsion system. But my concentration wouldn't gel. Designing a starship as therapy: it often worked, but not today.

I was deeply relieved when Shelley Magwood, my nominal boss, spotted I was online, and logged on to talk to me.

Shelley coalesced in my mother's study. She was sitting in a fashionable moulded-ceramic chair projected from her office in Seattle. She had heard about my troubles. 'I don't know what you're doing sitting there working on the damn Probe,' she snapped. 'The Probe can wait. The Kuiper Anomaly isn't going anywhere...'

Shelley was thin, intense, with a strong face, high cheekbones and a Roman nose. Her hair was dirty blonde, but I suspected she was already dyeing it, in her thirties. I always thought she worked too hard, burning herself up in her energetic pursuit of too many projects, but there always seemed to be a smile, just behind the door of her face. Nowadays she was more a manager, an entrepreneur, than an engineer, and I suspected she indulged in this proof-of-concept project as a sanity release, just as I did. I liked her a hell of a lot.

'You should be with Tom,' she said. 'Get your fat backside on a plane.'

'I've tried that,' I said. 'I have a seat lined up. The protocols—'

'Bugger the protocols. Look, if you need help—'

'Thanks. I just have to be patient.'

'I'm sorry about Tom.'

'Don't be. The work is helping.'

'Oh, is it?' Through some fancy projection-software interpolation it looked as if she was peering at the same diagrams I was. 'Just sit tight a minute,' she said sternly. 'I'll check over what you've done. The state you're in you'll probably screw the whole thing.'

'Thanks for your support.'

'I mean it,' she said. No doubt she did. She frowned, focusing on the schematics, and I sat back and waited.

So a kid who had once watched space shuttles launching from his backyard had finished up designing a real-life spaceship, after a fashion. It had been a long journey, though.

My primary ambition, as a small kid, had been to fly in space myself. But as I grew older it quickly became apparent that that would never be possible. Not only were the only manned space missions on the cards endless round-the-block tours on the Space Station, for which there was a whole generation of candidate astronauts waiting in line before I reached age twelve, but I soon learned that my personal spacesuit, my body, wasn't up to the task of taking me off the planet.

So my ambitions downscaled a bit. If I couldn't fly myself, maybe I could be involved in designing the next generation of ships. But even that got compromised.

I majored in math and engineering at college. But when I graduated in 2017, it was quickly apparent that there was no work to be had in designing spaceships. There were only a few design-study projects sponsored by NASA, ESA and the other space agencies. But even this was playing; there was no serious money in it. This was not a time for flying into space: it was an age of entropy, when the oil was running out and energy running down, and our attentions were increasingly absorbed by the need to cope with the Warming, and other hazards of the Earthbound future.

But I was an engineer. I wanted to work on something that would get *built* – and, incidentally, that would pay; I had no ambitions to be poor. So I looked for opportunities.

What was coming up at the time was a new generation of nuclear power plants. Whatever its drawbacks, nuclear power had become fashionable again, as it was not a source of carbon-dioxide emissions – and as a source of energy, a lot less problematical politically than chasing down the world's remaining oil supplies. So I went into nuclear engineering. I spent eight years working on a plant that eventually opened in 2027.

It was what we called a fifth-generation design. The core worked at nearly a thousand degrees, a temperature that would have signalled the start of a meltdown in early generations of reactor. Those high temperatures offered much greater efficiency, but to achieve them we had to go through a challenging programme of research and development, for instance in ultra-hard materials that were resistant to intense heat and neutron bombardment. We actually cooled the thing with a huge vat of molten lead; I learned a great deal about refrigeration principles on that project, principles I applied later to the Kuiper Probe.

When our meltdown-proof, terrorism-proof plant came online and started to feed its first watts into the grid, we were very proud of what we'd achieved. Super-safe and super-clean, we used to say. We even won the economic argument, although the costs of our competitors, at the time renewables like solar and wind power, were tumbling. That New York station is still operating today, even though its economic justification has gone away a little.

I was thirty-two years old. I was married to Morag, and we had a son, Tom. We were very happy. I didn't realise it at the time, but I guess that was in some ways the peak of my life. I would never have believed that things would fall apart so quickly.

My work suffered first. I admit I didn't see the Higgs revolution coming – but then, few others did.

Higgs technology came out of cosmology. The physics of the early universe was exotic. In our era some particles, such as the quarks that make up protons and neutrons, are massive, while photons, particles of light, are massless. It is an elusive critter called the Higgs field that gives objects mass. But when the universe was less than a millionth of a millionth of a second old, and it was still hotter than a certain crucial temperature of a thousand trillion degrees, the Higgs field couldn't settle. *Every* particle was massless. The universe was filled with them, flashing across unravelling spacetime at lightspeed. But when the universe expanded and cooled the Higgs field condensed out, like frost settling on blades of grass. Suddenly everything changed.

And when the Higgs field condensed it released a flood of energy, cosmos-wide. It is just as water freezing to frost must release heat energy: it was a phase transition, as the cosmologists say. That vast injection of energy powered the universe into a surge of 'inflation' that dramatically accelerated its expansion. All this is cosmology; it can be seen written in the relics in the sky – the remnant background Big Bang radiation, the gravity waves that slosh back and forth – a story deciphered when I was a boy.

What changed our world was the development in the 2020s of a new breed of particle accelerator so powerful it was able to emulate, in tiny spaces and brief instants, the tremendous energy density and temperature of the early universe – hot enough, in fact, to drive out the Higgs field from a bit of matter. And when the Higgs was allowed to recondense, it released a flood of energy – vastly more than the energy input, under the right conditions. If that sounds like something for nothing, it isn't: it is just as in a fission bomb the relatively small energy of conventional explosives is used to liberate the much greater energies locked up in atomic nuclei.

As soon as control of the Higgs field was achieved, even

on a small experimental scale, its potential was obvious. Here was an energy source of much greater density than anything we'd dreamed possible before – and we could tap it, tap an energy that had once driven the expansion of the universe itself. Furthermore it was as safe as you could wish, far safer even than our new-generation nukes.

When you try to predict technological trends, it's easy to follow straight lines. For instance computer power, measured in operations per buck, has been doubling every couple of years since long before I was born, and has continued to follow that trend, more or less, ever since. Maybe you could have foreseen some of the consequences: a world in which a machine equivalent of human-level intelligence has long been passed, a world in which artificial self-awareness has become a commodity, and a part of everyone's life. What's much harder to predict is what comes out of nowhere, out of left field. I was still a kid when the orbital astronomical observatories confirmed the universe's biography from the Big Bang to the present. And out of that great cosmological revolution has come a new power source for cars and planes and cities – and, maybe, starships. Who'd have thought it?

Not me, that was for sure. In the late 2020s, as I followed these sudden developments in the technical literature, I was alarmed.

In terms of my career, it needn't have mattered, maybe. We had only just brought that New York station online, and others of the same design were sprouting around the Great Lakes, and in Nevada and California. There is an asset inertia with big technology; you can't throw away your whole infrastructure just because somebody somewhere has a bright idea.

But the fact was, somebody *had* had that bright idea.

A new long-term national energy strategy began to emerge, born out of existing trends, notably the painful weaning of America off of oil, and the possibilities opened up by Higgs. 'Generation distribution' was the catchphrase. Every block, every home would be a source of energy, from photovoltaic cells, rooftop wind turbines, maybe even biofuel crops in the backyard. And everybody would be connected into a local microgrid, from which you would draw energy when you needed it, store energy in hydrogen fuel cells in your basement, and even sell power back when you had a surplus. The microgrids would be connected up to larger regional, national and international grids, supported by key nodes that would, in the first phase, be existing-technology power stations, including old hydrocarbon-burners and our new nukes, but these would be phased out as soon as they paid off their development costs, and replaced by Higgs generators. The energy supply would be distributed, robust at every scale, clean and environment-friendly, and soaked with smartness. The Administration began to fast-track enabling legislation, such as to force the utilities to purchase energy from any supplier. It was a marvellous vision.

But in the longest term there was no place for nuke technology, and I knew immediately that my chosen field was a conceptual dead end. Maintenance projects might have seen out my working life, but all the creative energies, and serious government R&D money, would be focused, quite rightly, on the new Higgs-field technologies. Even as it came online my New York station was obsolete – and so, in a sense, was I, in my early thirties. I couldn't bear it. I wanted to be in the front line.

I argued with Morag at the time. She pointed out we had a kid, and plans for more. The world didn't owe me a living, she said, no matter how hard I chased my dreams.

But I wouldn't listen. Aged thirty-four, I quit my job and took an academic post at Cornell. I would be teaching the fundamentals of physics to reluctant students, while researching the new Higgs-field technologies to advance my own career.

It didn't work out. There was already a whole generation of grad students armed with a hands-on knowledge of the new prototype unified-field energy systems – I was already too old, at thirty-four. I continued to make a living, but I'd got myself stuck up another blind alley, and was a lot less well paid. I was unhappy. Morag was justifiably unhappy too, unhappy at my choices, at the way it had worked out. We loved each other, but I guess we took it out on each other. We didn't mean to hurt Tom, but he was there. Call it friendly fire.

Then Morag got pregnant again. It was actually an accident, we weren't sure how we could afford it. But we embraced it. It was going to be a new start, we decided, us and the kids. As Morag's pregnancy developed I started to feel more content than I ever had before. Maybe I was learning that there is more to life than childhood dreams, and whatever disappointment I felt was fading in the light of a richer joy.

And then, and then. Morag died in childbirth; her child didn't survive.

Grief doesn't begin to describe it. It was like an amputation, a loss of half of myself. I went through the motions of my life, I ate and slept and rose again and got dressed and worked, but it all seemed purposeless, a charade. And my emotions raged, as uncontrollable and inexplicable as the weather. I even took it out on my memory of Morag, as if she'd somehow rejected me by dying. The ultimate jilting.

Oh, I looked after Tom, materially anyhow. I never disappeared into drink or drugs or VR fantasy-land, the way a lot of people expected me to, I think. I kept working, going through the motions of class after class, semester after semester, one faceless cadre of students after another, though I gave up on the idea of any original work. I kept functioning. Maybe it was 'stoicism', as one artificial-sentience therapist assured me. The way I see it, I just kept up the shell.

After Morag's death, I lost a decade. That's how I look at it now. Then, one day, I found myself inhabiting my life again.

When I looked around I was suddenly in my forties. Tom, in his late teens, had grown away from me, not surprisingly. And if I thought my career was stuck when I was thirty-four, it certainly was now. It's a depressing progression. By twenty I knew I would never be an astronaut. By thirty I knew I would never be a brilliant engineer. And by forty-five I was all I would ever be, for the rest of my life.

But I still needed money. I kept up my teaching at Cornell, and I put some feelers out for consultancy work.

I got a lucky break when Shelley Magwood contacted me, out the blue. She had been in one of my early cadres of students at Cornell, and she remembered me. Aged thirty or so she had already made herself rich with shares in a start-up company specialising in aspects of the new Higgs-field technologies. She carved me out consultancy assignments based on Higgs, and on my deeper experience in the nuclear field. For a transition period the two technologies would have to work together providing power to the common grid, and there were interfaces, protocols, loading balances and other technical details to be worked out.

So the work kept coming. I did it well enough. Shelley said I had inspired her, as a teacher; without me she wouldn't have found her own successful track, and so forth. I appreciated the morale boost, and the money. But we both knew Shelley was doing me a favour.

Then Shelley drew me into another of her ventures.

'I remember how you always used to throw space-technology applications into your classes,' she told me. 'It was obvious where your heart was. I think you might enjoy working on this.'

When the request-for-proposals for the project that became the Kuiper Probe arrived, Shelley's consultancy company was small and nimble enough to be able to position itself to grab the work, but smart enough to see the potential for the future. 'This is only a paper study,' she told me. 'But it might get picked up. And even if not, we're going to be *paid* to think about how to use Higgs to drive spaceships. We'll be like Renaissance shipbuilders, just as Columbus is about to embark, holding a patent on sail technology...'

Shelley quickly put together a team, with a number of freelancers, like me, and input from various other companies on specialised aspects. We rarely met; almost everything was done remotely, as Shelley's 'paper' study, actually a software abstraction, was driven to successive levels of design detail.

Kuiper was an obvious application for Higgs technology. But for me, it was no more than a start to use this miraculous energy source as a way to drive steam rockets. In the long term, I dreamed, control of the Higgs field could give us control of inertia itself: we could banish mass. I imagined a day when vast ships would float from world to world, light as thistledown.

My God, I loved the work. It paid pennies, but it kept me sane.

Shelley emerged from her quick review. 'So you haven't screwed up too badly. But your mind must be with Tom. Mine would be.'

I tried to tell her something of my relationship with Tom. 'Everything changed the day Morag died,' I said. 'I took ten years to get over that. If I ever did. And Tom—'

'Tom thinks you miss the dead baby more than you love him. Is that it?'

That shocked me. 'It isn't true,' I said. 'It never was.'

'Maybe not,' Shelley said. 'But these things get stuck in your head.'

'How would you know?'

She looked a little uncomfortable. 'When I was younger I had a lot of rivalry with my father. He was a tough character. Didn't suffer fools gladly, he always said. But the trouble was he couldn't distinguish between a genuine fool and a kid trying to learn.'

I listened to this carefully; she'd told me little about her past. 'I think I remember him.'

'Oh, you met him during my college days. Parent-teacher events when he was always on his best behaviour. And he was never cruel. He was loving, in his own way. But *his* way was a stream of put-downs. I grew up thinking I could never be good enough for him – until one day I decided I was going to beat him.'

'And that's why you work yourself to the bone.' We'd had arguments about her work-rate and its effects on her health right back to our college days, when I tutored her.

'Anyhow that rivalry stuck. And then he died, before I had a chance either to beat him or give up the chase... Now I'm stuck with it.' She glared at me. 'Nobody gets out of the past without scars. What you have to do is deal with it, and move forward. Right now Tom is all that matters.'

'OK,' I said. 'But things may be a little more complicated than that.'

I was thinking of my visitations by Morag.

I felt an impulse to tell her, to confess. I still hadn't even told John about it. I was starting to think I ought to open up to somebody. But, as well as I knew Shelley, I had no idea what her reaction would be. I guess I was afraid of losing her.

Maybe she intuited some of my confusion, if not the reason for it. She leaned forward. 'Focus on Tom,' she said. 'The project doesn't need you right now. But he does.'

I nodded. The moment passed, and my secret stayed intact a little longer.

Chapter 10

During their long interstellar jaunts in the monastic silence of his ship, Reath encouraged Alia to study the history of mankind. 'If you don't know where you've come from,' he would say, 'you certainly don't know where you're going.'

And in this study, as he had been throughout her life, it was the small, dark, unhappy figure of Michael Poole that was her companion, and her anchor point.

Humanity was thought to be some six hundred thousand years old – that is, six hundred thousand years since the root stock had diverged from ancestral forms. For the first hundred thousand years, a period that had actually ended in Michael Poole's own lifetime, mankind was confined to Earth. This era was a lengthy and mostly uninteresting saga of a groping towards rationality and material command, amid endless wars.

'The most interesting thing about mankind in this long Earthbound period is its fragility,' Reath said. 'Think about it. Humanity was confined to one rocky world in a remote corner of the Galaxy – indeed, imprisoned in a membrane of water and organics smeared over the planet's surface. Up to Michael Poole's time, that was all the life anybody knew about in the whole universe! Why, the slightest disturbance could have wiped us out – destroyed mankind before we got started – and that would have been that.'

The terrible contingency made Alia shudder. 'Poole's generation referred to his time as the Bottleneck.'

'They were right,' Reath said. 'But it wasn't the only age of crisis. There were several points in human history where things went badly wrong. Seventy thousand years before Michael Poole's time there was an immense volcanic eruption that disrupted the planet's climatic systems. Even earlier, while mankind was still only a species of upright ape among many others, a plague cut the root stock down to a few dozen. Mankind reduced to just fifty or so! Think of it. You can see traces of such times in our genetic legacy even now, evidence of a dreadful simplifying. The major difference with the Poole Bottleneck was that this was the first anthropogenic crisis – the first caused directly by the actions of mankind.

'It's no great surprise that as Witnesses we are drawn to Bottlenecks. They are the times of maximum danger for mankind, maximum drama – and yet of maximum flux and opportunity.'

Alia stared at Michael Poole, his troubled face trapped in stillness inside her Witnessing tank. In this particular incident Poole was outdoors, in a strange landscape. In hot, dense sunlight, he was climbing over a vast heap of wreckage, of smashed and abandoned machines. 'Here he is aged fifty-two,' she said. 'He is entering the most critical time of his life.'

'He looks troubled.'

'He often does,' she said wryly. 'Poole knew the dangers of his age very well. Most educated people of the time did, I think. But after the danger his son encountered, Poole came to grasp the implications better than most. He worked on a geoengineering project after all.'

'And he was a Poole,' Reath said, somewhat reverently.

'But they were so limited – all the people of his time, even Poole himself. The best you can say about them is that they were beginning to understand how little they *did* know.'

'And is it the problems of the Earth that are depressing him so?'

'More than that,' she said. 'His own work isn't going well. And it is a difficult time in his personal life...' She skimmed the projection back and forth; Poole stayed steady at the centre of the flickering images while people imploded around him.

When she was young Alia had focused her Witnessing on the more accessible moments of Poole's life: his joyous childhood, his discovery of love as a young man. With Reath's gentle coaxing she had been trying to concentrate on this period, the most difficult time of his life – Poole's own Bottleneck, perhaps. But it was very hard for her to get into the head of a fifty-two-year-old man from the middle of the twenty-first century. Everything about his life was so *different*. Her fifties would be the start of her young adulthood, a time of opportunity and growing command over her destiny. For Poole, more than half his life – and the more productive, enjoyable part – had already gone. He was running out of future.

Sometimes, when she studied Poole, all she seemed to see was his smallness. He was a dark, unhappy creature, shut in on himself, trapped in a world so impoverished of stimulus and capability it was a wonder people didn't simply die of boredom and frustration. 'He knows so little,' she said. 'He will die knowing so little. He suffers so much. And yet he will shape history.'

Reath touched her shoulder. 'This is just as Witnessing is meant to be. As you come to understand the life of another embedded in the past, you come to understand yourself better.

'But you must try to keep a sense of perspective, Alia. Mankind did pass through this terrible Bottleneck. And the future of this limited little species was remarkable indeed...'

After its long Earthbound prologue, mankind erupted off the planet, 'like a flock of birds lifting from a tree', said Reath.

There followed a wave of exploration and colonisation, in which Michael Poole's descendants played a significant part. But after the startling discovery of a Galaxy full of alien cultures, many of them ancient and malevolent, it was a wave of expansion that was pushed back several times. Once that reverse reached all the way back to Earth itself.

With the alien occupation of Earth overthrown, mankind re-emerged strong, united, focused – pathologically so, perhaps, Reath said. The government of the time, the most powerful central authority ever to emerge in human history, was known as the Coalition. A new expansion, a froth of war, conquest and assimilation, swept across the face of the

Galaxy. It took twenty-five thousand years, but at last the centre of the Galaxy itself lay in human hands, and legends of the victorious warriors, the 'Exultant generation', resonated down the ages that followed.

Alia said, '"Pathological"? That's a strange word to choose.'

'But it was a pathology, of a sort,' Reath said. 'Think about it. The Coalition dominated mankind for *twenty-five thousand years*! That's a period that was comparable to the age of the species itself, at the time. For all that time the Coalition controlled culture, politics – even the genetic destiny of mankind. The soldiers who finally broke into the Galaxy's Core were as human as Michael Poole, save for some superficialities. It was unnatural, Alia! That's why I say it was pathological. A kind of madness gripped mankind, as we became defined solely by the Galactic war.'

'But it was a successful madness.'

'Oh, yes!'

When the war was won, the centre could no longer control a Galactic mankind. Reath said darkly, 'It was as if a truce had been called among humans, for the purposes of the war against the aliens. But with the Galaxy won history resumed – history of the usual bloody sort.'

The great expansion that had climaxed in the Exultant victory had cleaned out or marginalised most non-human life forms, leaving the Galaxy an empty stage for a new human drama. New ideologies emerged, and successor states sprouted like weeds in the rubble of empire, each of them claiming legitimacy from the collapsed Coalition. The age of conflict had bequeathed a Galaxy well stocked with weaponry, and the wars that followed, motivated by economics and ideology, glory and ambition, consumed millennia and countless lives.

'It was not a noble age,' Reath said, 'though it threw up plenty of heroes. And it was played out in the shadow of the monumental achievements of the Exultant generation. Many were afflicted with a sense of shame at what they had become. But there was always somebody else to blame for the squabbling, of course. And time exerted its power. We are fleeting creatures, we humans!'

The river of time flowed on, bloodied by war, thousand-year empires bubbling like spindrift. The Coalition and its works were forgotten. And humans, flung upon a million alien shores, morphed and adapted. This was the Bifurcation of Mankind.

There were still wars, of course. But now different human species confronted each other. Some were so different that they no longer competed for the same resources – 'they no longer shared the same ecological niche', as Reath put it. But a more fundamental xenophobia fuelled genocidal wars.

'So much suffering,' Alia said. 'How terrible it all was.'

Reath said, 'I wonder what Michael Poole would have thought of it all, if he could have looked forward. Was his struggle worth it, merely to enable so much suffering to follow?'

'Michael Poole gave those who followed the opportunity to live their lives,' she said. 'He can't take responsibility for what they did with that opportunity.'

Reath nodded. 'Yes. When your children leave home, you can't live their lives for them. But you always worry.'

Alia wondered briefly if Reath had any children of his own. He said very little about his past – indeed she knew far more about Michael Poole, dead half a million years, than she did about the man who had come to share her life.

The age of Bifurcation ended abruptly.

Ninety thousand years after the time of Michael Poole, genetic randomness threw up a new conqueror. Charismatic, monstrous, carelessly spending human life on a vast scale, the man known to history as the Unifier saw only opportunity in the fragmentation of mankind. By using one human type as a weapon against another – and, somehow, by inspiring loyalty in soldiers as unlike each other as it was possible to be and yet still be called human – he built an empire. One of his many enemies took his life, his empire disintegrated, evanescent.

In the end he was defeated by the sheer scale of the Galaxy. And yet the Unifier's project had a long-lasting impact. If only briefly he had spread a common culture across a significant fraction of the Galaxy's geography. Not since the collapse of the Coalition had the successors of mankind recalled that they all once shared the same warm pond.

Reath said, 'Retrospectively historians call the Unifier's brief empire the Second Integrality of Mankind – the First being the Coalition. The Unifier planted the seeds of a post-Bifurcation unity. But it took a long time before those seeds took root.'

It was ten thousand years, in fact, before mankind began to act once more with a semblance of unity. And once again that unity required a common cause.

Mankind still controlled the Galaxy. But that Galaxy was a mere puddle of muddy light, while all around alien cultures commanded a wider ocean. Now those immense spaces became an arena for a new war. As in the time of the Unifier, disparate human types were thrown into the conflict; new sub-species were even bred specifically to serve as weapons. This war continued in various forms for a hundred thousand years.

'An unimaginable length of time,' Reath said, shaking his head. 'Why, those who concluded the war weren't even the same species as those who started it! And yet they fought on.'

The war didn't so much end as fizzle out. Like the Unifier, mankind was defeated by the sheer scale of the arena and, exhausted, fell back to its home Galaxy – though relics were left stranded to fend for themselves, far from home. The long unity of the Third Integrality was lost.

'But we didn't return to complete fragmentation, not quite,' Reath said. 'For now a new force began to emerge in human politics: the undying.'

Almost since the time of Michael Poole, there had been undying among the ranks of mankind. Some of these were engineered to be so, by humans or even by non-humans, and others were the children of the engineered. Of course none of these were truly 'immortal'; it was just that they couldn't foresee a time when they would die. They emerged and died in their own slow generations, a subset of mankind who counted their lives in tens of millennia or more.

The hostility of mortal mankind to these undying was

relentless. It pushed the undying together, uniting them for common protection – even if, often, in mutual loathing. But they were always dependent on the mass of mankind. Undying or not, they were still human; if the rest of humanity were to be destroyed, it was doubtful indeed if the undying could survive long. So while their view of the world was very different from that of the mortals, the undying ones needed their short-lived cousins.

The undying had rather enjoyed the long noon of the Coalition. Stability and central control was what they sought above all else. To them the Coalition's collapse, and the churning ages of war and Bifurcation that followed, were a catastrophe.

When, two hundred thousand years after the time of Michael Poole, the storm of extragalactic war at last blew itself out, the undying decided enough was enough. In this moment of human fragmentation and weakness, they began to act. They set about knitting the scattered scraps of mankind into a new Integrality – the Fourth – which they would call the Commonwealth.

The new Commonwealth crept across the bruised stars. It was a slow process. By Alia's time, since the founding of the Commonwealth three hundred thousand years had worn away; it was a remarkable thought that the great project of the Fourth Integrality had already taken *most* of human history. But the undying were patient.

And meanwhile they began a programme to share their own longevity with as many mortals as possible. Even this was dedicated to the interests of the undying themselves – for, whatever their origins among the multiple subspecies of mankind, the new undying would quickly inherit the values and concerns of those who engineered their emergence.

Reath was enthusiastic. 'It's really a wonderful vision, Alia. The undying are no elite. They are making us like themselves, giving us the gift of their own unimaginably long lives...'

But this cold calculation repelled Alia. It was as if the icy kiss of an undying transformed a mortal into one of *them*, causing her to become infected with their long inhuman perspectives. It was a plague of non-death, she thought uneasily.

Reath breathed, 'And they conceived of another tremendous project. At the heart of the Commonwealth the undying began to build the Transcendence. The undying dream of a new form of human life, a higher form – the betterment of us all achieved through a new unity. A dream, a wonderful dream!...'

Alia turned back to the Witnessing tank, set to a random moment in Poole's sixth decade, a three-dimensional slice cut out of his four-dimensional life. How strange it was that she should be united in this way with Michael Poole – he at the very beginning of mankind's great adventure, and she, perhaps, at its end.

It was a strange fact that for most of mankind the business of the Witnessing, and the wider programme of Redemption Reath had hinted at, was the most visible manifestation of the nascent Transcendence's ambitions. But, Alia thought now, how strange it was that the Transcendents, while reaching for the future, should be so obsessed with the past.

She tried to express this to Reath.

'Redemption is the will of the Transcendence,' he said peremptorily. 'And so to understand the Transcendence you must understand the Redemption.'

'But what difference does it make? Michael Poole never knew I've been watching him all his life.'

'It certainly makes a difference to you, doesn't it? The only alternative to knowing is *not* to know, to ignore the suffering of the bloodstained generations that preceded us. Wouldn't that diminish us?'

'I don't know,' Alia said honestly.

'We have time to explore this later.' He stood up. 'This has been a rich conversation. You've given me much to think about, Alia.'

'I have? But you're the teacher.'

He smiled. 'I keep telling you. The wisdom you need is within yourself, not in me. And I think you're learning how to find that wisdom... Do you feel ready for the Second Implication?'

She took a deep breath. 'Let's do it.'

'Tomorrow, then, we will make a new landfall.'

After he left, idly she let the tank projection run forward.

There was Poole, clambering over a strange reef of broken machinery. Hot, dirty, he seemed troubled, agitated; he seemed to be trying to reach something, or someone.

And then he turned and looked up, out of the tank, directly into Alia's eyes.

She gasped. She clapped her hands, and the Witnessing tank cleared. The image of Poole disappeared, that stern accusing stare evaporating in a blur of cubical pixels.

That was *not* supposed to happen.

Chapter 11

I ordered a pod bus to take me back to the airport.

The pod rolled silently up to my mother's front door, just a dozen seats in a gleaming glass bubble and a hydrogen-fuel engine hidden in the floor. There was one other passenger, apparently airport-bound like me. I clambered aboard with my suitcase. Embarrassingly my mother kissed me goodbye. The pod sealed itself up and hissed away.

We worked our way out into the road system, the bus's own local sentience tying into a system-wide intelligence mediated by a sky full of satellites and an invisible lacing of microwave signals. The traffic gradually built up, until we had in view, oh, at least twenty vehicles whirring away over the silvertop: pod buses like mine, cabs, delivery trucks, transports for disabled people, emergency vehicles like ambulances and fire appliances. My bus, as it swam into this stream, attached itself to more of its kind, nose to tail, until we were in a train of eight or ten pods, rolling easily along the road. I could see the heads of my fellow passengers in the bright blisters of the other pods. Every so often other pods would join us, or the train would crack open, releasing a pod to peel off down a slip road to perform some local pick-up or drop-off.

We moved pretty fast on the open road, maybe a hundred kilometres an hour, and in the few busy stretches we could be tailgating the vehicle in front, just centimetres away. It was traffic moving at speeds and with such closeness that would once have scared me to death. But of course nobody was driving, no human being. We passengers in our glass bubbles were precious treasures cradled by metal and ceramic and electronic intelligence, washed along the road system in safety and silence – and with no more pollution than a puff of water vapour here and there, the residue of hydrogen burning in oxygen.

We kept to the silvertop stripe. Painted down the centreline of the old tarmac it was modern smart-concrete, embedded with miniature processors: self-diagnosing and self-repairing, it should need no maintenance for decades. But away from the silvertop whole lanes had been abandoned, and the old tarmac surface was crumbling, the defiant green of weeds pushing through the black, the first stage of nature's recovery. There was a nostalgic tug when you looked out over those disintegrating acres of black stuff. I imagined the great unending streams of traffic, millions of tonnes of metal and glass and gasoline, that had once poured along these highways. And off the road you could see more haunting sights: abandoned gas stations and motels and shopping malls, all part of the vast infrastructure that had once sustained that river of traffic, and in turn fed off it.

How strange it is that all the cars have gone!

Of course it was economics that killed the automobile.

There was a tipping point in the 2020s. For decades the national economy, and our political freedom to move, had been utterly constrained by our dependence on oil. And now the oil was running out: the engineers had to start fires in the wells to force out the last of the oil, or send down microbes to detach it from pores in the reservoir rocks. At home we were suffering from price spikes, blackouts, sabotage, and abroad we were getting drawn into increasingly messy conflicts over the last dwindling supplies, in the Mid East, Central Asia. And then there was the Warming, whose link to the carbon economy was increasingly apparent. The coup in Saudi Arabia was the last straw. The non-OPEC oil had long dried up, and the taps being closed on the world's largest remaining fields, even briefly, was an economic blow that caused layoffs and stagflation.

Enough is enough, said President Amin, the second woman head of state. Taking the White House in 2024 Amin, the right woman at the right time, articulated a profound but deceptively simple dream of an America accepting a new destiny – an America that cared about its responsibility for the future of mankind 'as far as we, on our shining hill, can see'. One day this vision would lead to the Stewardship.

But first we needed to kick the oil habit. Amin put together the first version of our modern distributed-infrastructure energy strategy, reliant on hydrogen power and nukes. Of course there was resistance, a stupendous battle between the legislators and Exxon-Mobil-Shell-BP, the last of the great carbon conglomerates. And as OPEC saw its power base disappearing we faced external threats too.

Even more traumatically, we had to be weaned off the automobile.

It turned out to be simple, politically. In the longer term we were to switch to a new transport paradigm based on hydrogen, biofuels and electric cells. But for now Amin imposed new environmental and future taxes, reflecting the true price of an auto from its manufacture through to its injection of carbon into the air – a 'Full Social Cost Pricing' as the economists called it.

It was like a change of fashion. It was amazing how, when the cost of gas got high enough, you suddenly discovered you really didn't need to drive so much after all. Instead you caught the bus and the train, or you walked. You shopped where you lived: there was a revival of 'village ethic', as local clinics and schools and shops started to flourish, providing everything you needed within walking distance. And there was a boom in comms facilities. As our physical transport capacity declined we engaged in a 'virtual economy': tele-commuting at last matured.

It felt easy, day to day. But of course the dislocation was staggering. There was a massive relocation of businesses out of the city centres, and of people back in. Some more modern communities, such as whole stretches of Greater Los Angeles, were suddenly rendered uninhabitable without the car; property values went crazy. Agriculture was an industry as dependent on its distribution networks as any other, and food supplies boomed and crashed.

The impact on Detroit alone was bad enough, as the old factories either closed or painfully retooled for the manu-facture of a much reduced volume of smart new hydrogen-economy vehicles like pod buses. A whole slew of supplier industries had to pivot or fold. The old oil infrastructure had to be renovated to fit the new hydrogen-biofuel paradigm. Plastics, derived from oil, suddenly became precious. It was the end of the throwaway multiple-packaged culture I had grown up with.

I was pursuing my nuclear-engineering career through this whole period. Despite the boom in VR technology, I found myself spending a lot more time than I would have wanted to away from home. Maybe that contributed to the crisis my family faced later.

Of course nationally it was a huge risk. The nation as a whole had grown rich and powerful in a world economy built on hydrocarbon fuels; shifting that fundamental basis posed dangers politically and economically. But we had got through such vast economic transitions before, such as when oil had overtaken coal around 1900. After just a few years things began to get better, and the change became so embedded it seemed odd we hadn't taken the leap much earlier.

In the end giving it all up was just a matter of will, which Amin managed to assemble.

But Amin's policies, focusing on domestic issues, had a downside. It was a particularly nasty decade. It was all about the Warming, of course. Access to water was the focus of many battlegrounds, from the Nile to the Amazon and even the Danube. The changing climate wiped out whole nations – even the Netherlands was depopulated. America wasn't immune; there were droughts in the corn belt, one-off calamities like the New Orleans hurricane. All over the planet there was famine, disease and desertification, and drifting flocks of refugees. When the oil economy collapsed the petrostates imploded with startling rapidity, causing a whole new set of problems.

And in all this America, the only nation with the real power to help, obsessing over losing the automobile, did nothing. Our inwardness ended only with the Happy Anniversary flash-bombing of 2033, a real wake-up call. After that came the launch of the Stewardship under Edith Barnette, once Amin's veep: America's 'Marshall Plan for a bruised world'. It began by us baling out the petrostates as a few years earlier we had baled out Detroit. By then President Amin had paid her own price, in her assassination a week after she left office. But she had changed the world.

I used to try to explain all this to Tom. He was ten years old when Amin was assassinated; he remembers that trauma. I thought he would want to know about the lost freedoms of the automobile age – part of our birthright, we thought. I still remember how proud I was of my first car, a beat-up 2010 Ford, which I used to polish until it shone in the Florida sun. I missed driving – not just the freedom of it, but driving itself, a social interaction of a unique kind you got as you wrestled your way through heavy traffic on a Friday rush hour. Vanished skills, abandoned pleasures.

But Tom would stare at images of the vast streams of traffic that had flowed along the abandoned roads only a few years before, and at the poison that spread out from those crawling rivers of red lights and shining metal, blackening the land and turning the air the colour of a Martian sky. And he would flick on links to accident statistics: *how* many died every year? No dream of freedom could possibly have seemed worth the price to Tom, who had never owned his own car, and never would.

I only saw one private car during that ride to the airport. I recognised the model. It was one of the new Jeeps, with six tyres as tall as I am and a slick waterproof underside, and a little chimney stack from which vented its harmless hydrogen-fuel exhaust, water laced with a few exotic hydrocarbon by-products. Its cabin was perched on top of its body, a bright glass bubble. Some of these models had seats that turned into bunks, and little kitchens and toilets, and windows you could opaque to a silvery blankness. You could *live* in there. I felt an unwelcome stab of envy.

Its driver must have been seventy at least. Perhaps when the final generation of driver-nostalgics died off, I thought, so would the very last of the private cars. In the meantime, that guy was no doubt paying plenty for his fix.

But I still miss that old Ford of mine.

At the airport the check-in process was thorough, with cheek-swab DNA tests, neurological scans, and full-body imaging to make sure I wasn't carrying a pathogen in my bloodstream or a knife in a hollowed-out rib.

I finally got on the plane. The cabin was wide-bodied and fitted out with big fake-leather couches, around which people fussed and planted their in-flight stuff. There were no windows, but every wall surface was smart, although for now tuned to a drab wallpaper. It was like a lounge in some slightly cramped hotel; only the cabin's inevitably tubular architecture gave away the fact that we were on board a plane. My couch was smart too. As I sat down I felt pads move silently into place, fitting my body shape and supporting my back and neck and lumbar region. All very civilised, though that cheap-hotel feeling deepened. I settled in and spread my softscreen over my lap.

The plane filled up quickly. The couches were not set in rows but in subtly randomised patterns, so you had at least the illusion of privacy. But still my neighbour felt like he crowded into my space.

He was aged maybe forty, a round-faced man sweating so heavily his thinning hair was plastered to his scalp. His belly strained at his shirt. At one time you wouldn't have glanced at him twice, but in these days when everybody walked everywhere he was bigger than most. He had a lot of stuff, a pack he crammed under his seat, another he shoved into the locker in front of him, and he spread out a softscreen and a pile of papers on his lap.

He caught me watching him. He stuck out his hand. 'Sorry to disturb you. The name's Jack Joy. Call me Jack.'

I shook his hand, powerful but hot and moist, and introduced myself.

He snapped his fingers to summon the steward – a human, a retro symbol of a vanished age. Jack requested a bourbon, and asked if I wanted the same; a bit uncertainly, but feeling crowded by this guy, I agreed.

Slightly breathless, he gestured at the heap of stuff on his lap. 'Look at this crap. Every trip's the same, work work work.' He winked. 'But it costs so much to travel nowadays you have to make it worthwhile, even if somebody else is paying, right?' His accent was strong New York.

'I guess so.'

'You fly a lot?'

'I flew out here, to Florida. Otherwise not for years.'

'It isn't the unalloyed delight it once was. Watch this.' Without warning he slammed his fist against the fake leather armrest of his seat, making me jump. Immediately a metal band slid out of nowhere and snapped over his arm, and a blue light flashed over his head. A stewardess came running, fingering the weapon in her holster.

Jack apologised, waving his other hand in the air, sloshing his drink. 'Sorry, sorry. A nervous twitch! It always happens to me. What can I say?'

He had to submit to a scan from a hand-held sensor. But eventually the stewardess spoke into a lapel mike, and with some reluctance, I thought, caused the restraint to release him and slide back into the body of his seat.

Jack turned to me. 'You see that? By the time you get on the plane you've been through all the checks and the psycho profiling and all the rest, and you're in your damn seat, and you think they'll trust you at last. But no, no. One false move and wham, you're pinned like a lab rat. I mean, what could you do? Scratch somebody's eyes out? Lethe, even this shot glass is unbreakable. If I throw it against the wall—' He raised his arm.

'Don't bother,' I said quickly, 'I believe you.'

He laughed and sipped his drink. 'It's the way of the world, Mike – can I call you Mike?'

'Michael.'

'The way of the world, Mike. Lethe, it's the way of the world.' He settled back on his couch with a grunting sigh, and kicked his shoes off, which did nothing to improve my immediate environment.

Lethe. I'd heard that word used as an oath before, somewhere. John, I thought; John used it sometimes.

That stewardess came by again, checking we were ready for take-off. She caught my eye sympathetically. *You want more privacy?* I shrugged, subtly.

The plane surged forward and I was pressed back in my couch; I felt it adjust to accommodate me. I hadn't even heard the engines start up. With a word I turned my smart wall into a window, and watched the drowned Florida landscape recede beneath me, covered in pools and lakes that shone in the sun like splashes of molten glass.

Once we had settled into the flight I buried myself in a soft-screen study of climate change at the poles. It was a dull classroom subject, but, after Tom, suddenly it was personal.

It all started with the Warming, of course; all the searches I set off looped back to that. For decades carbon dioxide had been accumulating in the air twice as fast as natural processes could remove it. By 2047 its concentration was higher than at any time in the last twenty *million* years, an astounding thought. The consequences were depressingly familiar, ice melting, seas rising, ecosystems unravelling. All that heat energy pumped into the air and oceans had to go somewhere, so there were many more hurricanes and storms, floods and droughts than there used to be.

And so on. I skimmed all this, trying to find out about the Arctic.

At the poles the Warming is amplified. Apparently there is a positive feedback effect; as the ice melts the albedo of the ground is lowered – it reflects back less sunlight – and so the ground and the ocean soak up more heat. As a result temperatures there have been, at times, rising ten times as fast as in the rest of the world. In the north, the ice was all gone, and strange storm systems came spinning down from that rotating bowl of ocean to assault the land. Once the sea ice actually protected the land from ocean storms and the worst ravages of the waves. Now, all around the Arctic ocean, coastal erosion was 'rapid', 'dramatic', 'traumatic', so I read. At the same time the permafrost, the deep-buried ice cap, was melting. I'd seen some of this in Siberia; on a ground that undulated like the surface of the sea, roads collapsed, buildings just sank into the ground, and trees in the immense, world-embracing *taiga* forests tipped over.

Of course all this hit the people. As Tom had said, even fifty years ago many of the locals in Siberia still lived as hunter-gatherers, following the reindeer around. Now even the ground was giving way beneath them.

And then you had the methane.

The physics seemed simple enough. The peculiar geometry

of water molecules makes them difficult to pack into a solid structure when they freeze. So 'solid' ice contains a lot of empty space – room enough to trap other molecules, such as methane. And there is a *lot* of methane generated on the seabed; there isn't much oxygen down there, and anaerobic decay processes release a lot of the gas. So all around the poles huge quantities of methane, carbon dioxide and other volatiles were locked up in hydrate deposits, kept stable by the low ocean temperatures and the pressure of the land and water above.

When the temperature rose, that natural cage was broken open. The consequence was 'methane burps' of the kind Tom was unlucky enough to have encountered.

But that was a localised event, I realised, lethal as it was if you happened to be in the way. The Warming, however, was nothing if not global. There was more methane down there in the hydrate layers than in all the world's fossil fuel reserves, and methane, though it doesn't last as long in the atmosphere, is in the short term *twenty times* as potent a greenhouse gas as our old buddy carbon dioxide. So what would happen, I wondered vaguely, if this went on, if *all* that methane was released? I tabbed through pages on my soft-screen, following a chain of thought that had begun when Tom first had his accident. But my question strings petered out; my softscreen couldn't answer. I sat back, tugging at a thread of speculation.

I admit I didn't know much about the Warming, about climate change in the Arctic or anywhere else. Why should I? The planet was warming up, my body was growing older, it was all just part of the world I'd grown up in; you either obsessed about it, or accepted it and got on with your life. And besides, we had dumped the automobile, we had accepted the need to run the Stewardship. We were managing the pain, weren't we? But if those hydrate deposits did give way... I thought there was some very bad news buried in here. And on some level I just didn't want to know.

Was there anything to be done about it? I cleared the softscreen, took a stylus and began to doodle.

I kept being distracted by the environment of the flight.

If I miss driving, I miss flying more. When I was a kid

my parents flew all the time. At the peak of their careers they had pretty much sewn up the Miami Beach market for corporate eventing, and scarcely a weekend went by without them managing a sales conference or marketing strategy session at one resort hotel or another. All that was local, but to set up the deals they had to travel to where the customers were. When they got the chance, they would take us kids, John and me. Our teachers would kick up a stink, as in those days you were still expected to attend school for the regulation five days a week. But for better or worse my parents took the blows, and we flew.

We kids loved seeing the centres of business across the country, from New York to San Francisco, Chicago down to Houston. A few times we travelled overseas, to Europe and Africa and even Japan once, though my mother worried about the effect of such long-haul trips on our young bodies. The whole thing was a great eye-opener.

But most of all I just loved to fly. I relished being in a vast machine that had the energy to hurl itself into the sky. I was always fascinated to come into a major airport, and to glimpse all those other sparks of light in the sky, and the moth-like shapes of more planes on the ground; you got a real sense of the millions of tonnes of metal suspended in the air over the continental United States, every minute of every day. All gone now, of course. Now nobody flies – nobody but the very rich. It's the same logic that took away the automobile: we've had to sacrifice some freedoms to survive. I accept all that, and most of the time, like everybody else, I don't think about it. But I still miss flying.

Jack Joy was leaning over to see what I was doing. Some instinct made me blank out the softscreen.

He leaned back with his podgy hands up. 'Sorry. Didn't mean to pry.'

'It's OK.'

'Stuff about climate change? Work? This is your job?'

'No. It's my son's, in a way...'

I felt guilty about shutting him out like that. I told him a little about Tom's work, and the accident.

He nodded. 'Good kid. You must be proud.'

'I guess. Just relieved he's still around.'

'And now you're boning up on global warming?'

'I kind of feel the world has targeted me, or anyhow my son.'

'I get it,' he said. He tapped his nose. 'Know your enemy.'

'Not that I want the Earth to be my enemy.'

'Ah.' He waved a hand dismissively. 'Neither enemy nor friend. It's just a stage, right? A stage for us humans to strut our magnificent stuff.' He stuck out his belly as he said this.

I couldn't help laughing at him. 'I don't know if I'd say that. The Die-back—'

'Who cares about that? You see, there I would take issue with your son. That DNA cataloguing bullshit? Forget it! Let it happen. Let them all die off. So what?'

I couldn't make him out. 'Are you serious?'

'Of course I am.' He leaned closer, conspiratorially. 'Listen to me. The Die-back has been going on for millennia. Ever since the Ice Age. First we wiped out the big mammals. In North America, the mammoths and the cave bears and the lions? Pow, whole populations pop like soap bubbles when the first guy with a funny little spear wanders over from Asia. Australia the same. Asia and Africa it's different, but there the animals evolved alongside us.' He cackled. 'I guess they learned to run fast. But now we're working our way through them too, and the smaller critters, the birds of the air and the fish of the sea, the plants and the bugs. Whatever.'

'And you don't think that's a bad thing?'

'Two words,' he said. '*Morally neutral*. It just happened. There have been mass extinctions before, worse than this mother will ever be. And every time, you know what? Life bounces back. An evolutionary rebound, the biologists call it.' He winked at me. 'So you just have to let it fix itself, and in the meantime sit back and enjoy the view. They don't report this stuff—'

'But it's true,' I finished for him.

He glanced at me and grinned. 'Lethe, you know me already.'

'I don't often hear people curse like that. *Lethe*.'

112

'You don't? Actually there's a scientific hypothesis called Lethe. You've heard of Gaia?'

'Sure.' Named for a Greek earth-goddess, Gaia was a model of the Earth's unified systems and processes, from the rock cycle, to the exchange of gases between air and ocean, to the vast cycling of matter and energy which sustained life, and which life sustained in its turn. All this was the paradigm among biologists, and a staple in Eco 101 for everybody else.

Jack said, '"Lethe" is the opposite to Gaia. An anti-Gaia, if you will. The Warming isn't a simple event. Everything is working together, different effects reinforcing – just like Gaia. But now the Earth has begun working to *destroy* itself, as opposed to sustaining itself. Ask a biologist; you'll see.

'But you know what *Lethe* actually means? It's from Greek myth. Lethe was a river in Hades, which if you drank from it would wash away your memory. Later on it was used by Shakespeare, to mean "death". Lethal – you see. But the original meaning kind of makes sense, doesn't it?'

'Forgetfulness.'

'Exactly. As one species after another turns to dust, Earth is losing its biotic memory: look at it that way. But we, in turn, may as well forget it all too. I never saw a tiger, and never will, but I never saw T Rex either. What difference does it make that one died out thirty years ago and the other sixty-five million? Dead is dead.'

'That's a brutal viewpoint.'

'Brutal? Realist, my friend. And a realist deals with the world as it is, not as he wishes it to be. You just have to accept it. In the long term, from the viewpoint of history, all of this will be seen as an *adjustment*. It's just our bad luck to be living through it.' He grinned, wolfish. 'Or our good luck. In the meantime, why not enjoy life? Fuck it. I mean, if it's raining, grab a bucket.'

'So what kind of bucket do you carry?'

'Me? I deal in shit,' he said, evidently enjoying the look on my face.

If a Martian came down to Earth, he said, he might conclude that the main product of mankind was shit. Great rivers of the stuff pour out of our bodies and into the sewers of our towns and cities. In less civilised communities, we just dump it into the sea. In more enlightened places, Jack said, we stir it around and perfume it in sewage plants, and *then* dump it into the sea.

I could guess where this was going. 'Where there's muck there's brass.' It was an expression of my mother's.

Jack grinned. 'I like that.' He actually wrote it down on his softscreen. 'Muck and brass. But that's what it boils down to – literally.' Jack worked for a company that sold fancy reactors that treated excrement, by driving off the water that formed its bulk, and then extracting various useful hydrocarbons from the residue. 'It's an amazing technology,' he said. 'It's all a spin-off from space technology, those closed-loop life-support systems they use up there on the Space Station. Now here we are on Spaceship Earth using the same stuff. Inspiring, isn't it? Fresh water is short everywhere, and just reclaiming that is often enough to justify the cost of a kit.' He winked again. 'Of course we don't advertise the fact that we're selling your own shit back to you, but there you go.' He talked about how he sold plants small enough for an individual household, or big enough to handle a whole city block, and then he got on to payment schemes.

I wasn't very interested, and my attention drifted off.

He glanced at me speculatively. 'Here.' He gave me a card. It was black and embossed with silver: THE LETHE RIVER SWIMMING TEAM. 'My contact details,' he said. 'If you're interested. It will download into your implant.'

'I don't understand the name.'

'The Swimming Team is a group of like-minded thinkers,' he said.

'All realists?'

'Absolutely. Listen, I hand out dozens of cards like this. Hundreds. It's the way we work. No obligation, just like minds on the other end of a comms link. If you ever feel like talking over this stuff, give me a call. Why not? Of course some take the logic a little further.'

Intrigued despite myself, I asked, 'They do? Who?'

'I met a guy once, through the Swimming Team. Maybe I shouldn't tell you his name.' He winked for the third time. 'He called himself a Last Hunter. You ever heard of them?...'

The premise turned out to be simple. A Last Hunter aimed to take out the last representative of a species: the last eagle, the last lion, the last elephant of all.

'Think of it,' Jack breathed. His voice was almost seductive. 'To be the man to take down the last gorilla, a species that split from humans megayears ago. To end a ten-million-year story by writing your name across the end of it in blood. Isn't it a fantastic thought?'

'Are you serious? I've never heard anything so immoral—'

He wagged his fingers at me. 'Now, let's not start up on morality again, Mike. Illegal, I grant you. Especially if you have to sneak into a zoo to do it. You see my point, though. Even in a declining world there are ways to make money – a lot of it, if you are smart enough. And, more important, to find meaning, to define yourself.'

I had the feeling he was offering me something. But what? A finger or an ear chopped from the carcass of the last silverback gorilla? I found him overwhelming, disgusting – fascinating.

To my relief a hovering bot approached bearing food and drink, and I had an excuse to switch off. Jack Joy pulled down handfuls of sandwiches and began to feed.

Chapter 12

To introduce her to the next Implication, of Unmediated Communication, Reath brought Alia to a new world.

As Reath's ship slid into orbit, Alia peered down reluctantly. Orbiting a fat yellow star buried deep in the rich tangle of the Sagittarius Arm, this was a rust-brown ball surrounded by an extravagant flock of moons. It was an unprepossessing sight, even as planets went. The thick air was laden with fat grey clouds; it was like looking into a murky pond. The land was all but featureless, the only 'mountains' worn stubs, the valleys the meandering tracks of sluggish rivers. There were oceans but so shallow that the world's predominant ruddy colour showed through. And there were still more peculiar landscapes, such as huge circles of some glassy, glinting material.

There was life, though. It showed up in patches of grey-green flung across the face of the crimson deserts – managed life, as you could see by its sharp edges, and the neat bright blue circles and ellipses of reservoirs. Alia made out the greyish bubbling of urban developments around these agricultural sites.

The planet had a catalogue number, assigned to it on its rediscovery by the Commonwealth. And it had a name: *Case*, a blunt title that, it was said, dated back to the days before the Exultants' victory, when this place, close to the outer edge of the spiral arm, had been a significant war zone. Alia wondered vaguely if 'Case' had been a hero of that forgotten war. But, Reath said, the locals didn't use either the official name or the catalogue number; they just called their world, reasonably enough, the 'Rustball'.

As they orbited, Reath patiently taught her to read this planet.

The thick air, and the worn, low mountains, were symptoms of high gravity, he said: though this world was only a little larger than Earth, its surface gravity was much higher than standard, and so it must be denser. And that rust colour was the colour of iron oxides – literally rust. If the world looked old, so it was. The Galaxy, mother of the stars, was at its most fecund before Earth's sun was even formed. So humans moving out from Earth had found themselves in a sky full of old worlds, like children tiptoeing through the dusty rooms of a dilapidated mansion.

As for those glassy plains, said Reath, they were not strange geological features but the relics of war, a bloody tide which had washed over this world again and again.

After a day, a ship came climbing sluggishly out of the planet's steep gravity well. The shuttle, fat, flat, round, had the rust colour of the planet of its origin, and reminded Alia of a toiling beetle. Even before it arrived, Alia felt a deepening disappointment.

The two craft established an interface, and a tunnel opened up between them. Three men came drifting through into the roomier confines of Reath's ship. 'Welcome to the Rustball,' one of the visitors said. He introduced himself and his companions as Campoc Bale, Campoc Denh, and Campoc Seer. 'Reath has asked us to host you...'

The Campocs were squat, all of them a head shorter than Alia, with thick, powerful-looking limbs. Though their costumes were a bright blue, their skin seemed to have something of the murky crimson-brown colour of the Rustball itself, and their heads were as hairless and round as the planet of their birth. When they smiled Alia saw they didn't have discrete teeth but enamelled plates that stretched around the curves of their jaws.

Alia said, 'I'm guessing that "Campoc" is a family name? And so the three of you—'

'Two brothers and a cousin,' Bale said. But he didn't say which was which. 'And I know what you're thinking. You'll have trouble telling us apart.'

'Most visitors do,' said Denh.

'But we don't get too many visitors,' said Seer.

'And don't worry,' Bale said, 'I'll do most of the talking.'

117

'That's a relief.'

In the cluttered cabin, they made a strange collection of disparate human types: the long, elegant frame of Reath, the stubby, hairless Campocs, and Alia with her long arms and golden fur. And yet something united them, Alia thought: a curiosity about each other, a deep genetic kinship.

'So much for the formalities,' Reath said brusquely. He began to shepherd them towards the tunnel to the Rustball ship. 'Go, go! I'm sure you'll have much to talk about. As for me I've plenty to do up here.'

Alia followed the Campocs into their ship. Her luggage trailed after her. Inside, the beetle-like ship was as cramped and unadorned as the outside.

Reath said, 'Alia, if you need me, call. But you'll be fine.'

'We'll make sure she is,' said Bale.

The shuttle detached itself from Reath's ship with a noise like a broken kiss, and ducked without fuss into the thick atmosphere of the Rustball.

Alia had never felt so stranded.

On the ground, when she stepped out of the shuttle's protective inertial field, the heavy gravity immediately plucked at Alia, and she staggered. The air was thick and hot and smelled of ozone, and the clouds overhead were lowering and oppressive. It was like being at the bottom of an ocean; she felt as if she would be crushed. But a couple of moons sailed high, fat matching crescents identical in phase.

Bale was at her side. He took her arm. 'Give it a minute,' he whispered. 'It will pass.'

So it would. As soon as she had set foot on the planet, the Mist had swarmed into her, through her mouth and nose, and through the pores of her skin. Soon she could feel a subtle tingling in her bones and muscles and lungs, and the pain of existence on the Rustball began to recede.

The Mist lingered on every colonised world. The little creatures who comprised it were neither machine nor living; after half a million years the distinction between biology and technology was meaningless. As she stood here the invisible machines were busily swarming through her body, reinforcing and rebuilding and supplementing, equipping her to cope with the sheer work of survival. Alia didn't think about this. The Mist just worked.

The shuttle had landed on an apron of some durable black material, with crimson dust scattered thinly across it. A settlement of some kind clustered at the rim of the apron. Remarkably, the squat buildings seemed to be constructed of sheets of iron. There was dust everywhere, on the ground and on the buildings, even in the sky, which had a pale pink hue. The hot air felt dry and prickly, though she suspected precipitation was imminent from those heavy clouds – *rain*, she thought, digging out the planet-dwellers' word.

The Campocs were watching her.

Though Alia towered over the Campocs, like an adult among children, these strange little men were not children. There was a calm seriousness about them that was like nothing she had experienced before. It was as if they were listening to voices she couldn't hear. But then she was here for a purpose: to be made ready for the second stage of her training, the Implication of Unmediated Communication. Though she didn't yet understand how, these odd little men must have qualities beyond her; they must be at least one step closer to true Transcendence than anybody she had met before.

And beyond that uneasy realisation, she thought the three of them seemed calculating as they studied her, as if they had their own purposes for her visit. Bale, especially, stared at her, his nose small, his mouth a colourless line, his eyes like waveless pools.

Bale asked, 'Do you feel better yet?'

'I think so.' She didn't want to show him weakness, or nervousness. 'Are we going to those buildings?'

'Yes.'

'Then let's do it.' She ran forward, across the apron. To her astonishment she tired within a few paces. She looked back at Bale, baffled.

Gently he told her that she had to learn how to function in a high-gravity field. In low gravity it was easier to run, spending most of the time in the air as you paddled across the ground. But here, as on old Earth in fact, gravity was so high that it was actually energetically more efficient to *walk*, to clump along on one foot after another, than to run. This struck her as absurd, but she hadn't had to walk far enough on the water-world to learn this subtle lesson. Bale showed her how to do it, and a few experiments proved he was right.

They *walked*, then, to the township.

The buildings were just cubes and cylinders, as squat and massive as the people who had built them. None of them was large, just collections of a few rooms jammed together. And all the buildings were boxes of iron, mined from the ground. Servitor machines toiled in scraps of garden, bright green amid the predominant rust colour.

'Welcome to our home,' Bale said. He pointed at one nondescript building. 'That's where we live, where you will stay.'

Alia had come here to study; she had expected something more formal. 'Where's the seminary?'

'We don't have a seminary,' Denh said, or maybe Seer.

Bale put a massive fist over his heart. 'It's what's in here that we're interested in. Not buildings.'

Alia sighed. 'Fine.' She walked forward, trailed by her sluggish baggage, looking for her room. She had to duck to avoid the ceilings.

Chapter 13

We flew into Heathrow.

The huge airport was much diminished, as all airports were. Our plane was a gnat flying down onto an immense carpet of tarmac, where once a plane had landed every three minutes, day and night, and now nothing moved but mice and the grass in the wind. But on the fringes of the site I glimpsed some construction. The developers were putting up a theme park. The contents of all Britain's aviation museums were being emptied out here, Jaguars and Harriers and Tornadoes, venerable World War Two Spitfires and Lancasters and Hurricanes more than a century old but still flying, even a Concorde or two. From the air the old planes looked like birds forever pinned to the ground.

As we made our way through the terminal buildings, and more ferocious security checks by British immigration, Jack Joy approached me. He asked if I'd like to go into London with him; he had a hotel booked, he was sure he could squeeze out another room, maybe we could have a drink or take in a show, and so on. My plan had been just to wait for Tom to fly in – he was due in a couple of days. But now we had been released from the confines of the plane I was eager to get away from Joy and his 'realism'.

And besides, I'd already decided not to stay in London. As I had sat there in the humming quiet of the plane, mulling over past and future, deeper concerns had surfaced. I did take a train into London, but only to cross the city to King's Cross, one of the big rail terminals for the lines to the north of the country.

After my confrontation with her in VR Siberia, I'd decided to go in search of Morag. I had issues to resolve here, clearly. So I was going to York.

I don't remember when her visits started. Maybe she even came when I was very small, a time now lost in the shining mist of childhood memories. I don't think it was until I was a teenager, thirteen or fourteen, that I realised that other people *didn't* have this kind of experience all the time, that it was just me.

When I finally met Morag, I suffered a shock of recognition.

It was during a work trip to England. I was at a party, thrown by an Irish family, old friends of my mother's. I made a beeline for Morag, as if drawn by some invisible force. I think I actually frightened her with my intensity.

When I'd calmed down, we got on fine. With a strong streak of Irish in her, she was witty, bright, funny. Even her job was interesting. She was a bioprospector; she spent her time searching for new species of ascomycete fungi, a key source of antibiotics. It turned out she was actually a friend of John's, whose legal career had taken him in a similarly 'modern' direction, as he made money from the great shifting of wealth and population caused by the climate change. In some ways Morag had more in common with John than with me; after all at the time I was turning myself into that old-fashioned beast, a nuclear engineer. But Morag was always 'greener' than John. Later I always thought that side of her had carried on to Tom.

And with that flame of strawberry-blonde hair, she was beautiful.

As our relationship developed, she quickly became herself to me: *Morag*, not the fleshed-out version of my personal ghost. During the years of our relationship I didn't see any of my apparitions. After a time, and especially after Tom was born, other, more real concerns crowded into my head. I began to dismiss my visions.

I never told Morag about them. I always meant to. I just never really figured out how to say it without spooking her. How are you supposed to tell your wife that she has haunted you since you were a kid? In the end, as the visions receded in memory, the thought of even trying to talk about it came to seem absurd, and I put it all aside.

Then she died, and it was too late.

And the hauntings began again. The first, cruelly, was in a bleak hospital corridor where I sat with Tom, just moments after we had learned we had lost her, and the baby.

They were infrequent at first, maybe once or twice a year. They still didn't frighten me. But after I lost her they became unbearably painful.

In the last year or so, in the months leading up to Tom's jeopardy, they had been more frequent. Just in the last few days I had seen her on the beach in Florida, and even in my VR trip to Siberia. It felt worse than ever to be haunted. Maybe it was my shock over Tom that did it. A lot of stuff, deep disturbed emotions, had come welling up out of the frozen depths of my mind like Tom's methane burping from its hydrate deposits.

So I'd decided to do something about it before I had to face Tom in the flesh.

The journey was only a few hours. The train was smooth, clean, comfortable. We shuttled through Peterborough and Doncaster and a host of lesser places whose names I knew from similar journeys in the past, but about which I knew little or nothing. The countryside had changed since the last time I made this trip, though. In the vast fields of swaying wheat and rape and gen-enged biofuel crops there was hardly a tree or a bush to be seen; I saw more robot tractors than birds or animals. The biodiversity of countries like England flat-lined when I was a teenager, and isn't likely to recover any time soon.

And then there was the water.

You could see it everywhere, abandoned roads now permanently flooded to serve as drainage channels or as canals, and artificial flood plains that served as makeshift reservoirs. Much of South Yorkshire was now covered by a new lake. As we crossed it on a raised levee, the water receded to the horizon, and the waves that scudded across it were white-capped; it was like an inland sea. I could see the roofs of abandoned houses, the foliage of drowned trees, and the unearthly shape of the cooling towers of dead power plants looming above the water line. It was all so new the lake didn't even have a name – or maybe giving it a name would somehow confirm its reality. But geese flapped across the water in a neat fighter-bomber V formation. The geese, at least, seemed to know where they were going, and didn't seem spooked by this new geography.

The sun was setting, and the water glimmered, reflecting the sunlight in gold splashes. I glided across that drowned landscape in smooth silence, as if we were riding on the water itself, as if it was all a dream.

By the time we reached York it was growing dark. I joined a line at the rickshaw rank outside the rail station, and soon I was being hauled around the outskirts of the city by an unreasonably athletic young woman. In this post-traffic era, in their wisdom the city authorities had repaved many of the streets with cobbles. It might be fine for pod buses, but by the time we reached my hotel my ass felt like tenderised steak.

The hotel was where I remembered it. It is a small place off the A-road that snakes south from York towards Doncaster, overlying the route of a Roman road. The hotel itself is old, some kind of coach house, eighteenth century I think. Because it's within a reasonable walk of the city centre it's stayed profitable where many similar businesses have folded. It's modern enough, but there's nothing glamorous about it. Friendly place, though; the only security check I had to go through was a DNA scan verified by Interpol.

The room I was given was just a bland box with the usual facilities, a minibar and a dispenser for drinks and a big softscreen showing muted news. I couldn't remember which room we'd taken, back then, Morag and I. Anyhow the interior looked to have been knocked around since those days, nearly thirty years gone. Maybe our room didn't even exist any more, in any meaningful sense.

Of course the staff here didn't know anything about me. I was just some guy who'd called to make a reservation from Heathrow, and I wasn't about to tell them why I'd come back here, why I remembered the hotel so well: that this was where I had stayed, with Morag, at the start of our honeymoon.

I sat in the one big armchair, with my suitcase sitting

unopened on my bed, the meaningless news flickering on the wall. It was late evening, but to my body it was the middle of the afternoon, Florida time. I felt restless, perturbed. I didn't want to face anybody, not even a room service robot.

Why was I here? For Morag, of course. I had come here, on impulse, to our honeymoon hotel, a place of great significance for the two of us. Fine. Here I was. But what was I supposed to do now?

On impulse I placed a call to Shelley Magwood.

I brought up her image on my big plasma screen. She was in the middle of her working day, but to her eternal credit she took time out to talk to me, a confused loser in a hotel room in England. But as I sat there, awkward, inarticulate, unable to broach the subject that was dominating my mind, she seemed to grow faintly concerned. Her background shifted around her; I saw that she had moved to a private office.

'Michael, I think you'd better come clean. I can see something's on your mind. So you're in York, because you had your honeymoon there. Right?...'

I told her about our wedding day. We had married in Manchester, to be close to Morag's family, and most of my mother's too. But her parents were both dead, and only one of her two siblings showed up. On my side my mother was restless; she always felt confined by England, by her past. Uncle George had turned up – but not my mother's other sibling, my aunt Rosa, whom I'd never met. Still, the day had gone well; weddings generally do, despite the family bullshit that always surrounds them.

And at the end of the day Morag and I headed off to York to begin our honeymoon, a couple of weeks of hopping around some of Britain's historic sites.

Shelley said cautiously, 'I don't know anything about York. Nice place?'

'Very old,' I said in a rush. 'It was a Roman city. Then it was the capital of the northern kings who dominated Saxon England for a while. Then the Vikings came, and this was the last of their kingdoms to fall, as England finally unified politically. And then—'

'I get the picture.'

I forced a laugh. 'A good place to come ghost hunting. Don't you think?'

She stared at me. She knew me well, but surely she'd never seen me in this agitated state before. 'Michael, digging into the past isn't a bad thing. People do it all the time. Everybody's family tree is online now, extracted from the big genome databases, DNA all the way back to Adam, and people are fascinated. Who can resist looking on the reconstructed faces of your ancestors? But, well, you can lose yourself in there. Isn't that true?'

I felt impatient. 'That's not the point, Shell. And that's not what I'm doing.'

'Then just tell me, Michael. Did you say something about *ghosts*?'

And I admitted to her that I'd come here to seek the ghost of Morag, my lost wife. It was a relief to express it all, at last.

Shelley listened carefully, watching my face. She asked a string of questions, dragging details and impressions out of me.

When I'd done, she said dryly, 'And so you thought you'd give me a call. Thanks a lot.'

'I never did have too many friends,' I said.

'Look, I'm honoured you told me. I am the first, aren't I? I can tell. And this is obviously very important.'

'It is?'

'For you, certainly.'

'*For me*. So you don't think it's real.'

'I've known you a long time, Michael and you never seemed crazy to me. An asshole maybe, but never crazy. And what do I know about ghosts? I've seen the same movies you have, I guess.'

I'd never discussed the supernatural with Shelley; she was hard-headed and practical, thoroughly grounded in a world she could measure and manipulate. The hypothetical alien builders of the Kuiper Anomaly had generally seemed enough strangeness for her. 'Do you believe any of that?'

She shrugged. 'The universe is an odd place, Michael. And we see only a distillation of what's out there, a necessary sensory construct that allows us to function. Nothing is what it seems, not even space and time themselves. Isn't that pretty much the message of modern physics? But it's a strangeness we tap into, with our Higgs-field drive. Do you ever think of it that way? As if we're slicing off a bit of God with our monkey fingers, using the Absolute as fuel for our rocket engines.'

No, I never had thought of it that way. But I was starting to realise that my intuition to call her in my confusion had been a sound one. 'So there are layers of reality we can't see. The supernatural. Eternity.'

'Whatever.' She was dismissive. 'I don't think labels help much. Some of our experiences are more profound than others. More significant. Times of revelation, perhaps, when you solve a problem, or when you figure something out, something new about the world – you're an engineer; you know what I mean.'

'You feel as if you've gotten a bit closer to reality.'

'Yes. Something like that. I'm quite prepared to believe there are times when we're more conscious, more *aware* than at other times. Especially since the neurological mappers and other bump-feelers freely admit they still have no idea what consciousness is anyhow. And if you follow that logic through,' she said doggedly, 'maybe you'd expect to find, um, hauntings associated with places where high emotions have been experienced.'

'As in classic ghost stories.'

'Yes. Who knows?' She studied me. 'So if you really want to confront this ghost you say is stalking you, maybe you've come to the right place.'

I nodded. 'I sense a "but".'

'OK. *But* you aren't really here to become a ghost-buster, are you, Michael? You're here because you want a release from the past. Redemption maybe. And surely there are other ways to do that other than to try to get yourself haunted.'

'I design starships as therapy. Now I'm ghost-hunting as therapy. I must be pretty fucked up.'

She smiled, but her scrutiny was unyielding, intense, a bit intimidating. 'Well, aren't you?'

'I think I have to do this.'

'Maybe. But, look, I'm worried you're going to come to harm. That you'll descend into some pit inside yourself that you'll never come out of.'

'I'll be careful,' I said.

'Now, why isn't that reassuring? When you come out the other side of this shit, it's obvious what you should do.'

'It is?'

She leaned forward, her giant-screen image looming over me. 'Talk it over with Tom. Your son. And then get back to work, for Christ's sake.'

She cut the connection.

Chapter 14

Alia woke early, her first morning on the Rustball.

She washed and ate. Swathed by the Mist which had spared her from the effects of the gravity, she had slept reasonably well, but the air inside the rust-walled little dwelling was as murky and still as outside. She felt stale and worn down, joyless, just like the planet itself.

Without ceremony Bale invited her to join what he called a 'conversation'.

She found herself in a large, plain room. It was all but full. Perhaps twenty people sat on the floor, informally. When Alia asked where she should sit, Bale just shrugged, and she picked a spot at random. The three Campocs sat close to her, giving her a welcome bit of familiarity. The others were more distant, their faces receding into the gloom. The room itself was as dark and enclosing as the whole planet seemed to be – and uninteresting, the strange iron walls unadorned.

There was a round of introductions. These people, it seemed, were all members of Bale's extended family: parents, children, siblings, cousins of varying complicated degrees. Alia effortlessly recorded the names, and built up a map in her head of this densely populated family network.

When the formality was done, she asked, 'Are we going to start now?'

'Start what?' Bale asked.

'My training. The Second Implication.'

Bale shrugged, his shoulders machine-massive. 'We're just going to talk.'

She said, irritated, 'I spend most of my time with Reath, talking.'

'Reath is a good man. But what is the subject of the Second Implication?'

'Unmediated Communication. I'm not sure what that means but—'

'You can't talk about communication,' Bale said gently, 'without communicating.'

She sighed. 'So what are we going to talk about?'

'What humans always talk about. Themselves. Each other. You're a visitor. We're curious.'

With all those gazes on her, she felt terribly self-conscious. 'What can I tell you? I'm ordinary.'

'Nobody is ordinary.'

Somebody spoke up from the back – a great-aunt of Bale's, it turned out. 'Who's the most important person in your life?'

She said immediately, 'My sister. She's ten years older than me...'

Once she had started she found it easy to open up. These 'Rusties', as they called themselves, were good listeners. And so she talked about Drea.

When Alia was small Drea had taken care of her, as a big sister should. But as Alia had grown that ten-year age gap became less important, and the sisters became more equal friends. Gradually Alia's interests had come to dominate the time they spent together – especially dancing, especially Skimming.

Drea had always seemed grave to Alia, a bit stolid, a bit *dull*. Alia was more exotic, perhaps, her mind livelier, her body always a bit more flexible. It had been up to Alia to pull her sister along with her, to involve her in things she mightn't otherwise have tried. It was a rivalry that added a spark to their relationship.

Gradually warming up, she told this story in anecdotes and in sweeping summaries. Sometimes one of the Rusties would give her something back, tell her a similar story from their own complicated family networks. There was nothing remotely judgemental about their reaction.

But, slowly, Alia began to feel uncomfortable. She wound down.

Twenty pairs of eyes watched her.

Bale said, 'Alia, are you well? Do you need a rest – a drink, perhaps, or—'

'What is meant by "Unmediated Communication"?'

For answer, Bale reached out and took her hand. It was the first time any of them had touched her physically; she felt an odd jolt, like a mild electric shock. She pulled back, startled.

Bale said, 'Most human communication is symbolic.'

She struggled to regain her composure. 'You mean language?'

'Language, art, music. Language is a legacy of our deepest past. With it we envisage past and future, build cities and starships – with language we won a Galaxy. But it is all symbolism. I encode my thoughts in symbols, I transmit them to you, you receive them, and decode them. You can see the limitations.'

She frowned. 'Bandwidth problems. Difficulties of translation.'

'Yes. What I say to you can only be a fraction of what I think or feel. But there are modes of communication deeper and more ancient than language.' Suddenly he snapped his fingers in her face, and she flinched.

'I apologise,' Bale said. 'But you see the point. That message was crude, just a gesture of threat. But you reacted immediately, from the deeper roots of your being. And when I took your hand you felt something beneath words, didn't you? We humans communicate on a tactile level. Even a cellular, even a chemical level...'

'It sounds scary,' Alia admitted.

'You don't know the half of it,' said Denh.

'What do you mean?'

'Before you can communicate with others, you have to be able to communicate with yourself.'

'I don't understand.'

'You will.'

'When will my treatment begin?'

'It already has,' called Bale's great-aunt, from the back of the room.

131

Chapter 15

I lay down in the dark and took a pill.

After I lost Morag I was prescribed medication. There were medicines, I was told, that can target the sites in your head where traumatic memories are formed. Something to do with inhibiting the formation of certain proteins. If I only took the pill, I was told, I would still remember Morag and all that had happened, as if I stored a narrative in my head, but I wouldn't *feel* it – not the same way, not so much that it would harm my functioning.

John had always pressed me hard to take the medication. For sure it's what he would have done. But I had refused. Memories are what make up *me* – even bad memories, dreadful memories. What's the point of 'continuing to function' if I lose that? When I refused to allow Tom the same treatment I faced a battery of counsellors who gravely advised me on the harm I was causing to my helpless son, the hurt I could help him avoid. I stuck to my guns. But sometimes, I admit, when I look back on Tom's life since, I wonder if I made the right choice for him.

So I refused the 'forget' pills. But I did learn that there are also such things as 'remember' pills.

There's a medication that can sharpen memories, rather than dull them, by getting glutamate or some such brain-molecule to work more efficiently. It takes some analysis by various therapeutic machines to figure out what you need, and you have to put up with counselling about the damage that might be done to your personality by too much memory. But it's over-the-counter stuff. When I found out all this I bought some pills, and put them aside, kept them in my bathroom bag. I'd carried them everywhere since, knowing they were there but not thinking about why I wanted them with me.

Now was the time. I popped my pill, and I lay in that bed, in that small hotel, in the middle of England, and I tried to remember.

Here I had been with Morag, that first night. We had gone to bed early, still full of wedding bonhomie and speeches, food and champagne. We made love.

But I remembered waking later, maybe three in the morning, the time your body is at its lowest, all your defences down. She was awake too, lying beside me, here in this hotel. The booze had worn off by then; I felt mildly hung over. But she was here. As we'd lived together for a year before I think we'd both imagined the marriage wouldn't matter. But we'd made a commitment to each other. It did make a difference.

So we came together again, in this hotel, in this English dark, right here. I remembered the scent of shampoo and spray on her hair, the softness of her skin, a slight saltiness when I kissed her cheeks – she'd done plenty of crying that day, as brides do. And around us the hotel breathed, centuries old, and beyond its walls the still more ancient pile of the old city thrust its stone roots deep into the ground.

Immersed in my pharmaceutically sharpened memories, I remembered it all, as if it was real again. Maybe I cried. Probably. Maybe I slept.

I thought I heard somebody calling.

It was a woman, outside the hotel, calling from the street below, the line of the Roman road. The room felt cold, terribly cold. Listening to that voice, I hugged myself to stop my shivering.

I found myself outside the hotel.

It was nearly dawn, and a blue light leaked grudgingly into the sky, totally lacking warmth. That light was mirrored in a flood of water that blocked the street, maybe fifty yards away from me, between me and the city centre. I was surrounded by the silhouettes of darkened houses. No traffic moved on the road, nobody was out there, nobody awake but me. The flood water rippled languidly, strewn with rubbish. The world seemed a drab, defeated place.

How had I got here? I couldn't remember dressing, or coming down from my room. I was disoriented, overtired.

Looking along the road towards the city, I saw a shifting shadow – a curve of back, a leg, the faint sound of footsteps.

Trying to catch her up I walked up the road towards the city centre. I stuck to the middle of the road. But those cobbles were big and smoothed with use and shiny with dew, and I had to watch every step I placed in the uncertain light. I tired quickly, mentally as well as physically.

Then I came to that flood. As I approached it I could see water bubbling up out of the drains and around the rims of manhole covers. I vaguely remembered that somewhere near here the two rivers that ran through the city, the Ouse and the Fosse, came to a confluence, and the place was notorious for flooding. The water looked old and dirty, covered with a layer of dusty scum. You get used to these things; once towns like this had probably flooded once a decade, but now it was a rare year when it *didn't* flood, and people got worn out with trying to fix things, and just accepted the change.

But this pond was in my way. I couldn't see how deep it got towards the centre. I walked to left and right, helpless. There was no obvious way around it. The side streets would lead me away from the way I wanted to go, towards Morag. Everything was mixed up, made chaotic by the water intruding into the land; I was stranded in a strange landscape, a place where nothing worked any more.

I realised I couldn't see Morag. Perhaps I had already lost her. I grew panicky.

Lawned gardens lined one side of the street. I decided to go that way. I made for an old, crumbling wall on the right hand side of the road. It was too high to be easy to climb. I jumped up, and had to use my arms to haul my bulk up so my belly was resting on the wall. Then, with a lot of swinging, I got my right leg onto the lip of the wall, and then the left.

I more or less fell down on the other side. I landed heavily on my side on soft, moist grass, hard enough to knock the wind out of me. I lay there for a few seconds. I could feel dew, or flood water, soaking my face, my jacket, my trousers. There were high-water marks on the wall, and somebody had chiselled dates into the brick beside the higher of them: *2000. 2026. 2032*. And I saw a worm, a long earthworm, crawling around on the grass. Maybe the rising water had forced it out of the ground. It looked as bewildered as I did.

I got to my feet. The side of my body I'd landed on felt like one long bruise, and I was wet and cold. I felt very foolish, a fifty-two-year-old man standing on somebody else's lawn in the dawn light. I had to get on, get out of there.

I stepped forward and walked straight into a tree.

The tree was a fern, no taller than I was, and the foliage around me was bamboo. I wasn't sure which way I was facing. I had been turned around in the fall. I stumbled forward again, but tripped on a skinny mound of moist earth sticking out of the lawn. It might have been a termite mound. English gardens aren't what they were. I felt stupid, befuddled, surrounded by clinging obstacles, and every step I took, everything I tried to do to make progress, just threw up more problems.

Right. The wall had been on the right-hand side of the street, so I should keep the house to my right. I turned and pushed that way. The grass was long and clung to my shoes, and now my feet were soaked through. But I kept going, and I came to a gate that led me back to the road.

I had come far enough to have passed most of the pond in the road, but the water still lapped at my feet.

Ahead, the road rose to cross the river at a bridge. I could see somebody on the bridge, I thought, a pale face looking back at me. She was too far away; her face was just a blur, a coin at the bottom of a pond. I was sure it was her, though. I wanted to shout, but I was aware of the sleeping town all around me, and somehow I couldn't. Anyhow it would do no good. I had to get to her; that was the thing.

The hell with it. I strode into the water. It didn't come much up my shins, but there was a lot of mud and garbage gathered in the bottom – maybe the road surface had collapsed here – and it sucked at my feet. Soon I was breathing hard, and my heart was hammering. At last I got out of the water. My feet and legs were soaked and muddy. I was exhausted. I couldn't have come more than half a kilometre from my hotel.

I could see the bridge, and the castle mound beyond with the tower on top, the relic of the old Norman castle, a gaunt silhouette against that blue sky. But she had gone from the bridge. Which way? Had she climbed the mound? If I could reach it maybe I could try to climb up after her.

The bridge was closed at its far end, for some reason. The rivers curled around both sides of the mound, and the water was high, frothing, blue-grey. The bank was eroded and lined with sandbags. Under the bridge itself the water reached almost to the top of the arches. Maybe I should cross the bridge. Or maybe I should find some way around the other side of the mound.

I couldn't think my way through it. And I couldn't see her any more. I just stood there, bruised, my feet sodden, panting.

'Are you OK?'

The voice seemed loud. I turned. I was facing a young man, maybe twenty-five. He was wheeling a bicycle. Under a fleece jacket he wore some kind of blue uniform; maybe he was a hospital worker on shift. 'You look as if you've had some trouble.' His accent was broad Yorkshire. I could see suspicion in his eyes. Not surprising; I must have looked strange.

I heard a crow calling. I looked up. I could see the bird wheeling over the tower on the mound. Suddenly the sky seemed brighter; high clouds were laced pink.

'Hey . . .'

'I'm fine,' I said.

'You're American?'

'Yes.' I looked down at myself, at the filthy water leaking from my shoes. I tried to think of something to say, something that would normalise the situation. 'Jet-lag plays hell with your sleep patterns, doesn't it?'

'Yes,' he replied, doubtful. He turned away, wheeling his bicycle.

I looked up towards the mound. It just looked like a hill now, the castle a ruin, not the centre of some kind of maze as it had seemed a moment ago. There was no sign of Morag, but I knew there wouldn't be.

That young man was still looking back at me. If I didn't want a police bot to be called I should get out of there and clean myself up. I turned and faced that flood in the road. In the gathering light it didn't look so daunting. I walked to the road's centre line and just strode straight through the water. The road had given way; this pool must have been there a long time. But the water came no higher than my knees, and in a moment I was through it.

When I woke the sun was high. It was around noon local time. I didn't remember how I had got there, got back into my hotel from the flooded road. The whole thing was like a dream.

But I was lying on my bed, not in it, and though I'd kicked off my shoes my trousers were muddy, my sweater smeared with green grass stains, and debris had rubbed off onto the bed's top sheet. The management wouldn't be pleased with me.

A corner of the big wall softscreen was flashing. A message was waiting for me from John.

I showered first, made a coffee, ate a cookie from the minibar. Then I sat in my armchair, faced the wall, and called John. Towering over me on the wall, he was furious – two-dimensional, badly coloured, but furious. 'Lethe,' he said.

I was struck by his use of that word, but now wasn't the time to talk about a stranger on a plane. 'Lethe to you,' I snapped back. 'What's eating you?'

'You are.' It turned out Shelley Magwood had called him last night.

I felt cold, wondering how much she had told him. 'She shouldn't have done that.'

'Why the hell not? She was concerned, asswipe, not that you deserve it. And wasn't she right to be?' He tapped a screen before him, out of my sight.

A corner of my wall filled up with an image, grainy, badly lit. You could see the castle mound, the flooded street, a figure standing there in muddy water up to his ankles. John had used his contacts to hack into the town's security cameras. He shouted now, 'You call this a responsible way to behave?

For this I paid a small fortune to send you to Europe? Are you crazy?'

'If you listened to what Shelley told you,' I said stonily, 'you'll understand that this is about me and Morag. It's got nothing to do with you. You have to let me work this out my own way, John.'

'Oh, do I?'

I studied him, growing curious. I'd rarely seen him so angry. 'What's eating you? Why are you taking this so personally?'

'I'm not.'

Despite his denial, I could see something was going on here. If I had felt lobotomised last night, today I was sharp. Was he angry I hadn't told him about my haunting by Morag first? Or was there something more? 'You're hiding something. *Is it to do with Morag*? Damn it, John, she was my wife. If you know something you have to tell me.'

He faced me again. 'I know I shouldn't have made this fucking call. Off.' The screen turned to sky blue.

So John had had a connection to Morag I knew nothing about. Another unwelcome ghost from the past, I thought. I sat in my armchair, in my hotel dressing gown, and sipped coffee that quickly grew cold.

Chapter 16

On Alia's second day on the Rustball, Bale took her to the sea.

If they went overland it would take a whole quarter of a day to reach the ocean. Bale offered to Skim there with her if she preferred. But she wanted to see more of this world. So she rode with him in a ground transport along a road that gleamed, metallic, running straight as an arrow across the gravity-flattened plain.

The landscape was all but featureless, the towns they passed identical to the one where the Campocs lived. It was like passing through a sparsely sketched simulation.

Much of what she saw was dictated by geology. When the Rustball had formed it had been a rocky world, rather larger than Earth, with a massive iron core and a mantle of lighter rock. In the usual way of things it had suffered multiple impacts during its formation – including one final collision with a second monstrous proto-planet. Alia learned that Earth itself had suffered a similar collision, a great rocky splash which had resulted in the formation of its Moon. The Rustball had been stripped of most of its outer layers, and had been left as a lump of iron as big as the Earth, with a flock of moonlets made of its own mantle rock. But iron was more dense than rock, and so this world was more massive than Earth, its gravity strong. Over time, comets delivered a skim of water and air, and the naked iron rusted enthusiastically. Without a rocky mantle there was none of the magmatic churning that characterised Earth's dynamic geology. Still, simple life had come here, brought by the comets, settling into oceans that gathered in impact-basin hollows.

And later, humans arrived.

Alia was discovering she wasn't interested in planets.

She had grown up on a ship, a human-made environment. The *Nord* was a small, liveable place, built to a human scale, where everybody knew everybody else. And the *Nord* was fluid, every aspect of its design shaped by human whim. As a small child she had loved to spend time in the *Nord*'s museum, where there was a display of all the ship's morphologies since its launch long ago, reconstructed from records, or archaeological traces in the *Nord*'s fabric. As the millennia ticked by the vessel had mutated and morphed like a pupa writhing in its cocoon, every aspect of its geometry shaped by its crew.

But a world was different, weighed down by its own vast geological inertia. Why, most of its mass was pointlessly locked up in its interior, useless for anything but exerting a gravity field you could have replicated with the most basic inertial adjuster!

If the Rustball had started out dull, its human colonists hadn't done much with the place, Alia thought. The plain drabness of the human environment here was striking. The towns, though separated by hours of surface travel, were very similar in their bland, squat architecture; there was no sense of local identity. And there was no art that she could see, nothing beyond the functional.

'Lethe, I hate planets,' she said. 'No offence.'

'None taken,' Bale said blandly.

It was a relief when they reached the ocean.

The water pooled in a complicated multiple basin cut in the iron by a series of impacts. On a shore of hard, red-rusted iron, waves broke; driven by the higher gravity the waves were low but fast-moving.

Alia was surprised to see people here, gathered in little parties along the shore. Bicycling vendors sold food, water, souvenirs and simple toys. It was a happy place, as happy as she had seen on the Rustball; people were enjoying themselves. But as she walked through crowds of running children, harassed parents and languid lovers, something was lacking, she thought. It took her a while to realise that there was no music to be heard, not a single note.

Following Bale's lead, Alia walked to the edge of the water

and stripped down. Alia couldn't help studying Bale's body, the broad limbs, the banks of muscles on his belly.

He caught her staring.

'I apologise,' she said. 'It's just that our bodies are so different.'

So they were. She was so much taller and slimmer, her arms almost as long as her legs, and her fur was languid in the heavy gravity. By comparison Bale was squat, broad, shaped by a lifetime of battling the relentless pressure of gravity. His arms were short, massive, but inflexible at the shoulder and joints. His spine was rigid too, a pillar of bone. This wasn't a world where you would do much climbing, she thought; Bale was actually more truly bipedal than she was.

'We're different because we live on different worlds,' Bale said.

'So we do.'

'But Reath sent you here because we aren't *too* different, because we are similar.'

'He did?'

Bale smiled. 'Unmediated Communication is challenging enough without a dose of alien-ness on top.'

She wondered, then, about *how* strange a human could get.

Naked, side by side, they walked into the ocean. The water was fast-moving and turbulent. Her fur, soaked, drifted around her. Alia had swum before, but only in zero-gravity bubbles on the *Nord*, where it was no more than hundred metres or so to the nearest meniscus. It was very strange to slide into a body of water orders of magnitude more voluminous, a bottomless pit of it. Bale's cursory warnings about treacherous currents and undertows did nothing to reassure her. It was an unexpected relief, though, when the water was at last deep enough for her to lift her feet from the bottom and float. She felt her muscles relax as they welcomed their first respite from gravity since orbit.

All around her the stocky bodies of Rusties, adults and children, bobbed in the water. They laughed and played. Even on this dull world the ocean was a place of pleasure. Perhaps, she thought, even after hundreds of millennia of adaptation, the people's bodies were responding to deep cel-

141

lular memories of a primordial ocean that lay far away and deep in time. But when the water got into her mouth, it was very salty, with the blood-like taste of iron.

Bale floated beside her, watching her.

'Bale, aren't you curious about other worlds?'

He shrugged. 'People are more interesting than worlds. Anyhow, we Witness. We find out about other people that way.'

'Everybody Witnesses, all across the Galaxy. It's another thing we have in common. It is the mandate of the Transcendence.' This was what Reath had told her.

'Yes.' But Bale was watching her, suddenly intense. 'What do you think about the Transcendence?'

'I don't know enough about it,' she said. 'It's just there. Like the weather, on a planet like this.'

'Yes. And the Witnessing, the Redemption?'

'I don't know. Why are you so interested in that?'

'There are people,' he said carefully, 'who question the value of the Redemption.'

'There are? Do you?'

He studied her a moment more, then seemed to come to some conclusion. 'You are innocent. I like that.'

'You do?'

'Yes. And I like Witnessing – the act of it, anyhow, if not the implications of the programme. I told you I am interested in people.'

She asked impulsively, 'And are you interested in me?'

He smiled. 'Sex would not be out of the question. I would take great care not to crush your ribs, snap your limbs or inflict other harm.'

'I'm sure you would.' She moved towards him, not touching yet, just staring at him, sensing his massive presence in the water. She had been with non-ship-born before. There was always a fascination between different human breeds, a deep longing for some kind of genetic exploration. Or maybe it was simple curiosity. She moved closer. He opened his mouth, and she ran her tongue over the edge of his teeth-plate. His arms were as powerful as she imagined, his hands as gentle. And in the water her zero-gravity litheness pleased him.

142

Chapter 17

I booked Tom into a hotel at Heathrow. A day ahead of his arrival, too anxious to hang around in York any more, I took a train journey back to Heathrow myself.

At the airport, I was the only passenger in a pod bus that rolled from the train station in a stately fashion over abandoned kilometres of roadway. The hotel was a long way out from the terminals, a measure of how busy this airport had once been. The hotel itself was a kind of extension of a vast multi-storey parking lot dating from the second half of the twentieth century, the age of monumental automotive architecture. It was as if the areas set aside for humans had been an afterthought. Now the cars had gone, but the hotel lingered on. There were no lines at check-in. I had the distinct impression that I was the only guest. It was an uneasy feeling, as if the whole hotel was a sham, an immense trap for unwary travellers.

The next day I met Tom off his plane. He seemed angry, at me, at Siberia, at gas hydrates; I supposed that to him this return was a defeat.

He let me hold him. It was like hugging a statue. But then, after a few seconds, he melted. 'Oh, Dad—' Suddenly we were embracing properly, all barriers down, no more bullshit, just father and son reunited. He was grimy, covered in stubble, and exhausted by his long flight. He actually stank a bit. But he was Tom, the reality of him, in my arms. Standing there with Tom in that empty airport concourse, I felt as happy as it's possible for a parent to feel, I think. I guess the genes were calling.

But the moment passed, too quickly, and Tom pulled back. I knew we had words to exchange, words that were going to be like bullets flying. But not now, not yet.

I took him to the hotel, checked him in, and let him go to his room alone.

While Tom rested up, I went for a walk around the old car lot, which was immense, a cathedral among parking facilities. There were ten, twelve floors, and there was parking space even on the roof. It was an open concrete frame, and from the outside you could look right through it to see daylight coming through from the other side. It was like a huge concrete skull.

I walked inside, past barriers that no longer raised, toll booths with broken glass and rusting ticket machines. Only a few bays on the ground floor were occupied, by electric utility vehicles nuzzled up against power sockets. The rest were vacant, bay after bay still marked out in fading white paint, all neatly numbered, plaintively empty. A half-hearted attempt had been made to extend the hotel itself into this vast area, but the conversion had apparently been abandoned.

Once elevators and escalators took you to the higher floors, but they no longer worked, and the stairs smelled of damp and rot. I chose to walk up the ramps which had once borne the cars. It was a long steep walk through that gargantuan architecture, exhausting for a mere human.

On the roof it was breezy, and I approached the edge cautiously. I looked out over the airport. The runways were neat straight-line strips, surrounded by the vaster acreage of the roads. Standing there on that parking-lot roof, I was the only human in sight in square kilometres of concrete and tarmac, stained by rubber and oil, now turning grey-green as it crumbled. The cars and planes had gone, and I remained; and on the breeze I could smell, not the old dense stinks of gasoline and rubber, but the poignant scent of spring grass. One day the car lot would vanish too. The small blind things of nature were already eating into the concrete fabric. Eventually the decay would reach the cables that held together this stressed-concrete structure, and when they gave way the whole place would explode, scattering concrete dust like dandelion seeds.

I turned back and wound my way back down the huge exit ramps, and returned to the hotel.

Tom slept, showered, whatever, for twelve hours. Then he called me through my implant. I went to his room.

He sat in the room's single armchair. He was bundled up in a tired-looking hotel dressing gown, watching news that bubbled quietly from one wall. His hair had been shaved at some point during his brief hospitalisation. He looked cadaverous, ill; he probably looked worse than he was. He had an aspirator in his hand, the only sign I'd seen of continuing medical treatment.

I sat on the bed, and he gave me a whisky from his minibar. It was midnight, but both our body clocks were screwed. With nobody else around, you make your own time.

There we were, the two of us, sitting side by side in an alien country, neutral territory.

'We need to talk,' I said tentatively.

'Yeah, we do.' The words came out as a growl. He leaned over and tapped the wall.

To my surprise, an image of the Kuiper Anomaly came up. It was a tetrahedron, an electric-blue framework that rotated slowly. Every so often starlight caught one of its faces, and it would flare up, iridescent, as if soap films were stretched across the frame.

'What's this?'

He said, 'I've been hacking into your logs, Dad. Seeing what you've been up to, the last few days.'

'You always did do your homework,' I said.

'Still this shit with you, isn't it? Starships and alien beings.'

I folded my arms – I know, a defensive posture, but he had gone straight on the attack. 'How can you call it *shit*? Look at this thing, obviously artificial, the only artificial object we know of in the universe not made by human hands. We're facing the biggest mystery in human history – and the answers may deliver the greatest change in human consciousness since—'

'Since we came out of the caves? Since we walked on the Moon? Since Columbus or Galileo, or the invention of the sentient toilet bowl?'

'But—'

'Dad, will you just stop *talking*? You've been talking all my fucking life. I remember when Mom left you that time. I was six—'

'Seven, actually.'

'She told me why she was taking me away from you for a while.'

'She did?'

'She always talked to me, Dad, in a way you never did. Even though I was only a little kid. She said you had two modes. You were either depressed, or else you were escaping from the fucking planet altogether. We would come back to you, she promised me, but she needed a break.'

I said grimly, 'It might have been better if she'd had that out with me, not you.'

'She's dead, Dad,' he reminded me. He snapped his fingers, and the image of the Anomaly scrunched up and whirled away. 'So you think it would have been better if I'd followed you, and devoted my life to this kind of blue-sky shit rather than the Library of Life?'

I still had my arms folded. 'If you had, you wouldn't have got yourself nearly killed by some burp of toxic gas in a godforsaken place nobody ever heard of. At least I'd know where you were, instead of having to hear that you'd nearly died through some friend of a friend...' I hadn't meant to say any of that. All this stuff, the resentment, the sense of abandonment, the hurt, was just tumbling out, having been penned up inside me since I'd heard the bad news.

Tom said, 'So it's not the danger to me that bothers you. It's the effect on *you*. You've always been the same, Dad.'

'Just don't get yourself killed. It's not worth it.'

He looked at me, almost curiously. 'Biospheric capture isn't *worth it*? Why not? Because we're through the Bottleneck? Is that what you think, that the worst is over?'

I spread my hands. Here we were, with a kind of dreadful inevitability, arguing about the state of the world, rather than our relationship. 'We're dealing with it, Tom. Aren't we? We gave up the damn automobile. We gave up oil! Some people will tell you that was the most profound economic transformation since the end of the Bronze Age. And then there's the Stewardship.'

146

He actually laughed. 'The Stewardship? You think that the Warming, the Die-back are somehow *fixed* by that vast instrumentality? Dad, are you really that complacent?'

'Tom—'

'We are fundamentally different people. Dad, you were always a dreamer. A utopian. You dream of space and aliens – the future. But I think the future in your head is a lot like the afterlife, like Heaven, both impossible fantasies of places that we can never reach, and yet where all our problems will just go away. And, like the afterlife, those who believe in the future try to control what we do in the here-and-now. There has always been a kind of future fascism, Dad. But the future is irrelevant.'

'It is?'

'Yes! Not if we can't get through the present. I'm different from you, Dad. I'm no dreamer. I go out there, into the world, and I deal with it like it is. And that was always beyond you, wasn't it? You never *liked* the present. It's just too complicated, too messy, too interconnected. There's nothing you can get your engineer's teeth into. And not only that, it's depressing.'

He rubbed his shaven scalp. 'I remember you once worked with me on a homework assignment on cosmology. Do you remember trying to prove to me that the universe must be finite? You spun me around on an office chair, fast enough for my legs and arms to go rising up. You asked me what was pulling my arms away from my body, and making me feel nauseous? It had to be the universe, the whole of it, a great river of matter and energy circling around my body, stars and planets and people, tugging at my legs through gravity, relativity, whatever. I thought that was a wonderful thought, how I was connected to everything else.

'But, you said, that showed the universe had to be finite. Because if it was *infinite*, it would load me down with an infinite inertia. I wouldn't be able to spin at all. I'd have been trapped like a bug in amber. You see, that's how I think you are in the world, Dad. You see the complicated real-world problems of ecology and climate and politics and all the rest like an infinite universe that pins you flat. No wonder you'd rather believe it's all been fixed. By the *Stewardship*, for God's sake, the last word in bureaucracy and corruption...'

Well, maybe so. I did wonder if Tom would have preferred me to be a brutal realist like Jack Joy, the Lethe Swimmer.

I got up, walked around a few paces, turned away until I was calmer. 'Maybe we ought to keep it down. We might wake the other guests.'

He didn't smile. 'What other guests? Nobody here but us ghosts, Dad. Which reminds me—' Reaching out he tapped another part of the wall screen.

He brought up John's picture of me, standing in that puddle in York in the middle of the night. So, suddenly, things had got even more messy.

I sat down. 'John sent you this?'

'Does it matter? I know what you've been up to, Dad. I know about the fucking – *ghost*. I can't believe you're doing this.'

'Believe me,' I said fervently, 'it's not by choice.'

'Oh, isn't it?' I couldn't read his mood. He sat back, apparently relaxed. But one fist clenched and unclenched.

We were entering uncharted territory in our relationship, I thought; put a foot wrong and I could do damage that would last a lifetime. 'Tom – I don't want this. But I see her. Or I see *something*. I don't know what to tell you. I'm trying to figure it out myself. But this has been happening to me for a long time...'

'I. Me. Myself.' He said the words in a dead tone, like a metronome, but his gaze was on the floor. 'Do you ever *listen* to yourself, Dad? Do you remember the funeral, when we buried her, and the kid? Did you know I snuck into the church early?'

I hadn't known he'd done that.

'I went to her coffin. It was in the aisle, before the altar. I tried to open that fucking box. I wanted to climb in with her. I didn't want to be left with *you*. Because I knew that all you would think about was yourself. You even gave more thought to the kid who killed your wife than to me.'

'Tom—' I spread my hands. 'Please. I don't know what to say. Everybody's fucked up, you know.'

'Oh, I understand that.' He actually smiled. 'You know, I forgive you. I'm an adult now, I can see you couldn't help it. But you should have tried to protect me, even from yourself. You should have *tried*.'

'I'm sorry.'

'And now you come to me and tell me you're being haunted by my mother. No, worse, you don't even tell me, I have to find it out from somebody else.' He was still, rigid with anger. 'How am I suppose to deal with that?'

I had no idea what to say.

At last he sat back. 'So what now?'

'I don't understand.'

'You dragged me home, Dad. You insisted on seeing me, talking to me. Fine. I guess I owed you that much. Have you got what you wanted?'

'I don't want you to put yourself at risk again.'

He laughed, contemptuous. 'You think you can stop me?'

'Not if you don't want to be stopped. Any more than you can stop me designing starships.'

'So where do we go from here?'

I shook my head. 'You know, the irony is, we're both right.'

'We are?'

'Sure. I'm right to believe in an expansive future for mankind. The Kuiper Anomaly is proof that it's possible: somebody else got through *their* Bottleneck and hung that thing up there. But you're right to try to deal with the problems of the present, because if we don't get through the Bottleneck there won't be any future at all. I've had enough of hearing about the differences between us. We should try to find some common ground.'

That took him by surprise. He seemed to think it over. In those few seconds I could feel some of the tension between us drain away. We'd both said what we had come in to say, we had both landed blows.

'All right.' He stood up. 'Anyhow we'll try not to fight.'

'Amen to that.'

'Dad, I think I need to do some physio, sleep a bit more.'

I took the hint. I stood and headed for the door. 'Maybe I'll see you in the morning?'

'Yeah. Look, Dad - you may be an asswipe, as Uncle John says, but you're still my dad, and I'm stuck with you.'

'Ditto,' I said fervently.

'But give up on this haunting crap, OK? Get some therapy, for Christ's sake.'

I sighed. 'You'll have to tell your mother that. Goodnight, son.'

I closed the door behind me.

Chapter 18

On the third day on the Rustball, Alia's inquisition resumed – for so she had come to think of it.

And today she finally learned what this strange, drab world had to offer her.

She was brought back to that dark, iron-walled room. The three Campocs were here again, Bale, Seer and Denh, surrounded by a subtly different sample of their relatives.

Once again they asked her to talk about her sister. She went back over what she'd said before, and tried to dig out more memories, tease out more meaning. But the exercise made her feel increasingly uncomfortable. Her jokey stories of how she'd tricked her sister, or out-competed her, or left her embarrassed, no longer seemed so clever.

'There is always a rivalry between siblings,' said Bale's great-aunt. 'It is part of the human condition, no doubt exported from old Earth itself.'

Perhaps. But again and again down the years, Alia had indulged that rivalry at her sister's expense. It was a kind of bullying, Alia thought now, for Drea had been helpless: Alia was her sister, and no matter what Alia did to her, dear stolid Drea would always come back for more. On some level Alia had known that, and had exploited Drea's loyalty.

'I've been awful,' said Alia.

As she reached this conclusion the Rusties' faces were watchful, interested, engaged, sympathetic: analytical, not judgemental.

'You're flawed,' Bale said. 'We are all flawed. But it's best to know about it, to look inwards, to see honestly.' There was something intense in the way he said that. He was guiding her, she saw, to a new insight.

Alia looked inward. And she started to understand.

Something was different: something about her perception of herself. Her own memories had never been sharper, more accurate; it was as if she had a scholar inside her head, refurbishing the muddled archives that made up her recollection of the past, her picture of herself. And at the same time she was seeing that picture with a pitiless clarity she had never known before.

She had changed, subtly, internally.

'How are you doing this? Is it the Mist? Or some chemical transfer when you touched me—'

Bale said, '*How* doesn't matter. Anyway you're doing it to yourself. Consciousness is the awareness of self, and self is recorded in memory. You are becoming *more* conscious, for the quality of your awareness is increasing. Your memories are more precise, and your perception of them is clearer.'

'But I hate it! I see myself better than ever before, but I don't like what I see. I feel like sticking my fingers in my ears, shutting my eyes, turning away. Distracting myself until I forget.'

Bale's great-aunt said, 'We have all been through it.'

She sighed. 'But turning away won't work any more, will it?'

'No. But,' Bale said, 'would you prefer *not* to know yourself?'

'Right now, yes!'

That night she lay awake, alone in the dark.

She had turned away Bale's gentle invitations to share his bed. Even hours after the inquisition she couldn't stop looking inward, couldn't stop thinking about herself. She tried to immerse herself in her Witnessing, but right now not even Poole's antics and endeavours seemed able to distract her.

And anyhow she envied him, she realised reluctantly. Poole had been unusually clear-sighted for his time. But even so he had walked around in a kind of dream. Like every human his memories were imperfectly stored in the biochemical mishmash of his nervous system. And he had endlessly edited the story of his life, unconsciously, to make logic out of illogical situations, to put himself at centre stage and in control of events. There were sound reasons for this.

A human memory had never been meant to be an objective recording system but a support for ego: without the comforting illusion of control, Poole's mind might have crumbled in the face of an arbitrary universe.

But all that was different now. Her consciousness had already been superior to Poole's, even before she had come to the Rustball. A half-million years of evolution had seen to that. And now the re-engineering initiated by the Campocs, as it subtly knit and re-knit her neurones, or whatever it was doing in her head, accentuated the gap. Her memory was as perfect a recording instrument as any technology could deliver. And her self-awareness was so clear, the mists banished, that the comfort of delusion was no longer an option. Her knowledge of herself was accurate, and utterly pitiless.

She called Reath, in orbit.

'Don't worry,' he said. 'It isn't, ah, permanent. You aren't stuck with this new self-knowledge, any more than you have yet taken what you call an "immortality pill". I have brought you here so you can feel how it may be to immerse yourself in this Second Implication. But you have taken no irrevocable step on your road to Transcendence.'

'I can see why it's necessary,' she said. 'This cold self-awareness. You can't make a super-mind out of a crowd of dreamers.'

'But it's uncomfortable, isn't it?'

'You've no idea.'

'When you see your sister again, what will you do?'

'Apologise,' she said fervently.

'Alia, your time on the Rustball is nearly over.'

'It is?' she asked, surprised.

'The Rusties have only one more development to show you – or rather, to help you discover in yourself. But you must decide if you want to take that final step.'

'Is it up to me?'

'It always has been, child. You should know that by now. Try to get some sleep.'

But try as she might, alone with herself in the dark, sleep didn't come.

Another day – her last day on the Rustball – and another

session in the gloomy room with the Campocs and their extended family.

But today it felt different. She gazed around at their faces, which seemed to glow gently in the soft pink light of the room. They were all turned to her, their expressions open. They were looking at her, they were thinking about her, and what she had revealed of herself since coming to this community.

And suddenly she was looking back at herself. It was a view from many angles, as if the eyes around her had turned to mirrors. She had gone through another sharp transition, another expansion of her awareness, as if a door had opened, admitting light. She quailed, battered.

Bale touched her hand. The shock of physical contact was there, but it was not as it had been before, just one more link in a web of connecting. And besides, since her intimacy with him there was tenderness in his touch.

'Do you feel it?' he asked.

'I think so...' As he held her hand the sense of an extended perspective wavered, but did not collapse.

He said, 'Now you can see yourself through my eyes. You can look into the memories, even of yourself, stored in me. The others, too. It is as if we are all one mind, in this room, one nervous system united, memory and thought processes distributed and yet joined. *You can look at yourself*, not just from within your own head, but through the minds of others.'

This was necessary, she was told, necessary for mind to grow. If consciousness was founded on the ability to look back at herself, now she could see herself through the eyes of others too – and so by definition her consciousness was enhanced by an order of magnitude.

'It takes some getting used to,' Denh said.

'You can say that again,' said Seer ruefully.

Alia asked, 'How?...'

The communication was not mind to mind, for that was impossible; mind was only an emergent property of the brain, the body. But it was as if the physical barriers between one nervous system and another became irrelevant. There was a technology, she was told, or perhaps it was a biology, very ancient, which could link humans on some level deeper than words. Some even said this faculty derived from an alien species long assimilated by mankind. But its origin didn't matter.

Bale said, 'This is Unmediated Communication. There are no symbolic barriers. You will know what I am thinking as I think it – and I will know your thoughts too, as if they were my own, as direct as an embrace, or a punch in the mouth.' He hesitated. 'It is not yet fully developed in you. Even if you go further you will be able to pull back. Do you want—'

'Yes,' she said, not giving herself time to think. 'Do it.'

Suddenly the mirror-minds in the room shone bright – all the barriers between them fell away – and she saw herself, not just in this moment, but in the Rusties' deepest perception. She rummaged through their memories of how she had been during her conversations. She could see her body language, her shyness slowly giving way to enthusiasm as she talked – and the times when her words hadn't contained the whole truth, and she had been evasive, breaking eye contact, turning away, laughing unnecessarily, fiddling with her body fur.

She knew what these people thought of her. It was shocking, bewildering.

But, as she looked at herself through her own eyes and others', the self she saw wasn't so bad. Yes, she had sometimes been spiteful to her sister, driven by rivalry. But such incidents, spiky in memory, had taken up only a small fraction of their relationship. She was just a kid, promising, flawed, unformed. She hadn't known any better.

And, she realised to her surprise, she forgave herself. Suddenly she was crying, her vision blurred by tears.

An arm spread around her shoulders: Bale's great-aunt. 'There, there,' she said. 'We all go through it. Three steps. You have to *see* yourself; you have to *accept* yourself; and you have to learn to *forgive* yourself. But forgiveness is as hard as blame, isn't it? There, there; this will pass.'

The Transcendents were linked as these Rusties were linked. The Transcendence was surely much more than this, in its antiquity, its complexity, its wisdom. But this extraordinary linking of minds was its foundation.

And now she thought she understood the strange community of the Rustball. There was no art, music, expression, no *individuality* here, because none was needed. Art was only a form of communication, and a symbolic one at that. Who needed the imperfect channels of art or music when you could directly access another's memories, thoughts, emotions? Why struggle to express yourself if you knew your own mind with a pitiless clarity? And why travel if you knew that wherever you went you would find nothing so fascinating as other people?

But how limited this community was as a result, she thought. How introverted, how drab their lives were. Was this really the future of mankind?

Bale watched her, a kindly concern mixed with pride. But it struck her now that every second they had spent together, even those moments when they embraced in the water, had been shared in the heads of his brothers and cousins. They had never been alone, even when they were most intimate. She felt a qualm of unease, a stab of revulsion.

Chapter 19

I had twenty-four hours before my flight back to the States. Tom had a few days more. Tom wanted to see London.

I decided to go visit Uncle George.

George lived alone in a smallish town about a dozen kilometres south-west of Manchester. I took the train up from London. On arrival, consulting my softscreen map, I decided to skip the pod buses and rickshaws and walk the couple of klicks to George's home.

When I was a kid George was fond of telling me that it's foolish to imagine that the future is going to be disconnected from the present or the past, as if everything will be ripped down and rebuilt. He was right. In this town, all the old housing stock was still there, the boxy twentieth-century commuter houses crammed side by side into every available square centimetre. In the age of the automobile this had been just another dormitory suburb for the nearby big city, its historic roots swamped by residential developments. Now, sensibly enough, if you wanted to work in the city you lived in the city, but that meant places like this had lost their primary function. Now wooden doors had been replaced by massive weather-proof steel shutters, brickwork coated by silvery Paint, windows bricked up.

There was nobody around but me. It was eerie to walk through the quiet streets. Fifty years ago the place would have been carpeted by automobile metal, cars parked in every drive and bumped up on the sidewalks. Now the cars had gone, and the houses with their blanked-out windows were like backs turned.

Tom and I had made peace, of a sort. Or we had agreed to disagree. Or something. But now I found myself obsessing about our arguments about the Stewardship.

The Stewardship was a legacy of Amin's Administration, though it was set up after she died. It was a new international body, a 'green UN', assembled with the power and authority of the US government. Its central task, the challenge of the century, was to feed everybody: to raise per capita food production while reducing our consumption of materials and energy.

It had started with simple quick-return initiatives, like buying up land high in ecological value but in danger of over-exploitation. Right now the Stewardship was working on two mighty flagship projects: to save what was left of the Brazilian rainforest, a hotspot of biodiversity and evolutionary innovation, and to stabilise China, so parched and overcrowded that the Yellow River was poisoned when it didn't run dry, and whose vast lowlands were one massive hydro-engineering project.

But there were plans to go much further, to establish an ethical framework and new economic rules to rebuild the world – the kind of work John was involved in. It really was a new 'Marshall Plan for a bruised world,' a bold interplay of environmental management, economics, diplomacy. Gradually the big religions had come on board, and a decades-long tide of conflict spawned out of aggressive and triumphalist tendencies in all the major faiths had begun to turn. The Stewardship had even been given a limited democratic legitimacy when the rest of the world was allowed to participate in US presidential elections, a 'fifty-first state' with as many electoral college votes as California – more than enough to turn close elections.

I believed the Stewardship was the greatest achievement of statesmanship of my adult life. I was able to talk about this passionately. But Tom didn't appear to agree with me, even about this. How could the two of us be so different?

Well, I told myself, a relationship is a process; you crash through dramatic stages now and then but you never reach a conclusion, not this side of the grave anyhow. But I wasn't sure how to follow it up with Tom, what to do next. Or what to do about Morag, come to that.

As I walked, all the issues in my life churned around in

my head, seeking focus, interconnection: work, the starship, Tom, Morag, the niggling issue of the gas hydrates. Also, though I didn't quite want to admit it, it was faintly disturbing that everything seemed to centre on *me*.

I think I imagined that talking to George would help me get this straight in my head.

George's home was just another brick box in a row of boxes. He had kept a few windows as windows, even if the glass was dusty and his paintwork, smart or not, had seen better days. And he still had a garden; little sprinklers watered his lupins, asters and delphiniums. His lawn looked healthy enough, but the holly bushes which had once separated the garden from the sidewalk had been replaced by a line of bamboo.

He took a couple of minutes to answer my ringing. He greeted me with a broad, toothy smile. 'Michael! So you turned up.' He led me into his hallway, and through to the kitchen. 'Come in, come in. I'm glad to see you. But then, old people are always glad of visitors. Pathetic, isn't it?'

George was the same sort of build as me – compact or squat, depending on whether you're looking out or in. He still moved pretty well, but his upper body was bent over, his neck jutting forward, and there was a kind of uneven fragility in his footsteps.

The hallway was narrow, the walls coated with yellowing wallpaper, and there was a musty, damp, unmistakably old-person sort of smell, despite the labours of a spider-like cleaning robot that scuttled upside down over the ceiling. The place was noticeably flood-proofed. There were no carpets downstairs, just tiles and a few roll-up rugs and mats, and the electricity sockets had been reinstalled halfway up the walls.

The kitchen was clean and bright, and I could smell garlic. George once lived in Italy, and he picked up some good cooking habits there. But with its safety-conscious ceramic covers, rounded edges and bright primary colours the kitchen looked oddly toy-like. George had grumbled about that before: 'The social workers turn your home into a chuffing nursery,' he would say. But in alcoves on the walls there was a collection of Catholic artefacts, a plaster statue of the Virgin Mary, a little plastic bottle labelled 'Lourdes Water'. These were relics of George's parents, I believed, who had been devout.

George was eighty-seven years old. His wife, my Aunt Linda, had died a few years earlier. He had actually remarried her after they divorced; aged twelve I was hauled over to England to attend the second wedding – 'a joke', my mother called it, 'typical George'. As far as I could tell George and Linda had been happy. But then, a few years back, she had died. 'That's the trouble with happy endings,' he told me after the funeral. 'You just live on and on until you've sucked all the juice out, and it turns out not to be so happy after all.'

He sat me at his small breakfast table and began to fuss with a kettle. 'So what do you want, tea, coffee? A beer? Have a beer. Go crazy.'

'A beer will be fine.'

He rubbed his hands and cackled, his open mouth revealing even white teeth, probably regrown from buds. He bent stiffly, opened his refrigerator, and hauled out a couple of brown bottles.

The refrigerator protested in a soft whisper. 'George, are you sure that's wise? It's a little early, don't you think?'

'Chuff off,' he said cheerfully, and slammed the door shut.

The beer was strong and gritty. I asked, 'Wheat beer?'

'The only kind I can afford. The hop harvest never recovered from the milt. But it's five per cent proof.' He took a long pull. 'So,' he said, 'tell me about your Kuiper project.'

That was what I always liked about George, even when I was a kid. He never acted like an uncle, never like *family*. He wouldn't ask you polite, bored questions about how you were getting on at school. Over the years he developed common interests with us – with me it was spaceflight and all things extraterrestrial – and so when he visited we always had something real to talk about.

Not that my mother appreciated that, I don't think. 'You treat Michael as the son you never had,' she once yelled at him. 'Bollocks,' George had replied succinctly, to my huge pleasure.

George always said he was pleased I was working on Kuiper, even if it was only a small-scale design study. He found the Anomaly particularly fascinating, because, he told me, its discovery in the first decade of the century had come at a strange time in his own life. His father had just died, he had gone looking for a sister he had never known he had, and the discovery of Kuiper and the great philosophical transformation it had brought had seemed to him to parallel the upheavals going on in his own heart.

Also, he told me once, it was particularly appropriate that *I* should work on Kuiper. He didn't elaborate. George could be a bit mysterious at times. Well, he was a Poole.

As we sat there talking about Kuiper a toy robot came rolling into the room. It was a real antique, all shaped tin and plastic and little glass eyes, and as it rattled along a flywheel sent friction sparks shooting from a grill in its belly.

George snapped at the robot, 'What do you want?'

'Well, George, you aren't following your routines. Normally you take a walk to the shops this time of day. I wondered if you'd forgotten.' The robot's voice was comically melodramatic, intended to intone interplanetary dangers, devoted to domestic trivia.

George said to me, 'You see what I mean? They turn your home into a nursery.' He barked at the robot, 'No, I hadn't forgotten. I'm just not a chuffing robot like you. I have free will.'

The robot said, 'Well, so do I, George, but we can discuss philosophy later. Wouldn't you like to take your walk? Perhaps your new friend could go with you.'

'It's not a friend, it's a nephew. And we're drinking beer and talking. So clear off.' He aimed a kick at the robot. His foot passed clean through it, scattering it to pixels that quickly coalesced. The robot, grumbling, rattled out of the room. 'Little prick,' said George.

The design turned out to be a VR copy of a toy from George's long-gone childhood, a robot from some forgotten TV show called *The Link*.

'I never imagined you as a nostalgia buff, George.'

'Well, you have to have a *personal care assistant*,' George said, spitting out the words. 'You should have seen the other designs. But if it didn't play a mean game of chess I'd have scrambled it long ago. Little prick.'

As we talked, and George made me lunch – a light Italian dish of pasta with baked fish, good if a little heavy on the garlic – the house and its contents continued to fuss around him. George responded to most of this with a cheery curse, but he took his pills and obeyed the rules.

He only had to live like this because the family, *I*, wasn't around to look after him any better. The population of the elderly had hugely expanded during George's lifetime. He liked to say that the commuters who had once journeyed daily out of here had all come back in their old age, 'like a flock of elderly gulls returning to their nesting cliff'. But there weren't enough youngsters around to look after them all, even if our hearts had been in it. So it was up to the robots. Without artificial sentience, if the machines hadn't been able to fulfil the state's duty of care to its citizens, George said he didn't know how we would have coped. 'Maybe put us all to work, in the Sunny Vales Gulag of the Twilight Years. Although euthanasia would be simpler.'

I was silently thankful for the empathetic intelligence of the designers who had made George's mandatory companion a chess-playing, bickering toy robot rather than a bland, soulless nurse.

After lunch we took a walk. George said he would show me the new managed forest that was growing up on the outskirts of town. 'Off the Stockport road,' he said. 'Only a mile or so. Used to be a golf course. Nobody plays golf any more. Good.'

So we walked. The day was mild, the sunlight hazy and washed out. The air seemed reasonably fresh, with only a faintly polluted tinge to it, an acidic smell like crushed ants.

The hike wasn't that easy. The road surface was mostly silvertop to allow the pod buses and rickshaws to pass, but the sidewalks, or pavements as George called them, were little used, cracked and weed-infested. You had to watch where you stepped. George had been supplied with exoskel-etal supports, but he said he had locked the 'clanking splinty things' in a spare bedroom. He walked with a stick well enough, however.

That home-help robot tailed us, grumbling to itself, pro-jected from a dog-tag around George's neck.

As we walked our talk gradually spiralled out from my work on Kuiper. I began to tell George about Tom and his accident. Actually George had known all about it. He followed the news about Tom and other family members; in a wired-up world nobody is far from a camera. I tried to tell him how we'd got together in that dismal hotel in Heathrow. George listened, and though he didn't say much he seemed to understand.

He dug into the issue of the waterspout and the gas hydrates. 'How are these gases stored? Is there a critical temperature at which they will be released? *How* much is there exactly?...'

He asked smart questions, having once been an engineer himself. He had worked in software until he had been made redundant by Moore's Law, he liked to say, the relentless expansion of computer capacity. His career had spanned the milestone time when the first human-level sentience systems came on the market at a budget an average household could afford. Now nobody designed software any more; for many of its generations it had designed itself. And there were no more analysts, programmers, or software engineers; instead there were 'animists' and 'therapists' who sought to understand the strange new kinds of minds that permeated the world.

George had been too old for any of that. He had seen out his career working on the 'legacy suites', some decades old, that still lay at the heart of many major systems, and were now threatening us with the digital millennium. The present is built on the past, even in software; George said he finished his career feeling more like an archaeologist than an engineer.

Soon his questioning about the hydrates exposed the limits of my knowledge. But he agreed with me that Tom's experience might be a bellwether warning about more serious dangers to come.

'Michael, if you're concerned about this, you should go find out what the implications are. I find it hard to believe nobody's thought of this before.'

'Find out from who?'

He could be sarcastic sometimes. 'Forgive me for stating

the obvious. But maybe you could start with the Centre for Climate Modelling. You'd think *they* would have some handle on it all since it is their job. They're based in Oklahoma, aren't they? We can check it out back at the house.'

'They'll never listen to me.'

'Oh, I bet I can find a way in. I still have contacts with the Slan(t)ers.' This was a dubious old conspiracy-theory organisation, scattered around the planet like a terrorist network, with whom George had had dealings long ago. 'Small-world networks,' he would say. 'Whoever you're trying to reach, there is a Slan(t)er who knows another who knows somebody, and so forth. The Slan(t)ers are a bunch of old nuts. But then so am I.'

'But even if the climate modellers are mapping the hydrate issue, if the whole polar ocean is going to blow its lid, what is there to do about it?'

He snorted. 'You design chuffing starships. Can't you think of anything?'

'Not offhand,' I said heavily, 'no.'

'Then start thinking. If you do dig into this business of the gas hydrates, *if* there's a significant threat and *if* you can think up some way to stop it, you might do some good.' He winked at me. 'And of course you will be building up a connection between you and Tom. But, you know, I think you ought to find some way of talking to your son other than through megaengineering... In here.'

We had come to a gate in an iron fence. Beyond lay a park, with trees scattered over a lawn-like expanse. We walked in, stepping onto the grass. George sighed with a stiff pleasure at the softness of the ground.

Small black shapes moved purposefully through the grass at my feet. They looked like ants, but I saw the flash of metal jaws and even the spark of tiny lasers; they were miniature bots, nano-gardeners, patiently tending the forest of grass around them.

We came to the shade of a tree, a sycamore. I helped George to the ground so we could sit for a while, leaning on the bark. George was breathing hard, and I realised with a pang of guilt that the kilometre or so we had walked was a long journey, for him. My feeling wasn't lightened by the accusing glare of the robot.

The prospect was attractive, just trees and some low bushes and the grass. But further away I saw what looked like fencing, lines of rectangular panels turned to the sun. They were engineered trees. We controlled genomes so exquisitely that we no longer bothered to grow a tree and cut it down and chop it up; we just grew panels that could be snapped off, taken away and used immediately. I'd read that in Sweden they had developed living houses, just sprouting from the ground with saunas attached. And in one Chinese lab they were growing whole books on trees, complete with text, like bundles of leaves.

When George got his breath back he sang a few lines from a plaintive song. '*All the leaves are brown / And the sky is grey…*'

'That sounds pretty.'

He shrugged. 'This whole place is totally transformed from when I was a kid. See these trees? They're sycamore. And the undergrowth is rhododendron and Japanese knotwood.' He pointed with his stick. 'There used to be a big old oak tree over there. Edge of the fifteenth green.' There was nothing left now but a hollow in the ground, faintly shadowed. 'As a kid I came out here to meet a girlfriend who lived nearby. I'd cycle over and sneak in and read in the shade of that old tree. Sometimes I'd pinch golf balls that came sailing by and sell them back to the punters, but that's another story.

'Well, I came back, Christ, I must have been in my fifties, your age, to clear up some last bits of business after my father's death. I took a walk out here. And that old tree was dying. I always thought it would live for ever, or at least outlive me. But it actually looked like it was bleeding; there was this awful tarry sap leaking out of cankers on its trunk. All the leaves were brown.

'Later I found out what it was. *Sudden oak death*, they called it. It was a kind of fungus that kills by cutting off the flow of nutrients in the trunk. Back then we were shipping plants and trees all over the planet, and bringing their pathogens with them. Now you only see oak trees in hothouses in Kew Gardens.' He waved a hand at the sycamore above him.

'Instead we have this spindly crap. And all the wildlife you used to get with the old stuff has gone too, woodpeckers and butterflies and toads. The world seems emptied out.'

I knew what he meant. Monocultural and silent, England was like an abandoned theatre stage, the actors all gone. Much of America was the same.

'But when I first noticed that poor bleeding tree all I could think of was that silly old song. *All the leaves are brown.* But there is no warm LA sunshine to escape to, is there?'

'I guess not.'

George leaned back against the tree trunk and sighed. 'Listen, Michael. I hate to sound like an old man, but you ought to know this. I've been thinking of getting myself written into a tree...'

I'd heard of this. The idea was you would embed a coded version of George's genome into the DNA of a sycamore, say. It would make no difference to the tree: there were ways to do this without changing the length of a tree gene, or the protein it spelled out. But the tree as it grew would be a kind of living memorial, with every one of its trillions of cells carrying a genetic echo of George himself.

The robot said sourly, 'He's not just thinking about it. He's put it in his will.'

'I never thought you'd be so sentimental, George.'

'Sentimental? Maybe. I don't have any kids, you know.'

That was the selling point, of course. Across Europe and North America childbirth rates were falling, and an increasing number of people faced the prospect of dying childless. So they were being sold other 'ways' of having their heritage living on.

'I think it's some deep genetic thing,' George said, his voice fading a bit. 'I don't have any regrets about not having kids – not for the sake of the kids themselves, because they never existed, and even if they had they'd probably have turned out to be arseholes like me. But behind me there is a queue of grandmothers and grandfathers going all the way back to some low-browed *Homo erectus*. Why should that long line end with *me*? It doesn't feel responsible that I should let it all just go without a fight.'

On impulse I touched his hand; the flesh was papery,

liver-spotted, but warm. 'We share a lot of genes, George,' I said. 'What, a quarter? You live on through me. And through Tom. But if you want the tree, I'll make sure you get your tree.'

'Thank you,' George said.

The robot, standing beside us, whirred softly. I wondered what it made of our talk.

'So anyhow,' George said carefully, 'it isn't just Tom and gas hydrates that's on your mind, is it?'

Immediately I understood what he meant. 'John called you too, didn't he? He told you about Morag. That asshole.'

'He means well,' George said, a bit dubiously. 'At least I think he does. That's family for you. They can lift you up and smack you in the mouth with the very same gesture.'

'And what about you? Do you think I'm crazy too?' The robot looked at me warningly, and I realised I'd snapped. 'Sorry,' I said.

'Of course not,' he said. 'I believe you. Why not? The world's a strange place; I haven't lived so long and not figured that out. And you always seemed sensible to me. I have some advice, though. Go see Rosa.'

'Rosa?'

'My sister, your aunt. Look, her background is – odd.' He'd once told me how she'd been taken away from home to be brought up by a holy order in Rome, a peculiar, introverted society of matriarchs of some kind; he'd called it a 'Coalescence'. 'She left it all behind years ago. By the time she got back in touch with me she was ordained, and working as a Catholic priest in Spain.'

'I should go see a *priest*?'

'You think you're haunted. Who else are you going to talk to? Look, I'll set up the contact for you. She's family. And I bet yours won't be the only ghost story she'll have heard in her life.'

'I'll think about it,' I said, uncertain. 'And she'll be – um, sympathetic?'

George said ruefully, 'We Pooles don't do sympathy, Michael, even those of us who take holy orders. But you may get some truth from her. If you want therapy, I'll sell you the robot.'

'You chuffing won't,' said the robot.

'So,' George said, 'how are you feeling now?'

'I have all this stuff swirling around in my head,' I said hesitantly. 'Tom. The hydrate deposits, that might end this world. The Kuiper Anomaly, an emissary of another world. Morag, perhaps a visitation from another level of reality altogether. Each of these things seems extraordinary, or tremendously significant, or both. And they are all somehow focusing down on *my* life. Sometimes I wonder if there is some connection between them.'

His eyes, still the family smoky grey, were bright. 'Of course there's a connection. *You.*'

I hadn't wanted to say it out loud. I looked down at my body, my paunchy belly, my fat legs. 'That makes no sense.'

'Actually it's halfway to madness,' the robot pointed out.

'We *aren't* all created equal, Michael. Let me tell you something. You know that the Kuiper Anomaly was discovered in the first decade of the century. But it actually showed up on some old records, images and infra-red searches, dating from before the formal "discovery". It had just never been recognised for what it was. But we have a date, I mean to within a day, when that thing appeared on the edge of the solar system. And you know what that date is?'

Suddenly I felt cold. It was like the feeling I sometimes got before one of Morag's visitations. 'Tell me.'

'The Anomaly appeared *on the day you were born*. Coincidence?' George leaned back and laughed. 'We're a peculiar lot, we Pooles, a damn peculiar lot. Stuck in history. We can't help it. Now, are you going to help me up, or do I have to rely on the robot?'

The toy robot watched as I struggled to help him rise, its blank artificial eyes fixed on me suspiciously.

I took the train back to London the next day. I would never see George in the flesh again.

Chapter 20

The next day, back aboard Reath's ship, they prepared to leave the Rustball.

Reath had promised to take Alia back to the *Nord*. After her disturbing experiences on the Rustball she longed to go home for a while, back to the familiar sights and smells of the ship, to relish its conceptual freedom compared to the dreadful chthonic rigidity of planets. And she longed to see Drea, above all, to put things right.

But before they left orbit Reath came to her. He seemed uncomfortable. Plans had changed, he said.

The Campocs said they felt she was unready to proceed to the next stage of her Transcendence training. She should see more of the post-human Galaxy, if she aspired to join the body that governed it. So she was to be flown off to some other dismal rocky speck of a world.

Not only that, it turned out, the Campocs wanted to come along too.

She was bewildered. 'Reath, can't you – I don't know – appeal to somebody?'

'It doesn't work like that,' Reath said. 'I have to accept what the Campocs say. Otherwise there would be no point coming here.'

'But I want to go home.' Alia was embarrassingly aware of the whine in her voice.

Reath sighed. 'I know. Everything will be fine, you'll see.'

She allowed herself to feel reassured. But as she watched the Campocs' ugly, beetle-like shuttle climb up out of their planet's gravity well once more, she thought back over the exchange. Reath's control of the situation had somehow been challenged by the Campocs, by Bale and the others. She worried at this disturbing development, a shifting in the alignment of the unseen powers that had taken over her life.

And what could the Campocs possibly want?

The planet to which the Campocs directed them orbited an undistinguished star some three hundred light years closer to the Galaxy's centre than the Rustball.

The journey was uneventful. Alia spent most of her time immersed in the travails of Michael Poole, trying to shut out the unwelcome complexity of her own life. The Campocs weren't good company; they kept themselves to themselves throughout the trip. In fact Alia was relieved about that. She had felt uncomfortable with Bale ever since she had figured out that their intimacy must have been shared with his kin. But, faintly suspicious of the Campocs, she tried tentatively to use her new abilities to sense something of their thinking. It felt eerie to probe for the thoughts and feelings of others, with no more difficulty than she might grope for an elusive memory inside her head. But it worked.

She could sense a kind of disciplined excitement shared by the Campocs. It was true they had never travelled much before; this jaunt away from the Rustball was a novelty for them. But there was something else under the surface, she thought, something darker she couldn't bring into focus. It added to her sense of unease about them.

No doubt they could sense what Alia was feeling too. She tried not to think about that.

At their destination they all crowded to the windows to see the view.

This new world was called Baynix II, after its parent star. It had no name of its own. 'Or rather,' Reath said mysteriously, 'those who live here have never told us what they call their world – if they are still aware they are on a world at all...'

It was another ball of rock and iron, more or less like Earth, with a scattering of oceans, ice caps, clouds. But where the Rustball had been almost all iron, this world was almost all rock, right to its core.

'It is a Dirtball,' Denh snickered.

Reath said, 'Another result of the vicissitudes of planetary impact processing.' He speculated that Baynix II was more like the Moon than Earth, a secondary product of a giant collision, sculpted from the mantle of some larger world.

Alia peered down uneasily. All these worlds seemed to be the products of random acts of immense violence. She couldn't imagine how it must be to live on such battered fragments.

They crammed into a small shuttle, and Alia descended into the air of yet another planet.

There were oceans here, delivered as usual by comets, and a layer of atmosphere, mostly carbon dioxide. But the land was ancient, littered with the eroded shadows of features billions of years old, palimpsests of craters and mountain ranges. The native life, battered by radiation, had never progressed beyond single cells, hardy little radiation-resistant bugs. The circumstances of the Dirtball's difficult birth had left it inhospitable: that shrunken core meant no significant tectonic renewal, and no global magnetic field.

And as far as Alia could see, humans had made little impression here. There were no cities, no farms. A couple of automated monitoring stations, themselves unimaginably old, stood silently, eroded and half-covered by drifting sand. And that was all.

'So why are we here?' Alia asked.

Reath grinned, and allowed the shuttle to dip close to the ground. 'For *them*,' he said, pointing.

Alia thought the formations on the ground were just geological. They were ridges, low, lumpy and irregular, the same colour as the sandy ground from which they rose. Reath gave her no more clues. Irritated by the mystery, and the sense that everybody knew more about what was going on than she did, Alia refused to ask any more questions.

The flitter landed. The gravity was a little less than standard, not uncomfortable. They disembarked, and waited for the local Mist to prepare them. Alia felt filters in her nose and throat close up against the corrosive dust suspended in the air, and oxygen coolly hissed into her lungs.

She walked up to the rocky formations. From the ground they looked like low, eroded ridges, pushing up from the flat earth. There might have been fifty of these features, lying parallel, their worn summits rising some forty metres into the air.

It wasn't until she was almost climbing on the first of them that she recognised what it was. Suddenly it snapped into focus – that thin ridge that pushed into the ground, those deep craters, the smooth bulge above – this worn morphology wasn't random at all.

'Lethe,' she said. 'It's a *face*. A human face.'

The 'ridges' were like statues of human forms, fallen statues each two or three hundred metres tall. Tremendous arms, legs, torsos rose out of the dirt. On one especially well-sculpted hand four fingers and a thumb were clearly visible. The drifting sand had half-buried the figures – or perhaps they had been left this way deliberately, for the sculptors' own unimaginable purpose. The great face before her was shoved into the dirt, so only one eye, one nostril, half of an open mouth was left exposed. Around half-open lips was a spill of sand of a different colour, a denser, blue-purple hue, as if it had been vomited out of that rocky mouth. She could have climbed into the great socket of the one exposed eye. But there was an odd sense of watchfulness about that empty pit, she thought uneasily.

'It's astounding,' she said.

Bale nodded. 'I know.'

'But what is it *for*?'

Bale only smiled.

Reath seemed less interested in the statues than in the sand in which they lay. He squatted on his haunches and lifted a handful of dirt, letting it run through his fingers. 'This was the bed of a lake, once. Or perhaps an ocean. These grains are clearly water-formed – see how they are rounded? But the ocean surely vanished billions of years ago.'

Alia confronted him. 'What have these monuments got to do with me?'

'Monuments?' He got to his feet, a bit stiffly. Pooling ocean-floor sand in his palm, he rubbed the rounded grains gently. 'Almost all these grains are of silicate materials. Silicon is ten times more abundant than carbon in Earth's crust, you know – and presumably several times more abundant still here on this ball of sand. Have you ever wondered why it should be the scarcer carbon, then, and not the more abundant silicon, that emerged as the basis of Earth life?'

Alia snapped, 'Everybody knows that. Because carbon can form multiple bonds. Carbon can make molecules that are complex enough to store a genetic code.'

'True, true. But you *can* form complex structures of silicon, at least in its crystalline form...'

'So what?' Alia knocked his hand, scattering the sand grains. 'Reath, I've had enough of this. What are we doing in this sculpture park?'

Reath seemed a little lost. He looked down at his feet, as if the grains she had spilled were the only ones on the planet. 'It was the Campocs who brought you here,' he reminded her.

Alia was distracted by a spark of light that shot over the arc of the sky. It was a ship, she saw immediately. Moving gracefully it descended towards this plain of sand, and as it neared she made out its details, complex, fragile, beautiful.

It was undoubtedly a shuttle from the *Nord*. As soon as it landed a hatch popped open and a woman climbed uncertainly out. It was Drea. Alia ran.

Drea stumbled a little in the unfamiliar gravity, and she coughed as the Mist kicked in. But then she ran too, heavy-footed across the sand towards Alia. The two of them collided in a tangle of limbs, laughing.

Alia felt unreasonably joyful to see her sister. 'Thanks for coming all this way,' she said.

'I'm not sure if I had a choice.' Drea smiled. 'A summons from Reath is pretty forceful. Anyhow I missed you.'

'And I you. You'll never know.'

A dusty breeze stirred Drea's hair body fur. 'I've got to tell you - on the *Nord* they're having a constellation naming ceremony.'

This happened every decade or so, as the stars, slowly shifted across the *Nord*'s sky by the ship's sublight crawl, adopted new configurations. The names of the new patterns were chosen by popular votes, amid much friendly rivalry.

Alia winced. 'I wish I could be there.'

'They are going to name a constellation for you, Alia!

173

It will be called "The Skim Dancers". Everybody voted for it.'

Alia grabbed her sister's hands. 'So you're in it too!'

'But it's you they are proud of, Alia. Everybody is. Although nobody's quite sure what you're doing out here.' She glanced around. 'Not much of a place, is it?'

Alia said, 'Mostly I've finding out unpleasant things about myself. I'm sorry.'

Drea looked mystified. 'Sorry for what?'

Alia smiled. 'For pulling your fur when I was three...'

'And I'm sorry too.' It was Bale; he had come to stand a couple of metres away from the sisters.

Alia introduced him quickly, and the other Campocs. But the Campocs didn't acknowledge Drea, who suddenly seemed lost, turned in on herself. Alia's unease quickly deepened. She glanced at Reath. He looked very uncomfortable now, but he stared at the ancient sand at his feet.

She turned back to the Campocs. 'What's going on here, Bale? Why is Drea here? And what are *you* sorry for?'

His smile was thin. 'For what we have to do.'

'What are you talking about?'

Drea staggered.

Alia grabbed her sister's shoulder to support her. Suddenly it was like handling a doll; Drea's limbs shook loosely, her head lolled, and a line of spittle leaked from the corner of her mouth.

Alia turned on Bale. 'What have you done to her?'

'Alia, you must understand that—'

She hit his shoulder. With her long space-dweller's arms she was capable of delivering a powerful blow, and she sent him sprawling in the dirt. He gaped up at her, his mouth a round circle of shock.

Denh and Seer came to stand between her and Bale, and stared at her warily. 'Don't hit him again,' Denh said. 'She isn't being harmed.'

'But you're *doing* this to her.' This was the other side of their interconnection, she thought, the dark shadow of the cosy family gatherings she had seen on the Rustball – this power to reach into the head of a stranger.

174

Bale got shakily to his feet. 'She's in there. She's safe. It's just that she can't – connect.'

Alia stared at Drea's slack face. '*Safe*? She must be terrified.' She turned on Reath. 'Did you know about this?'

He looked shocked. 'Of course not. They asked me to bring Drea here, but for you, not for *this*. I knew of this world, the statues – I thought it would be educational. I didn't anticipate this!'

For the first time she saw truly how weak he was, and how little help she was going to get from him to resolve this sudden crisis. 'Do you know what they intend?'

Reath grimaced. 'Don't *you*?'

She stared at him. Then she closed her eyes. She was aware of the minds of the three Campocs, but they were closed to her, hard black spheres in her universe of thought. And Drea was there, a tiny bright thing, trapped and struggling in a cage.

She opened her eyes and took deep breaths. The Campocs were not Transcendents, but they were powerful beyond her knowledge, and they were malevolent. She was effectively alone here, beyond help from anybody. And all the time she was aware of that frightened, trapped little creature in her sister's head, who utterly depended on what she did next. She was trembling, as much from fear as from anger. Some Transcendent she was going to make! But she had to find a way through this. She clung to her anger; it would be more useful than fear.

She glared at Bale. 'All right. What do you want with her?'

'Why, nothing. We want you. Or rather we want you to do something for us.'

'Then why not just take me, rather than her?'

'That wouldn't be enough,' Bale said. 'We need you to act freely.'

'I'm not free if you are holding my sister!'

'Then without our conscious commands. You have to want to work for us, Alia.'

'How long are you going to hold her?'

'As long as it takes.'

'For what?'

Reath stepped forward. 'I think I understand. *As long as it takes for you to join the Transcendence*, Alia. Do you see? Through your sister they hope to control you, and through you they hope to gain some leverage over the Transcendence itself.'

The thought seemed shocking to Alia, almost blasphemous. 'How dare you challenge the Transcendence? And to do it in such a base way, through taking a hostage–' The contrast between the audacity of their ambition and the shabbiness of their methods was astonishing.

'We have no choice,' Bale said grimly.

'We are frightened,' Denh said.

'By the Redemption,' Seer finished.

'The Redemption? Witnessing? What's that got to do with anything?' She stared at them, baffled, angry, increasingly scared.

Reath said with a trace of his old firmness, 'I think we need to talk this out. But not here, standing in the dirt. Come. Let's go back to my shuttle.' He looked uncertainly at Drea. 'Can she—'

Alia took her sister's hand; her fingers were limp. 'Come, dear. It's OK.'

Perhaps the Campocs' grip on Drea's nervous system relaxed a little. Her gaze was as unfocused as before, but in response to her sister's gentle pressure she took one step, two, stumbling like a baby. Alia sensed that the trapped creature in its cage was a little calmer, slightly reassured. But, glancing down, Alia saw urine trickling helplessly down Drea's leg, soaking her fur, pooling on the sand of the Dirtball. 'I'm sorry,' Alia whispered to her sister as they walked. 'I'm so sorry.'

Chapter 21

I endured another flight back across the Atlantic, again at John's expense. This time I mostly slept through the journey, though that seemed a waste of the facilities on offer. Back in Florida I slept off my jet lag over a night in a Miami hotel: sooner that than face the family again so soon.

Then I set off on a train journey to Oklahoma City.

I was taking George's advice. Trying to find out about the impact of gas hydrates, I was going to consult the oracle – which was an artificial sentience called Gea, the 'Global Ecosystems Analyser', being run out of the University of Oklahoma. Gea was the keystone of the Centre for Climatic Modelling, which reported to a Stewardship agency called the Panel on Biospheric Change.

It was a long ride. The train took me across the Oklahoma flatlands, vast stretches of scorched brown earth littered with abandoned farm buildings. Green things grew only where sprinklers sent sprays of water high into the air. This was the twenty-year drought, as the media called it. Old news. I turned away to read a novel on my softscreen.

When I got to the end of the line, I was astonished to find Shelley Magwood waiting to meet me off the train.

I'd booked myself a hotel room, but when I told her the name of the place Shelley tapped her ear, cancelled my reservation and booked me somewhere better at her company's expense. 'Call it an investment,' she said.

At the hotel she gave me an hour to unpack and shower. Then she hired us a big two-person rickshaw and took me through the city.

The centre of Oklahoma City turned out to be quite attractive. It was a mixture of lakes, parks, landscaped hills and stylish buildings, all connected at the very centre of the city by a peculiarly elaborate system of walkways and tunnels. The place seemed to work on a human scale, which meant that it had survived the disappearance of the automobile pretty well. But many of the buildings were twentieth-century stock, and they showed their age in crumbling concrete and cracked fascias. There was plenty of Paint, too, glittering silver or gold in the sunlight.

And the scouring of the twenty-year drought reached even here, the heart of the state capital. Sprinklers spun and spat, and many of the green spaces were roofed over with filmy plastic envelopes. The city was a vision from one of my old science fiction novels, I thought, a domed colony stranded on a desert world.

Shelley kept up a kind of tourist patter as we travelled. It seemed she had spent a year here on a consultancy assignment, and she was fond of the place. 'You ought to go see Route 66,' she said. 'Have you ever heard of that? Once the most famous road in America, the Mother Road – who said that, was it Steinbeck? Now stretches of it are an automobile-age theme park.' She grinned. 'They actually have working gasoline cars, and motels and roadside diners. They even have halls where they pump in toxic fumes so you can smell how it was when we were kids. It's a long, thin museum. You have to see it to believe it.'

She took me to a frontier-age restaurant and ordered us T-bone steaks, rectangular slabs of meat so vast they literally covered the plates they were served on. 'But don't worry,' she told me as she tucked in. 'The cows are cube-shaped and the meat is gen-enged. You can eat this stuff all day and you won't get fat.'

She was good company, small, neat, bright, her cropped-short dirty blonde hair gleaming with gel. Her energy and enthusiasm for her life and her work always lifted me. But she hadn't answered any of my questions.

'Shelley – what the hell are you doing here? I'm not sorry to see you. But why?'

'What you told me about the gas hydrates made me think. It does sound like we're all sitting on a time bomb, doesn't it? I'd like to know what Gea, the big computer suite, has to say about that. I'm curious.' She grinned and wiped her mouth; she'd reduced her steak to a few shreds of gristle. 'Also I'd like to see Gea herself.'

'*Her*self?'

She shrugged. 'Her choice to be female, apparently. She, it, is one of the most powerful software suites in the world, after all. Computer science could be revolutionised, if they ever figure out how she works.'

'And that's all,' I said heavily.

She took a mouthful of her gen-enged steak to stall answering. Then she said, 'Well, Michael, there are a lot of people out there concerned for you.'

'Oh.' I sat back. 'I get it. The ether has been buzzing with chatter about me again. Who called you? John? Uncle George?'

'If you don't like people talking about you, you ought to make your address books private.'

I felt impatient. 'Shelley, I'm not meaning to offend you. Really, I'm glad you're here. But I'm fifty-two years old, for God's sake. I don't need nursemaiding.'

'I'm not offended. If you offended me I wouldn't be here. OK, your uncle asked me to keep an eye on you. But I wouldn't have come just to babysit. Anyhow I like the steak,' she said pragmatically.

Hovering trays came scooting silently over the floor, and long killer-robot tentacles snaked out to clear away our plates. Shelley waved her hand over the tabletop; a small embedded softscreen glowed with numerals, showing our tab, and she tapped the screen a couple of times to add a tip.

From the capital we took a pod bus south to Norman, the base of the University of Oklahoma.

On the edge of the campus we were met off the bus by Doctor Vander Guthrie. He was a software animist by profession, and, it turned out, a kind of customer liaison officer for the facility of which Gea was the heart. Aged maybe thirty, he was tall but stocky, powerfully built. He was plainly dressed in a check shirt, jeans and cowboy boots. And he had a startling, completely inappropriate shock of sky-blue hair.

Vander embraced Shelley, a bit stiffly. Of course they had

worked together before; sometimes I got the impression that Shelley had worked with everybody on the damn planet.

Vander led us to a small electric bus which would take us to the computer centre. We crowded in, facing each other, knees touching. The bus jolted forward and carried us through the campus. Vander was nervous, his movements abrupt, even clumsy. But he seemed genuinely glad to see us. It turned out that meteorology had been a specialist study of this place for decades, even before the Warming had kicked in at the end of the twentieth century. Back then they used to think the big problem was tornadoes.

'So this was a logical place to found the world's premier climate-modelling software suite,' Vander said. 'However most of our visitors are politicians looking for an excuse not to sign up to some treaty or other, or else media types looking for yet another gosh-wow end-of-the-world story. Not that we don't come up with plenty of *those* here,' he said with bleak humour. 'So to have a couple of engineers come visit is a vacation for me.'

Vander Guthrie was a mass of contradictions. When he moved I could see the bones and muscles working under his checked shirt, as if he was some over-engineered simulacrum of a human being. But his diction, vaguely Bostonian, was very precise, academic. And he had that mop of electric blue hair, which I couldn't help staring at. He was obviously an early casualty of cosmetic genetic engineering.

His eyes darted nervously; his character cowered within that huge sculpted body.

If this was a prime choice for a customer liaison worker, I wondered what kind of meatballs they must have *behind* the scenes here. Some things about software projects never changed, I supposed.

The bus decanted us at a fancy-looking theatre. Inside was a brightly lit auditorium, with banks of seats, a deep stage that looked capable of displaying big three-dimensional VRs. 'I have to put you through our orientation session,' Vander said apologetically. 'Federal law.' He ushered us to the middle of the front row, and with an odd spurt of athleticism he vaulted over the seat backs to take a place in the second row. Then he clapped his hands, and the lights began to dim.

On the stage, a huge imaged-from-space portrait of the Earth assembled, finely detailed, heartbreakingly beautiful. I could see the big swathes of spreading desert around the mid-latitudes, the peculiarly spangled effect over much of South America that showed the break-up of the rainforest, and the deep blue of the North Pole, a spinning ocean without a trace of ice. A grave voice began to intone, reeling off statistics about changes in forest cover and ocean temperatures.

'You say it's the law that we have to sit through this,' said Shelley sarcastically.

'Well, so it is,' Vander said defensively. 'For one thing your reactions to the displays are being monitored, non-invasively. There are plenty of crazies out there who seem to think climate change is a good thing, or anyhow something ordained from on high. To them Gea is a kind of quantum-computing anti-Christ. Also the indoctrination stuff might actually help you figure out Gea's results, assuming she actually produces something in response to your query about those methane hydrates.'

'She doesn't always?'

He seemed offended I even asked. 'She isn't a calculating machine, you know. You don't just turn the handle. Anyhow the overview is often useful. You wouldn't believe the fantastic ignorance of some of the pols and other celebs we get trooping through here.'

Before us, the automated presentation was getting into its stride.

The Global Ecosystems Analyser was the pinnacle of efforts to model and predict the Earth's dynamic natural systems in toto that dated back to various pioneering turn-of-the-century studies. Gea was sponsored and run by a consortium that included the World Resources Institute, the World Bank, and UN development, education, refugee, environment, agriculture and other agencies. All of this was coordinated by the Panel on Biospheric Change, a central committee of the Stewardship itself.

'The politics behind Gea are a mess,' Vander said ruefully. 'It's nearly as complicated as the climate modelling, and a lot less useful...'

Data poured into Gea from a whole range of sources.

There were real-time downlinks from satellites, and from a mesh of miniaturised systems embedded in the fabric of the planet. 'Inside every softscreen sold since 2040,' Vander said proudly, 'there is an environmental monitor with a direct link to the Gea suite.' Then there were streams of secondary data, slightly less current but no less vital, on demography, biodiversity and agriculture. Even relevant peer-reviewed science papers were thrown into the mix. Thus Gea monitored every aspect of the world's climate and geography, the oceans and atmosphere and the global circulation patterns – and, not least, the impact of humanity.

Vander said, 'The trick is to think of the ecosystems as vast machines. Gea captures information on their inputs, such as climatic conditions, geological changes and human-induced changes, and on the outputs they provide for us, such as food, water purification, nutrient cycling, even tourism income – and less direct benefits such as biodiversity. She follows trends as transient as day-to-day fashions for wearing different gemstones in your ear stud, which might impact mining activities, all the way up to the gradual billion-year heating up of the sun, which will – might – one day render the Earth uninhabitable altogether. This is hard science, however. Everything is interconnected, in a messy way.'

I understood what he meant. The science of the very big and the very small are relatively simple: stars and quarks alike are governed by simple laws. It's in the middle scales that things get tricky. This was why I had always been attracted by engineering. You couldn't compress life, or indeed the weather, into symbols or codes: the biosphere was its own story – and so it was unknowable to any human mind. Maybe not to Gea, though.

The display moved on to some partial solutions Gea had already generated. Vander grimaced. 'The sales pitch,' he said. 'You wouldn't believe it, but we have to fight to keep our funding up.'

Gea had produced some assessments on what was called a 'sub-global' scale. We were shown examples from North America – chosen, no doubt, because we were in an American facility. All over the world glaciers were melting. In the short term the release of huge volumes of pent-up glacier-lake waters could cause catastrophic flooding; that had happened in Peru, Nepal and northern Italy. But in the longer term the melting was even more disastrous, for the glaciers actually served as frozen reservoirs. The presentation – with dismal images of shrinking patches of old brown ice, floods, dwindling rivers, people queuing at standpipes – told of how Gea's modelling had helped communities in California adjust to a thirty per cent loss of drinking water over the last decade without catastrophic dislocation.

The presentation moved on to an even more local problem: the twenty-year drought that afflicted the central plains of America, including Oklahoma. The crucial causative factor was, again, the heat delivered by the Warming. Hotter seas pushed moist air higher than it used to go, causing heavier rain in the tropical regions, but that meant a paucity of rain for a mid-latitude belt around the globe. In America this was actually a reversion to conditions that had prevailed eight thousand years ago, when the corn belt had been a 'prairie peninsula'. American farmers had it tough, but again warnings by Gea had given them time to prepare. Images of dust bowls and bleached cattle bones from Tajikistan in central Asia showed how bad it might have been.

'Gea can't *solve* the climate problems,' Vander said. 'That's not her job. But by showing us the future reliably she can help us cope with the human consequences.'

We listened to this dutifully for a while. It was even well presented. But it was very familiar stuff. And as Shelley whispered to me, 'Why is it that the collapse of the environment always reduces to a set of dreary lists?'

Vander Guthrie seemed more interested in the software engineering that lay behind Gea than the climate modelling itself. As the show went on he leaned forward and began to gossip in whispers. 'Shelley tells me your uncle worked through the Age of the Help Desks.'

Vander seemed to have a genuine interest in the history of his discipline. His job, though, was only a remote descendant of the software analysis George had once made a living out of. He described for us new design paradigms based on something called 'surface binding'. This meant breaking down Gea's model of the world into self-contained modules. 'So Gea has a model of global rainfall patterns, say,' Vander said, 'and another on ocean heating. One affects the other, of course. But to figure out how, Gea has to let her model oceans "drive" the rainfall models in a realistic way. It's not a question of software protocols, you see. It's as if it were real. The communication between sub-models is not symbolic, it's experiential. And that offers Gea a much greater richness of consciousness and experience than we have. You see? She is like a community of minds, but minds linked by direct experiential channels.'

I exchanged a cautious glance with Shelley, keeping my face carefully straight. The geek with the blue hair was actually something of a mystic, it seemed. However there was something quite moving in the way he described all this, as if he actually envied the complex entity he devoted his life to serving.

He went on, 'Of course design philosophies are only at the bottom level of the creature we know as Gea. You don't *program* Gea, any more than your mother programmed you. My job title is *animist*. Remember we're dealing with a mind here, a conscious entity. I didn't design her; none of us did. I can't even necessarily *measure* her output. How do you calibrate playfulness, joy, beauty, sorrow, fear?'

'And you can't control her?' I asked uneasily.

'Why do you use that word? This is a climate-modelling system,' Shelley said scornfully. 'She isn't a killer robot with laser-beam eyes. What harm can she do?'

I shrugged. 'Lie to us? If she's so smart, how would we even know? And then, when we build the flood barrier in the wrong place, or stimulate algal blooms in the ocean when we should be containing them—'

Vander Guthrie smiled, a bit wearily. He'd heard all this before. 'The Frankenstein complex? I wouldn't worry. Gea is actually sentient, remember. And with sentience comes responsibility. Conscience, if you will. And, believe me, for a creature as aware as Gea, that's a deep inhibitor indeed...'

The image froze. Vander raised a hand to his ear, as if someone had called him. He grinned at us. 'She's ready to see us.'

To reach the Gea facility itself, Vander led us across a broad, empty plaza, eerily bare of trees or benches. At the centre of this circle of concrete was set a building, an unprepossessing box, squat and windowless. As we hurried across the empty plaza I was aware of camera drones flitting in the air, and before my eyes smaller motes danced in the bright daylight – more security drones, tiny ones. Even the floor beneath our feet looked smart.

Vander talked nervously as we walked. 'You can see we wrap our baby up pretty tightly. Ideally she would be dispersed, maybe even buried underground. But the logic of her architecture dictates that's impossible.' With a super-powerful computer, aiming for the highest processing speeds, you always designed for small distances to minimise lightspeed delays between components. But that very density made for its own problems – notably the production of an immense amount of heat, which was no doubt why Gea's physical manifestation was stuck out here above ground. Vander said, 'But we've done our best. This block is as robust as most nuclear power plants. You could drive a plane into it and we wouldn't even notice.'

I felt terribly exposed out there. But I could see the logic; this open space, saturated by sensors, was so wide it would have been impossible to smuggle across any kind of harm-making device. Vander also warned us that our behaviour was being monitored for evidence of 'inappropriate feelings'. I hoped that awe and dread would not be regarded as too 'inappropriate'.

We reached the blockhouse. The wall itself sparkled with embedded processors. Vander palmed a control set in the wall, and a door slid aside out of sight. We hurried inside, with Vander waving us in anxiously; a deafening buzzer sounded the whole time the door was open. As the door soughed shut behind us drones clustered in the air around us, glittering with lenses.

Inside, the blockhouse was brightly lit by strips set in the roof. It looked even smaller inside than from outside, and was crowded with scaffolding where technicians in white coats and hairnets laboured at terminals, or waved their hands in the air to manipulate VR interfaces. Some of them peered down at us suspiciously.

Vander led us to a corner of the blockhouse. A small room, not much bigger than a toilet cubicle, had been partitioned off; a light shone red above the door. We had to wait outside until Gea was ready for us. Vander seemed tense, as if his god was stirring.

At the centre of the facility was an installation of support gear and instrumentation. The heart of it was a sphere, jet black, only a couple of metres across. The sphere was embedded in a framework of clumsy-looking engineering, ducts and pipes and huge flaring fins. Most of this gear seemed to be refrigeration plant, labouring to keep that central sphere cool. But wires snaked out, and laser light flickered around it, the visible signs of data chattering into and out of the sphere.

At the core of Gea was a quantum-computing processor, Vander told us. Inside that jet-black sphere the intertwined strands of possibility that make up our actuality were picked apart, and each separate strand used, remarkably, as a computing channel. The subtle use in computer processors of strange quantum effects like entanglement and superposition had actually driven forward the basic science of quantum physics. But still, nobody really understood how these machines worked – nobody human anyhow.

'Gea and her kin have already far surpassed us in raw intellect,' Vander said worshipfully. 'Take mathematics, for instance. There hasn't been a single basic proof achieved by an unaided human in thirty years. Nowadays the computers do the proofs. Our job is to dig into what they've discovered and prise out the implications. We are intuitive, emotional; we still have a guiding role to play. But the computers are the intellects now. We will never again be able to grasp what they are doing.'

'Never? That's a strong thing to say,' Shelley said.

'I mean it. At the heart of Gea's biospheric modelling is a nonlinear problem with millions of interacting variables. But our brains are hard-wired for a world with a mere three dimensions, so we can go no further than problems with a handful of variables, because we can't visualise the solutions. And that's our fundamental intellectual limit. Gea can *see* the qualitative content of an equation: she sees the babbling brook in the equations of fluid mechanics, the rainbow in the formulae of electromagnetism. We just can't do it.'

'OK,' I said uneasily. 'So what's the future for us?'

He laughed. 'Frankenstein again? There's nothing to be afraid of. I told you. I know Gea as well as anybody can. The smarter you are, the more you comprehend, the more you love.'

'*Love*? You really think Gea *loves* us?'

'Oh, yes,' said this strange guy with his cowboy body and blue hair and geek-scientist manner. 'Gea won't let any harm come to us, if she can help it.'

Shelley asked, 'So what are we waiting for?'

'For Gea's response.'

I glanced at Shelley, who shrugged. I said, 'Vander, are you kidding? You have to wait around until she feels like coming online?'

He looked faintly embarrassed, and he tousled his mop of blue hair. 'Gea is, um, contrary sometimes. There's a basic contradiction in her existence which torments her, I think. You see, she's a climate modeller. She knows that heat dumped into the environment worsens the problems the climate faces. But she knows that when *she* runs, her hardware stratum itself generates a lot of heat. You see the paradox? And therefore—'

Shelley said, 'You have to coax her to come online, and as soon as she gets the chance she turns herself off again for fear of making the problems worse. Do I have that right?' She stared at me, and we both burst out laughing.

Vander seemed offended. 'Believe me, in the brief fractions she is online she can achieve far more than most minds on the planet, artificial or otherwise—'

The light on the wall flashed.

Vander whooped and punched the air. 'There she is!' He tapped his ear.

Shelley asked, 'Is that her? What's she saying to you?'

He glanced at me. 'It's not me she wants to talk to. Michael Poole – it's you.' He actually looked jealous.

With a faint horror-movie creak, the door to the little partitioned booth swung open.

Chapter 22

Reath set up a low tent alongside his shuttle. Servitor machines brought out seats, and bowls of food and drink.

They sat in the shade: Reath, servant of the Commonwealth, the three Campocs as stolid and alike as the enigmatic statues that lay in the dirt, and Alia and her mind-neutered sister. Alia tried to feed Drea, but the Campocs' control remained too tight to allow it.

And they talked about the Transcendence of Mankind.

Bale said, 'We all do it, you know. Witnessing. Every human in the Commonwealth is a Witness; every child is given a subject, somebody from the past to study. *Everybody*. This is the law, the mandate of the Transcendence.'

This was a commonplace. 'And? So what?'

Bale said heavily, 'Have you never wondered *why* the Transcendence wants us all to peer into the past?'

Alia looked uncertainly at Reath, who returned her gaze calmly. 'Studying the past helps me understand the present. Michael Poole helps me understand myself—'

Denh guffawed. 'You think the Witnessing programme – the huge *expense* of giving every kid in the Galaxy a Witnessing tank – is for the benefit of you, of us?'

Seer said, 'Nothing the Transcendence does is for your benefit, but for its own. You must always remember that.'

Alia frowned. 'All right. So why is the Transcendence so interested in the Witnessing?'

'Because,' Bale said, 'the Transcendence is tortured by regret.'

The Transcendence was at a cusp in its destiny, they told Alia. Coalescing out of a gathering of humans, it already soared far above the capabilities, even the imaginations, of its constituent members. This was an extraordinary moment

188

in the evolution of life itself, so it was believed, as the Transcendence looked forward to the possibilities of an unlimited future – literally; it anticipated infinity and eternity. Soon, in any meaningful sense, the Transcendence would become a god.

But not yet. In these final brief moments, the Transcendents were still human. And they were not content.

All this was an abstraction to Alia, a matter of theology. Despite her training with Reath the Transcendence itself was still only vague in her imagination. What could a god *want?*...

The Campocs thought they knew.

The Transcendence understood the cause of its own anguish very well. *It was the past.* Of the trillions who had lived, most humans' lives had been dominated by pain and fear, their only saving grace being that they had been short. But the past was the root from which the mighty tree of the present had grown. So how then could the Transcendence give itself up to the bliss of an unlimited future, while its base was stained with the blood of all those who went before, and had lived and died in misery? Somehow the past had to be *redeemed*, for if not the goal of perfect Transcendence could never be reached; there would always be a deep flaw beneath the shining surface, a worm in the apple.

And so, under great programmes administered by the Commonwealth's Colleges of Redemption, every human child was made a Witness, as Alia had always studied the life of Michael Poole. You were assigned one character, one life thread drawn from the tapestry of the past, perfectly imaged with unimaginable technology. Any and every life was available to be remembered in this way – and not just the significant and famous, like Poole. Every last one of them needed to be treasured, and remembered. *Every one.*

Alia shook her head. 'I never thought it through. To catalogue the whole of the past, to make *everybody* a Witness – and to Witness *everybody*—'

Despite the tension of the situation Reath smiled. 'We humans have always been bureaucrats. And the Transcendence must be supreme in this aspect of our nature, as it is in everything else!'

But it was expensive. Though it was far from complete, soon the Redemption programme, in all its manifestations, was absorbing a significant portion of the energy budget of the Transcendence itself, and so of the combined powers of mankind.

Bale was watching her carefully. 'And that's what we're worried about.' He stood up. 'I will show you something. Come, we will walk to the statues. Your sister will be safe here, I promise.'

Alia glanced at Reath, who shrugged, out of control of events once more. Drea just sat passively. Reluctantly Alia pushed back her chair.

They returned to the fallen statues. Once more Alia stood before that monumental face.

Bale stepped forward. He bent and gathered up some of the strange bluish sand she had noticed piled by the mouth of the statue, and dug out a little more from its eye socket. 'Alia, do you know what this is?'

'Sand,' she said bluntly.

He shook his head. 'No. *This* is breath. And *these* are tears.'

The fallen forms were more than statues. They were humans.

In the age of Bifurcation that had followed the triumph of the Exultants, most post-human forms had been more or less similar to the basic human stock – like the heavy-gravity forms of the Rustball, or the aquatic creatures of the water world, even Alia's own low-gravity design. And rarely had the bounds of carbon-water chemistry been broken.

But in some places even those basic parameters had been ignored.

Though silicon chemistry was not as favourable a substrate for life as carbon, in some places, by chance, it did arise, such as here on Baynix II, the Dirtball.

There had been silicon-based life forms on this silicon-rich world, native forms, long before humans arrived. And when humans came here, they chose to download their children into the silicon, rather than any carbon-chemistry medium: they had made them into these statues.

What a strange thing to do, Alia thought.

'Silicon isn't an ideal information storage medium,' Bale said. 'Not as good as carbon molecules. But in its crystalline form you can make complex structures, store as much data as you like. There are ways to copy the lattice structure, so you can reproduce; there can be divergent forms, mutations – evolution. Of course while we breathe out carbon dioxide such creatures would breathe out *silicon* dioxide – sand.'

Alia stroked the immense sandy cheek of the stone form before her. 'Life would be so terribly slow.'

'Oh, yes,' Bale said. 'But time is only perception. If you watch them over a century or so you can see them churn around in the sand...'

'Why keep the human form at all?'

Reath shrugged. 'Sentiment? We evolved with human morphology, after all; perhaps we are more deeply wedded to it than we know.'

Alia walked around the head of the statue. She felt compelled to keep away from the line of sight of those immense graven eyes, though surely they could not see her; to this chthonic man she would be a flash of motion, gone in an instant. 'So now I know what these statues are. I still don't know why you brought me here.'

Bale regarded her gravely. 'These people made their children into crawling things of stone, a form as remote from the basic human as it is possible to imagine. Why do you think they would do such a thing?'

Alia thought it through. 'Because they were refugees. They had to hide.'

'Yes. And by abandoning the carbon-chemistry substrate they made themselves all but undetectable, even by a remote sweep for life. Nobody would expect to find humans hiding in stone.'

'Who were they hiding from?'

'Who do you think?' Bale said.

'Oh. Other people.'

Bale touched the huge hand of the statue. 'We don't know why they were fleeing. But after all this time, the desperation remains. Now can you see how much the Transcendence has to regret?'

Yes, Alia thought. And no matter how you try to achieve Redemption – no matter if every human who ever lived from now on spent her entire life on Witnessing – there would always be more pain: a bottomless pit of it.

Bale watched her sharply. 'There. You see it, don't you? *The Transcendence is striving for a goal that is unachievable.* That's what we think. Yes, we are suspicious of it – and we aren't the only ones. More and more of mankind's resources are being poured into this sink of pointless ambition. Is there no better way to spend our wealth and power? And - what if full Redemption *can't* be achieved – what will the Transcendence do then? Alia, we think the Transcendence is approaching a crisis.'

Reath seemed shocked by this talk. 'You must not anthropomorphise in this way. *The Transcendence is not human,* remember. It is more than human. And it has a cognisance beyond our petty comprehension. Even its regret is super-human! You must not imagine you are capable of under-standing it.'

Bale bowed his head. 'Perhaps not. But we fear it. We are all affected by the Transcendence, as a planet is ruled by the sun it circles. And if the sun becomes unstable... *We want to know,* Alia. We want to know what the Transcendence plans to do next – and perhaps we can have some influence over it.'

Reath said heavily, 'And that's where Alia comes in, is it? You see her as your way into the Transcendence.'

Bale spread his hands, looking helpless despite his squat, powerful build. 'We don't know what else to do.'

Reath stood before Alia, anger flaring in his eyes. 'If you become a Transcendent, Alia, it must be for your own pur-poses, your own desires, not for *his.*'

Alia stared at them. Much of this discussion went far above her head, this philosophy, abstraction. But these theo-logical disputes obviously meant a great deal to these men, enough for them to have put her sister's life at risk. So what was she supposed to do?

She looked inside herself for guidance – and she thought of Michael Poole, the subject of her own Witnessing. *What would Poole have thought if he could look ahead to this strange future of ours? What would he think of us, this obsession with the past – would he think we were insane?* And she remembered how Poole had looked at her, looked out of his Witnessing box, as if aware of her scrutiny. Perhaps the Campocs were right. Perhaps there was more to Witnessing and Redemption than she had been told.

There was only one way she could find out more, perhaps only one way to resolve all this.

She faced Bale and Reath. 'I will go forward. I will continue on this path; I will go on to the Transcendence. But you are right,' she said to Reath. 'If I do enter the Transcendence it will be for my own purposes, not anybody else's. Not even yours, Reath.'

He bowed his head.

'Bale, I have listened to what you say. But I will promise you nothing. *Nothing.* And I will not act under duress. You will release my sister *now.*'

He faced her down for a heartbeat. Then he, too, bowed his head.

Alia heard a gasp. She looked back to the shuttle. In the shadow of the tent, Drea had slumped forward. The Campocs were clumsily attending her.

Alia turned back to Bale. 'I thought you cared for me. But you betrayed me.'

'Oh, Alia—'

'If you ever harm any of my family again, I will make you pay.'

He said nothing, and he tried to keep his mind closed to her. But she sensed fear. Good, she thought. Perhaps there will be advantages to being a Transcendent after all.

She began to walk back to Reath's shuttle. 'Are we done here? What's next.'

Chapter 23

I peered through the door into darkness.

I glanced back at my companions. Shelley watched me with a lively curiosity, Vander with obvious envy. In their different ways, both of them longed to step through this door. But it was me Gea had asked for.

I stepped through the doorway—

Wham.

I was standing in the open air, under a glaring sun, beside a river bank. The ground was crowded with vegetation. The air was ferociously hot and humid.

When I looked back, the door and its frame had disappeared. I guessed I was in some kind of immersive VR. But there had been no sense of transition, none of the usual preparation, no lying down in a darkened place or a sensory-deprivation tank. I was simply here. Wherever *here* was.

I stepped forward. The river was broad, meandering, sluggish, working its way through a wide valley littered by marshes and swamps. Vegetation crowded, green and lush, vigorous. My fake-leather shoes slipped on the bare rock, or stuck in patches of mud. Sweating hard, I felt ridiculous in my shirt and jacket, clothes for Oklahoma City. I was *not* equipped for this.

There was nobody about, no sign of buildings or vehicles. As far as I could see nothing moved, no animals crawled; there was no sound but the chirping of some insect. And not a single bird flew in the sky.

But with the shock of my immersion wearing off, I started to tune in to strangeness.

There were lots of mosses and ferns, and lining the river

bank stands of what I thought might be bamboo, but on closer inspection looked more like horsetails. Away from the river itself taller trees crowded in thickets, surrounded by an undergrowth of ferns and mosses. The trees were some kind of fern, I thought, with a woody trunk and leaves clustered in strange starbursts at the ends of their branches. They looked like ginkgoes, maybe. Elsewhere there were patches of scrub, low-lying ferns and something like heather. The place was oddly drab. Everything was a deep muddy green: there was no other colour anywhere, no flowers. And there was no grass, oddly.

I stepped close to the water and squatted down. I rustled the undergrowth, moving it aside. The leaves and fronds were heavy and damp; if this was VR the detail impressed me.

At last I found movement. I disturbed plenty of insects: centipedes, cockroaches, beetles. Snails and worms crawled through the mud by the water's edge, and a dragonfly fluttered into the air on filmy wings. Again I was struck by what was *not* here: no bees or wasps, no ants, not a single termite mound. I made out a ripple in the water, a ridged back breaking the surface. It looked like a crocodile – but the head I glimpsed, the tail, didn't look quite right.

Then something scuttled out from between my legs. I jumped back with a start. It was a little creature no larger than my hand, running on splayed legs. With four legs and a tail, it looked something like a lizard. But the shape of its head and body were subtly off, like a sketch made from memory. It scuttled back into the undergrowth.

And as I stared after the lizard thing, I heard a bellow, a deep, mournful sound. My heart pounding, I turned around.

Animals moved across the landscape, perhaps half a kilometre from me, a dozen of them in a scattered herd. They had massive barrel-shaped bodies, but their weak-looking limbs sprawled out to either side of them, and they moved slowly, clumsily. Their heads were big shovel-shapes with broad mouths. They were the size of cows, although there were a couple of smaller individuals, infants. But on those splayed legs they had a reptile-like gait; they looked like fat, land-going crocodiles.

The cow-crocs gathered around the tree ferns and dragged at their leaves with their big plated mouths. They didn't seem to have any teeth. My anxiety subsided. Herbivores, then; I should have no trouble with them unless I got in the way of a stampede.

But then I made out a low, lithe shape slinking through the shade of a tree. It was smaller than the cow-crocs, maybe the size of a dog, with a bulky body and stubby tail. It had sideways-askew legs, another variation on the theme of crocodile. But there was nothing sluggish or ungainly about the way this creature moved, nothing stupid about the sharp eyes I could see gleaming in that blunt head.

I stood stock still. It was foolish to be afraid. This must be a VR, and VRs were full of safeguards; I should have nothing to fear. But this VR was of a density and richness like none I'd experienced before – and it wasn't under my control.

'Do you know what you're looking at?'

I was startled. The voice was small, metallic, and it came from near my feet.

A toy robot, fifteen centimetres tall, stood on a patch of bare rock. Its shell was painted gaudy colours, red and blue and yellow, but the paintwork was chipped and scuffed, heavily played with. It had eyes like glass beads that lit up when it talked, and a tiny grill from which its insect-sized voice emanated. It didn't even have legs, just moulded shapes concealing wheels. It rolled towards me now, and a friction mechanism crackled and sparked. It was pointing a ray gun at me, but I didn't feel too concerned, as the ray gun and the arm which held it were just shaped tin shells.

'I know you,' I said. 'You're Uncle George's companion. His home help.'

'Not quite.'

'What are you doing here?... Oh. You're Gea, aren't you?'

'You can think of me as Gea if you like.' She spoke with that ridiculous cod-American toy-robot accent.

'And you chose to manifest yourself as Uncle George's robot?'

'I used a form you are familiar with. What did you expect?' She ran back and forth a little, sparking. 'Actually this form does the job. Although it's sometimes tricky getting around.'

'I bet it is.' I glanced up the valley towards the shambling herd of cow-crocs. 'Am I in the past? What are those creatures, dinosaurs?'

'Not dinosaurs. Dinosaurs haven't evolved yet.'

That *yet* chilled me. 'They behave like mammals but they walk like reptiles.'

'They are neither. They are a class from which true mammals will one day evolve. The palaeontologists call them mammal-like reptiles. The big herbivores are called pareiasaurs. Those you see on the far side of the river – ' a huddle of smaller, more nervous-looking creatures '– are a kind of dicynodont. The predator is a type of gorgonopsian.'

I glanced at my feet. 'And the little lizards?'

'They aren't lizards. Lizards haven't evolved yet, either. Some of them are reptiles called procolophonids. Others have no name. Only species which have left a distinguishable trace in the fossil record have names assigned by human palaeontologists.'

'So how can you reconstruct them?'

'Extrapolation, from traces in modern genomes, ecological-balance calculations, other sources. I am confident in the veracity of what you see.'

'Oh, are you? Where am I, Gea?'

'You are some two hundred and fifty million years into the past. This is an era known to the geologists as the Permian. If you want more precision—'

Two hundred and fifty million years. 'That's precise enough.'

'Much that is familiar has yet to evolve. The whole hundred-million-year history of the dinosaurs, their rise and fall, follows after this time. There are no grasses yet, no flowering plants, no wasps or bees or termites or ants. There are no birds. And yet there is much that is familiar, deeper qualities.'

'Yes.' I thought it over. 'All the animals have four legs, one head, one tail.'

'The tetrapodal body plan is a relic of the first lungfish to crawl out of some muddy river onto the land, a choice once made never unmade; presumably all animal life from Earth will always follow this plan. And there are deeper, persistent patterns in the nature of life: the dance of predator and prey, for instance.'

At the base of this ancient food chain were plants, insects and invertebrates. Little lizard-like creatures, like my pro-colophonids, ate the plants and insects, and in turn various carnivores munched on their bones. At the very top of the food chain were the gorgonospians, like the dog-like critter I had seen; gorgonospians ate pretty much everything, includ-ing each other.

'This is the first complex ecosystem on land,' the robot said. 'But it is based on a web of food and energy flows nearly as complex as today's. For such an ancient scene, it is remarkably rich.' The tiny B-movie voice sounded even more ridiculous when she used words like *ecosystem*.

'So why are you showing me all this?'

'Because it is about to be wiped out.' The robot rolled back-wards. Her glass-bead eyes flashed. And the world changed.

I staggered. It felt as if the land surface beneath my feet melted and flowed.

And suddenly it was *hot*, a sweltering heat much more severe than the tropical humidity I had suffered earlier. It was dry, airless, and I found myself gasping; I tugged at my shirt, ripping buttons to open the neck.

The land had changed utterly.

The basic topography remained, the river and its valley, the eroded hills further away. But the river was low, a trickle in a plain of dried and cracked mud. And the green-brown blanket of life had shrunk back everywhere. The stands of ginkgo-like trees were bare trunks, lifeless. Only scattered bushes and low ferns, and smaller undergrowth plants, weed-like, seemed to be surviving. I saw none of the big cow-sized herbivores, or the dog-like carnivores that had hunted them. Suddenly this was an empty stage.

But still there was life here. An animal poked its nose out of a burrow, cautiously, like a badger emerging from its sett. Snuffling, the animal managed to expose a stand of mush-rooms, pale and sickly, and it dug its face into their white flesh. This was a low-slung reptilian, about the size of a cat,

with the age's characteristic croc-like splayed legs and wedge-shaped head. There wasn't much flesh beneath its warty skin, and I could see the bones of its spine and ribcage.

It looked up at me, at the only biped on the planet. Its eyes were glazed, incurious. Then it shambled towards the river, seeking water.

The little robot was still at my feet, her glass eyes blank.

'So what's happened?'

'There have been major eruptions,' the robot said. 'Far from here, in Siberia, too far away to hear or see. But they have had a global influence.'

They had not been volcanoes, I learned. Magma, 'flood basalts', had come seeping from fissures in the ground, and had covered vast areas.

'When the eruptions began, the injection of dust into the air caused a snap freeze, a couple of cold summers. But since then the huge flows of basalt have been emitting carbon dioxide and sulphur dioxide.'

'Greenhouse gases.'

'Yes. The result is a rise in air temperatures, all around the planet. Life here was always precarious. Even a one-degree rise in temperature has been enough to kill off many plants, and the herbivores that fed off them—'

'And the carnivores that fed off *them*.'

'There have been few actual extinctions yet, but biotas have been disrupted, and populations of plant and animal species have crashed. The creature by the river is a dicyno-dont. Its habit of burrowing in the ground to aestivate has enabled it to ride out the worst of the heat where others have succumbed.'

'Let me guess,' I said. 'Worse is to come.'

'Bingo.'

Another snap transition; I staggered, shocked.

That baking sun had disappeared. Suddenly rain poured out of a cloud-choked sky, hammering on my head and shoulders hard enough to hurt – and I realised that the water was actually stinging me, like a mild acid. Hastily I dragged my jacket over my head. But there was no relief from the sweltering heat; the air was so humid it was actually difficult to breathe.

The robot stood patiently at my feet, rain splashing from its paintwork.

'Shit,' I shouted. 'You might have warned me.' I could barely hear my own voice above the roar of the rain.

'The dicynodonts had no warning.'

'More eruptions?'

'Yes. The basalt traps are pumping out chlorine, fluorine, sulphur dioxide, as well as carbon dioxide. These gases are combining with the high air to form a cocktail of acids, hydrochloric, sulphuric, carbonic—'

'Acid rain.'

'Yes. The last of the trees and the larger plants are now being burned off. Animals are being flayed alive. Those dicynodonts still shelter in their holes, but there is nothing to eat but a few ferns and moss and lichen in crevices by the river.'

'And it's going to get worse again, isn't it?'

'Would you prefer a warning this time?'

'Just do it.'

Another bewildering change.

The rain had cleared, the sky stripped of cloud to reveal the sun once more. But the sky was tinged a washed-out orange-brown, with barely a scrap of blue. I still stood beside the river valley, but it seemed much broader than before, its banks roughly scoured away. Its floor was littered with boulders and banks of gravel, and further downstream it was incised by channels that cut across each other like braided hair.

The land was bare rock. I couldn't see a scrap of green anywhere: there wasn't even soil cover. It was as if a great knife had scraped over the ground, cutting away all the soil and plants and trees, the animals and insects.

That robot still stood at my feet, unchanged, patient. I felt irrationally angry at her, as if she had caused all this devastation. I took a deep breath – and my lungs ached. 'Jesus. I can barely breathe.'

'Actually,' the robot said, 'I have used some artistic licence. If you tried to breathe the authentic air of this period you would shortly die of anoxia.'

'What happened, Gea?'

'Gas hydrates,' she said simply.

The carbon dioxide injected into the air by the Siberian volcanic event had caused global temperatures to rise by several degrees. Eventually, at the poles, the ocean margins and tundra began to thaw out. Just as Tom had experienced in 2047, there had been an immense release of the methane and carbon dioxide trapped in the ice – a hundred-fold expansion in volume when that great lid of cold was released. All over the polar regions there had been vast bubbles, water spouts, the very ground crumbling and cracking open as geysers of the stuff spewed into the air. It must have been a hell of a sight.

The effects were disastrous.

Gea said, 'The injection of the first of these deposits into the air fed back into the greenhouse cocktail already working in the atmosphere, and warming increased further—'

'Which thawed out more hydrates, which released more gases, which increased the warming effect.' Any engineer would recognise a positive feedback cycle. Around and around it went, getting hotter and hotter, the air filling up with the noxious gas.

When all the hydrate banks had emptied, a violent warming pulse followed. Not only that, there was now so much carbon dioxide in the air that the levels of oxygen were reduced to far below normal.

'The last of the dicynodonts probably suffocated rather than starved,' the robot said. 'At least it was quick. The ferns and cycads and other opportunistic species that took the chance to propagate during the warming pulse – even they have gone now. A few plants survive, just weeds, clinging on in pockets of soil.'

I looked around at the barren landscape. 'It's like being on Mars. Nothing but rock and dust.'

'That isn't a bad comparison,' the robot said. 'Look at the river. Can you see the heavy debris, the braiding effect in the channels? There is no life here, nothing to bind together the soil. When the rains came the remaining soil was quickly washed away, and heavy debris scoured the channels. You can find such braiding in rivers on Mars, which likewise formed their courses in the absence of life.'

The oceans had suffered too. When the rains came all the dead and stinking vegetation was washed away into the rivers and swept downstream to the sea. Around the mouths of the rivers the sea beds were covered in a carpet of organic matter, the rotting corpses of animals, the dead vegetation, all mulching down to a thick black slime that choked the life of the seafloor, the molluscs, shrimps, worms, arthropods. As it decayed this foul stuff drew down yet more oxygen from the air and emitted yet more carbon dioxide and other foul gases. Meanwhile the excess carbon dioxide poisoned the plankton, the tiny organisms that were the basis of all marine food chains. Thus oceanic populations imploded just as had those on land.

Gea said, 'Biodiversity was reduced to about a tenth of what it had been before. Ninety per cent of marine species went extinct, seventy per cent of land vertebrates. The numbers are approximate, of course; we will never know it all. It was far worse, by an order of magnitude, even than the dinosaur-extinction event. This disaster must have come close to ending the story of multi-celled life altogether.'

'But life recovered,' I said. 'Didn't it?'

'Oh, yes. Eventually.'

After this end-Permian extinction event the world was a desolate place, its complicated ecosystems imploded – and its ruins became dominated by a single animal. The lystrosaur, a kind of dicynodont that looked something like a pig, was a chance survivor that took its extraordinary opportunity; soon ninety-five per cent of all the animal flesh in the world was lystrosaur meat.

Recovery came as the descendants of such survivors, shaped by time and evolution's scalpel, diversified to fill those empty niches. A new world of dinosaurs and pine trees would emerge from the rubble of the old, and at last, after the flowering plants and the grasses and the true mammals, mankind.

But it took time. For some ten million years the world remained empty, dismal, its old richness gone. And biodiversity would not recover the levels it had lost for *fifty* million years.

'Much was never to be replaced at all,' said the little robot.

'The old order of the mammal-like reptiles and the spiky trees under which they grazed was gone for ever.'

'Why show me this? You aren't claiming that the eruptions in Siberia are about to kick off again?'

'No. But a similar causative sequence may be unfolding. The root cause of the Permian extinction was the Siberian-trap eruptions. Their emissions of carbon dioxide and methane began a global-warming pulse, but the tipping point came when the temperatures rose so high that polar gas hydrate deposits began to be released. After that a positive feedback effect did the rest.'

'There are no basalt eruptions going on today,' I said. 'But instead of the Siberian traps—'

'Mankind,' the robot said. 'Your activities, by injecting heat and greenhouse gases into the air over centuries, have had precisely the same effect as the Permian-era eruptions. And similar consequences.'

Standing there on that baked, dead plain, I tried to think it through.

I had grown up with the Warming, laden with guilt over extinctions and environmental degradations that had happened long before I was born. Like most people, I guess I got bored with it, and got on with my life. 'It's like living with original sin,' Uncle George once said to me. 'We're all Catholics now, Michael.'

Then along came President Amin. We all went through the great wrench of giving up our automobiles, and we were smugly proud of the Stewardship. The Warming stopped seeming so bad, the Bottleneck not quite such a hazardous highway. Oh, it was a drag for anybody caught in a flood or a hurricane. But we were muddling through, so I'd thought. Even the parts-per-million projections of the final greenhousing load of carbon dioxide in the air were starting to fall.

Now here was Gea telling me that I had been fooling myself – that Tom was right. I couldn't believe it, on some deep intuitive level.

Gea said, 'Perhaps you aren't thinking about the Warming, the Die-back the right way. Perhaps, deep down, you imagine that the Earth's processes are linear. That the response from the biosphere will be proportionate to the pushing you give it. But that isn't necessarily so. The Earth's systems are only quasi-stable. For example the Amazon forests, drought-stricken, are dying back rapidly. The injection of their locked-up carbon into the atmosphere raised temperatures, which will in turn accelerated the dying of the forest. This is biogeophysical feedback. And so it goes, on a global scale, geospheric and biospheric systems flipping suddenly to other states.

'Not only that, the various factors, themselves nonlinear, interact with each other in a nonlinear way: habitat destruction, over-population, over-harvesting, pollution, ozone destruction, all working together—'

'*Lethe*. You're talking about Lethe. The anti-Gaia.'

'There comes a point where if you keep pushing you don't get more of the same but something new entirely, events of a different quality.'

'You know, I think I imagined that you would be like an electronic Gaia. Here we are talking about death.'

'I contain both Gaia and Lethe, in my imagination,' she said.

'OK.' I had to ask the final question. 'And if temperatures were again to reach the point where the hydrate deposits are released?'

'The normal interactions between life and the physical world will break down completely. Gaia will nearly die.'

'The end of the world?'

'Oh, I wouldn't put it as severely as that! It won't even be the end of mankind. You are far more widespread than the lystrosaurs ever were; humans are smart and adaptable and able to recover. You are hard to kill off completely - though it is easy to kill vast numbers of you.'

'But our culture will be destroyed. *Most* of us will die. Billions.'

She rolled back and forth, emitting showers of sparks, her little wheels scraping across a lid of post-Permian bare rock. 'You know, it's a lot easier to move around now that everything is dead,' she said. 'No foliage to clog up my wheels, no insects to get in the way or hopping amphibians to knock me over. Perhaps we should give the world to robots—'

'Shut up,' I said.

She stopped still.

'How long do we have?'

'That's hard to say. A decade? Probably less.'

'This can't be allowed to happen.'

'I tend to agree.' A thick bound report popped into existence on the rock surface before her. 'Today I am delivering a definitive study to all my sponsoring agencies, and all governments and inter-governmental agencies. Not that I expect this to make a difference by itself; people have a tendency to dismiss bad news.'

'Is that why you brought me here?'

'*You* asked to see *me*, remember,' she said. 'You came to me asking questions about the polar hydrates.'

'OK. But what now? Do you want me to argue the case for you?'

'More than that.' The tinny voice lacked tone, colour.

I knew what she wanted of me. 'You expect me to *do* something about it, don't you?...' Was that what this was all about? Did Gea, this superhuman artificial intelligence, expect me to come up with a way to save the world?

The robot rolled back and forth. 'I am a biosphere modeller. I have my specified goals: monitoring, not modification. But it is difficult to limit sentience. I am curious. I am concerned not just with my models but their implications. But I cannot initiate any action in the wider world; I have neither the means nor the authority.'

'You need a human to do it.'

'I needed a human to come asking the right questions, yes. You selected yourself, Michael Poole.'

I said harshly, 'What do you care about the destiny of life? You have never been alive yourself.'

'Michael Poole, I am fearful.'

'Fearful? You?'

'I am facing extinction too, I and the other sentiences you have brought into the world. Hasn't that occurred to you? Probably not. None of us can survive without the infrastructure of human society. If this goes on, artificial intelligences will be one with the mammoths and the cave bear...'

I thought I saw movement in the corner of my eye

– movement, here on this lifeless VR world, inhabited only by me, a tin robot and lystrosaur bones. I turned.

A human figure, slim and silent, stood at the summit of one of the low, bare hills. She was so far away the mist obscured her. But I knew who she was.

I whispered, 'Do you see her, Gea?'

'You are important, Michael Poole,' Gea said. 'Significant.'

'I don't want to be significant... You see her, don't you? Tell me. *You see Morag.*'

'You stand at a crossroads. A tipping point. The world and its cargo of life faces the gravest danger in human history – perhaps even since the Permian. And yet you have strength, unprecedented, greater than at any time in history. One day the future will be as you imagine, Michael Poole. But first you must make the future come to pass.'

'How can I shape the future when I'm haunted by a ghost from the past?'

'But the deepest past and furthest future merge into one...'

Morag stood still, and yet she seemed to be receding from me, sinking deeper into the unreal mist. I longed to run after her, but knew it would be futile. In this lifeless world, alone with an utterly alien mind and a virtual ghost, I shivered.

Two

Chapter 24

I invited Tom and Shelley to my home in upstate New York. I wanted them to help me try get my head around the problem of gas hydrates.

Over a VR link to London I gave Tom a bald summary of my private consultation with Gea. I left out the wu-wu stuff, the mixing up of past and future, Gea's vague hints about my own cosmic destiny. I *definitely* said nothing about Morag.

But even this sanitised version was enough to send Tom's antennae twitching. 'One of the world's finest artificial sentiences said this to *you*?'

'Why not me?' I snapped back. 'Gea has to start somewhere. I do have access to some of the world's most advanced technological capabilities, the Higgs engines. And I have *you*, Tom. You were right in the middle of that hydrate blow-off in Siberia. Maybe Gea is a good judge of character. Maybe she thinks that as your father I will be motivated to do something about this, to take her seriously.'

'You really think she's capable of that kind of manipulation?'

'You didn't meet her,' I said fervently. 'Besides, no matter how smart she is, she doesn't have any kind of formal power in the human world. She doesn't even get to vote. She can only get things done through people, by persuasion. If you think about it, she's behaving exactly the way you'd expect her to.'

He looked doubtful – in fact he looked at me as if I was crazy. But in the aftermath of Siberia we had agreed, kind of, that we would try to work together on stuff, rather than use our interests and motivations as a way to pull apart from each other. So he agreed to fly over to New York, at John's expense. But, he said mysteriously, he wanted to bring a guest of his own.

My visitors converged on my house, by plane and train and bus, for my amateur brains trust session.

I'd been here a little over five years. The place was only an hour's commute out of Grand Central Station, so I was hardly remote, but I was happy enough to be away from the stretched-to-the-limit overcrowding of the city itself. My house was the modern kind, a weatherproof concrete brute suffused with intelligence. With solar cell arrays, a wind turbine I could unfold from the roof and fuel cells in the basement, I was pretty much self-sufficient in electricity. There was a big chest freezer, and a cellar I kept stocked with cans and dried food. I had deep foundations and high sills and doors that sealed shut; I could have ridden out a metre-deep flood. And so on. I was no survivalist, but you had to think ahead. I'd insisted on puncturing the walls with windows, though – real windows, despite the architects' complaints – and I'd faced many of the walls with wood panels. It was still a home, not a spaceship.

Tom, though, had always seemed to disapprove of the place.

He had never lived here. After Morag's death the two of us had never really been comfortable in the old family home; it had room for the larger family Morag and I had always planned, and now it was too big for us. I took a smaller apartment in New Jersey, but it never felt like home either, and was of such old building stock it became increasingly costly. When Tom started college I was happy enough to move out.

Also I'd hoped my new place was different enough that both Tom and I would be spared any unpleasant memories. But Tom said it reminded him of *my* family home, my mother's house in Florida where I'd grown up. It was 'a nostalgic facsimile in concrete and gen-modified wood', as he acutely said.

'Well, I think it's cosy,' Shelley said to me when she arrived. 'A kind of cosy bomb shelter, but cosy nonetheless.' Shelley was a pleasure to have around, as always, a bustling knot of sanity and intelligence who brought light into my sometimes darkened life.

My greeting from Tom was more guarded. And I was surprised when Tom produced his guest: Sonia Dameyer, the American soldier who had helped him out in the first hours after his injury.

It turned out that she and Tom had formed a relationship during his recuperation. She said, 'I know it's a little sad for the only two Americans in a foreign country to glom onto each other, but there you go. I had some furlough due, and a free plane ticket from Uncle Sam. So when Tom said you'd invited him over here, I couldn't resist. I thought it would be good to meet you in person, Mr Poole. I hope you don't mind.'

'Call me Michael. Why should I mind?'

She was in civilian clothes, a neat, attractive jumpsuit. But she was one of those soldier types who always looked military, even out of uniform; her posture was upright, her manner correct, her intelligence obvious, her attention focused. I hadn't seen any hint of her relationship with Tom when I'd met her during my VR jaunt to Siberia – though maybe I should have. I liked her, as I had immediately in Siberia, but I found her a bit formidable.

We gathered on the living room sofas with mugs of coffee, heaps of cookies, flipcharts, scratch pads and softscreens, and got down to business.

'So,' said Tom. 'The world is going to flip its icy lid. What are we supposed to do about it?' He meant to be ironic; he just sounded out of his depth.

To my surprise Sonia leaned forward. 'Can I make a methodological suggestion?...' She began to outline an approach to problem-solving she said she'd used before. 'We'll break the day into two halves. It's eleven a.m. now. We'll work until lunch – one, say, or one-thirty. And we'll use that time to open up the problem. We'll just throw in everything we know, and anything else we come up with – any suggestion or idea, however tentative.'

Tom said dryly, 'Are we allowed to giggle at other people's suggestions?'

'The whole point is to develop ideas. But there are two rules. One is that *everything* gets recorded. And the second is, before lunch anyhow, that if you do comment you do it in a positive way. You have to start by saying what you *like* about the idea. We're trying to find ideas and build on them, not destroy them. After lunch we'll pull it all together more coherently and critically.' Tom laughed, but Sonia said firmly, 'Those are the rules.'

Shelley grinned. 'Fine by me.' She leaned to me and whispered, 'I think we're going to be glad she's here.'

I was impressed. For sure, if I had suggested this, Tom would have shot it down in flames at the get-go. I imagined Sonia working like this out in the field, pulling together her own motivated, trained-up, overbright staff with a few unhappy or angry locals, to fix whatever was broken. Now she was using those same management skills to handle our awkward father-son dynamic.

So we began to pool what we knew about gas hydrates. Tom had his personal experience, and what he'd picked up on the ground in Siberia. I had what I'd learned from Gea, and in follow-up studies since. Sonia for now acted mostly as a recording angel.

The most interesting new facts came from Shelley, who, typically, had been doing some burrowing. She'd found that the end-Permian extinction, through which Gea had walked me so painfully, wasn't the only instance in which gas hydrate releases had made a mess of Earth's climate. She displayed graphs of temperature and atmospheric composition. 'This spike is known as the "initial Eocene thermal maximum". It happened about fifty-five million years ago, ten million years after the dinosaurs died off.' There had been a sharp increase of global temperatures, a hike of five or ten degrees in a 'geological instant' – a time so short it couldn't be distinguished in the rock record, perhaps as fast as decades, maybe even just a few years. And at the same time there had been a big pulse of carbon dioxide injected into the air. It had been a major gas-hydrate release, just like the end-Permian event.

And just as the end-Permian event had been kicked off by the immense Siberian traps volcanism, so in the Eocene, volcanism had again, it seemed, been the trigger. Off the coast of Norway, in deep sediments under the ocean, lava had funnelled up from deep magma chambers and seeped into the hydrate layers along the continental slopes. The lava hadn't even broken the surface; this was minor as volcanic events go. But as the lava had dumped its heat, the ice-like crystals that contained the gases had melted, and the lid had come off the hydrate deposits. We stared at images of layers of sediments that had collapsed over emptied-out hydrate layers, and at great vertical ruptures, the remains of conduits where the released gases had forced their way to the surface.

The methane had reached the ocean floor, bubbling up in immense spouts like the one that Tom had lived through, and causing, no doubt, plenty of local damage. But that was just the start. Once the methane reached the ocean and the air there had been a complicated series of chemical reactions. The methane cheerfully reacted with oxygen, a process that itself released heat. The products of the reactions were more hydrocarbons, water – and carbon dioxide, gigatonnes of it, more greenhouse gas.

'And the rest,' Shelley said, 'is history. The event wasn't nearly so severe as the end-Permian catastrophe, because only a fraction of the global hydrate load was released. But it was a huge sloshing, a perturbation of the entire carbon pool of Earth's surface. You can still see traces of it in isotopic imbalances and the like. Eventually the excess carbon dioxide was drawn back down out of the atmosphere by Earth's systems – photosynthesis, weathering. But that took millennia, maybe megayears. And in the meantime there was a spike of warming.'

Sonia said, 'So in the Eocene the trigger was this undersea volcanism. But in the present day—'

'In the present day,' Shelley said, 'the trigger is anthropogenic global warming. Gea is right, as far as I can tell, Michael. The carbon dioxide and other crud we've dumped into the air has done the damage, more than enough to replicate the volcanic perturbations of the past. The anthropogenic warming of the climate we have already induced *will* cause the hydrate deposits to become unstable. At least we know what's coming,' she said sepulchrally. 'Different causes but same effects: the fossil record can teach us that much.'

Tom said, 'And the timescale?'

'As Gea said,' Shelley told us. 'A decade or less. In fact the destabilisation is already happening. As you know.'

We let this sink in.

As she went about her self-appointed task of recording all this Sonia's small face was pursed into a frown. The practical soldier was having some trouble with thinking about these huge scales in space and time, I thought. 'OK,' she said. 'So we can't afford to let these hydrates go up. That's the consensus, right? So what do we do about it?'

We all looked at each other warily. This was the crucial question – and the tricky part.

We were a guilt-ridden generation. President Amin and the Stewardship had taught us we had to change our ways; now we all lived a lot cleaner, and had stopped fouling the pond. But a legacy of the new thinking was that one of the worst insults was to be called an *instrumentalist*, in jargon that dated from Amin's time: a meddler. To imagine that we could actively *fix* planet-sized problems seemed as hubristic and arrogant as the mind-sets that had got us into this mess in the first place. So to ask Sonia's question – what do we *do*? – was to confront a modern taboo square in the face.

Shelley said reasonably, 'Look at it this way. We don't trust ourselves not to make a mess even worse. But those gas hydrates have no conscience, no soul, no sympathy; they will blow however we feel about it.'

Tom surprised me. 'All right, so let's play the instrumentalist game. If the crud we're injecting into the atmosphere is going to cause the hydrates to tip over into instability, let's just stop doing it.'

I caught Sonia's eye and remembered her rules. I said, 'What I *like* about that is that in the long term it has to be the right solution. To remove the root cause of a problem has to be a better strategy than to tinker with the symptoms.'

Tom said cautiously, 'Let's hear the *but*.'

'But it's too late.'

Shelley backed me up.

214

We'd already done a great deal by eliminating most of the automobiles. But even if we shut down all the factories and power plants tomorrow, carbon dioxide would still be injected into the air from, for instance, rotting deposits on the dying seabeds. We were dealing with planet-sized systems; the vast inertia of Earth's processes would ensure that the rise in carbon dioxide content continued for decades, and the warming with it.

Sonia recorded all this. 'So it won't help if we stop putting the stuff into the air. Why don't we try taking it out again?'

Shelley said, 'That's such a good idea that people are already doing it.'

It was true; there were 'geoengineering' projects going on in various corners of the globe – tentative, deeply unfashionable. Most of them focused on modest efforts at what was called 'carbon sequestration', drawing down carbon dioxide from the air faster than natural processes could manage.

'So we just accelerate those programmes,' Sonia said. 'Maybe we should make the carbon dioxide snow out, like it does on Mars.'

That was one from left field, the kind of wacky idea that I imagined Sonia's own process was supposed to generate. We played around with it a bit. The difficulty was that Mars is much colder than the Earth. You'd have to reduce the global temperatures to make carbon dioxide freeze, which was precisely the problem we were dealing with anyhow. Or maybe you could somehow tinker with the atmosphere, add some kind of freeze factor to the air... None of us knew enough chemistry to come up with a plausible way of making this happen.

Tom clasped his hands behind his head and sat back in his chair. 'I hesitate to say this in front of an arch-instrumentalist like you, Dad, but maybe we're thinking *too* big here. After all we aren't interested in cooling down the whole damn planet. Just stabilising the hydrate sediments would be enough – wouldn't it? So why don't we just think of a way to refrigerate the poles?'

Shelley said, 'Actually there have been a lot of schemes proposed in the past for cooling down selected portions of the Earth's surface.' She ran through this quickly, what she could remember or retrieve through her softscreen, and we chewed it over.

Most of these ideas involved shadowing a chunk of Earth's surface, thus cutting it off from the sunlight. You could inject crud into the air, aerosols of various kinds to screen out the light. Or, even more simply, you could send fleets of planes over the poles dropping shards of some silvered material onto the ice or the water. If you made the material smart, we thought, you could make it self-assembling, a self-knitting, self-repairing mirrored cap. You could even programme it to break up on command. It was quite a thought, to wrap a significant chunk of the world in silver foil.

Or, we thought, you could put some kind of solar-shield system into orbit. The Russians had played with this idea in the past. You would get a lot more control over the light you let through than with systems in the atmosphere or on the ground. For a few minutes Shelley and I disappeared into happy elaborations of this idea. You would be looking at a massive, unprecedented programme of space launches, but we knew that if we turned our minds to it our Higgs-energy engines could fuel the booster fleet required. But the dynamics of positioning a shield so as to provide an effective screen to the poles would be tricky. The equator would be comparatively easy to protect; there you could throw your shield up to geosynchronous orbit where, orbiting once every twenty-four hours, it would seem to hover over a single point on the surface of the turning Earth. Geosynchronous wasn't the only solution, though; Shelley dug up some esoteric material on complex orbital patterns the Russians had once used to provide twenty-four-hour comsat coverage to their scattered, far-from-the-equator domains.

Eventually Sonia timed us out. We were getting too deep into specifics, she said.

'OK,' Shelley conceded. 'But we must get in touch with some of those geoengineering groups, whatever we decide to do. They have got to have experience of these mega-projects we can tap into.'

Tom was shaking his head, in a world-weary way I'd seen too often as he was growing up. 'Geoengineering. Terraforming. Wet dreams.'

I snapped, 'What use is it to sneer, Tom? And besides it was *you* who suggested we cool the poles.'

'I didn't say *cool*,' he said. 'I said *refrigerate*.'

Shelley jumped in between us, damping down the fire before it started. 'You're quite right, Tom. A refrigerator is a machine for extracting heat from a volume. So how does it work? You pass your working fluid, your refrigerant – ammonia, say – around the volume you want to chill. The refrigerant is vaporised with heat from your target volume, so extracting the energy. As a gas the refrigerant is passed to a condenser, where it is returned to liquid form and so gives up that heat. And then the liquid is pumped around the loop again to suck more heat out.'

Sonia made notes, but she looked dubious. 'How could you refrigerate the hydrate deposits? They are buried deep, and they cover millions of square kilometres.'

'It needn't be so difficult,' I said, thinking fast. 'You'd pass a network of pipes into the substance of the hydrate deposits themselves. It wouldn't take long to build up a functioning network.' I drew rapidly, producing a sketch that looked a little like a road network, with big arterial routes and smaller side roads branching off. 'Your working fluid needn't be ammonia, of course. In these volumes it probably couldn't be. Liquid nitrogen, perhaps – you could just draw down the nitrogen from the air...'

Tom was shaking his head again, and I was on the point of snapping at him, and I knew that despite all Sonia's hard work we were falling into the elephant traps of our relationship.

Sonia and Shelley seemed to come to the same conclusion simultaneously. We needed a break. They both stood up. 'Lunchtime,' Shelley said. 'Michael, you're the cook.'

'Fine,' I said with bad grace. Tom clambered out of his chair looking as grumpy as I felt.

Sonia made one last note. '*Refrigerate*. Hold that thought.'

Lunch was a buffet, cling-filmed plates of stuff I'd prepared earlier in the day: smoked snake meat, a green salad with big, bright leaves of out-of-season gen-enged lettuce. We filled our plates and our glasses. I had some of those little clip-on drinks holders that you fix to the side of your plate, and I let my guests wander around the house.

Shelley said to me around a mouthful of snake meat, 'It's going well, don't you think?'

'The session? We're coming up with some ideas, I guess. I think you're right we ought to contact those geoengineers if we're going to start treading on their turf—'

She shook her head. 'Not that. The important stuff. You and Tom. You seem to be getting on OK. The real reason, the *only* reason, you're interested in saving the world is because it gives you something to talk to your son about. Isn't that true?'

Just as George had said, I remembered. 'I guess so. But why else would anybody do it? Anyhow we're both on our best behaviour with you two around.'

'Sonia is quite a find, isn't she?'

'You like her?'

'I think she's terrific,' Shelley said. 'Smart, obviously competent, healthy – what more could you want? She'll be good for Tom. How close do you think they are?'

'I can't tell. I never could...' I've always had a complicated view of relationships, either subtle or confused, depending on your point of view. It seems to me that there is a whole spectrum of possibilities between the poles of platonic and lover, whole levels of intimacy, sharing, degrees of distance. When I was younger I always enjoyed the early days of a new romance as you both reach out to explore, trying to understand what you had, where on that spectrum of possibilities you sat.

I tried to explain this to Shelley.

'"A spectrum of relationship types",' she said. 'Even when you talk about love you sound like an engineer.'

'Is that a bad thing?'

'Not necessarily.'

'Looking from the outside Tom seems to be just the same,' I said. 'Maybe he's at the early stages still with this Sonia, you think?'

'Oh, I think they've gone further than that.'

'How do you know?'

'The way they look at each other – or rather the way they

don't. The way they sit together. They're aware of each other, but in an accustomed way, they don't need to check. They're used to each other, Michael.'

Now I thought it over, I saw she was right. 'I hope they'll be happy.'

'Oh, I think they will be. So where do you think *we* are on your spectrum?'

I was taken aback; I'd never thought of Shelley that way. She squeezed my arm. 'I didn't mean to frighten you. Don't worry, Michael. I do understand, you know.'

'You do?'

'Sure. Because for you, the spectrum isn't there any more, is it? For you there is only Morag, and that's all there can ever be. Morag, wrapped in a rainbow cloak. But I'm here anyhow.'

'I—'

'You don't know what to say? So don't say anything.'

Tom, followed by Sonia, came walking through from the lounge. His face was ominously hard. 'Dad, you had a message. I took it for you. Sorry, I obviously wasn't meant to hear it.' His tone dripped with insolence, or contempt.

'What message?'

'From Rosa in Seville. My great-aunt,' he explained to Shelley and Sonia. 'Another bat in the family belfry. She said your immigration checks have been completed, and she's been passed as a suitable personal mentor for you while you're in Spain. Oh, and she said she looks forward to "swapping ghost stories" with you.' His anger was obvious, cold.

Shelley took a step back from me and sighed. 'Oh, Michael.' Sonia avoided my eyes, a sane person giving a nut some space. My embarrassment deepened.

'I thought you were done with this stuff, Dad,' Tom said bitterly. 'Didn't we have a deal?'

'I'm sorry.'

'But you're going over there even so.'

'I have to.'

Shelley sighed again. 'I thought we had you back too, Michael. But you were fooling us, weren't you?' Somehow her disappointment in me hurt more than Tom's reaction.

She dumped her plate on the table. 'OK, that's enough bull-shit – and enough of this rabbit food, thanks all the same, Michael. Let's get back to work.' She put an arm around Tom's shoulders. 'I want to follow up this idea of yours. *Refrigeration...*'

She led him into the lounge, and Sonia followed, without so much as glancing at me. I was left alone in the kitchen.

I took a few minutes scraping garbage into the recycler and stacking dishes, time I needed to calm down. I found myself trembling. It might have been easier if Tom had actually screamed at me.

Then I followed them back into the lounge, where they had started to work again, filling pages and screens with sketches and notes, as, slowly, an inchoate dream of a refrigerator system big enough to encompass the pole of a planet took shape. But for the rest of the day I felt excluded, as if I had committed an awful transgression, an exile in my own home.

Chapter 25

For the third part of her training, the Implication of Emergent Consciousness, Alia was to be brought to a world at the heart of the Galaxy. She was dismayed at the thought of being taken to yet another dull mass of pointless geological stasis. And like so many others this world seemed to have no name, only a number assigned to it in the vast, growing catalogue of the Commonwealth.

But this, Reath said, was a world of Transcendents.

To Alia's relief, during the journey on board Reath's austere Commonwealth ship the Campocs kept themselves to themselves, and didn't try to discuss their strange obsession with Witnessing and the Redemption. They seemed ashamed of how they had treated Drea. Bale kept out of her way, and made no attempt to revive their physical relationship.

Drea spent most of the journey asleep. She seemed to have been wounded on some deep level. Alia tended her sister with a complex mix of concern and shame.

And during the journey Reath continued his coaching of Alia.

He seemed irritated by the presumption of the Campocs in trying to figure out the motives of the Transcendence – even trying to manipulate it, through Alia. 'The Transcendence is not a human mind at all,' he said testily. 'It is already far, far greater than that. And it has ambitions reaching still further.'

At the heart of the Transcendents' project was what he called *entelechy*, a belief that humans contained a potential, a stupendous possibility, that could be realised in full only through unity. 'What is the purpose of the great churning of human history – all our striving, our wars and our peace, our colonising and our retreats? Surely it is to explore ways in which humans can become the best we can possibly be. And the Transcendence is the highest expression of that deep ambition.'

For now the unifying of mankind was a process, Reath said, a gathering in, a connection and sharing. But that process was not simple, not linear. It was believed that when the interconnection of the community of Transcendents reached a certain level of complexity, a critical mass, it would go through a phase change.

That didn't mean much to Alia. 'What will it be like?'

Reath looked absent. 'I am not a Transcendent. I can't imagine. But it will be a different order of reality, Alia.

'Think of a cone. Imagine taking slices through that cone, higher and higher, approaching the apex. You make circles, don't you? They shrink as you get higher – but then when you reach the tip itself, those circles transmute suddenly into a point, a quite different geometrical entity. It is a discontinuity, a step change.

'So it is with the Transcendence. It will proceed from its present scattered imperfection to a new level of awareness, a totality that will be a crystallisation of mind, a full comprehension of the universe, and of ourselves. When it goes through its phase change, the Transcendence will become infinite, and eternal. *Literally.* Already it is planning on such scales.'

This sounded wonderful to Alia, if scary, but baffling. 'How can you *plan* to be infinite?'

'What do you know of infinities, Alia?'

'What do you think?...'

Infinity was a way of thinking, he said, not so much a number as a process. And the process of infinity shaped the way the Transcendence was laying its plans for the future. 'Infinity gives you *room*.

'Imagine this. Suppose you owned a starship, bigger than the *Nord*, an immense ship with an infinite number of cabins. You number the cabins one, two, three... You have one passenger in each of the cabins – an infinite number of passengers. But now another ship docks, with a *second* infinite set of passengers, all of whom want lodging. What do you do?'

'Turn them away. I'm already full up.'

'Are you? Try this. You work along your infinite corridor. You tell the passenger in room one to move to room two. The passenger in room two goes to four. The passenger in room three goes to six...'

'Everybody shuffles up,' she said. 'To the cabin with the number twice their old one.'

'Is there room for them all?'

She thought it over. 'Yes. Because I have an infinite number of even-numbered cabins.'

'And how many cabins have you freed up?'

'All the odd ones.' She thought about it. 'An infinite number of them too.'

'So what do you do with the new set of passengers?'

'Welcome them aboard...'

He smiled. 'You see? Infinity plus infinity equals infinity. Infinity lets you do things finitude would forbid. Infinity is a mapping; it is a way of doing things, a way of thinking, apparently paradoxical. The Transcendence is not yet infinite, but after its singularity it plans to be. So this is the way the Transcendence thinks, Alia. And if you wish to understand the Transcendence, it is the way you must think too.'

'There isn't an infinite amount of room in my head.'

He held up his thumb and forefinger a few centimetres apart. 'How many real numbers are there between zero and one?'

'An infinite number?'

'An uncountably infinite number, in fact... There are many orders of infinity; we won't go into that. So you *can* cram infinity into a finite space.'

'All right. But this is the real universe! What about the granularity of space and time, of matter and energy? What about quantum uncertainty?'

He winked at her. 'I won't worry about that if you don't.'

They arrived in a spectacular sky.

They had come some distance into the Core, the Galaxy's central bulge, and there were stars everywhere, stars and turbulent clouds of gas and dust. You could still see a curtain of darkness hanging behind the stars, a black sky not completely obscured by the light. But towards the centre itself there was a still denser crowding.

In that bath of light and sleeting radiation thousand-year battles had once been fought, and trillions of humans had lost their lives.

Against such an astounding background, the world of the Transcendents, as it loomed out of the crowded light, was unprepossessing. It wasn't even a planet, really, not much more than an asteroid, even though inertial generators buried in its heart gave it a gravity close to standard, and a layer of air thick enough to breathe. Reath's shuttle swept over a landscape crowded with buildings that clustered in craters and ravines. Many of the buildings were massive, with walls of blown asteroid rock fixed on foundations that dug deep into the dirt. But the buildings were mostly dark, unadorned, with only small clusters of lights within their hulking shadows.

In a sky full of stars this worldlet didn't even have a sun of its own. Alia learned that orphaned worlds were in fact common here, for the stars were so crowded that close encounters and even stellar collisions were frequent, and planets were often torn away from their parent systems.

But this nameless, homeless fragment had its own history. Huge energies had been spent in turning it into a munitions factory – and even vaster energies expended on flattening it again. The modern buildings were built into the relics of those long-vanished days, structures so massive and solid it was likely the asteroid itself would erode away before they did, leaving the blocky buildings to drift off.

And now these buildings once devoted to killing had been rededicated as the temples of a new god.

As the shuttle descended Alia grew increasingly uneasy. With her new faculty for listening beyond the confines of her own head, she reached out, tentatively. She could see the bright minds of the Campocs, open to her now, and she could read their poignant emotions as clearly as if they were her own – their apprehension at being here, their strange, complex concerns about the Redemption, and their muddled guilt over their treatment of Drea. In the foreground too were the minds of Reath and Drea. They were still mostly closed to her, like silvered spheres drifting in her mental sky; it would take her some time to build up her skills before she could see into the minds of non-adepts.

And beyond all that there was a greater roar, inchoate and confused. It was as if ten thousand voices were calling at once, their words merging into a roar as meaningless and as thunderous as the crashing of the waves on a shore. This was the Transcendence, the churning of multiple interconnected minds.

She recoiled, trying to shut out what lay beyond the walls of her head.

The shuttle came down at the edge of a township, small and very quiet. Nobody was in sight. And after they landed, nobody came to greet them.

They clambered out of the shuttle and took a walk. It was a strange experience. This battered world was very small, with a horizon as close as the curve of a hill; you could have walked all the way around it in a couple of days. The gravity was artificial, and felt like it; Alia could feel lumpiness, subtle discontinuities, as she passed from the influence of one Higgs-control inertial field to another. Even the clouds that littered the cramped, dark blue sky were orderly, artificially formed. Lamps hovered in the lee of buildings to dispel shadows.

It was a drab, shabby place. Dwellings had been built into the ancient ruins without much sense of beauty or elegance or individual style – nothing but functionality. There was no art anywhere, Alia noticed, just like the Rustball.

They came upon people, but the people ignored them.

Everybody from the children upwards wore clothes of a dull, machine-manufactured uniformity. They passed a kind of refectory, a public eating place. Few people prepared their own meals, it seemed. Everywhere was quiet, lifeless. Nobody even seemed to talk.

In one shallow rubble-filled crater, a group of children played a game with bat and ball. They ran and threw and caught, working hard enough to sweat. But their faces were empty, and they ran without calling out, or laughing, or clapping, or bickering over dropped balls and missed swings.

And their movements were oddly coordinated. You could see there was something *higher* about them, Alia thought, something that distracted them – or controlled them, she thought uneasily. But there was something missing in them too. They flocked like birds, somehow less than human.

'Everybody goes around as if in a dream,' said Drea. 'Even these kids.'

Bale said, 'Wouldn't you?'

'Most of the children are Transcendents too, of course,' murmured Reath. 'From before they were born, the moment of conception. Many Transcendents breed true, though not all. They play only because of the needs of their growing bodies; it is more a structured exercise than a game as you would understand it.'

Drea said at last, 'What a dull place! Is this really how superhumans live their lives?'

Reath muttered something about how the richness of a Transcendent's individual life was as irrelevant as the cultural milieu of a liver cell.

Alia walked on stiffly, uneasy, a complex shadow cast before her by Galaxy-centre light.

Drea said dryly, 'Your imminent godhood doesn't seem to be improving your patience.'

'Wouldn't you be churned up? I keep waiting for it to happen.'

'What, exactly?'

'For them to come get me. The Transcendents.'

Reath laughed, not unkindly. 'It isn't going to be like that. There are no teachers, no guides. This is the Transcendence, remember, a manifestation of the group, not of individual actions.'

'Like a Coalescence,' Drea said.

'Like a Coalescence, yes – although a Coalescence is a mindless machine, and the Transcendence is the essence of mind. *There's nobody in charge.* Alia, I called this a "Transcendent world", but that's just a simplifying label. It isn't a headquarters, or a capital. It's just that many of the population here happen to be Transcendents. But there are Transcendents all over the Core – indeed all over the Galaxy. Just as individuals don't matter, nor do places; the Transcendence is everywhere, or nowhere... Even I'm not in charge; I'm only here to point out your choices. It's always been up to you.' He sounded wistful – even envious, she thought.

They walked on until they came to a kind of compound. Here, behind a low fence, was a group of very old people. Though dressed in the same dull robes as everybody else, they were bent, slow – most of them were in fact immobile, on chairs or beds set out on a scrubby lawn. They looked small to Alia, as if they had sublimated with age. Younger attendants walked among them, adjusting blankets and offering them bland-looking food. But the attendants seemed as distracted as everybody else.

Then, for a moment, the old people seemed to move in a coordinated way, blank faces lifting, twig-like limbs moving, a ghost of the energetic flocking of the children. Alia thought she could see the spirit of the Transcendence move through them, as it had through the children. But the moment passed, and all she saw were old people, muttering and stumbling in the dirt.

'The undying,' said Reath softly. 'Survivors of history, and now the heart of the Transcendence, a new form of mankind altogether... Nobody knows quite how old some of them are. That immortality pill works wonders, Alia!'

Drea asked, 'But who wants to live for ever if it's going to be like this?'

Still nobody approached them, or even acknowledged their presence. Tired, disappointed, deflated, they trailed back to the shuttle.

Chapter 26

Another flight, more airports and processing and online booking-system therapists. I got through it.

From the air Seville was like a jewel glittering on the breast of a desert. A river, the Guadalquivir, cut through the city, but its waters were low, brown, sluggish. The city itself, much of it gleaming silver with Paint, seemed oddly static, even for these traffic-free days, like a vast movie set. As the plane banked for its final descent I glimpsed the countryside stretching off to the east, across southern Spain towards the true desert of Almeria. Its barrenness was broken by patches of grey-green, maybe olive groves. Further out I saw dazzling silvery rectangles that might have been greenhouses, or solar farms – and one spindly needle shape that must have been the famous Sundial, all of a kilometre tall. But these signs of life were sparse in a huge empty landscape.

The airport terminal was a big box of glass and concrete, turn-of-the-century chic, but the concrete was cracked and stained. Spidery cleaning bots clambered stiffly over the windows, but they just seemed to be pushing the dirt around. Even inside the terminal building there was reddish dust on the floor, like fine-grained sand, swept carelessly into the corners in tiny dunes.

The disembarkation processing was straightforward enough. My exit interview from the plane took only thirty minutes, with the usual blood, DNA and retina scans, psychological profiling and neural probes. But there was a lot of walking to be done from one stage of the induction to the next, and only a dribble of us passengers to do it. I felt I was in the guts of a vast machine, devised to process herds of humans that had now vanished.

Once I'd collected my bags, I made it through customs.

And there was my Aunt Rosa to greet me.

She was a small, compact old woman, slow-moving, oddly muscular, her shoulders rounded, her movements stiff. Her face was a disc of rumpled flesh, tanned like leather, but her eyes were pale and clear, tiny grey stones. She looked like Uncle George, her brother, far more than my mother, her sister. Her hair was a scattering of grey threads, roughly cut. She was in the uniform of her profession, a black shirt, black slacks, and a cardigan of black wool, heavy-looking despite the heat of the afternoon. Even her shoes were black, brightly polished on her small feet. And around her neck she wore a pale slip of stiffened cloth.

She looked me up and down, her gaze critical; after the long flight I felt murky, crumpled. 'So you're Michael. Gina's boy.'

'I'm glad to meet you, Aunt Rosa.'

'*Aunt.*' She snickered. 'Great heavens, you must be fifty years old. What kind of word is that to use?'

'Actually I'm fifty-two—'

'"Rosa" will do, I think.' Her accent was odd, British-tinged English rather than American, but with unfamiliar cadences.

We stood there facing each other. I felt awkward, uncertain. In the end I bent to kiss her on her left cheek, and then her right, in the European style. She didn't flinch; she looked amused. Her skin was hot and very dry.

She stepped back. 'So we got that over with. You have all your luggage? Good. Follow me...' She led me out of the terminal building.

When we stepped out of the air conditioning it was like walking into a wall. I'd never felt anything quite like it, a dry, heavy heat that seemed to drag every bit of moisture out of my skin, and the air had a dusty, almost aromatic tang. It was almost like my jolting virtual-Permian experiences. Rosa just stomped her way through the heat, oblivious. I struggled to follow.

She brought me to a rank where a cab waited for us, an empty white pod with tinted glass. I touched the metal handle of the trunk, and was zapped by a static shock that made my hand jerk backward.

Rosa raised almost invisible eyebrows. 'It's the dryness of the air,' she said. 'Occupational hazard. You'll get used to it. Or not. Get in.'

Rosa lived in an area called La Macarena, in the north of Seville, crowded with tiny, baroque churches and tapas bars. But even here, as our cab wormed its way through narrow streets, there was nobody around. Many of the bars and shops were boarded up, and the only signs of motion were insects and cleaning robots.

A few of the grander residences, behind high walls and railings, showed signs of life. Some of them had trees growing, olives or oranges, or even scraps of lawn; the heads of sprinklers showed everywhere. The place was clean, the streets free of litter and the walls scrubbed clean of graffiti. But there was a general feeling of decay. It was as if the city was populated only by machines, robots who mindlessly, pointlessly, scrubbed the streets and the walls, but all the while everything was rotting away, slumping back into the dry ground. And despite the obvious efforts of the cleaning bots, everything was covered with a fine patina of orange dust.

Spain was losing its people. Its population had halved since the beginning of the century, and by the end would halve again. I had known this, that here was an extreme case of the general depopulation of the west. But I hadn't expected it to be so obvious, the city to feel so empty.

We reached Rosa's apartment. It was a small, rather poky place on the third floor of a tenement block, close to an avenue called the Calle del Torneo that followed the line of the river. The tight security was opened up by a sweep of Rosa's palm and the sacrifice of a few cells from her fingertip to a DNA tester. Even within the building I saw nobody around, as if Rosa was Seville's last resident left standing.

The apartment's conditioned air was cool, moist, fresh. Rosa had a small kitchen with a dining area that opened onto a balcony with a view of the city, and a spare bedroom where she allowed me to make camp. A couple of bots crawled around the place, equipped to cook, clean. Her support equipment seemed much simpler than George's – but then, I could see, Rosa had aged better than George. And she seemed to have disengaged some of the higher sentience functions in her various machines. There was no backchat from this lot, and nothing like George's faintly irritating toy robot companion.

The bathroom was tiny. I showered, in a trickle of water that got steadily more lukewarm. Orange-red dust washed out of my hair and skin and pooled at my feet. Later I learned that water was inordinately expensive here – which was why those grander residences, the homes of the rich, made such a show of its conspicuous consumption. With Rosa's blessing I lay down for an hour and napped. My dreams were turbulent, and I woke unrefreshed.

Rosa prepared me a meal. We sat at her table, near the window that looked out over the city. A sunset towered into the sky, a smear of dusty light. The buildings before me were silhouetted by the setting sun, making a lumpy, cluttered skyline, but lights showed in only a handful of them.

Rosa's food was surprisingly good. They were local dishes, she said. She served me a fish soup with bread and twists of bitter orange peel; she called this *carrochenas*. Then we ate bowls of broad beans with chunks of cured meat, *habas de la rondena*. But the meat was gen-enged ham, chunks hacked from some brainless, cubical, undying mass in a factory somewhere; I found it a little bland, watery.

We exchanged small talk about the family. Rosa didn't seem very interested. In that she was more like my mother than George. But she knew about Tom, and his escapade in Siberia.

And she knew all about Morag. She raised the subject even before we'd finished the beans.

'Let's get this out in the open before we go any further.' She tapped her dog-collar with a bent finger. 'Is this what you're looking for, Michael? Bell, book and candle?'

'I came because George thought it would be a good idea.'

'Ah, George, my dear long-lost brother. The ultimate family man. This is his instinct, you see; when faced by a problem, you should wrap it up in the clinging webs of family. Maybe if he'd had children of his own the antics of his siblings and nephews wouldn't matter so much to him – not that *I'm* one to talk. Well, perhaps he's right. If I take what you say at face value, we're dealing with a haunting here. Who better to come to than a priest?

'And where better to come than such an old country as this?' Columbus himself had a tomb here, she told me, in Seville's cathedral, which was itself built on the site of a mosque erected by the Muslims who had once occupied southern Spain. 'We're soaked in history, drenched in ghosts. Why, once Seville was known as a centre for necromancy, which is the art of calling up ghosts deliberately, to gain information about the future. Queen Isabella put a stop to that! Now the crowds of history have receded, and we have new populations of ghosts to deal with.' She leaned towards me, staring, and a deeper silence seemed to seep into the room. 'Can't you *feel* it? The stillness of an empty city?'

I felt claustrophobic, resentful. I sat back and pushed my food away. 'Look,' I said. 'I'm grateful for your hospitality. The food. But—'

Her eyes glittered. 'But you don't feel I'm being respectful enough about your precious experience.'

'Precious?' I shook my head, my irritation growing. 'Do you imagine I'm some neurotic old fool? Believe me, I don't want this to be happening to me.'

'I think you'd better tell me about Morag,' Rosa said quietly.

I calmed myself down. 'All right. I met her, oh, twenty-seven years ago. She was a couple of years younger than me. She was actually a friend of John, my brother.'

Rosa raised an eyebrow at that. We'd married, and we were very happy, and we had Tom. After that my work had kept me away from home a lot, but Morag had got pregnant again even so. And then – well, Rosa knew the rest. She listened patiently. That skill was the result of forty years as a priest, no doubt, but it was effective nonetheless.

'And now she's come back to you,' Rosa said.

'So it seems.'

'Why, do you think?'

'I don't know! I wish I did.'

'And do you want it to stop?'

I could answer neither yes or no; either would have been true, either a lie. 'I want to understand,' I said at last.

She reached out. When her dry fingers touched the back of my hand I felt a jolt, like the static shock I felt earlier. 'Try to be calm,' she said. 'I just needed to be sure you were sincere.'

'Of course I'm sincere.'

'Well, now we both know that, don't we?'

While she learned about me, I found out about her. Uncle George had told me something of Rosa's story. During that meal I began to learn a little more.

She had been born in Manchester, England, as George had been, nearly ninety years ago. But when very small she had been sent to Rome, and given into the care of a Catholic fringe group called the Puissant Order of Holy Mary Queen of Virgins – *the Order*, as George referred to it. George himself had been so young he had forgotten he even had this second sister, until by chance he came across a photograph in the effects of his deceased father. The Order were a teaching group. Among other things. Rosa had been raised by them, and when she grew up had gone to work for the Order.

When he was in his forties, George had discovered Rosa's existence, and he went to Rome to look for her. This had coincided with some kind of crisis in the Order. The following sequence of events had resulted in Rosa being expelled from the group, and for a time she faded from George's life again.

It turned out that Rosa had stayed within Catholicism. She had gone to a seminary and eventually taken holy orders to become a priest. Now, I learned, she served a scattered parish that covered much of the northern suburbs of Seville, and poorer communities outside the city boundaries. She had been here for three decades, and she was still working, with no intention of retiring as long as her strength held out.

Her story struck me as strange, in those first tellings. The Order had been prepared to take her in because, it seemed, there was some deep and old family connection between the Pooles, my mother's little nuclear family in Manchester, and the Order in Rome. But for a family to send away a child, for *good*, was a bafflingly painful thing to do. For the parents to lie about it to George, their son, to keep secret the very existence of a sister, seemed a terribly cold and calculating deception.

And then, I considered, my own mother, that bit older than her brother George, probably remembered it all. Had she never thought to tell George about Rosa, before he stumbled across the secret for himself? But my mother had never discussed any of this with me either. Generations are like that, I suspect; even though I was in my fifties my mother still kept her problems from me, as if I was a child.

Still, Rosa's account of herself was a hollow story, I thought, a listing of events without real heart. I wondered how much more of it I would have to learn before I was done – and how much I really wanted to know.

'Are you a believer, Michael?'

'In the Christian God? I guess not. I'm sorry.'

'Don't be. I'm not sure if I am, despite this.' She flicked her collar. 'But I'm convinced that everything we humans do has some evolutionary purpose, or else we wouldn't do it. And I believe that priests, and the witch doctors and shamans that came before them, have a crucial role to play, regardless of their theological justification.

'When I first came out of the seminary, and accepted my first post at a parish here in Seville, I imagined I would be strong enough to cope with what the job threw at me. After all I had been through some gruelling experiences myself.' Her face worked briefly, but she didn't elaborate. 'I was wrong. I was shocked.

'I found I was a conduit, Michael. That was my role. A conduit into which people were able to flush their pain and their fear. And, believe me, there is plenty of that, even in this place where there are hardly any people left. I was nearly overwhelmed, a mote in a dust storm. But my seniors counselled me, and I came to understand my duty, which was to stand firm in the face of that great wind of misery.'

'And,' I said cautiously, 'experiences like mine? You've come across such things before?'

'My faith teaches us that the world is a subtler place than is revealed by our blunt senses, Michael. You have to believe that much, whether or not you buy the Christian explanation. And, yes, sometimes I have been exposed to experiences that you would describe as beyond the natural. You're an engineer, aren't you? You are probably uncomfortable that something so irrational is happening to *you*.'

I never enjoyed being pigeon-holed. 'I like to think I'm broader minded than that,' I said.

'Well, perhaps you are. You're here, after all. And now that I've met you I'm quite prepared to believe that you aren't mad, or delusional, or a liar; something really is happening to you. What we must work out is what it means.'

'So what do we do?'

'Why, nothing. You say that Morag comes to you, without your choosing it. Then let her come to you again, and we will see what we will see.'

'And if she doesn't come?'

She smiled; I thought I detected a trace of contempt in her expression. 'Then you've nothing to worry about, have you?'

We had been drinking wine. It was fortified, a kind of sherry, but light and very dry, with a strange salty tang. Rosa took hers with a little water. She said the wine was called *manzanilla*, and was matured only in a town to the south-west, where the Guadalquivir met the Atlantic Ocean, which perhaps explained the subtle saltiness.

Rosa opened the glass doors to her balcony, and we walked out. We were looking west, where the sky was still stained by the dusty sunset, but at the zenith bone-white stars were starting to appear. The air was cooling, but it was still so dry it burned my throat. There were few lights to be seen in the darkened landscape of buildings, homes and shops, restaurants and bars, and a kind of dense silence settled over the town, a silence so rich it seemed to roar, dully, like the blood in my ears.

Rosa had brought a little jug of water with her, and now and again she tipped some into her wine. 'You are sure you don't want any of this?... Customs are changing, you know. In some houses these days good fresh water is presented as the finer drink. You *wine* your *water* rather than the other way around!' She held up the jug to the sky, peering into the water; it was slightly cloudy. 'But this wouldn't pass muster in the best households. Desalinated ocean water, pumped up here from Almunecar on the coast.'

'Water's scarce here?'

'Of course. A mid-latitude, mid-century blight,' she said. 'Spain is a big square box of land and mountains, and for twenty years, I suppose more, it has been drying out, desiccating. I remember when I first came here there was a vast scheme to water the Almeria, the desert region to the east. It would be the world's greatest tourist resort, greater than Florida, with golf courses and holiday homes by the tens of thousands. And they promised to make plants and grasses so salt-resistant you could irrigate them with untreated sea water. Ha! Now it is all gone, and we are plagued by dust.'

'I noticed it today.'

She ran her finger over the balcony rail; the pad came away pink with grime. 'The cleaning machines polished this only this morning.' She rubbed her fingers together, and the dry dust trickled to the floor. 'Here it is,' she said. 'All those golf courses and holiday homes, and the salt-resistant rice and alfalfa and corn, all blown up into the air... Hush.' She raised a finger and peered into the dark.

I heard a rustling, coming from the alley below me. 'What is it? A mouse, a rat?'

'Possibly. Though there isn't much for them to eat any more. It may be a robot, another of our guardian-angel machines, earnestly keeping the streets safe for old folk like me. I sometimes wonder – I'm told that the machines are as smart as dogs, or even some cats. When they have run out of vermin to eliminate, what will they do for sport? Will they turn on each other?...'

'Why is Spain so empty? What caused this depopulation?' I was faintly ashamed of my ignorance.

'The drought hasn't helped,' Rosa said. 'But the change has come from humanity, Michael, from inside us.'

Some time around the turn of the century, people all over the world just stopped having so many children. For a while the effect was masked; the end of the last century saw the biggest population bulge in human history, and as that vast cadre grew to child-bearing age they flooded the world with yet more kids. But the bulge soon worked its way through the demographics, and the decline cut in.

Rosa said, 'In Spain, the government became alarmed. It was thought at first that it was simply a choice of women taking control of their own bodies, on a mass scale perhaps for the first time in history. Spain, along with other countries, put in place more civilised child-care facilities – robots helped with that. More subtly they tried to renegotiate gender roles, the unspoken contract between men and women. I watched all this from outside, of course. Quite a spectacle! Some of this social engineering worked, for example in the US. But not in Spain, Italy, Greece, the more conservative, patriarchal countries. There traditions are too deeply rooted to be shifted, even in the face of population collapse.

'But I think it's all a lot deeper than a simple matter of stay-at-home fathers and day-care nurseries – don't you? After all profound instincts are being defied here: the instinct to propagate the tribe, to fill the world with your brood, the antique Iron Age drives that have enabled us to cover the planet. But now some other, more mysterious motivation is taking hold. Once people came here in great waves, the Romans and the Visigoths, the Moors and the Christians. And now they are leaving again – not *going* anywhere, just disappearing into lost potentialities. And when they've gone, there will be nothing but this aching emptiness. But it feels *right*. Don't you think? It suits the times.'

'I'm surprised you're happy to live alone like this.'

'At my age, you mean? Oh, I'm safe enough. I'm surrounded by machines, as we all are. Pointlessly intelligent, all of them. Machine sentience is now omniscient and omnipresent, just as we once imagined God to be – ha! I am sure they would not let me come to any harm.'

'What about crime?'

'I have no fear of that. Criminals prefer crowds too. I prefer the silence. Sometimes you can feel it rise up around you from a thousand abandoned buildings, a million rooms empty of everything but garbage. I feel as if I'm in a tiny lifeboat, adrift in emptiness.'

'And you *like* to feel that way?'

'Where I grew up was rather different,' she said.

'You mean the Order?'

'It was somewhat crowded. Perhaps, late in life, I am enjoying the contrast.'

'Aunt Rosa, I think you spend too much time on your own.'

That won me a laugh. 'Perhaps I do. Am I morbid, do you think? But I still have work to do here. You asked me about experiences beyond the natural...'

She told me a story. She said that once the city authorities were working their way through the depopulated districts, trying to make them safe. There was some demolition, but usually, more wistfully, what was called 'mothballing', as buildings were secured and sealed against the day when the people would return. And sometimes, in this patient cleaning-out, the fire-fighters or police officers or environment managers found things that induced them to call on the services of a priest like Rosa.

'In one case, as they approached a ruined old house, the workers thought they heard children singing, in harmony, like a school choir. But there were no children there. Then they found a cellar. It turned out that it had been used by a man who had taken children over a period of years. You don't need to know the details. His crimes had never been discovered, not until now. The workers would not, could not enter that cellar. It wasn't because of rot or decay or the danger of disease; their equipment would take care of that. But there was a deeper blight which they hoped I would confront, with my prayers.' She paused. Her small, closed-in face was quite unreadable now. 'Have you ever been in the presence of evil, Michael?'

'I don't think so.'

'You would know. In fiction, evil is portrayed as stylish, clever. The devil is a gentleman! But evil is banal. In that cellar, the dirt, the blood, the bits of hair and clothing, even the scattered toys – it was nauseating, literally revolting.' She turned to me; her body stayed motionless while her head swivelled like an owl's. 'Your ghost. Morag. Is she evil, Michael?'

'No,' I said with certainty. 'Whatever it is, she's not that.'

She seemed to relax, subtly. 'Good. At least we will not

have to face *that*. Then we must seek out another explanation, a different interpretation. Perhaps you are a necromancer, Michael, in this capital city of necromancy; perhaps you are a man who speaks to ghosts to discern the future – what do you think?'

I thought I needed some more of that sea-water wine.

Rosa had promised me that the next day she would take me to see the sights of Seville. We would climb *La Giralda*, a Moorish tower stranded in the middle of a Gothic Christian cathedral, and view the city. Or, better still, perhaps we would ride up the Sundial, the symbol of Spain's number one export industry, electrical power. I thought it was interesting that Rosa's ideas for a day out were all about going to high places. She sought out isolation and height, a contrast, it seemed, to her strange early life, which, as far as I could make out, had been in conditions of crowding, and deep underground.

I looked forward to seeing the Sundial, though. It was a solar-power tower a kilometre tall, rising from gleaming hectares of solar-cell farms, a modern wonder. Air heated at its base rose up through the tower and drove turbines. It was a simple design, if horribly inefficient – but who cared about efficiency when the sunlight was to be had for free?

But in the event we didn't go anywhere, for the next day was a 'dust day'.

I was woken not long after dawn by a rumble of traffic that wouldn't have seemed unusual save that it was *here*. Looking out through the closed balcony windows I saw robot lorries rolling down the street, spraying water. Loudspeakers broadcast warnings in precise, clipped Spanish. In the middle distance the whole skyline obscured by an orange-red haze, and the rising sun was a pale disc that threw only faint shadows on the empty road surface. We would likely be stuck indoors for the day, Rosa said.

We had breakfast. I sat beside the closed window, with cups of coffee made of desalinated ocean water, watching the storm. The dust was coming on a wind from the north, from out of the peninsula's desiccated interior, blowing the last of the country's topsoil into the sea. When it hit us we were sunk in darkness. Even the day after that, the dust still lingered. Holed up in Rosa's apartment, we heard the buzzing of planes. They were seeding clouds over the reservoirs, Rosa said, spraying liquid nitrogen and silver iodide, trying to magic up some rain. Rosa was cynical. She said the planes were just a stunt, designed to reassure the populace that the government was doing something. There was a regional election coming, she said; that was why they were seeding the clouds.

At times it got so dark it was like being under the sea. I looked up at waves gathering and breaking on top of the layer of dust that overwhelmed the city, vast waves towering between earth and sky.

Chapter 27

There was no true night on this world of Transcendents. Enclosed within the opaqued walls of her cabin, with her sister sleeping soundly nearby, Alia was restless. In the silent dark, with no distractions, it was even harder to shut out that unending roar outside her head.

But as she drifted between sleeping and waking, she found at last what she had been brought here to discover.

It was like a dream. She was aware of herself, lying comfortably on her pallet. She even knew that her sister lay still in the corner of the room, her body a warm mass, her mind folded over on itself.

But the nugget of consciousness that always lodged behind Alia's eyes seemed to have floated free to drift through the rooms of her mind. The walls of those rooms were porous – flimsy, translucent – so that a brighter light shone through them. And she heard voices, many of them. It wasn't the formless clamour that had upset her before, but like distant singing, a massed choir perhaps, the merged voices sweet but scattered by the winds.

The glow out there was warm and welcoming, the voices gentle and harmonious. With an effort of will she pushed her way out through the walls of her head.

Her mind threw up analogies for what she experienced. She was floating over a landscape. It was dark, but over that velvet ground lay patterns of light, like a system of roads, a glowing threadwork in multiple colours which connected a multitude of brilliant points.

She wanted to see more. She rose up effortlessly. The floor below was like a starry sky, but inverted, with a vast constellation map written over it. Here and there tightly connected clusters of nodes glowed like cities. She saw that the map was not infinite. It closed on itself – not like a sphere, that would be much too literal for this dreamy vision, but with every point connected to every other. The map was dynamic, the links sparking, twisting, reconnecting and changing constantly. The constant flux was part of the pattern too; this was a map in time as well as space.

And though the topology of the network changed constantly, none of those shining points was ever left isolated. Each was always joined by two, three, four links to its neighbours, and through them to the totality.

This was the Transcendence, the shining nodes human minds, the links that joined them channels of shared thought and memory. This visual map was a crude analogy, and incomplete, for the merged mind was greater than a simple aggregate of individuals. And yet it helped her to begin to see.

She saw nothing threatening in this warm interconnectedness. Suddenly she longed to be one of those nodes, to be joined for ever in the tremendous friendliness of that topology. She sank down, out of the invisible sky. She passed into the netting, through layers of it, until she was surrounded by glowing mind-nodes. Tendrils of interconnection reached out, probing at her from all sides.

She felt unexpected fear, and for a moment she was back in her body, which turned and twisted on her pallet.

But then the metaphor changed.

There were no more stars and laser-beam threads. Faces turned to her. They were smiling. And they all looked like Drea, her sister, she thought – or even like Alia herself. As those familiar eyes shone, hands clasped hers, or rubbed her back, her neck, her arms. They moved in closer, until she was surrounded by a comfortable warmth. It was briefly suffocating, and she thrashed again, but the pressure eased.

Different metaphors now: hallways opened up all around her, as if doors were flung open to reveal them receding into the distance. Every way she chose to go was open, and every way looked inviting. She picked a direction. She went that way – not walking, not even Skimming, simply travelling.

Now she was in a kind of library, a place where shelving and stacks receded in every direction as far as she could see, side to side, up and down. People worked here patiently, consulting records, moving them from one corner of this vast archive to another. The librarians' forms were undefined, their attention devoted to their work. She couldn't see how they moved about, as there was no floor to walk on – but that was irrelevant; it was only a dream. And though the archive stretched off to infinity in every direction, she could somehow see other archives beyond its remote walls, other centres of knowledge, remembrance, wisdom.

This was another obvious metaphor, constructed by her mind as it struggled to interpret the flood of information it was receiving. This was memory, the pooled memory of the Transcendence. And all of it would be accessible to her, as accessible as her own memories always had been, whenever she willed it.

Now there was a change in the way the patient librarians were working, she saw. Some were making a space in one block of shelves, and others were bringing in a new stack of material, its details too remote to make out. She knew what they were doing. That was her own pitiful heap of memories, her whole life of a mere few decades dwarfed by the great banks of knowledge here. And yet she would be given a place here; she would be cherished. Others would be able to access her memories as easily as she could, just as she could reach the memories of others – and even the greater collective experiences of the Transcendence itself, which she now perceived as shadowy mountains of information looming beyond the bounds of the archive.

And, for ever preserved, the memories that defined her need not die with her – and so *she* need not die, not ever. She had no need of Reath's 'immortality pill'; in this chill, remembered sense, she was already an undying.

Even now she was still outside the Transcendence, in a sense. She was still herself, still small and closed-over and complete. But there was a place for her here in this immense cathedral of mind. All she had to do was take one last step.

She had a final moment of doubt. It was as if she looked back at herself, her body lying peacefully now on its pallet.

And then she let the embrace of the Transcendence enfold her at last.

The Transcendence was a body. She could *feel* its limbs, the bodies of its human host already counted in the billions and scattered over thousands of worlds. And yet in another way she was barely more aware of the individual bodies that made up this great host than she was of the cells of her own body.

And its consciousness was not just a network of pooled minds. It arose *from* that network, like a frost pattern emerging from the interactions of ice molecules. She, the spark that was still Alia, felt bewildered by the scope and grandeur of its thoughts. The Transcendence was a symphony orchestra overwhelming her with its mighty themes – and yet her lone piping was an essential part of the whole.

She didn't lose herself. She was still Alia. She was even aware of her own body, lying on its pallet. When she became more adept she would be able to function normally, live a fully human life, while still engaging in the greater community of the Transcendence. It was like doing two things at once, like walking and holding a conversation at the same time. It would be a life lived on two levels, just as she had seen of the Transcendents on this worldlet.

And now she glimpsed the mighty purposes of the Transcendence, the design behind this grand architecture. She felt its tremendous ambition of joining every human mind into its own grand confluence of thought, a gathering into the ultimate embrace of the Transcendence. Then would come the day when the Transcendence, arising out of humanity, would become the highest conciousness of this cosmic age, and it would apprehend the form of the whole universe. This was the dream of a young, unformed god – a dream of power, but not what to *do* with it, not yet. There would be time enough, a literal eternity of it.

And in the meantime there was reflection.

She found memories. There were the firefly sparks of individual lives – she sensed birth, death, love, sex, despair, triumph. Rising above these small rememberings were the vaster memories of the young mass mind itself, as it emerged from a misty unawareness to a cognisance of itself. The most striking note was a huge joy, surprisingly simple, a joy to be alive: a triumphant shout of *I am!*

And yet there was a grace note of sorrow, a trill of regret.

She became aware again of the host of bodies, the heads from which the mass mind had sprung. She saw that there were knots in the distribution of minds – knots of density, of resistance, of a kind of stubbornness, of *age*. They were the undying, the ancient core of the Transcendence. And it was here that the regret was centred.

Alia was drawn to the pain, wary but curious, like the tip of a tongue probing an aching tooth. And suddenly she was bombarded by screams, trillions upon trillions of anguished voices calling out together. She screamed in response.

Even in her torment she knew what this was. This was the Redemption, the Witnessing of the blood-soaked past. This dark pit, right at the heart of the Transcendence itself, was the place to which all those carefully retrieved memories drained. It was superhuman. It was unbearable. She spun and thrashed. This was wrong, terribly wrong. *The Campocs were right—*

She was awake, only Alia again, lying on a sweat-soaked pallet. A face hovered over her like a lantern, full of concern. It was Drea. Her sister brushed her brow, and Alia felt her fur plastered to her forehead.

Drea said, 'You were yelling! Was it a nightmare? Are you all right?...'

Alia grabbed her sister and held her close.

Morning came.

Beyond the walls of the shuttle the worldlet looked even drabber, the people even more dull. There may have been fire in their heads, Alia thought, but their bodies were impoverished. It was impossible to believe that such complex magnificence as the Transcendence could arise out of the shabbiness of this thinly populated rock.

Nobody spoke to her, not Reath, not even Drea. They all seemed frightened of her.

Alia went to her Witnessing tank. It lit up to show her the wormlike thread of Poole's whole life. At least he wouldn't turn away from her. Impulsively she picked out a single moment.

Here was Poole, with his son, in a hospital ward. Their

faces slack, they sat side by side, holding hands, subtly distant from each other, frozen in time. Seconds ago they had received the news that Poole's baby had died, after only moments of life, and that Morag, Poole's wife, had died with him. Alia believed that this was the crux of Michael Poole's whole life, his personal singularity, his moment when the conic sections diminished to a point, a new quality. The moment when he lost everything.

In Michael Poole's time, you were born alone and you died alone, but you spent your life trying to get through to others, through love, through sex – or even through violence, the bloody intimacy of killing. In his love of Morag, in the oceanic few months in which their baby had come to term, Poole had come as close as he ever would to reaching through the barriers to another human. But with these deaths he was already falling back into himself, even now, just heartbeats after hearing the dreadful news. And Alia, with her unwelcome knowledge of his future, knew he would never recover, never get so close to anybody ever again.

What would Michael Poole make of the Transcendence?

What would he have thought of her, as she sat hiding in the cabin of a shuttle, cowering from her destiny? Would Poole envy her this opportunity to reach out to the Transcendence, and to allow it to embrace her? Would he have longed to touch other people so closely? Or would he understand her deepest, most fundamental fear, which she hadn't even been able to express to Drea – that in joining so closely with others, she would ultimately lose herself? And what would he make of the terrible, obsessive, self-inflicted pain of the Redemption?

Absently she let the image in the tank run on. Poole and his son sat side by side, heads down. But now he looked up vaguely, as if searching for something in the air, a disturbance in his world that somehow broke through to his consciousness even at this terrible moment. Again Alia had the strange impression that somehow *he knew she was watching him*.

She waved her hand, and the images dissolved.

Reath approached her cautiously. 'How do you feel?'

Alia frowned. 'It's as if I'm trying to remember a dream.

But the harder I try, the more elusive it is.'

Reath said gently, 'It was a superhuman experience. Literally.'

Or it was like being drugged, Alia thought uneasily.

'You have fulfilled the three Implications. You're one of the Elect now, Alia. You have entered the outer circle of the Transcendence itself.' Reath's expression was complex, full of pride and longing. 'I envy you.'

'Then why don't you join me?'

He smiled sadly. 'Ah, but that's impossible. There are some of us who can never join the Transcendence, no matter how we try.' He tapped his skull with his forefinger. 'Something missing in here, you see. The defect occurs on worlds scattered across the Galaxy, following patterns we can't make out. Is it genetic? Or perhaps there are more subtle determinants of human destiny than genes.'

'I didn't know. I'm sorry.'

'Don't be. We have our place, we *eunuchs*. Do you know that term? We can serve the Transcendence in a unique way. We are useful for we are no threat to it, you see.'

She frowned. 'The Campocs were right.'

'About what?'

'It's full of regret. The Transcendence. That's why it's driving the Redemption. It's as if it is tortured... But I had thought all that regret arose from the Transcendence itself.'

'It doesn't?'

Alia remembered now, a bit of her dream-like experience becoming more lucid. She had glimpsed those deep dark knots of folded-over awareness, like pellets buried in a loaf of bread. And from those pellets, poison leaked. 'Not from all of it. *From the undying.*'

Reath said, 'Remember the undying initiated the joining in the first place. They are the foundation stones of the edifice of the Transcendence. And so, of course, they are shaping it. The Campocs are afraid of the impulse to Redemption. But you've seen it now. Are you afraid?'

'Perhaps. I don't know enough to be afraid. The Transcendence may be like a god. But even as it is being born, it is a wounded god. Isn't it rational to be afraid of that?' And maybe, she speculated now, somewhere in its deepest, secret heart the Transcendence was developing its obsessive Redemption in new and strange ways she had yet to understand.

Reath said, 'Will you go back? You must, you know. It must be difficult – I can't even imagine! But the only way to cope with it is to try, to grow—'

'I want to know more about the Redemption,' she said briskly. 'Perhaps that way lies a deeper truth.' Perhaps, she thought, a truth not even known to the Transcendence itself. In which case, it was surely her duty as a good Transcendent-Elect to increase its own self-awareness.

Reath nodded gravely. 'Then,' he said, 'if that is your feeling, we must take you to the engine of the Redemption.

Chapter 28

The dust storm subsided, and the forecasters said we could expect a clear twenty-four hours. At least I thought they said that; the forecasts were littered with unfamiliar symbols and novel dust-storm jargon. In a Spain slowly turning into a bit of Mars, the weather forecasters had to learn new tricks.

In that clear slot, Rosa offered to take me on a jaunt out of the city, to 'a kind of outer suburb', she said. 'It's become the heart of my mission here. Even though you won't find it on any map.'

'What's it called?'

She treated me to a little Spanish. 'The locals call it *the Reef*.'

I was puzzled. 'Sounds like a theme park.'

'Not quite. Oh – you'd better take this.' She handed me a pill.

I studied it dubiously. 'What is it?'

'Protection. General-spectrum. Some gen-enged antibiotics, a little nano tinkering, that sort of thing. The US Consulate insists you're covered before you're allowed within five kilometres of the Reef. Probably over-cautious, but why take a chance?'

After three days with Rosa her ghoulish humour irritated me. And I was starting to feel nervous about this new leap into the dark. I took the damn pill.

A small cab pulled up outside Rosa's apartment building. A sleek, silent bubble of plastic and ceramic, its hydrogen engine emitting the subtlest puffs of white water vapour, it was done out in papal yellow and adorned by a stylised Christian cross. We clambered inside. The air conditioning was cool, crisp and moist, the seats were soft and deep, and there was a fragrant new-carpet smell.

The pod slid silently away. The streets of Seville were empty as usual, and I was childishly disappointed; I don't think I'd ever ridden in such luxury, and I would have been pleased to have an audience. This pod was actually a private vehicle, fabulously expensive, owned and run by a consortium of the local churches, to whom this Reef was evidently important.

As we moved out into the city's hinterland I looked back. All but the grandest buildings were coated with Paint, silver or gold; in the harsh Spanish sunlight Seville shone like a gaudy movie set. Rosa told me that the photovoltaics attached to all those empty buildings garnered more energy from sunlight than the Sundial itself. Even abandoned the city made a profit for the nation.

Travelling north, we left the city proper and headed into a landscape that opened up around us, bare and flat. Our road, modern, surfaced with silvertop, arrow-straight and quite empty, cut across the dirt. We passed abandoned farms, where the dust had overwhelmed low walls or piled up in the lee of the buildings. There were signs of past dust storms, drifts like dunes that had been bulldozed from the road. In some places there had been attempts to stabilise the dunes with grass, but the grass looked yellow, sparse, dry. Along one stretch of road the dunes had been entirely coated with pitch. They looked very unearthly, like huge black sculptures.

I saw a plume of smoke rising up from beyond the north horizon, where we were headed.

'Methane burn-off,' said Rosa simply. 'Been burning for decades. Don't worry about it. Your pill should protect you.' She tapped a small pack at her waist. 'Or if not, I brought masks.'

We began to pass buildings. They were just shacks, boxy constructions strung out beside the road. Spindly TV aerials poked at the sky. Some of the plots even had little gardens, where stunted olives or orange trees struggled for life. Children came running out. Some waved, or made coarser gestures at us, sealed in our high-tech bubble.

When I looked more closely I saw that the shanties and shacks were made of ceramic and metal, sheets of it shaped and battered: material obviously sliced from the carcasses of automobiles. Their 'windows' bulged; they were windscreens or side windows. One woman in her front yard ground some kind of corn in a metal bowl that had obviously once been a hubcap. A group of children ran by, playing with a kind of cart that ran on 'wheels' made of sliced-up bits of an exhaust manifold.

Everything was constructed almost entirely of bits of dead car.

As we drove on the shanty town shuffled closer to the edge of the road. Some of the shacks became shops and stalls with open fronts. There were still a few kids giving us the finger as we passed, but here they were crowded out by adults. Shopkeepers yelled at us and held out samples of their wares, unidentifiable bits of meat on sticks. They seemed to be of all races, as far as I could see, a real melting pot. And many of these people were young; there were plenty of teenagers, adolescents, young adults. Compared to the antique stillness of the traditional city, it was like being driven through a vast nursery.

Safe in our glass cocoon, we could touch, smell none of this. Even the voices were muffled. It didn't seem real, like a VR theatre arranged for our benefit.

'Don't be afraid,' Rosa said. 'Many of them know me. Anyhow surveillance here is pretty good these days.'

'I'm not afraid. Spooked, maybe.'

'Perhaps you haven't been in Seville long enough. Even I feel disturbed sometimes by the crowding here... Ah. We've nearly reached the centre.'

We passed over a low ridge, and began to descend into a broad, wide valley. From this elevation I could see how the shanty town spread out for kilometres around me, the rough shacks carpeting the earth. Smoke rose up in isolated threads, from fires or methane burn-off. I saw a few better-constructed buildings, blocks of concrete studded among the rubble shacks. Perhaps they were clinics, schools, police stations, welfare offices. And drones flew overhead, glittering insects hovering over this plain of garbage. I felt reassured by these signs of governance. I guess I'm really not terribly brave.

Our road cut through all this, following its own straight line. But a kilometre or so ahead of us it came to a dead end. A ridge pushed up out of the plain, terminating the road and blocking our way. It glittered, as if covered in broken glass.

It was a wall, metallic, glassy, crumpled, that stretched to left and right as far as I could see.

Rosa was watching my reaction. 'That is the Reef,' she said. She leaned forward and tapped the pod's windscreen. 'I think this jalopy has some imaging facilities...' A disc of the screen showed us a magnified image of what lay ahead.

I saw that the Reef wasn't natural at all. It was man-made. It was a heap of automobiles.

Cars upon cars upon cars, piled up, crushed down on each other, glittering with bits of smashed windscreen and gaudy paintwork, the whole thing laced together by a patina of orange rust: there were so many cars they were beyond counting. It was like a vast heaping of dead beetles. And as I learned to work the controls of our pod's imaging system and turned my gaze, godlike, I saw people crawling, digging, climbing, working at the Reef, everywhere I looked.

The pod rolled to a stop. Its blister popped open, and suddenly the pod was full of a clamour of voices. You could hear individual shouts close by, and beyond that massed voices like the cries of gulls – and then a wider roar, like waves breaking, the sound of a million voices merging into one. Then there were the *smells*. It smelled like a road. I smelled tar and asphalt and rubber, and a sharper stink that might have been tyres burning somewhere. I felt immediately nauseous, but I tried to hide it.

Rosa sniffed up this toxic mix with a look of pleasure. 'Ah, bliss. Once the whole world smelled like this, of *car*. A few hours of it won't do you any harm.'

Before me the Reef rose up. We were only in its foothills here, and the constituent cars, crushed, mangled and stripped, were pressed into the dirt, but its shoulder rose mountainously above.

Rosa was watching me. 'I know it's all somewhat over-whelming.'

I felt uncomfortable to be under the protective wing of a bent old woman close to ninety. I insisted, 'I'm fine.'

'Just remember, I have masks.' She clambered out of the pod, and I had no choice but to follow.

Away from the smart road surface the ground was dirt. But it gave slightly as I stepped out onto it, and beetles and spiders and even a few brown-skinned rodents fled from my feet. The ground was *warm*, warm beneath my feet. I was standing on the crust of a vast midden, I realised. It was profoundly uncomfortable to walk over that soft, moist, warm surface.

Now we were out of the pod, some of those vendor types crowded closely, yelling, competing for our attention. Most of them bore sticks and skewers with bits of broiled meat. I didn't like to think about where that meat had come from, but its smell wasn't as bad as the general old-car stink. I was taller than almost everybody here, even the adults. The people were dressed in rags, but looked healthy enough, well-fed. But the crowding people brought a secondary smell of sweat and body odour that washed over me. I could hear that some of the vendors' cries were yells of greeting for my aunt. *'Mama Rosa!'* She replied in a guttural Spanish; I wondered if this place had its own dialect.

Rosa glanced back at me, grinning, and pushed on into the crowd. There was a danger I would lose her, even in this diminutive mob. I hurried through the sweat and the waving sticks of meat.

We came to a kind of staircase cut, astoundingly, into the heaping of dead cars. Rosa started to climb. I tried to copy her brisk strides, but I stepped gingerly on beaten-flat wings and doors and hoods, and crunched over patinas of broken glass.

Above my head I heard a confident cawing. A line of big, black, powerful-looking birds peered down at my slow toil with silent menace.

'Crows,' Rosa said. 'They're a hazard here. They'll mostly leave an adult alone, but if they see a child they will some-times try to cut it off. They fly at your head. They *herd* you.'

'I never heard of crows behaving that way.'

'This is a novel landscape, Michael,' Rosa said. 'You adapt or die. Keep an eye on the birds.'

'Oh, I will.'

Maybe a hundred steps above the ground we arrived at a kind of cave, walled by bits of car, cut into the steepening face of the Reef. There were chairs, tables, and a rough-cut doorway leading through to more chambers within.

Rosa entered the cave and, with relief, threw herself down on a chair. I followed suit. My legs were stiff from the climb; I thought Rosa had done remarkably well.

Even the chairs here were old automobile seats, heavily patched with duct tape.

A woman came bustling from the back chambers. She was dressed in an ancient, shapeless smock, and she was healthily fat, though her face was streaked with grime. When she saw Rosa she fussed over her immediately. '*Mama Rosa! Mama Rosa!*' They exchanged a few words, and then the woman receded to her back room, to come bustling out with a tray of glasses and a bottle.

As she poured, Rosa said to me, 'I took the liberty of ordering ahead. The dish of the day, so to speak. The water's local stuff but don't worry, it's clean; engineered bugs see to that.' She held up a glass. 'Look, it even sparkles.'

'Rosa, I don't believe it. Is this is a restaurant?'

'I don't think I'd give it as grand a description as that. But they serve good food. The best on the Reef!'

As we waited for the food to arrive, me nervously, Rosa with anticipation, we talked about the Reef, and its strange history.

In the late 2020s, as the Americans had ended their long love-affair with the car, the Spaniards had followed suit.

In those pre-Stewardship days Seville had already reached a garbage crisis, and dumped millions of tonnes of the stuff in vast overflowing landfills. So for the people of Seville there was only one logical place to get rid of their suddenly useless cars, and that was in the foul-smelling, rat-swarming trash city just over the horizon. The dumping had caught on, and soon cities in the rest of Spain were paying Seville to take on their own refuse too. 'An early example of negotiating for ecological credits,' Rosa said dryly. Eventually the detritus of the automobile industry of a modern nation had drained here, gathered up by the mechanical muscles of grinders, diggers and crushers into this great ridge of dead cars. And all the time garbage had continued to pile up around it.

'So the Reef was born. People were already here, picking over the garbage, trying to make a living out of it. But then there was a flood of newcomers. In the 2020s southern Spain was wide open to refugees, especially from Africa. At the Strait of Gibraltar you only have to cross a few kilometres of water...'

The final days before the Stewardship had been a time of increasing panic, of a sense of helplessness as problems spiralled out of control. Among the worst was the spread of infectious diseases out of the tropics, like dengue fever, encephalitis and yellow fever. Uncle George used to say it had been bound to happen. As the world warmed up and mosquitoes and ticks were able to survive at higher latitudes, the diseases spread out of their traditional ranges, driving human populations before them like herders.

Floods of refugees had broken into Spain and headed for the cities of the south, seeking work, succour, help. 'And of course the refugees brought with them the diseases they had been trying to flee,' Rosa said grimly. 'The authorities couldn't keep these plague-ridden undesirables out of the country. But they could keep them out of the towns.'

In the Seville area the refugees had gathered here on the Reef, for there was no other place for them to go in the desiccating countryside, nowhere they were welcome. They slept in the warmth of the vast rotting heaps of garbage, and they had begun to burrow into it, alongside the rats and gulls and the crows and the beetles, a whole community of scavengers who had got there before them.

'And, of course, the scavengers began to eat other scavengers,' Rosa said. 'Before long a kind of food chain established itself.'

'With the people at the top?'

'Not necessarily,' Rosa said. 'Remember the crows.'

They survived, or some of them. People bred young and

died early in such a situation. Soon there were children running around, whole generations of them who had known nothing but this garbage-world.

But the city had kept on dumping its trash here regardless. It was a vast denial of reality, that the citizens of a still-prosperous city like Seville could simply ignore the gigantic heaps of rot they continued to create, and the hapless people who now lived there. And this wasn't the only garbage-dump city on the planet; there were others near Lagos and Manila, Beijing and Vladivostok – even a few, Rosa told me to my surprise, in the USA.

Rosa had been one of the first local priests to try to make contact with the inhabitants of the Reef. 'In those days it was like a circle of hell,' she said. 'There was famine and disease, and no government, no control, no policing. The police and army just fenced the place off, and left whoever and whatever was inside the perimeter to consume themselves, and rot. So crime was rife. The bad guys from Seville used this place as a mine of human flesh to do what they wanted with - even just target practice. Imagine that.'

Things had changed in the late 2030s when the Stewardship money had started to flow. Suddenly people discovered they had a conscience after all, and Seville turned its attention to the vast blister on its doorstep. But those early do-gooders, following in the steps of Rosa and others, found their efforts were not welcome. 'The Reef had become a home,' Rosa said, 'a way of life.' After that the authorities had taken a more subtle approach. The police had worked more carefully to establish a presence, and Stewardship money was used to establish a basic human infrastructure, schools and hospitals and the like.

'But the local economy is still the same,' Rosa said, almost proudly. 'And the ecology. People live off the garbage – and not just by barbecuing rats, either.'

She said that gen-enged bacteria had been loosed on the Reef. Bugs that could eat oil were working their way through the contents of the leaking engine blocks and fuel tanks in the mound beneath me, cracking waste oil and gasoline into more useful hydrocarbons and other chemicals. Other bugs devoured polyurethane plastics and other 'non-biodegradable' components of the car corpses. Even hydrogen could be harvested, she said. Collection plants had been set up around the base of the Reef, at the outlet of systems of drainage pipes through which this reclaimed treasure was collected. 'All very modern, don't you think? We live in an age of margins, where there is money to be made from reprocessing the garbage of richer times.'

As the population of Spain continued its precipitous decline there had been an obvious motive to open up this community: the families of the Reef were unusually fecund for the time and there were lots of kids running around, kids who might be employed usefully to keep the nation functioning.

After a vast citizenship programme, some Reef babies had grown up to become lawyers and doctors and engineers and politicians. Many had gone to live and work in more salubrious parts of the country, or even abroad – but not all; some had stayed to work for the strange community that had fostered them. By now, Rosa said, the Reef was integrated into Spanish society. It even had zip codes.

Something scuttled over my foot, startling me. It was an insect. I bent down and grabbed it between thumb and forefinger. It looked like a beetle, but it had an unfamiliar blue-green sheen to its carapace; I'd never seen anything like it. I showed it to Rosa.

'Keep it. It might be a new species.'

'Really?'

'Garbage tips are the modern crucibles of evolution.'

I tried to make out Rosa's fascination with this place. 'You keep talking about the Reef – ecology, evolution, food chains – as if it's one big ecosystem. And you talk as if the humans here are part of the ecosystem themselves, just another kind of scavenger.'

For a moment, as she peered out over the metallic slopes of the Reef, she was silent. I had time to smell the food cooking, an aroma of hot butter and seafood.

Rosa said slowly, 'An ecosystem. So it is. In a way, now that the government has moved in, the place has lost some of its fascination for me. It's safer, yes, and life expectancy has shot up. But not so interesting...'

Even when she had first come here, she said, the place hadn't been as lawless as she had feared.

'I imagined either simple chaos, or gangsters and warlords, chieftains wielding crude power based on threats and intimidation. There was plenty of that, of course. But from the beginning the Reef was simply too *big* to be governed in such a way. And the refugees were not a homogenous mass; they trickled here from all over. Chances were you could talk to your neighbour, but not to somebody on the other side of the mound. Without communication centralised power was impossible. Nobody knew what was going on; nobody was in overall charge.'

Instead, she said, the nascent community had organised itself.

If you worked on the Reef, struggling to survive, your best bet was to do what your neighbour was doing. If you saw her digging, you dug; if you saw her fleeing, you fled. 'And that way,' Rosa said, 'through local interaction and feedback, a community *emerged*, evolving bottom-up.'

When the government first began to open up the place, they sent in sociologists and complexity specialists to study what was going on. They found a collective organisation that made almost maximally efficient use of the resources of the Reef as a whole. And this was achieved by groups who shared no common language. They just worked it out as they went along.

'Like an ant colony,' I said, with faint disquiet.

'And it worked almost perfectly. A perfect human machine.' She actually sounded wistful.

It was a tone of voice I had heard from her before, when she had hinted at aspects of the Order in Rome which had taken her in. *Crowding. Underground. Swarming with people.* I wondered what the Order truly was – and why it had expelled Rosa. Whatever the truth, it was evident to me that she had spent her life since seeking either its opposite in isolation, or its reflection in other things, even in this extraordinary place, the Reef: she had spent her life longing to go back.

Our lunch arrived, heaps of steaming food served on clean hot plates by our grubby-faced landlady. Rosa told me it was a local variant of paella, called *fideos a la malaguena*, peppers and shellfish, with spaghetti rather than rice. The pasta and peppers were fine. But the shellfish, mussels and clams, were gritty. I wondered from what dark ocean they had come, and pushed them aside.

Our lunch was cut short by an alarm. It was a mournful siren that sounded from far away, like the cry of some immense beast raising its head from the sea of garbage. The landlady came out of her kitchen, wiping her hands. She peered up at the sky and muttered.

Rosa and I stepped outside the cave-like restaurant. The cause of the alarm was obvious. Coming from the north was a murky red cloud that towered high above the glinting shoulder of the Reef; its upper levels thrashed and writhed, purple. The light was already failing.

'This wasn't forecast,' Rosa said.

Looking down the slope of the Reef I saw people running for shelter, the shopkeepers and stallholders battening down and grabbing their wares. They swarmed everywhere, racing over their midden like the ants Rosa seemed to think they were. The sky grew darker. Bits of loose garbage began to blow about on the surface of the Reef.

And then, as the light failed, I saw her. She was standing at the foot of the Reef proper, where the lowest strata of doomed cars were sinking into the ground. She stared up at me.

I had never seen her so close. *It was her*, no doubt about it; I could make out her eyes, her nose, the laugh lines around her mouth. I could even hear her voice, though I could make out no words. It was typical of her to come to me now, in the storm, in a time of confusion.

Rosa stood beside me. I dared take my eyes off Morag for a second – I was fearful she would just vanish back where she had come from if I looked away – and I saw that Rosa was staring in the same direction as me, her small mouth open.

'Rosa – *you see her*, don't you?'

Rosa took my hand; her leathery grip was reassuring. 'I think so.'

I was overwhelmed. It was the first time anybody else had

shared my visions. 'Can you make out what she's saying?' All I could hear was a kind of jabber, very rapid; Morag almost sounded like a speeded-up recording.

Rosa listened closely. 'No words,' she said. 'But it sounds like information. Structured. Very dense. We should have brought a recorder.'

'Yes...'

Morag turned away, took a step away, and looked back at me. I thought her expression was pleading.

'I have to go to her.' I looked down, seeking the staircase. It was getting very dark now, and wind-blown sand scraped the back of my neck, a premonition of what was to come.

The landlady gabbled agitated Spanish.

Rosa said, 'She says we must go inside. The storm—'

'No! Morag's down there. Let me go!'

But they were surprisingly strong, especially the landlady, and they began to drag me back towards the shelter of the restaurant.

Morag was walking away, her hair whipping around her face. Still she looked back at me. But she was blurring into the darkness, becoming indistinct again, and I could no longer hear her voice.

Then the dust descended. Suddenly it was everywhere, in my eyes, mouth, ears, hair, and the world was full of the wind's stupendous bellowing. Rosa and the landlady hauled me backwards into the cave, and a door slammed, shutting out the storm.

We sat in that darkened cave, illuminated only by a lamp that burned Reef methane. The landlady gave us water to wash the dust out of our hair and mouths and off our skin, and we drank a hot, flavourless tea. Rosa had to pay for all this, of course.

'So,' Rosa said gently. 'I feel privileged. I've heard many ghost stories, Michael. But I've never *seen* somebody else's ghost before.'

I felt powerful, confused emotions. I was disappointed to have lost Morag, when she had seemed so close. But I clung to that electrifying understanding that *Rosa had seen what I had seen*: whatever was going on, I wasn't crazy or delusional.

I was relieved, I guess. But I was even more scared of the whole thing than before.

'I have to get this straight in my head, Rosa. It's in the way.'

'In the way? – Ah, yes. Your gas hydrate project.' She touched my hand. 'You are trying to balance your own needs, the issue of Morag, with the wider needs of us all. You feel confused. But that's because you are a good man, Michael.'

I snorted. 'Good? Me?' I thought of my relationship with Tom, that terrible flawed mess. 'Believe me, I don't feel it.'

'You don't need to. Saint Augustine said that if you don't *feel* you are good then you must *pretend* you are. You practise, you do good things. And then, one day, you wake up and find you are good after all.'

The landlady nodded, muttering; perhaps she picked up some of Rosa's child-like sermonising.

'I don't want to lose Morag again,' I said. 'Not if I don't have to. But I need to understand.'

'Well, since I saw her too, I now need to understand also,' Rosa said. 'Let me do some research.'

That surprised me. 'Research? I expected you to say you'd pray for me.'

'I will, if it will help.' She tapped her forehead. 'But God didn't give us brains for nothing. Let me see what I can figure out.'

The landlady, muttering, opened the door a crack. But the storm was still howling, and a scattering of sand hissed on the floor.

Chapter 29

This time Alia and her uneasy crew travelled more than a thousand light years away from the centre of the Galaxy, and returned to the plane of the spiral arms, where the sky's equator was a thick band of light, the compressed glow of the arms seen edge-on, and the Galaxy centre itself was a huge sun that glowered behind scattered stars.

They had come in search of the engine of the Redemption, Reath said enigmatically.

They approached a world, another world with no name but only a number in the Commonwealth's catalogue. It was just another rust-red globe, a scrap of desert folded over on itself, calmly circling a shrunken sun. This world was old, far older than Earth. It was a long time since even the sparking flowers of impacts had disturbed the slumber of this world's worn plains; billions of years of collisions had scoured this system clean of comets. It was all a bit depressing to Alia, but she was learning it was typical.

Reath's shuttle slid low through dust-laden air. The landscape was unprepossessing, worn away – and dominated by mounds that pushed out of the sand, low but neatly circular. They were just heaps, the same dull crimson colour as the rest of the landscape, but they were regular, like perfect spheres buried in the dirt. The mounds were everywhere, peppering the shadows of worn-down continents, filled-in seas. Some of them were kilometres across.

Life had never advanced far on this shrunken world. But humans had come here, of course; in time they had been everywhere. Those low mounds were their signature.

Reath said, 'Water is the key to our kind of life – and most kinds of post-human life too. On a world like this any surface water or ice has long since been lost, disassociated in

the higher atmosphere. When the first colonists came, only the very deepest aquifers remained – so deep they hadn't been dug out even by asteroid impacts, and so very difficult to reach – and there was more water bound into the mineral structures of the deeper rocks, perhaps hundreds of kilometres down.'

'So if you wanted to live, you'd dig,' Drea guessed.

'And that's what the colonists did. Their settlements were mostly subsurface, with deep stalks going down hundreds of kilometres in search of water. Such settlements are always going to be cramped, confined...'

They all knew the story, the fate of such enclosed societies. And they knew what the mounds must conceal.

The shuttle hovered over one of the larger mounds. Commonwealth monitoring posts ringed it in a loose circle. There were no landing facilities, no docks, but Alia could see the scars of previous landings splashed over the dirt. The breeze of the shuttle's descent blew sand in snaking ripples over the surface of the mound.

Alia thought she saw hands, small human hands, push out of the mound to pat the dirt back into place.

'This mound will do,' Reath said. 'Coalescences are different in detail, but all essentially the same. I don't think it makes any difference which mound we pick.' To Alia's surprise he started handing out face masks. 'You'll need these.'

Alia had never worn such a thing; she had to be shown how to put it on. 'Why? The Mist—'

'The Mist doesn't work in a Coalescence,' Reath said. 'The air in there is special. Many Coalescent types use the air to communicate. Biochemicals. Scents, pheromones.'

Bale adjusted Drea's face mask for her, making sure it fit snugly all the way around. 'And you don't want stuff like that in your lungs,' he said, his voice muffled by his own mask.

They faced each other, Alia and her sister, Reath, the three Campocs, their faces obscured by their translucent visors. Drea said, 'We look like bugs!'

They stepped out onto dirt that crunched softly under their feet. The gravity was low, only about a third standard, and Alia felt comfortably light on her feet. Theirs were the only footsteps to be seen. The pale brown sky was cloudless, and the stale air didn't stir. Alia had the impression that there was little weather here.

The mound rose up before her, as if growing out of the dirt. Commonwealth monitoring stations, boxes of bright blue and yellow, sat impassively before it. 'How do we get into this thing?'

Reath said, 'I don't imagine it's hard.' He faced the mound, spread his hands, and called into the empty air, 'This is Alia, a Transcendent-Elect. You are here to serve her. She wants to speak to you.'

For long heartbeats nothing happened. Then the curved surface of the mound dimpled, and sand hissed away. A doorway opened up, a low archway, revealing a corridor that led off into darkness.

Reath glanced at Alia. 'Will you take the lead?'

Alia could think of nothing she'd less rather do than walk into that mouth of strangeness. But she had her duty – or maybe it was just that she didn't want to lose face. She stepped forward, into the archway. Loose sand trickled down over her, pattering on her faceplate.

The dark corridor led to an inner door, like an airlock. When they were all inside the outer door closed. Alia glanced back at the closing door; she saw nothing but sand shifting into place, an unobtrusive technology.

For an unpleasant heartbeat the six of them were locked in darkness, the silence broken only by the scratch of their breathing behind the masks. Then the inner door slid open. They crowded through the hatch.

They emerged into another corridor, low-roofed and with rounded walls of what looked like ceramic. Illuminated dimly by lamps inset into the walls, the corridor curved out of sight. They had to duck to avoid the low ceiling, even the squat Campocs.

A few paces from the door a figure was waiting to greet them.

Alia stepped forward. This was a woman, she thought – but slim and sexless, and dressed in a bland white robe. She was without hair; the naked skin of her face and scalp startled blue eyes, and a wide mouth set in a monstrous face. That mouth gaped open, so the water washed into it with its cargo of sewage, and then the mouth clamped closed. A muscular back broke the water surface, with knobbly vertebrae and short hairs folded flat. As the creature swam away, vast slow bubbles broke the surface behind it.

Seer laughed coarsely. 'Rocket propulsion!'

Now Alia made out a whole school of the swimmers pushing languidly back and froth through the dense mess, chewing, farting, shitting. There were breaks in the far walls through which the swimmers passed. Perhaps this chamber was just one of a whole network that laced through the mound.

Reath smiled at Alia. 'You're starting to see it, the purpose of the place?'

'I think so. This is a sewage treatment works, isn't it? But they don't use machines, but *people*.'

The waste of the mound community poured into chambers like this. The swimmers chewed it up, shat and pissed it out, and chewed it down again. Their organs were specialised to filter and separate organic material from water, waste from recyclable goodies.

Reath said, 'It isn't so strange if you think about it. Human mothers have always produced milk for their babies. Animals pre-digest food for their young – and some even eat excrement to extract minerals. The details vary, but to do things with humans rather than machines is the way of communities like this. Somewhere in this mound there must be big-lunged air recyclers, waste removers, builders and demolishers, drones for carrying and fetching – even for disposing of the dead. And after all a human sewage processor isn't likely to break down.'

'*Drones*,' said Bale, with an expression of disgust.

'So,' said Seer, incredulous, 'if these guys keep on padling around this toilet bowl long enough they'll turn it into oup?'

Alia leaned down, ducked her hand at the surface of the ater, and raised it towards her lips. 'Needs salt, I think.'

Drea recoiled. 'Oh, you *didn't*.'

Alia grinned and showed her a clean hand.

was blotchy. It was hard to tell how old she was, though her smallness and a certain delicacy about her features made her look young. Her eyes were her most striking feature, large, watery orbs with wide, watchful pupils: eyes adapted to twilight, Alia thought. She was expressionless.

Reath nudged Alia. 'Ask her who she is.'

'I am Alia. Tell me your name.'

The woman had to think it over. 'My name is Berra.' Her accent was strong, but easily comprehensible. But she spoke slowly, enunciating each syllable separately: *Be-rra*. It was as if it was the first time she had heard the name herself. 'You are the Transcendent-Elect.'

'Yes. My companions are—'

Berra wasn't interested. 'I am an Interface Specialist,' she said. 'I will answer all questions.'

'I'm sure you will —'

'Please do not speak to anyone else you meet. Or any*thing*. Please speak only to me. You need not doubt my veracity.'

'I wouldn't dream of it.'

'What is it you want to know?'

Alia took a breath. 'I want to learn about the Redemption.'

Berra nodded. 'Ah, yes. We all serve that mighty cause. Then you will want to see the Listeners.'

'I will?'

'Please come.' Berra turned and led them away, along the corridor.

Reath walked beside Alia and Drea. The Campocs clustered behind. Curious, watchful, they seemed to be enjoying the adventure.

Alia said to Reath, 'We can only speak to her, she will only speak to me. I suppose it's fair.'

'Don't jump to conclusions,' Reath said. 'The protocol here has nothing to do with human manners.'

'Power must be scarce,' Bale said. 'Not too warm, not too bright, cramped corridors.'

Seer whispered, 'And it's been this way a *long* time. You see how small she is? And those big pupils: she is adapted for these dingy passages.'

Denh asked, 'What do you think the power source is?'

was blotchy. It was hard to tell how old she was, though her smallness and a certain delicacy about her features made her look young. Her eyes were her most striking feature, large, watery orbs with wide, watchful pupils: eyes adapted to twilight, Alia thought. She was expressionless.

Reath nudged Alia. 'Ask her who she is.'

'I am Alia. Tell me your name.'

The woman had to think it over. 'My name is Berra.' Her accent was strong, but easily comprehensible. But she spoke slowly, enunciating each syllable separately: *Be-rra*. It was as if it was the first time she had heard the name herself. 'You are the Transcendent-Elect.'

'Yes. My companions are—'

Berra wasn't interested. 'I am an Interface Specialist,' she said. 'I will answer all questions.'

'I'm sure you will —'

'Please do not speak to anyone else you meet. Or any*thing*. Please speak only to me. You need not doubt my veracity.'

'I wouldn't dream of it.'

'What is it you want to know?'

Alia took a breath. 'I want to learn about the Redemption.'

Berra nodded. 'Ah, yes. We all serve that mighty cause. Then you will want to see the Listeners.'

'I will?'

'Please come.' Berra turned and led them away, along the corridor.

Reath walked beside Alia and Drea. The Campocs clustered behind. Curious, watchful, they seemed to be enjoying the adventure.

Alia said to Reath, 'We can only speak to her, she will only speak to me. I suppose it's fair.'

'Don't jump to conclusions,' Reath said. 'The protocol here has nothing to do with human manners.'

'Power must be scarce,' Bale said. 'Not too warm, not too bright, cramped corridors.'

Seer whispered, 'And it's been this way a *long* time. You see how small she is? And those big pupils: she is adapted for these dingy passages.'

Denh asked, 'What do you think the power source is?'

Bale shrugged. 'Geothermal? But on a planet like this you'd have to dig deep.'

Reath looked back. 'The details don't really matter. Every Coalescent colony is like this, more or less. And the crowding isn't just for economy. It's purposeful. You stay cramped; that way you stay locked into the eusociety.'

'Yes, but—'

Reath snapped, 'Stop your chattering!'

Berra led them deeper into the complex. The corridors were empty, save for themselves; there was no noise, no disturbance – no dirt. Most of the walls were unbroken by doors. The corridors branched and bifurcated at forks and T-junctions and complex intersections. The party even changed levels, climbing ladders and descending staircases. It was a three-dimensional maze through which Berra led them confidently.

The Campocs started to seem lost: 'Have we just come around three sides of a square?' 'Haven't we been here before?...'

But Alia and Drea, born on a starship, shared a good innate sense of direction. Alia always knew where she was in relation to the outside. And she could picture the path they were following; though tortuously, Berra was leading them deep into the heart of the mound. It was a comforting thought that she and Drea could Skim out of there in an instant, if need be.

At a confluence of corridors they came upon activity. High on one wall a recessed light was flickering. Creatures clung to the wall, a tangle of long limbs, three or four of them evidently working on the light. Berra clearly wanted to go on, but the visitors slowed to a halt, staring up curiously, and she had to wait.

In the dim light Alia had trouble seeing the workers clearly. Their hands and feet had five splayed digits each, but each finger or thumb was tipped by a broad pad which clung easily to the wall's smooth surface. Their limbs were very long and thin, longer than their skinny bodies, giving them the look of spiders. They seemed to be *licking* the broken light, with pink tongues which unrolled from their mouths. Their skulls were small, their brain pans shrunken, Alia thought.

But their faces, especially their eyes, were their most human feature, and even as their tongues worked at the lamp they glanced down at the visitors with fear.

Bale said, 'Remember, we aren't supposed to speak to them.'

Reath snorted. 'I doubt if they would understand you if you did.'

Drea asked, 'What *are* they?'

'Specialists,' Reath said. 'Like everybody here. Post-humans adapted to their roles in keeping the whole functioning.'

Berra was growing anxious. Mutely she walked back and forth along the corridor she wanted to take, away from this junction.

At last Alia took pity on her. With backward glances at the workers on the wall, she led her party away.

After another hundred paces, Berra halted. They were in a stretch of corridor as bland and featureless as the rest. But Berra patted the wall with her small hand, and a door opened up like lips parting. Fetid air gusted out into the corridor. Hot and moist, its stench was unmistakable, even filtered by the face masks. They all recoiled, save Berra.

'Lethe,' Drea said. 'That's shit!'

Berra patiently waited by the door, her eyes locked on Alia's face.

Alia asked, 'What's through here?'

Berra said, 'The way to the Listeners.'

Reath said firmly, 'Come on.' He stepped forward through the door.

Alia reluctantly followed – and was immersed in a fug of stinking air. For the first time she was grateful for her face mask. The chamber was huge, its far walls lost in a mist of humidity. But the room was dominated by a tank of fluid, presumably water, so large it was almost a lake. The water was cloudy, brownish, and warm enough for steam to come coiling up from its surface. Small waterfalls erupted from the walls, spilling more fluid into the brimming pond, and big low-gravity ripples washed with low gurgles against the walls of the tank.

A head pushed out of the water. Alia glimpsed a low brow,

startled blue eyes, and a wide mouth set in a monstrous face. That mouth gaped open, so the water washed into it with its cargo of sewage, and then the mouth clamped closed. A muscular back broke the water surface, with knobbly vertebrae and short hairs folded flat. As the creature swam away, vast slow bubbles broke the surface behind it.

Seer laughed coarsely. 'Rocket propulsion!'

Now Alia made out a whole school of the swimmers pushing languidly back and froth through the dense mess, chewing, farting, shitting. There were breaks in the far walls through which the swimmers passed. Perhaps this chamber was just one of a whole network that laced through the mound.

Reath smiled at Alia. 'You're starting to see it, the purpose of the place?'

'I think so. This is a sewage treatment works, isn't it? But they don't use machines, but *people*.'

The waste of the mound community poured into chambers like this. The swimmers chewed it up, shat and pissed it out, and chewed it down again. Their organs were specialised to filter and separate organic material from water, waste from recyclable goodies.

Reath said, 'It isn't so strange if you think about it. Human mothers have always produced milk for their babies. Animals pre-digest food for their young – and some even eat excrement to extract minerals. The details vary, but to do things with humans rather than machines is the way of communities like this. Somewhere in this mound there must be big-lunged air recyclers, waste removers, builders and demolishers, drones for carrying and fetching – even for disposing of the dead. And after all a human sewage processor isn't likely to break down.'

'*Drones*,' said Bale, with an expression of disgust.

'So,' said Seer, incredulous, 'if these guys keep on paddling around this toilet bowl long enough they'll turn it into soup?'

Alia leaned down, ducked her hand at the surface of the water, and raised it towards her lips. 'Needs salt, I think.'

Drea recoiled. 'Oh, you *didn't*.'

Alia grinned and showed her a clean hand.

Reath said, 'It would probably have been safe. Shall we go on?'

Berra led the way through the chamber and out to another corridor. Before they had walked much further they were taken through another door.

They found another lake, but this was of a white substance like milk. Through this paddled more swimmers. They were not big-mouthed and hairy-backed like the shit-eaters of the sewage lake, but more delicate, with thin limbs and big watchful heads. They had webbed fingers and toes. And every one of them had a swollen belly.

Drea walked forward curiously. The swimmers reacted nervously, paddling away through their lake of milk.

Reath said quickly, 'Check your face masks. Any pheromones in the air will be concentrated here.'

Drea asked, 'What is this place?'

'Can't you tell?' Alia pointed.

In the middle of the lake a woman leaned back, supported by two others. She lifted her bare hips out of the milky fluid, spread her legs – and babies slid out, two, three of them. The newborn swam around confidently, eyes open. They seemed to have no umbilical cord, no placenta. One of the babies seemed to be laughing, just heartbeats old.

The attendants who had helped with the delivery had bellies as swollen as everybody else here: they were all female, and they were all pregnant. And it was no particular coincidence that this woman had given birth the moment the visitors had walked in the door, Alia thought: no doubt there were births here all the time, every second of every day. This, of course, was the very heart of the mound.

'These are the mothers,' Berra said simply.

Alia understood. This was not really a human society at all. It was a Coalescence: it was a hive.

Chapter 30

I got a call from Shelley Magwood.

She said she had fixed a meeting with Earth Inc., the nation's largest private geoengineering concern. The purpose would be to explore ways we could leverage their expertise in macro-projects to get our nascent hydrate-stabilisation scheme off the ground – 'Actually into the ground,' as Shelley quipped. It was a crucial step for us.

But the meeting had to be face to face, Shelley said. The two of us had to go out to EI's headquarters in the Mojave desert.

I dreaded the thought of yet more flying. I complained, 'Given that these guys aspire to rebuild the Earth, demanding a meeting face to face is a bit twentieth century.'

Shelley, projected virtually to Rosa's apartment, shrugged. 'Look, we need to follow EI's lead. These guys know how to get these big projects accepted and done, and being shy about their methods at this stage isn't going to help.' She grinned, the lively-minded engineer, curious. 'Anyhow I hear they have some spectacular stuff out there.'

'Yeah, a regular save-the-world theme park,' I groused.

'Oh, come on. It's an adventure. Anyhow they have a point. Primate politics still works. Did you know that you can't fool a chimp with a VR? They just wave their hands through the images. They are too dumb to be taken in.'

'Or too smart.'

She reached out, as if to ruffle my hair. I flinched, I couldn't help it. But when it hit my flesh her VR hand broke up into pixels, little cubes of light that scattered in the air. She laughed. 'Isn't real life better? I'll meet you at JFK. We can fly on together from there.'

I said my goodbyes to Rosa.

Of course our business was unfinished, but I had caught her attention with my ghost. Rosa was a much darker character than Shelley, much more cynical and remote, and so much older, of course. But when she focused on a problem that interested her she was bright, sharp, curious, intense, just as Shelley was. They had a lot in common, I saw – even though Shelley the rationalist engineer would have been suspicious of the arcane strangeness of Rosa's life.

I endured the hours of the flight into JFK, where Shelley met me. We only had a couple of hours on the ground before we set off again on another immense seven-league-boots jaunt to LAX, and Shelley gently coaxed me through the airport processes. Already jet-lagged, I managed to sleep on this flight, but by the time we were vomited out at LAX I felt even worse.

And after that yet another flight, this time a local hop aboard a small dozen-seater passenger jet, owned and operated by EI themselves. The plane was adorned with the corporation's somewhat tasteless logo, of an Earth cupped in the palm of a human hand – 'like a wrestler illegally squeezing a testicle', as Shelley aptly said.

From LAX I had expected us to cut inland towards the Mojave, but to my surprise we headed west, out to the coast and over the ocean.

Shelley and I were the only passengers, and our drinks were served by a little rubber-wheeled bot. The plane was a very modern design, a shell of glass and ceramic full of light and air, and I could barely hear the discreet thrumming of its hydrogen-burning engines. It felt as if we were in a bubble, suspended over the sea.

The afternoon sun was low, and the water seemed like it was on fire. When I looked back towards the coast, LA was a carpet of streets and buildings, a rectangular grid like circuitry coating the contours of the land. Over the city the air was discoloured, but the vast orange smog dome I remembered from trips out this way when I was a kid had pretty much dissipated.

Shelley noticed something in the ocean. 'Look at that.' A city-sized area of the water was stained a deep green. 'What do you think it is? Maybe a sewage outlet?' But the area was a neat straight-edged square, artificial.

'Actually we'd call it a plankton bloom.' A VR popped into existence on a seat facing us. It was a man, aged maybe fifty, blond, blue-eyed, trim, his skin pale and healthy-looking. He was dressed in a neat, nondescript business suit of a style that can't have changed significantly for a century and a half. He smiled in a sensible sort of way. 'EI welcomes you to California.'

Shelley scowled; she was notoriously intolerant of such VR stunts. 'Who the hell are you?'

'Forgive me. My name is Ruud Makaay...' He was a senior executive at Earth Inc., he said, responsible for what he called 'outreach'. 'Of course this is a VR projection. I, the flesh-and-blood Ruud, will be your host today at EI – in person, once we land.' His English was smooth; later I learned he was actually Dutch.

Shelley asked, 'And that algal bloom in the ocean?'

'It is a demonstration of one of our simpler techniques. The productivity of the ocean can be stimulated with the judicious injection of certain iron compounds. The "bloom" you see is the result. The purpose is to draw down carbon dioxide in the air into the microscopic bodies of the little creatures that make up the plankton. If it's down *there*,' he said, grinning, 'it can't be up *here* in the air contributing to the greenhouse effect. To increase the effectiveness of the take-up we are experimenting with various gen-enged developments of plankton species – of which there are many, it's a whole ecology down there, you'd be surprised. Now, look over there.' He pointed to his right.

Peering down I made out a row of structures, vast but skeletal, floating on pontoons on the surface of the ocean. Each was an upright hoop within which long windmill blades turned in the wind off the sea: each a hundred metres tall, they looked like vast egg whisks. As the plane dipped over the turbines, I saw that a pale mist, like a bank of fog, lingered around the machines. Close to, the sheer scale of these lacy engines was stunning, and their shadows, cast by the setting sun, were long and graceful.

'Spray turbines,' Makaay said. 'Another of our simpler

ideas. You just spray sea water into the air, to make clouds.'

'Why?' Shelley asked. 'To trigger rain?'

'Actually the opposite,' he said. 'The purpose is to stimulate the production of the clouds themselves, and so to make them more reflective. The clouds are meant to block the sunlight...' Water droplets formed in a cloud when vapour gathered around seed particles, 'dust condensation nuclei' in Makaay's terms. The idea was to load so many nuclei into a cloud that the droplets multiplied, but none got big enough to fall as rain. So the cloud got whiter, and kept out the sunlight.

The geoengineering solutions promoted by Earth Inc. could be vast in scale, Makaay said, but were based on two simple principles. Earth intercepted heat from the sun; and an excess of carbon dioxide in the air trapped too much of that heat. So EI solutions were based either on reducing the amount of solar energy the planet soaked up in the first place, by making the Earth more reflective – 'abedo manipulation', Makaay called it – or drawing down carbon dioxide from the air, 'carbon sequestration'.

'And here, in one glance, you can see two of our solutions at work, on a demonstration scale anyhow. This is why we do our best to bring people out here in person. There is nothing like seeing things with one's own eyes to make an impression.'

Shelley eyed me. 'Primate politics,' she said. 'I told you.' She turned on Makaay. 'Even you. You're a great big tall man in a suit. Even now, all the guys at the top are just like you. When I started my working life I got a crick in my neck from looking up at my bosses all the time. It was like being in a forest.' She seemed a little out of tune to me, a touch over-aggressive, even rude. But she had never been very tolerant of managers, bureaucrats and marketeers.

Anyhow I knew what she meant. Makaay was a tall, bulky man, his sheer physical presence impressive, and his broad, heavily boned face seemed to ooze control. He was like my brother John, or my father – one of the competent-looking big men who make serious waves in the world. Not me, though. I somehow always knew I wouldn't turn out that way.

Makaay didn't seem insulted; he even seemed amused. 'Ms Magwood, I know very well I'm a walking cliché. But you have to understand I spent half my working life inside the Beltway, or in the UN and Stewardship complexes in New York or Geneva. And there, believe me, you have to wear a uniform like this –' he indicated his body – 'to be taken halfway seriously. By looking like I work for IBM, I've won half the argument already.

'It also helps that I'm Dutch, by the way. We Dutch have been geoengineers since the Middle Ages, ever since we reclaimed half our own country from the sea, and we've been exporting our expertise for as long. These days we're somewhat in demand, to help bale out drowning countries from the Pacific islands to Bangladesh.'

We were silent for a moment. It helped his moral authority, of course, that in our lifetimes Holland itself had given up its own centuries-long battle against the sea, and the Dutch had become a nation of exiles.

'You're quite a package, Mr Makaay,' Shelley said dryly.

'But, you know, it's not me who's the throwback,' he said mischievously. 'It's the pols and bureaucrats I have to deal with who have some serious evolving to do.'

Even Shelley smiled at that.

Leaving the spindly spray turbines behind we returned to the coast and flew inland.

Once we were over the Mojave we flew a circuitous route that took us over more of EI's pet projects, set up on a demonstration scale across the face of the desert. There were windmill-like factories lined up in a row; Makaay said these were designed to strip the wind of carbon dioxide by passing it over absorbing chemicals, such as calcium hydroxide. Then, following the line of a canal, an arrow-straight lane of blue cut into the desert, we flew over patches of green, fields and forests, neatly squared off and contained. I learned later that this was a land-based analogue of the plankton bloom we'd seen in the ocean; these virulently green grasses, shrubs and trees were gen-enged to soak up a lot more carbon dioxide than their wild, unmodified ancestors. The key, it seemed, was to enhance lignin content.

The most impressive constructions were silver domes, sitting in patient rows like vast golf balls. More carbon sequestration, Makaay said. The principle here was simple: to freeze carbon dioxide out of the air, thousands of tonnes at a time, and then coat it in an insulating cladding – and, well, just leave it sitting there in the desert. 'Hardly attractive, but it works,' he said.

Shelley argued with VR Makaay about the practicalities. Running a vast refrigeration plant to freeze down all that carbon dioxide was itself going to inject more heat into the atmosphere, wasn't it? Yes, but if you took a longer view, over a decade or more, the net effect was a reduction of the atmosphere's heat load through removal of the greenhouse gas. And then, no matter how efficient your insulation, there would always be some leakage, wouldn't there? So in the end you weren't actually removing the carbon from the air but just adding a time lag. Yes, admitted Makaay, but this was a simple method to apply large-scale, and at least you were buying some time while you figured out a better solution...

We had all fallen into a sceptical habit of mind, I thought, even Shelley, perhaps even myself. Geoengineering solutions always tended to brush over the complexity of the real world, notably the tangled intricacy of the biosphere – and so it was easier to do nothing than to do something big and risk making things worse. But Shelley and I were here to ask for help with some macro-engineering of our own, on a scale that would make these silver-clad golf balls look like toys.

I switched out of the conversation. As we dipped over one of those domes I could see the plane's reflection, a moth that slid across a curving face of sky blue.

Before it began its landing approach the plane banked, to head into the wind from the coast. We looped over an arid landscape populated by nothing but scrub and Joshua trees. And suddenly the ground blazed with reflected light. I made out cars, neatly parked, a carpet of glass and brightly painted metal. They looked perfect, intact and unmarked, row upon row of them.

After the Amin policy announcements had effectively robbed the gasoline automobile industry of its future, there had been years of adjustment and bale-out. In Detroit and other motor cities the assembly lines had continued to roll like a tap nobody could turn off, pumping out vehicles for which there was no longer a market. The federal government had simply bought up the excess stock and shipped them to such places as this. And here these exquisitely engineered vehicles sat, rust-free in the dry air, as if in expectation that the smog-choked days of the twentieth century might somehow return. Some of the later models were very smart, I knew, smart enough to be self-aware. I wondered if they knew where they were, if they were waiting like abandoned pets for owners that never came.

We emerged from the plane into a flat blistering heat; it was worse than Seville. I was even more impressed that EI had managed to turn bits of this desert green. Ruud Makaay met us in person at the foot of the aeroplane steps. He seemed oddly bigger than his VR representation, and his handshake was firm.

EI's buildings, at the edge of the smart tarmac of the small airfield's runway, were boxy white blocks, unimpressive. They were air-conditioned, though, and we stepped indoors with relief. Makaay led us through what looked like a regular office environment, an open-plan clutter of partitions and desks and people working at softscreens and terminals. Most of them seemed to be here in the flesh, though one or two had the fake sheen of VRs.

Makaay brought us to a small office. We sat; Makaay poured us both a coffee.

'Your place is smaller than I expected,' I ventured.

'Well, this is only the head office,' Makaay said. 'Corporate HQ. We have design facilities, labs, manufacturing plant all over the country – all over the world, in fact. And we kept this place low-key by design. We didn't want to make the mistake of having our visitors distracted by the place itself, by fountains and pot-plants and statues of the founder. Have you even been to St Paul's Cathedral, in London? The tomb of Wren, the architect, has a Latin epitaph: "Visitor, if you seek my monument, look around you." Something like that. It's the same with us. We want to make sure that what's out the window is more interesting than what's in here.'

'So,' I said, 'do you think you'll be able to help us?'

'Too early to say. Your proposal's a little thin right now,' he said dryly. 'But we'll get to that. However, now you've seen something of us, what do *you* think – do we look as if we can make your project fly?'

I thought that over. 'You're certainly more prosperous than I expected.'

'Actually I wouldn't say so. We're not rich yet, not given the size of operation we run. It's just that we play big. Everybody is surprised we have achieved any success at all, however. I think we have all got locked into a mindset that says there is no way to make money in this contracting world of ours.

'Look at it from the point of view of an industrialist in, say, 2020. The shift to hydrogen, the need for new power generation systems, the dislocation of getting rid of the automobile – even if you could get your head around such vast changes, you didn't have the infrastructure in place, the raw materials, the patents to exploit them; you didn't have things sewn up the way your daddy used to. So it was better to resist change, to keep your head down, hoping it would all go away, or at least hope the storm wouldn't break until you had finished your own career.

'It was Amin's Administration that changed all that.' He smiled fondly. 'I was in business school at the time, at Harvard. Amin's policies laid the foundation of new growth industries, in bio-infrastructure, compensation, environmental mitigation. There was money to be made in saving the world! When people realised that you saw a flurry of patents to protect technologies that were going to be key in the new political, legislative and economic environment. At Harvard our instructors told us we were privileged to be living through a shifting in the economic paradigm, perhaps the most profound since the Industrial Revolution. And people started to get rich.'

'Like EI,' Shelley said.

'Look, this company has greened an area of the Sahara the size of Texas. You only need to siphon off a little of the proceeds from such an enterprise to bring in some major profits. But it's nothing to what we could be achieving, I believe.'

There was still scepticism about EI's work, he said. The

carbon-sequestration projects had generally proven more readily acceptable because it was relatively easy to make money out of them, by earning carbon credits, or reducing your liability to carbon taxes. But, he said, the schemes appealed because they were essentially passive. 'You are fixing, not *changing*. Of course it's true that the risks of changing things are more unknowable, and therefore greater.'

Shelley said, 'Such as Cephalonia.'

Makaay leaned forward, passion showing in his pale eyes. 'I was on the clean-up team. I haven't forgotten. We are engineers, the three of us; you understand. *Things go wrong*. We learn from mistakes. We fix them. Nothing like Cephalonia has happened again, or will. And it mustn't stop us trying again.

'But we do need to reassure people, I accept that. Our lawyers are trying to agree a code of conduct for geoengineers at UNESCO. A kind of Hippocratic oath, if you will, a pledge that we will use our powers responsibly. If that is accepted perhaps we can start to build trust once and for all. And then we can really get on with the job.'

Shelley said, 'OK. But do you think we've a chance of getting the support we need for the hydrate-stabilisation project?'

He sat back. 'It's not impossible. It's a question of how you sell it. Your project is vast in scale, and that will instinctively repel a lot of people. But it's essentially passive, like our carbon-sequestration programmes. You aren't meddling; you're simply trying to maintain an equilibrium. So perhaps we can avoid a few philosophical obstacles on the way. We have a lobbying firm we use in Washington; they'll be able to advise.'

At his use of the word *lobbying* I quailed; the world of high politics was not one where I would feel comfortable.

Shelley noticed this and smiled. 'We have to do this, kiddo. We're talking about a major international effort here – billions of dollars of investment. We have to deal with the big boys.'

Makaay's expression was friendly, engaged, but reserved, consummately professional. 'I can't say yet if we'll support you. Our board has to make the decision. It's a big ask for us. But I do believe that your project is exactly what EI was founded to do in the first place.' He stood and paced around the little office. 'I see an opportunity, for all of us. We need a success. And once we have shrugged off our anxiety about "meddling", the opportunities are vast.

'Look – call me a progressive. I want to build a world with room for as many happy, well-fed and healthy people as we can cram in. What's wrong with that? But obviously I also want to do it without wrecking the environment in the process.' The two levers of geoengineering, he said, carbon sequestration and albedo control, were actually independent of each other. 'Now, an increase in carbon dioxide has some beneficial effects: plant growth is stimulated, for example. So suppose we let the carbon levels rise, but kept the temperature under control with albedo modification? *That* might be the way to advance our civilisation to a new optimum, while protecting the planet.

'And we can go further,' he said. 'This Bottleneck will teach us to cooperate on a planetary scale. Then we will be able to reach beyond the Earth altogether. We can reserve the Earth simply for doing what it is best at, to support the most complex biosphere we know, and use the resources of space to escape the constraints of closed planetary economics...'

Shelley stood up to stop his flow. 'Terrific. But in the meantime, do you have an office where we can set up?'

He grinned, self-deprecating. 'Quite right. Let's get to work.'

As we followed him out of the room, Shelley whispered to me, 'Call him Prospero.'

'Who?'

'Don't you remember your Shakespeare? *The Tempest.* Prospero called down a storm; he was an early geoengineer.'

'Didn't he cause a shipwreck?'

Shelley raised her eyebrows, and we walked on.

Chapter 31

By Alia's time eusocial living was nearly as old as mankind. The first human eusociety, the first hive, had in fact been born on old Earth, in the brief interval before spaceflight.

It was a solution to the dilemmas of cramped living which tended to emerge when a community was isolated, when resources were short, when it was difficult to strike out away from home. Reath said, 'Anywhere you can't get away from Mom, this is the way you end up living. It's a feature of our neural processing, I believe – some would say a deep flaw. But it's undoubtedly a part of the human story.'

It always began with social pressures. If adult children stayed home, they would compete with their parents for resources. So a mother bullied her daughter into having fewer children, or none at all, and made her devote her energies to her sisters. Families extended into great conflations of sisters and cousins and aunts, all childless, all tending the needs of the children of a single mother.

Ultimately this served the needs of the genes, or it would never have worked at all. A human was more closely related genetically to her daughter than to her niece. But if by living eusocially you could preserve more nieces than you would have had daughters, you could give your genes, though indirectly, a greater chance of survival.

And then, when the social pressures were locked in, natural selection took over.

As the generations ticked by, as a drone you adapted to the environment you found yourself trapped in: the environment of the Coalescence. Individual creatures, the building bricks of a higher organism, were modified in different ways to serve the needs of the colony as a whole for nutrition, physical support, locomotion, excretion, even reproduction.

And why waste energy on the vast bodily reengineering of puberty if you were never going to have a child? Daughters were born in whom the ability to reproduce was postponed – or never cut in at all.

And then there was intelligence. Eusociality required a tight central organisation. With the mother and her precious babies at the heart, concentric circles of childless workers served the mother and infants, constructed and maintained the colony, gathered food, fended off predators. But there was no command structure. Workers picked up cues from those around them and acted accordingly, and out of this network of endless local interactions arose the global structure of the colony as a whole. This was emergence: from simple rules, applied at a local level and with some feedback, large-scale structures could develop.

Minds were not necessary for this. Indeed, it was better *not* to know what was going on globally; the colony, emergent from everybody's small-scale actions, simply worked more effectively that way.

Better not to know that you were in a hive.

Alia gazed at the swimming mothers. 'All this in half a million years. What will they become in five million years – or fifty, or five hundred?'

Reath said, 'Up to now no human hive has become more closely integrated than a colonial organism. But the evolutionary process has barely begun. Alia, in a sense *you* are a hive! You are a composite of perhaps a hundred trillion cells, each of them one of several hundred different specialist types – muscle, blood, nervous. You are the ultimate outcome of an evolutionary decision of the ancestors of your cells, which were once individual entities, to cooperate some six hundred million years ago... I suppose there is no limit to the integration which is possible with time.' He shook his head. 'The end result is unimaginable.'

'I don't understand why we're here.'

'Alia, hives are repulsive things. But they are useful.'

Eusocieties were *stable*, and very long-lived, typically enduring many multiples of the lifespans of their members. And that made Coalescents good archivists. A Coalescence was a mound of natural clerks and librarians. 'Coalescences have been used as information processors and stores for most of human history. That's why they are so useful for the Redemption project.'

The Campocs were more sceptical. Bale faced Alia. 'Hives are useful, yes. But if you want to know what it *feels* like to be a drone, go back to the Transcendence.'

Alia was shocked by Bale's comparison of the mindless fecund swarming of the Coalescents with the lofty ambition of the Transcendence. There was no similarity – was there?

At last Berra took them to the mound's deepest levels, to the chamber of the Listeners.

This chamber was low and flat. Its floor was empty save for a few low constructions, and it was lit by lanterns studded at random in the roof. But as Alia peered around she saw that these dim constellations went on and on, blurring in the distance into a single band of light. This one chamber had to be kilometres wide, perhaps more.

Bale stared at the ceiling. 'I wonder what's holding up the weight of the mound.'

Drea snorted. 'You're very literal, aren't you, Rustie?'

Alia walked forward to the nearest of the low structures on the floor. It was a box no more than waist-high. She found a disc of some translucent substance set in its wall. When she passed her hand before the disc a spot of light, a very faint blue, showed up on her palm. She asked, 'Lasers?' Glancing around, she imagined a network of the beams criss-crossing the huge chamber.

And now she heard a scuttling, glimpsed a hunched form. It ran through the shadows, hurrying from the cover of one of the laser boxes to another. It had huge eyes, eyes like saucers.

Drea said dryly, 'I take it that was a Listener. Another specialist drone type?'

Alia said, 'I suppose so. But what do they listen to?'

Berra said, 'To the echoes of time.'

The Listeners were here to help the Transcendence achieve Redemption.

The Transcendence did not see itself as an end for which the desolation of past lives had merely been a necessary

means. It believed it must somehow redeem the past, if it were to be cleansed – if it were to be perfect. But once the goal of Redemption had been formulated, the nascent Transcendence had had to face profound questions. *How* was the past to be redeemed?

Colleges of Redemption were established to address this question. At the very least, it was soon realised, the Transcendence – and indeed the mankind from which it arose – must be aware of the past, so that the past could be taken into the awareness of the Transcendence, a part of its eternal whole.

In the first attempts, vast museums were established. Many of them were virtual, shared between worlds, with no single physical presence. And in these museums immense dioramas were shown, great events of the past brought before the eyes of the present, based on the best reconstructions of the historians and archaeologists.

But it was not enough.

For one thing the present was an imperfect window on the past. Human records were always incomplete, and often full of lies. Of course there were physical traces to be retrieved, and legions of new archaeologists descended on all the worlds of mankind, and especially Earth. Some elements of the past were recorded in the genetic legacy of mankind itself, still carried within human bodies, even though they had been scattered across the Galaxy, morphing and changing as they went. But various catastrophic events, natural or otherwise, had left huge blanks in all such records.

And no matter how complete the records might be, there was still the question of interpretation – of the meaning of the events, the motivations and intentions of the characters of the times, many so remote from the Transcendents as to be practically another species. A new generation of historians sprang up, arguing over differences of meaning great and small.

It was all very unsatisfactory. So, even as the first dioramas were established, efforts continued to deepen and widen the Redemption. And at last a new way to excavate the past was discovered.

On the *Nord*, only very small children thought the universe was infinite. Just because it *looked* that way didn't make it so, any more than the apparent flatness of a planet meant it really was an infinitely flat plane. The universe was finite: closed, folded over on itself. To Alia the finiteness of the universe was as obvious and intuitive as, to an Earthborn child, it was obvious that the sun was a star.

And this was useful. As the Transcendence had sought ways to recover its past, it had fallen on the closure of the universe. For time and space were not separate entities but merged into one unity, spacetime. And so in a finite universe *the closure must be complete in time as well as in space*. Just as one side of the universe was connected to the other, so the very far future was connected to the very remote past.

And that was how you could detect the past: by listening for its echoes.

The finite universe had a topology, a connectedness imposed at the Big Bang, the instant of the initial singularity. Sitting inside the universe, you couldn't see that topology directly. But there were ways to sense its presence. Alia had once had a toy, a virtual game. It was like a slab of sky inside a cubical box. Battling spacecraft, black alien bad guys and heroic Exultant greenships, would slide through the sky, firing cherry-red beams at each other. But the game wasn't confined to the walls of the box. If a ship hit a wall, it would disappear – but would reappear on the other side of the box, heading the same way. So, even though they were separated in space, the points on each wall mapped precisely onto the corresponding points on the opposite wall. It was as if the whole of the universe was tiled, filled with identical copies of the game, joined side to side. Once you got used to it you could use the strange folded-over property as part of your tactics; you could send your greenships to sneak around the universe's 'curve' and fall on the aliens from behind.

And you could play other games. You could imagine setting off an explosion somewhere in the box. A spherical shock wave would set off in all directions. It would stay a simple sphere until the front passed through the walls of the box, after which it would fold around and intersect itself, forming circular arcs all over the place. Alia could see that if you sat in the middle of the box and watched those shock-circles blossoming all over your sky, you could use the pattern to figure out the geometry of your box-cosmos. The whole of spacetime was a lens, shaping the radiation that washed through it.

The Listeners' purpose was to explore the tremendous diffraction of spacetime. They mapped gravity waves, ripples in spacetime itself, deep and long, spreading at lightspeed from the universe's most titanic events: the explosive deaths of stars and galaxy cores, the collisions of black holes and galaxies. Gravity ripples passed further than any other, and they offered, indirectly, the clearest possible map of the universe, its structure, and its contents.

'Remarkable,' Reath breathed. 'And so these "Listeners" watch the laser light with those big eyes of theirs. These long light beams are sensitive to disturbance by the gravity waves which wash through the core of the planet.' Strangely, some gravity waves, when converted to sound, were audible to human ears. The Listeners actually heard the chirp of colliding neutron stars, the warble of one black hole absorbing another.

The gravity-wave echoes washed around the closed universe, from pole to pole – and from future to past. The information the Listeners sought from their gravity waves wasn't just about the great physical events of the universe. It was about the history of mankind.

The Transcendence had conceived a great project. It would build a probe which it would send into the furthest future, and thereby hurl it into the deepest past. And there, hiding in the dark at the rim of Sol system, this monitor from the future would witness the unfolding of mankind's deepest history – and it would send the whole complex story back around the curve of the closed universe to the great entity that had constructed it. The Listeners recorded these whispers, sent from the deepest past to the furthest future. Once retrieved, the news from history was analysed and stored in Coalescent archives.

Thus the past was brought into the present of the Transcendence. And, buried somewhere in that immense lode of data mined from the past, was the wormlike thread of Michael Poole's biography.

*

Reath disturbed Alia from her absorption. It was as if she came back to herself, back to the dismal cavern of the Listeners, from a dream of cosmic unity.

Reath studied her, analytical but uneasy. 'Have you learned enough?'

She frowned, thinking. 'I've learned how we recover the past. But I've yet to learn how we use that information. It isn't over yet, Reath.'

He sat beside her. 'So we go on. Alia, I'm concerned you're becoming sidetracked from your true purpose.'

She returned his gaze blankly. 'What does it matter to you? I thought you said it's up to me to find my own way into the Transcendence. Isn't that exactly what I'm doing?'

'You have tasted the Transcendence, but you are still alone, still Alia. And it is *Alia's* curiosity you are indulging. If you only gave yourself up to the Transcendence, all your doubts and questions would wash away. I've seen it many times before.' He clearly meant that to be reassuring, and perhaps it would have seemed so once, but now his bland assurances chilled her. 'And besides,' he went on, 'are you sure these questions you have come from your own heart? Don't forget these Campocs blackmailed you into this whole line of questioning about the Redemption.'

She said coldly, 'The Campocs' methods were primitive. Brutal. But the questions they raised are valid. Reath, I want to resolve all my doubts before the Transcendence swallows me up. Is that so hard to understand?'

Reath frowned. 'Your language of "swallowing up" is inappropriate. The Transcendence is an augmentation, not a diminishing.'

But I'd rather be alone and sane, Alia thought darkly, than conjoined into a vast insanity. I have to be sure. But she couldn't possibly say that to Reath, of course.

The Listeners seemed to be getting used to the visitors' presence. They scuttled back and forth across the floor of their chamber, their huge eyes capturing the flickering of their light beams.

Drea stared at them in disgust. 'This is a terrible place.'

Suddenly Alia felt confined, trapped, buried under this great mound of tunnelled-through dirt. She turned to Reath.

'Let's get out of here—'

Berra gasped. She reached out to Alia, who recoiled.

Reath took Alia's arm. 'Try to be calm,' he murmured. 'Don't alarm her further. We need her guidance to get out of here before—'

'Before what?'

'Before she fulfils her final duty to the hive.'

'What final duty? What's wrong with her?'

'Why, don't you see? She needs to keep us here, for as long as she can. She needs *you*, Alia.'

Berra had been born with the potential for intelligence. But she had probably never been fully conscious, self-aware – not before Alia arrived.

'Because,' Alia said slowly, 'it's best if a drone doesn't know she's a drone.'

'Yes. Which is why, in most hives, drones shed their higher cognition. But there are circumstances when intelligence is too useful to lose altogether – when the Coalescence is attacked, for example, or has to be moved.'

'Or when a Transcendent-Elect comes asking questions,' Alia said.

'Yes. Alia, Berra lucked out. She was just the interfacer who happened to be closest when we came calling. She may not even have known our language before she was needed. She probably didn't even have a *name* before, because it was better that she didn't. It was as if she woke up, for the first time in her life, the moment you walked through the door.'

'But now we're leaving,' Alia said. 'She can go back to the way she was. Can't she?'

Reath shook his head. 'Alia, Berra has served the hive well. But now she knows too much: she knows who she is, *that she is a drone*. And she has nowhere else to go. Alia, she will be dead before we leave the planet.'

Alia stared in horror at Berra. The little drone seemed to be collapsing on herself, as if imploding, still staring at Alia. Alia couldn't stand it. She Skimmed away, right out of there, out of the heart of the hive.

She found herself standing on the rusty plain once more. She ripped off her face mask and sucked in the dust-laden air.

Chapter 32

While we worked with Ruud Makaay on fleshing out EI's involvement in our gas-hydrates project, Shelley and I stayed in Palm Springs. We were guests of EI in a grand, somewhat faded hotel. Its outer shell had been Painted so that it glittered silver in the dry sunlight like a vast, complicated Christmas-tree bauble. Inside there was a gigantic pool, and an even bigger bar, where a robot pianist gently played Chopin. But no guests.

Shelley had a lot of work to do, as always. She worked eight or nine hours every day, some of it with Makaay and the EI staff. But she also kept in contact with clients, suppliers and contacts all around the world, and those nine work-hours were scattered randomly through each twenty-four. She worked in the hotel's small computer-aided-design booth, in her swimsuit or a fluffy hotel bathrobe, surrounded by VR visitors, or ghostly circuitry plans, or mock-ups of intricate mechanical assemblies. She had an admirable capacity to function well at three in the morning, and catnap at four in the afternoon.

So I spent a fair bit of time alone. It was close to midsummer and off season, and Palm Springs had an echoing, empty feel. The twentieth-century wealth and ease of transportation that had built the place had drained away, leaving a glittering relic in the desert air. It wasn't so bad for me. I felt as if I'd been through a lot, and Palm Springs, big and depopulated, was a good place to let the tension drain away. If only I played golf the place would have been perfect, I thought; the robot pros would have let me win every time.

Shelley and I did spend spare time together. We ate, swam, walked, talked. I was always fond of Shelley. Competent, engaged, humorous, at ease in her life and her work, she was the kind of human being that I'd always aspired to be. And I think she was fond of me too, even though compared to her I was a no-hoper – never reliable, always inclined to flakiness. But I was 'never short of ideas', she would sometimes say. You needed somebody around to come up with the impulse to *do* things, and I was a source of that – as witness our hydrate-stabilisation project itself.

For sure a life with Shelley, who was sane, engaged, and *alive*, would have been good for me – if not always for her. But it was never going to happen, because, as she had said herself, Morag was always there, for better or worse as attached to me as my right arm, and there was no point behaving as if it wasn't so. I sometimes regretted that fact. I think Shelley did a little too. But our relationship had its place in my notional spectrum of possibilities. So it goes.

I talked to Rosa in Seville a few times. She was 'digging up old ghost stories', she told me a bit mysteriously. Sometimes she spooked me herself: behind her small face, so accurately reproduced by the hotel's VR systems, I felt I glimpsed the shadowy conclaves of the Vatican, great mounds of knowledge that had accumulated for two millennia – and, perhaps, even stranger archives still.

After seven days Ruud Makaay called us back to his Mojave headquarters, where, he said, he was calling a seminar on our proposals.

We gathered in a conference room in the EI compound. The room itself was a clear-walled cube. There was a long table with a dozen chairs, evidently a mix of real and VR seamlessly joined. That was all there was; the room felt unfinished, a sketch. But in a virtual economy you flaunted your wealth by showing less.

Makaay, Shelley and I were the only flesh-and-blood attendees. Tom and Sonia Dameyer projected in. I took a seat beside Tom, real and unreal side by side at the same table. I was inordinately glad to see him; I still hadn't got over that Siberia experience, if I ever would. Tom looked uncomfortable to be here, though.

Vander Guthrie from the Global Ecosystems Analyser facility in Oklahoma materialised out of the air. He looked as awkward as ever, his hair's sky-blue tint ridiculous, and he grinned nervously at me. And he carried a little toy robot that he set on the tabletop. The robot rolled experimentally back and forth, friction sparks emanating from its plastic belly. In a tinny outer-space voice it proclaimed, 'The table's a little slippery, but I think I can cope.'

'Oh, for God's sake,' Tom groused. 'Dad, what is this, a circus?'

'Gea is supporting us. It's significant, Tom.'

'It's ridiculous, is what it is. What am I doing here?'

I longed to touch his hand. 'If not for you none of us would be here. Just take it easy and follow your heart.'

Tom snorted, but sat still.

On his other side, Sonia caught my eye and smiled faintly. *He'll be OK.* I was grateful for the wordless message, and glad she was there, sane and calm. Sanity and calmness do seem to be in short supply in my bloodline.

Ruud Makaay, sleek and competent as ever, pinged the water glass in front of him with his fingernail. 'May I call us to order? Thank you all for being here, one way or another...'

Our purpose, he said, was to review the work done so far on fleshing out the hydrate-stabiliser scheme, and to decide on next steps.

Tom was immediately suspicious, even hostile. 'Next steps? Such as you taking the whole thing over so you can get rich drilling fucking great holes in the North Pole?'

I said quickly, 'Tom, take it easy. The EI people are helping us out here.'

'Oh, *sure.*'

If Makaay was perturbed by this unpromising opening he didn't show it. 'For now let's build on what we have in common, rather than focus on our differences. Can we agree on that much?'

The Gea robot rolled back and forth. I wondered what she made of all this interpersonal, typically human bullshit. And yet, I supposed, she depended absolutely on people, with all our imperfections, to get things done; she had to put up with us.

Shelley took the cue. 'Shall I start?' She stood, walked to

the head of the table, and with waves of her hands began to conjure up VR images of complicated bits of engineering, gleaming and flawless. The core of it was a device shaped something like a bullet, with a complicated tracery of flanges and ducts engraved on its nose. At its heart I saw a spark, a soul in the machinery. Shelley produced a variety of representations of this thing, some transparent, cutaway or exploded. 'We call this a mole,' she said. 'It's the cornerstone of our design. But each mole will be small, no larger than a clenched fist...'

To stabilise the hydrate strata it would be necessary to thread it with coolant pipes, just as in our original back-of-the-envelope sketch. The teams Shelley had gathered to flesh out the idea were adhering to that basic design. And they were still assuming that liquid nitrogen, drawn down as a gas from the air and then cooled and liquefied, would be the working fluid. You'd pass the nitrogen through the underground pipes where it would evaporate back to a gas, in the process drawing in heat from the hydrate layers, and then it would be sucked out of the pipes for recondensing. That way you would effectively pump heat out of the ground.

But to stabilise a band of hydrates that passed right around the pole of the planet we would need hundreds of thousands of kilometres of pipe. It just wasn't practical to fabricate and implant so much.

'Which is where the mole comes in,' Shelley said. 'It will be like a self-propelled drill bit.' The flanged nose on the most solid representation whirred, its function obvious. 'And it will lay tunnels, not pipes. It will simply burrow its way through the ground, just like a mole. But the tunnel it digs out won't be allowed to collapse.' She indicated a range of little devices attached to the side of the mole. 'We will shore up the tunnel as we go, using local materials. The precise technique will depend on what we find down there, which is going to vary according to the local geology... The walls of the tunnel will themselves be smart, of course, and capable of some limited self-repair, though in case of major breaches such as through seismic movement we can always send down more moles.

'We will send in hundreds of moles, thousands maybe.

Each mole will make most of its own decisions down there, learning as it goes. But we can communicate with it through the pipe it leaves behind. We're also experimenting with sonar and electromagnetic pulses, so the moles can communicate with each other even without a direct connection.'

Sonia said, 'So they will hear each other digging away in the rock. A whole community, tunnelling, tunnelling.'

'That's the idea,' Shelley said. The overall design was straightforward. The moles wouldn't be going terribly deep, and wouldn't face challenging temperatures or pressures; the materials technology we needed was well within the envelope of experience of the mining industry. 'And the smartness, of course, is trivial.'

Makaay asked, 'And what about power?'

Shelley nodded at me. 'That's where Michael's expertise comes in.' She tapped that glowing spark at the heart of her conceptual mole. 'This is a Higgs energy reactor, the most concentrated energy source we have. The mole's heart will be a cube the size of a sugar lump, which will deliver it enough energy to tunnel through ten thousand kilometres – that's our design goal, we may achieve more.'

Tom turned to me. 'You can build such things, the sugar lumps?'

I said, 'We can take them off the shelf, almost. We've been working towards such devices for a long time, Tom. For a while we've been good at making very small, very smart gadgets. So if you can make a power source equally compact you have a powerful technology...'

Now that power supplies were catching up with miniaturisation, the agencies and companies I consulted for were developing, among other things, miniature robotic engineers designed to go places humans couldn't, such as to check out undersea pipes and cables, or the interiors of antiquated nuclear reactors. The space community was designing a new generation of unmanned exploratory robots, swarms of them the size of oranges or smaller, which could be scattered on the surface of Mars, or in the clouds of Venus or Jupiter, or sent swimming in the ice-cloaked seas of Europa. These tiny probes would work for years, individually and cooperatively, smart enough even to design their own science programmes

on the spot. Even on Earth tiny distributed sentiences were even making new kinds of science possible. You could spray smart motes around a forest, let them self-organise, and begin to gather data, in three dimensions and real time, on the detailed behaviour of macro-climates and macro-ecologies across a significant volume. All of this would be enabled by Higgs technology, by grains of an energy field that had once caused the universe itself to expand, each providing years of power.

Tom seemed impressed despite himself. Perhaps he did have some engineer's genes in him after all.

With most components coming off the shelf, Ruud Makaay thought it would be possible to have some kind of field trial up and running within mere weeks. Earth Inc. took on immense projects, but it was a nimble organisation, it seemed, capable of reacting quickly.

The discussion descended into technicalities.

Vander, prompted by Gea, pressed Shelley with some tough questions. Vander, as he spoke, had a strange way of sitting, alternately lounging then coming bolt upright, startling you. It was the way you might behave if you were alone, not in company. And that shock of blue hair made him hard to take seriously, despite the sharpness of his mind.

I suspected that Vander's problem came from that ill-advised genetic engineering, performed long before he was born. Changing the colour of his hair was one thing, but I was pretty sure Mr and Mrs Guthrie had taken the opportunity to upgrade little Vander's IQ as well. The problem with that was what the neuro-anatomists and behavioural geneticists called pleiotropy: most genes perform more than one function, and that's certainly true of the complexes of genes that seem to control levels of intelligence. So you could boost IQ, but we still weren't smart enough to avert unwelcome side-effects. It was an irony that only parents not smart enough to be able to grasp this in the first place would inflict such risky genetic meddling on their unborn children. Poor Vander.

Tom seemed fascinated by Vander, his peculiar, twitchy manner, his uncertain voice. I thought he ought to be grateful Morag and I hadn't been so dumb as to do this to him.

Shelley handled most of Vander's questions, though we had to flag some issues to resolve later. Most of the problems Vander and Gea raised came from the fact that the design was still at a conceptual level, and Shelley just didn't have the depth of detail yet. I couldn't see that any showstoppers emerged, however.

When the technical questions ran down, Sonia leaned forward. 'You said these moles will be smart enough to make their own choices. *How* smart?'

Shelley checked a softscreen. 'Each mole will be three times as smart as a human. But in a narrow way. Special-ised.'

Sonia said, 'But smart machines have a way of thinking for themselves, don't they? Military systems are gener-ally kept dumb, you know. Everybody jokes they are even dumber than the brass. But you can see why they have to be that way. You don't want a weapon system or a piece of armour to be thinking about what it should do; you want it to do what you tell it, the instant you tell it. And now we're going to let loose a swarm of these super-smart moles into the crust of the planet? How do you *know* they will do what they're supposed to do?'

Shelley said evenly, 'Because it will be in their own best interests. A mole is designed for burrowing, for laying tun-nel, for talking to its fellows. It will be as natural as walking, talking, hugging a child is for you. The mole won't *want* to do anything else. And as for the greater goal, each mole will be smart enough to understand the greater mission, the impelling problem. We'll put each one through an education programme to make sure.'

Sonia said, 'OK, but they can still make choices, can't they?'

'Sonia, I understand your concerns, but I wouldn't worry about it,' Shelley said. 'To us this is a detail. Motivation en-gineering is a well-established discipline – in fact a subset of animism, Vander's speciality.'

Sonia couldn't have looked less reassured. But I knew Shelley was right. There were actually philosophical argu-ments that endowing our machines with all this sentience and self-awareness was morally wrong, especially since their choice was usually limited, their freedom illusory. And I remembered my own helpless suspicions when first confronted with Gea. But there was nothing to fear from our artificial sentiences: despite our innate worries, the ghost of Frankenstein was laid long ago.

Makaay called a bio break. We pushed our seats back from the table, and dispersed.

Tom and Sonia approached me. Tom had a mug of coffee; the vapour curled up convincingly from his virtual mug, and it struck me as odd that I couldn't smell the cinnamon.

Tom said, 'Dad, these are seriously scary people you're dealing with here.'

'You mean EI?'

'Have you never *heard* of Cephalonia?'

I repressed the urge to snap back. 'We live in complicated times, Tom.'

'Yeah, right.'

Ruud Makaay touched my arm. 'Michael, I'm sorry to take you away from your son, but there's somebody here who wants to meet you...'

It was another VR presence, of a bulky, business-suited man, sweating heavily. 'Hey, Mike. I bet you don't recognise me.'

I did, but he was such an incongruous presence I took a moment to place the name. 'Jack Joy. The Swimmer.'

He made a shooting-the-gun gesture at me with one fat hand. 'We shared a plane journey together.'

'How could I forget?'

'Listen, you're surprised to see me here, right?'

I shrugged. 'Of course I am.'

'After our talk on the plane, you never used that card I gave you.' I tried to apologise, but he waved it away. 'No matter. I'm a curious guy,' Jack said. 'And you interested me. You told me about your kid in Siberia, remember. After that I looked up about those gas deposits, and the danger, and all of that. And then I heard from a friend of a friend that you were involved in some kind of scheme to stabilise them. I was intrigued. So I found you.'

'How?'

'Through your brother John.' He grinned. 'I never met him before, but he's a Swimmer too. Did you know that?'

Lethe. 'I suppose I suspected.'

'Anyhow, through him to you, and here I am. And I've been watching the show. Very interesting.'

'I hope you don't mind me inviting Mr Joy,' Makaay said, but he had nothing to apologise for. He had warned us in advance that we would be monitored by others in his organisation, and by representatives of potential supporters and sponsors.

I said, 'It's fine. But I don't see what interest the Swimmers have in a project like this.'

Jack shook his head. 'Oh ye of little faith. You really should look us up, Mike. I'm here to see if we can help, we Swimmers.'

'*You*? You want to support the stabilisation project?'

He shrugged, as if graciously accepting my gratitude. 'Any way we can, if we think it's the right thing to do. We have deep pockets, actually. You might be surprised.'

'But why would you want to?'

'Because it's serious, if you're right about these damn gas deposits blowing their stack. We're pragmatists, OK? We don't believe in denial. Your brother is a pragmatist too. And also we may be able to act long before our various governments and intergovernmental bodies and all the rest of the bureaucratic mound on top of us get their thumbs out of each others' asses. You may need us, Mike,' he said, with a kind of overweight persuasiveness.

'Michael,' I said. 'Call me Michael.'

'Actually Mr Joy may be right,' Ruud Makaay said smoothly. 'We are critically short of funding. We need money to develop the concept to the point where the governments will give us money to develop the concept...' He shook his head. 'It's a vicious circle, an old story, I'm afraid.'

VR Jack said, 'We want to be your friends, we really do. I'll be waiting.' And with a nod to both of us he disappeared.

Tom approached me. 'More complications, Dad? How long a spoon do you need to sup with the likes of *him*?'

Makaay called us back to order. Confused by Jack's intervention I took my seat again.

Shelley presented the next logical level of our tentative design.

She showed how moles, inserted into the earth and dispersing from some central point, would fan out, spreading their narrow tunnels behind them as they did so. Some of the moles would move around circumferential arcs as well as radially, so that a multiply-connected network, rather like a three-dimensional spider's-web, would develop within the hydrate beds.

'The network will grow incrementally,' Shelley said. 'We have to follow a phased approach, simply because it's going to take time to ramp up the industrial capacity to churn out all those moles, all those condensers and collectors. And besides, nobody has ever run a pipe network on anything like this scale before. The moles will take some time to figure out the best way to do it.'

This was the modern approach to engineering. You let your machines, loaded with as much smartness as possible, figure things out for themselves, and then learn from the way they did it. That way, not only was there a good chance you'd end up with an optimal design at the finish, but you could expect that at every stage you would move from one optimum configuration to another. It was like climbing a hill, Shelley said, in such a way that you didn't just aim for the peak but at every stage took the best path available.

'So in the end,' Tom said, 'it will all merge together into a single vast cap of silicon brain embedded in the floor of the polar ocean. Talk about hubris!'

Ruud Makaay said ruefully, 'Believe me, that word is already carved on my tombstone. All I can say is that we geoengineers would never take on a project like this if there was any choice.'

'But there is no choice,' Gea said in her small, absurd voice.

Tom said, 'There's still something I don't get. I'm no engineer, but I do recall some high school thermodynamics. You're keeping those hydrate deposits cool; you're pumping the heat out with your liquid nitrogen. But where is all that heat going *to*? It can't just disappear, can it?'

'It certainly can't,' said Shelley. She patiently explained that our mechanism would end up dumping its heat into the ocean, and the air.

'This will be the hardest part of the sell, I fear,' Makaay said. 'Because it is going to be very hard for our paymasters to understand.'

'Well, there's no magic involved,' Shelley said. 'All that heat has to go somewhere. But the net injection of heat into the environment will be trivial compared to the catastrophic rise in temperature that would result if the hydrates' vast store of greenhouse gases were released to do their worst. And anyhow we can always mitigate the effects of any heat injection with albedo control... It's a necessary evil,' Shelley said.

Sonia said, 'I don't think I understand.'

Tom laughed. 'They're going to pump all that heat out of the hydrate layers and into the air. The whole point is to stop the world from heating up. But to do that we're going to have to make the problem *worse*. What a joke.'

The Gea robot said, 'There are many aspects of the present predicament of mankind that are ironic,' she said. 'It is indeed all a vast joke. Ha ha.' And she rolled back and forth, friction sparks cascading.

Chapter 33

Alia, seeking guidance, sought the Transcendence.

To rejoin the Transcendence was easy, even here, on the hive-world. When she called, the strange constellation of minds simply gathered around her. Once you had been a part of the Transcendence, you never really left it; it was always in the background of your life, always waiting to take you in once more.

It was exactly like an addiction, Alia thought uneasily.

But now she sensed a kind of restlessness. The Transcendence, aware of its own imperfections and incompleteness, struggled to be born – and laced through it all was that nagging guilt over the bloodiness of the past from which it was emerging.

She looked back at herself, Alia, her own nugget-like awareness embedded in the greater whole. To be part of the Transcendence was to be overwhelmed by perspectives, human and superhuman, that overlapped and clashed. On one level she struggled to maintain her sense of identity and purpose, and to unravel her doubts about the Redemption – but at the same time she was faintly ashamed of herself. Who was *she* to question a mass mind founded on the wisdom of others far older and wiser than she was? Even now, unready as she felt, she could simply give herself up to the greater whole. She could put aside Alia, like a memory of childhood; she could immerse herself in the Transcendence, and never surface again...

Which was what it wanted, she realised. For her nagging questions, lodged deep within its own consciousness, made the Transcendence uncomfortable. She couldn't take credit for causing this conflict within the Transcendence, but her questions were opening wounds, sharpening a conflict that already existed.

She clung to herself, like a defiant child who wouldn't say sorry. This was a genuine dilemma for the Transcendence, and she had a duty to keep asking her questions: *What is the true purpose of the Redemption? What is its ultimate goal? What does it cost? And – how far will you take it?*

The constellations of pinpoint minds seemed to swim around her – and then they came together with a shocking rush. She saw a human face, a small, round, worn face, with eyes like bits of diamond.

And she heard a voice, resounding inside her head. 'You won't give up, will you, child?'

'I only want—'

'What you want doesn't matter. What the Transcendence wants is for your doubts to be replaced by certainty. For, you see, it seeks certainty itself. You know that the impulse for Redemption comes from the communities of the undying. And so you must meet the undying, the oldest of all. You must meet *me*. My name is Leropa. Find me.'

'Where?'

Suddenly she was pushed out of the Transcendence.

She was back in her own body, back on Reath's shuttle. She lay on a couch. Reath and Drea hovered over her, concerned. But the three Campocs had backed against a partition, huddled together like frightened children. It struck her that joining the Transcendence was like being ill.

And that strange face, Leropa's face, hovered in the air before her. Alia cried out. It was as if she had woken, but her nightmare still haunted her.

It, *she*, Leropa, glanced dismissively at the Campocs. 'They can hear me, with their little web of minds. I'm invisible to the others.'

Alia struggled to sit up. 'Where must I go? Tell me.'

'Earth,' the woman said.

And then the face was gone – not broken up or dispersed, simply gone from Alia's field of view, as if she had turned her head away.

Had any of it happened? Had this strange woman Leropa

really come swimming out of the Transcendence to address her? Had she really talked of Earth?

The Campocs remained jammed up against each other, trembling, watching her fearfully, and Drea stared at her, baffled, concerned.

Chapter 34

I spoke to Rosa again. She told me, 'There has been an up-surge in sightings – hauntings, poltergeist phenomena, you name it – all over the planet.'

'Really? I had no idea.'

She snorted. 'Why would you? You would not look in the places where you might discover such things. Nor would I, in normal times. But, prompted by your experiences, I have been researching. You aren't alone, Michael, for better or worse. The whole world is suddenly haunted! *And this has happened before.* History shows it; there have been previous plagues of ghosts. Now, what do you suppose this means?'

I had no idea. I didn't know whether to be reassured or terrified.

I felt guilty about working on this stuff in the middle of the hydrate project. I kept it a secret from Tom, Shelley and the others. It was like I was looking at porn. But I did it. And I summoned Rosa, like raising a VR ghost, to my Palm Springs hotel room.

In the flimsy gaudiness of the room, with its late-twentieth-century American tourist chic, Rosa was a dark, sullen mass, small and hunched, her priest's robes so black they seemed to suck the light out of the air. When she first appeared she seemed disconcerted. She looked around as if finding it hard to focus. Then she saw me, and nodded, unsmiling.

'Michael.'

I asked, 'Are you OK? You look a little travel-sick.'

Her mouth twitched, a characteristically minimal expression from Aunt Rosa. But her response came a discernible fraction of a second after the cue, enough to remind me that this was not real, that we were far apart and separated by lightspeed delays. 'I'm fine. But the older I get the harder it is for my system to accommodate multiple realities. As you will learn.' She looked down at her black eroded pillar of a body, spread her liver-spotted hands. 'Just think! I do not actually need to look like this. I could have materialised as Marilyn Monroe – have you ever heard of her?'

'Perhaps we should sit down.'

Rosa rested her hands on something – it materialised when she touched it, a light, high-backed chair – and dragged it towards my table. 'We may as well look as if we share the same universe,' she said.

I walked to the table and sat stiffly. I described EI's conference room to her. 'It was a hell of a lot better than this. You wouldn't have known who was really there and who wasn't, the interfaces were that good. Of course the illusion relies on the human factor, on protocols. You have to make sure you don't break the rules, do things that are impossible in the consensual reality—'

'Like this?' She reached out of shot and picked up a mug. Like the chair, it appeared out of nowhere, captured by her imaging system as a contiguous part of her extended self. 'As a Catholic priest I spend an awful lot of my time on protocols, of one kind or another. I don't imagine we could run our lives, or manage our souls, without them. I wonder if your apparitions follow their own protocols. Are they systematic, confined by rules?...'

And so we were getting to the point.

Rosa conjured up a VR reconstruction of those strange moments in Spain, as the dust storm had closed in. A miniaturised slab of the Reef coalesced out of the air over my table-top, and I cleared the water jug and other junk off the table to save confusing the system.

Lumpy and massive, the virtual Reef looked like the papier-mâché hillsides I used to build as a kid to drive my toy cars over. But the representation was finely detailed. I could see the glittering of crushed automobile hoods and smashed windscreens, and I picked out the crudely hewn stairs that led up to the cave where Rosa and I had eaten. And when I bent down to peer into the mouth of the cave,

I saw two little figures sitting at a table. Each the size of my thumb nail, they were charming, like toys in a doll's house; I had an impulse to pick up the tiny model of me and examine it more closely.

'This is a reconstruction,' Rosa said. 'The records are sparse. The Reef is thinly monitored, relatively. This is the best we can do, for now.'

The projection ran forward. The dust storm came, a crimson cloud descending in silence, like weather on Mars.

Then she appeared – Morag, the visitor, at the foot of the Reef. I saw that toy representation of myself try to descend from his metal-walled cave in pursuit. The little Rosa and the burly landlady dragged him back, and Morag retreated into the dark shadows of the storm. All this was played out in silence. As Morag was on the cusp of vanishing into the dust cloud, Rosa froze the image.

'Can you magnify this thing?' I touched the doll image of Morag; my finger brushed her, scattering tiny pixels.

The image ballooned, but as it enlarged it became increasingly fuzzy. When the face expanded it was no more than a sketch, a default female human. It could have been anybody. I was crushingly disappointed.

'This is based on the available records, and on what I saw,' Rosa said. 'My eyes are good, better than I deserve at such an age. But the figure was simply too far away, the dust swirling and obscuring.'

'You are painfully honest,' I said.

'Extraordinary claims require extraordinary validation.'

'So you can't be sure it was Morag.'

'I'm sorry.' The magnified image of Morag dissipated. 'And I wasn't able to capture any of her speech – that strange high-speed monologue we heard.'

I rubbed my chin. 'So this is all we have. If only the surveillance density had been greater! Bad luck she showed up in a place like that.'

'It might not have been a coincidence,' Rosa said. 'If she, or whoever is behind the apparition, is determined to remain obscure – to tantalise rather than to reveal – then she would naturally do it this way, in a place where surveillance is sparse, in glimpses through dust clouds, retreating.'

'Why do you call it an *apparition*? It's a ghost – isn't it?'

She sat back in her chair. 'Not necessarily. Michael, I'm afraid to deal with this we will have to delve into the pseudo-science of the supernatural...'

Humans stick words on things, like bright yellow labels. It is our way of dealing with the universe. And even phenomena which are not part of our consensual reality have accumulated a vocabulary of their own.

'An apparition is just that, an appearance of *something*,' Rosa said. 'If you want an even broader label for what is happening here, you can talk of a haunting as an interaction between an agent and a percipient – your Morag-figure is the agent, you see, and you the percipient. The agent could be some external phenomenon, either natural or supernatural, or maybe something emanating from inside your own head: all of these are agents. The language is non-judgemental. Now, a true ghost is something more specific: a ghost is one class of apparition, a manifestation of somebody deceased.'

'Morag is dead.' Absurd how difficult it was to say that, even after all these years.

'Yes,' Rosa said. 'But we don't know if this *is* Morag in any sense. And there are other types of apparition.'

You could also have visions of people who were still alive: there were 'wraiths' and 'crisis ghosts', manifestations of living people going through some trauma. You had ghosts of the specialised kind, like poltergeists. You had animal ghosts. And so on.

Hauntings of all kinds had a long history, she said. Arguably you could trace the idea of ghosts back to the tale of Gilgamesh, four thousand years ago. The ancient Greeks and Romans told each other ghost stories, and the more rational of them tried to investigate hauntings and other spooky phenomena.

'The early Church accepted the idea of ghosts, of spirits that could be detached from the body. This was bound up with competing theories of the nature of our immortal souls. In the end the early Church fathers came up with the notion of Purgatory, a place somewhere between Heaven and Hell, where restless souls could lodge. Such ideas were attacked by later thinkers – during the Reformation, for instance. But they, or rationalised versions, remain part of the Church's corpus of beliefs.

'And the apparitions seem to keep up with technological advances,' she said with her characteristic dry humour. 'As soon as photography was invented ghosts started showing up in images – never clear enough to be used as proof of the ghosts' existence, of course.'

Thomas Edison had tried to invent machines to detect apparitions. I was intrigued by that; after all, it seemed no more fantastic a thing for Edison to try than other astonishing things he *had* succeeded in doing, such as lighting up cities with electricity, or capturing human voices in wax.

'When the internet spread that was immediately haunted too; people received spectral emails from senders who never existed.'

'And now they show up even in virtual reality,' I said ruefully.

'But still leaving no trace,' Rosa said.

Talking this way helped me deal with the whole issue, I think. It wasn't so much that Rosa took me seriously, but the reassurance I derived from her patient analytical probing. As Rosa analysed and classified, and picked apart cause and effect, motive and design, she was breaking open the mystery and arbitrariness that had baffled and distracted me from the start. This needn't be overwhelming, a nightmare: that was the subtext of her dialogue with me.

But I felt more uneasy to be discussing ghosts and hauntings in that gaudy Palm Springs hotel room than I had in Spain. A place like Seville, steeped in millennia of blood-soaked history, was a place where it had felt right to contemplate deeper orders of reality. Palm Springs, bless it, was a monument to the trivial, the sensual; defiant in its own shallow reality it seemed to consume the whole universe, leaving no room for mystery.

Or maybe I was just feeling guilty about spending time on this 'spooky stuff', as Tom persisted in calling it.

'Complicated thing, guilt,' Rosa had said when I tried to tell her about this. 'We Catholics have been thinking about it for two thousand years, and we still have not figured it out. My advice is to embrace it. Good for the soul.'

'Ah,' she said, smiling. 'Now that *is* an engineer's question. What's the function of all this? Oh, I can think of a whole range of interpretations... Try this. Everything about us, from our toenails to our most advanced cognitive functions, is shaped by evolution. You've heard me argue this way before. If a feature didn't give us some selective advantage it wouldn't have emerged in the first place, or would have withered away long ago. Do you accept that?'

I wasn't sure I did. 'Go on.'

'If that's true, and if these visitations, and their timing coinciding with great crises, are real phenomena, then one must ask – what's the evolutionary advantage? How can these visitors *help* us?'

'By providing continuity?'

'Perhaps. A linking of the better past to a hopeful future, through a desperate present... Perhaps an intelligent species needs some kind of external memory store, an external mass consciousness, to help it ride out the worst times.'

'That sounds very fishy to me,' I said. 'I thought selection wasn't supposed to work at the level of the species, but the individual, or the kin group.'

'Maybe so. But wouldn't it be an advantage if it *did* emerge? If there were lots of bands of intelligent animals running around the planet when a global crisis hit, wouldn't the pack with the cultural continuity offered by a halo of ghosts, no matter how imperfect the information channels, have a clear advantage?' She was smiling. I could see she was enjoying the speculation.

But I was floundering. 'So Morag could be a ghost, of some kind. But not a ghost from the past. *A ghost from the future.* Is that what you're saying? But how is that possible?'

Rosa said, 'A Catholic thinker would have no real trouble with that idea. Theologians don't believe in time travel! But we do imagine eternity, a timeless instant *outside* time altogether, like the constant light that shines through the flickering frames of our movie-reel lives. So a visitor from eternity, an angel, can intervene at any time, historically, she chooses, because it's all the same – it is all one to her, all in one moment, like a reel of movie film held in your hand. There is no difference between past and future to God.'

'You think big, don't you?'

With her right hand she pointed up to Heaven. 'There's nowhere bigger than Up There.'

We were disturbed by a chime, the VR equivalent of a knock on the door. I was almost relieved to take a break from all this spookiness.

It turned out to be my brother John, who had logged on to give me a hard time.

Projected from his office in New York, John's VR was of an altogether higher quality than Rosa's. It was the middle of his working day, and he was dressed in a dark business suit. I was struck how big and solid he looked, just like Ruud Makaay.

John greeted Rosa civilly enough. He even cracked a joke. 'If you shared my VR protocols I could give you a kiss.' But their manner with each other was watchful.

I realised that I had no idea what contact there had been between the two of them. After all she was John's long-lost aunt as well as mine. Was it possible this was the first time they had 'met'? But I felt intimidated even to ask.

You could have cut the atmosphere with a knife, VR or otherwise. Two brothers and an aunt, suspicious, wary, facing each other down like rival gangland bosses: what a cold family we were, I reflected, what a damaged bunch.

'What do you want, John?'

He sighed. 'It's a little tricky. I saw you were logged on, and I saw who you're speaking to. I don't mean to snoop but I am paying for the calls. Can I speak freely?'

Rosa said sharply, 'As long as you get to the point, fine.'

'Michael, people are concerned about you.' He waved a hand. 'About all this. You know what I mean.'

'And they spoke to you, right?'

'Don't be resentful,' he snapped. 'I'm trying to help.'

'But I am resentful, you asshole. Who spoke to you?'

'Shelley Magwood, if you must know. And through her, Ruud Makaay.'

Of course I should have expected that John would hook up with a man like Makaay. They were of a type.

John said, 'All this is a distraction. You have work to do,

Michael. Responsibilities. This hydrate-stabilisation proposal you've initiated seems to have genuine merit. I think there's every chance it will gain some support, and maybe even do some real good, if presented in the right way.'

'But if I disappear up my own backside in pursuit of the spooky stuff, I'll be harming that process. Right?'

'Of course you will,' he said irritably. 'You're talking about a very expensive engineering project here; it's a hard enough sell as it is without hints of flakiness from its initiator.'

Rosa watched us both. 'Your rivalry is deep-seated, isn't it?'

I said, 'You have to remember that when we were kids John was a couple of years older than me. Now we're in our fifties, and he's *still* a couple of years older than me.'

Rosa laughed softly.

John glared at us. 'Yeah, yeah. Just don't forget who's been bankrolling you. And look, Michael, it's not just the project.' He clearly tried to soften his tone; he leaned forward, resting his elbows on his knees. 'You have to think about the effect you have on others. Tom, particularly. Your pursuit of this –' he waved a hand '– this chimera is hurting him. She was your wife, but she was his mother, you know.'

'You've got no right to talk about my relationship with my son.'

He held up his massive hands. 'OK, OK.'

Rosa had an air of amused suspicion. 'What is really going on here, John?'

He glowered back. 'I'm concerned for Michael.'

'Oh, perhaps there is truth in that. But I am sure you would be quite happy to see your little brother take a prat-fall, as long as no permanent harm was done. So why are you interested in this business of Morag?'

Characteristically he went on the attack. 'And what's your angle, Rosa? What's your motive in messing with my brother's head?'

'Will you believe me if I say I actually want to resolve this issue, to help my nephew, that I have no higher motive? Other than simple curiosity, of course; I always did like a good ghost story... No, you probably won't, will you?' I was obscurely pleased that she wasn't fazed.

John stared at her. 'Do you actually believe in ghosts?'

It was a simple question that, in our increasingly sophisticated pursuit of the mystery of Morag, I'd never quite framed that way, and I was interested in her answer.

She thought for a moment. 'Do you know what Immanuel Kant said about ghosts? "I do not care wholly to deny all truth to the various ghost stories, but with the curious reservation that I doubt each one of the sightings yet have some belief in them all taken together..." As a priest you soon learn that there is a whole spectrum of credulity, that total acceptance and utter denial are merely two poles, two choices among many.' She smiled. 'Or to put it another way, I have an open mind.'

John seemed angered by this. He stood up. 'You're full of shit.'

I said, 'John, watch your mouth. She's your aunt, and a priest. She's a priest who's full of shit.'

He turned on me. 'You really ought to get your head clear of this garbage, Michael. For your own sake, and the rest of us.' He clapped his hands and disappeared, like a fat, business-suited genie.

Rosa stared at the space where he had been. 'So many issues, so many conflicts. Even for a Poole your brother is unusual.' She turned to me, her gaze direct, probing. 'Michael, I think your brother is hiding something from you – something that's troubling him about all this more than he's telling you. You have to resolve this, the two of you, whatever it is. You are stuck with him, you know. Stuck with each other for life. That is the doom of family.'

I stared, surprised. I'd had this feeling about John before; it was disturbing to hear it confirmed. But in this dense, dark tangle of me and Morag, Tom and a ghost, what secret could John possibly hold?

Rosa stood up. Her chair vanished in a haze of pixels. 'Perhaps that is enough for now.'

'OK. But our ghost story – what next?'

'I am sure you will agree that we need more data. I suggest you wait for another visitation. Or, if you have the courage, seek one out, as you did in York. But this time, make sure you record everything you can – especially that strange rapid speech.'

'I'll try,' I said dubiously. 'I don't know how easy it will be.'

She smiled. 'You'll have help. Another of your friends contacted me.'

I frowned. 'I really hate the idea of everybody talking behind my back. Who this time?'

'Gea,' Rosa said simply.

Even given the context of the conversation that surprised me. 'So a sentient artificial intelligence is investigating the ghost of my dead wife. Could my life get any weirder?'

She leaned forward. The VR illusion of her presence was so good I thought I could smell her musty, exotic scent, a mix of old lady and priest, perhaps through some synaesthetic confusion in my muddled head. 'But we are all on your side, Michael. You are the hub of a wheel, you see. We are all connected to you. Even if we bicker among ourselves.' She stood straight and tucked her hands into her black sleeves. 'We will speak shortly.' And she disappeared.

Chapter 35

Alia had never cared much *where* she was. She grew up on a ship, sailing on an endless journey; she had been born in transit. And through Skimming she had learned that all differences in space could be banished with an act of will. But now she was coming to the one place in the human Galaxy where she couldn't help but know *exactly* where she was.

As Sol itself loomed out of a sparse Galaxy-rim dusting of stars, she was already seeing a sky Michael Poole himself might have recognised, even though the constellations had shifted and morphed since his day, and the stars themselves showed signs of the passing of mankind, some of them greened by orbiting shells of habitats, others lined up in rings or belts, still others detonated and scattered in the course of war.

And soon she would come to the very centre of it all: Earth, the home world of mankind – the place where, it was said, in the end all undying flocked.

Reath's ship cut across the plane of Sol system, like a stone rolling across a plate. The sun's planets, so significant in memory and legend across the Galaxy, were scattered in their orbits about their star. Alia was disappointed; she had no instinct for the dynamics of planetary systems, and somehow she had expected all the solar worlds to be lined up in a neat row ready for inspection.

One world did swim by to become bright enough briefly to rival the still-distant sun. They crowded to the windows to see. The planet remained a mere point of light to an unaided eye, but they used the ship's enhancement features to see better.

It was a giant, a ball of murky gas that swathed a rocky

core larger than Earth. The planet's colour was a dull, washed-out yellow-brown, but you could see streaks and whorls in the cloud tops, sluggish storms curdling that thick blanket of air. Reath pointed out moons, balls of rock and ice that were minor worlds in their own right. And, strangest of all, the planet was circled by a ring, a band of light centred on the planet.

This planet, Reath said, was called Saturn. It was the system's largest surviving gas giant; there had been one larger, but that had long been destroyed, and was anyhow hidden on the far side of the sun. Saturn had once been central in the planning for the defence of Earth itself. 'It's a fortress,' Reath said, 'a vast natural fortress circling on the boundary of the inner system.'

Alia asked, 'And what about the ring?'

'Orbital weapons systems, very ancient. They break down, collide, smash each other up. In time their fragments have been shepherded into ring systems by the perturbation of the moons' gravity. It's odd,' he said. 'Once Saturn was one of Sol system's most spectacular sights, for it had a *natural* ring system – fragments of water ice from a shattered moon. When mankind came here, bringing war, those rings didn't last long. But now Saturn's rings have been reborn in these bits of smashed-up weaponry.'

On the planet itself, huge machines of war had been constructed beneath the cover of the eternal clouds. But the war had never come here; those immense machines had never been activated.

'But the machines are still waiting for the call to arms,' Reath said.

Drea said, 'I wonder if they will know who to fight for, after all this time. Would they recognise *us* as the heirs of their builders?'

None of them, not spindly Reath or the squat Campocs or furry, long-limbed Alia had an answer. Saturn swam away into the dark.

It was half a million years since mankind had first ventured to the stars. For much of that time humanity had been locked in war – and although in the end a Galaxy had been won, it had always been Sol system, even Earth itself, that had been the principal mine for the resources for that war. So the system was left depleted.

Once, between Jupiter and the inner rocky worlds, there had been a rich asteroid belt: now it was impoverished, mined out and scattered. The iron of the innermost world, Sol I, called Mercury, had been dug out so long that the little world had been left misshapen by quarries and pits. Earth's two neighbours, Sol II and IV – Venus and Mars – had been used up too. Mars had been stripped of what volatiles it had retained from its chill birth, and even Venus's thick air had been transformed to carbon polymers and removed. Now, abandoned, both worlds looked remarkably similar, two balls of rust-red dust, naked save for only a thin layer of air, and with no signs of life save the abandoned cities of a departed mankind. It was a strange thought, Alia reflected, that in a mere half-million years after the humans arrived, all these worlds had suffered a greater transformation than any in the vast ages since their births.

At last the ship made its final approach to Sol III: Earth.

Even from afar the planet didn't look quite as it had in Poole's time. The horizon was blurred by a deep, structured layer of silvery mist: in this age, Earth was surrounded by a cloud of life. The ship cut through this community. Alia watched, bemused, as translucent animals, all amorphous bodies and clinging tentacles, attached themselves to the ship, spraying acid to get at whatever lay inside. The ship was forced to charge its hull to repel these swarming, vacuum-hardened creatures.

This unlikely ecology was an unintended consequence of mankind's long colonisation of near-Earth space. Once, engineering structures had lifted up out of Earth's atmosphere to provide access to space. There had even been a bridge that had spanned many times Earth's own diameter to reach to its Moon – but the Moon itself was lost now. All those mighty engineering projects had long since fallen into ruin, but they had lasted long enough to provide a route for Earth's tenacious life forms to clamber out of the atmosphere and to leak out into space, where, hardened and adapted, their remote descendants still remained.

The ship fell towards the planet itself.

The world that came spinning up out of the dark was still recognisably Earth. Alia could even name the continents, so familiar from Poole's maps. She knew that the continents were rafts of rock that slid around the surface, but even half a million years was but a moment in the long afternoon of Earth's geology, and the essential configuration was unchanged.

The continents' outlines had subtly altered, though, she saw. The land had pushed out to sea, and where the great rivers drained into the oceans, fat deltas crowded into the water. The oceans, steel grey, had receded since Poole's time. Not only that, there was no trace of ice, at either north or south poles; in the north there was a cloud-strewn ocean, and the southern continent, Antarctica, was bare green and grey. A good fraction of Earth's water must have been lost altogether.

In the temperate regions most of the lowland was inhabited. The ground was coated by a silver-grey broken by splashes of vivid green. The habitation was so widespread, crowding from mountain peaks to river valleys, it was hard to distinguish individual cities or communities. But in the sprawl of urbanisation there were distinctive patterns – circles, some of them huge, which shaped the development around and within their arcs. Roads like shining threads cut across the plains of habitation, linking the circular forms, and Alia could make out the sparks of flying craft.

Reath pointed to the ground. 'See those circular forms? In the time of the Coalition, they built all their cities that way, low domes on circular foundations. Conurbations, they called them.'

'They were copying the architecture of alien fortresses,' Drea said. 'And they gave their cities numbers, not names. They didn't want anybody to forget that Earth had once been occupied.' It was a familiar story, a legend told to children across the Galaxy.

When the Coalition fell the great domes had been abandoned, mined for materials, left to rot. But the first post-Coalition cultures had established their towns and cities inside the old circular foundations. That was half a million years ago, and since then Earth had hosted a thousand cultures and had fought numberless wars; the people thronging its streets probably weren't even the same species, strictly speaking, as the folk who built the Coalition. But still the circular patterns persisted. On Earth, Alia thought, everything was ancient, and everywhere reefs of a very deep antiquity pushed through the layers of the present.

The only exception to the general pattern of habitation and cultivation was South America. On its descent towards its landing site in Europe, Reath's shuttle cut south of the equator and swam across the heart of this continent. The land was covered from mountain-peak to shore by a bubbling carpet of crimson-red; only the bright grey stripes of rivers cut through the dense blanket.

Alia pointed this out to Reath. 'It looks like vegetation,' she said. 'Like *wild* vegetation. But there's no *green*.'

Reath shrugged. 'It probably isn't native. Why should it be? Earth is the centre of a Galactic culture. For half a million years life forms from all across the Galaxy have been brought here, by design or otherwise. Some of them found ways to survive.'

Bale said, 'So it's an alien ecology down there. Why don't they clear it away?'

'Maybe it's too useful,' Reath said.

'Maybe they *can't*,' Seer said with a cold grin.

The shuttle cut across the Atlantic, sweeping from south to north. In the last moments of the flight Alia peered down into a great valley that she found hard to identify from her memories of Poole's maps. Then she realised it was the basin of the sea once called the Mediterranean, now drained of water. As elsewhere the urbanisation crowded down from the higher lands, but much of the basin floor was colonised only by wild greenery. Here and there she made out lenticular shapes, stranded in the dried mud and grown over by green. They might have been the remains of sunken ships, she thought fancifully, wrecks that had outlasted the sea that had destroyed them.

The shuttle left the basin and flew north over the higher land. They were somewhere over southern Europe – Alia thought it was the area Poole would have called France.

They came to a densely developed area that straddled a river valley. Here those circular patterns of development crowded closely, and the ground was textured with buildings and roads, as if carpeted by jewels.

The shuttle descended, and Alia found herself falling through a sky that was full of buildings – impossibly tall given Earth's gravity, surely saturated with inertial-control technology. Drea peered out in awe at one vast aerial condominium. 'Look at that. It's bigger than the *Nord*!'

Bale said dryly, 'They don't believe in economising on energy, these Earth folk, do they?'

The shuttle found a clear area to land, and dropped without ceremony to the ground. They clambered out and stood still a moment, allowing Earth's Mist to interface with their bodies' systems.

This landing pad was just a clear, shining floor. There were no facilities, nothing like a dock or replenishment station. The nearest buildings looked residential. Further away more buildings floated, huge and glittering.

Bale sniffed. 'Funny air. Not much oxygen. Lots of trace elements, toxins.'

Reath said, 'This is an old world, Campoc…' He fell silent.

The little party was being studied. A small girl had popped into existence a few paces from Alia – literally popped, Alia could hear the small shock of the air she displaced. She was wearing a jumpsuit of some substance so bright it shone. She stared at Alia, then disappeared again.

Alia whispered to Drea, 'Skimming?'

'I think so.'

Another visitor Skimmed in, this time a man, grossly fat. He glanced at them all, spied Drea, and walked up to her. He leered at her breasts and said something Alia couldn't hear. Drea snapped, '*No.*' He shrugged and disappeared.

But he was soon replaced by another, a younger man who gazed at them curiously for a few seconds before disappearing. And then another, an older woman – and then a party, a family perhaps, adults and children hand in hand, who Skimmed in as one.

All around the shuttle people flickered in and out of existence. Alia could feel the air they displaced washing gently over her face. The party clustered together nervously.

'They're just curious,' Reath said. 'Come to see the visitors – us.'

'They have no manners,' Seer said.

'Or attention span,' Denh said.

'Then ignore them,' Alia said.

'Quite right.' The voice was a dry scratch.

Alia turned. One of the visitors remained while others flickered around her, evanescent as dreams. It was a woman, though her figure was all but masked by a shapeless brown robe. She was small, dark, somehow very solid, Alia thought, as if she were made of something more dense than mere flesh, blood and bone. She walked through the transient throng towards Alia. Her face was round and worn, and her head was hairless, with not so much as an eyelash.

Alia said, 'You're Leropa.'

'And you're Alia. I've been waiting to meet you,' said the undying.

Chapter 36

It took Ruud Makaay and his people only a few weeks to set up a prototype test rig of the stabiliser technology. He summoned us to Prudhoe Bay, on the Arctic coast of Alaska, for a trial demonstration.

I was impressed by the speed with which we had got to this point. But then Makaay had insisted from the beginning that EI was going to use off-the-shelf technology wherever possible. Even the moles weren't entirely new. In the dying days of the oil industry, smart mechanical critters much like our moles had gone burrowing into the earth and beneath the seabeds all over the planet in search of the last meagre reserves. Similarly the big condensation and liquefaction plants we were planning to set up would, in principle, have been immediately comprehensible to a Victorian engineer: 'Gaslight-era technology,' Makaay said. It was just the scale of what we would be attempting that was new – the scale, and the intrinsic smartness of the system.

As well as its technical goals this trial demonstration would be a 'bonding session' for us, the project's champions, Makaay said. And, more seriously, it would give us a chance to rehearse, to begin developing the case we were going to have to make to the world's power-brokers if our project was ever to get off the ground.

But for now we were still in development mode, and Makaay was keeping the press out. It was all a question of perception. In advanced engineering, you expected failure; you learned as much from failures as from successes – indeed if you never suffered a failure you probably weren't pushing the envelope ambitiously enough. But Makaay, after half a lifetime spent trying to sell the unsellable, knew that the public, media and politicians rarely understood these truths.

So, for now, the only witnesses to any disaster would be the core team.

Plus one potential ally, he told me.

'*The* Edith Barnette? You're serious? She must be eighty if she's a day.'

Barnette had been Vice President in the momentous Amin Administration. She had been deeply unpopular at the time, and had taken much of the flak for the pain of Amin's mighty economic restructuring; she never followed Amin to take the White House herself. But historians had come to recognise Barnette as a key architect of the whole Stewardship programme, and as a driving force in getting the necessary policies through Congress and into international governance. Of course all that was a long time ago.

'She has no formal power. But she has contacts all over the Hill, and in the UN, and the Stewardship councils.' Makaay smiled, his VR image flawless. 'In my world, Michael, opinion is currency, worth far more than gold – far more even than conventional political power. And if we can get Barnette on our side we will go a long way to swinging the debate our way, believe me.'

'But what if we fail?'

'If it isn't a showstopper Barnette will forgive us. She's one of the few of her breed smart enough to do so. And she's always had her heart in the right place, Michael. She understands what we're trying to do here – or she will by the end of the day of the test.'

Even though Barnette would be there, personally I would much rather have stayed home. I had had my fill of travelling, and had no desire to haul my weary ass all the way up to Alaska, the roof of the world. But Shelley talked me into making the journey. We had to trust Makaay's instincts, she said again. Otherwise why work with him?

So I acceded; I travelled to Alaska. But as I slogged through my long journey, a whole series of more or less dreadful plane hops, I kept in mind my other agenda, the mysterious and spooky business of Morag. The whole issue was upsetting, and was isolating me from my family and friends, but I couldn't wish it away. I had a deep gut instinct that my strange contact with Morag was just as important as anything else in my life. I was determined not to let it drop – though I had no real idea how I was going to pursue it. Somehow, I knew, Morag would come to me.

It turned out I was one hundred per cent right.

The plane flew in over a vast brown plain, and the ocean was a steel sheet across which waves rippled tiredly. There was not a speck of blue or green to be seen on land or sea.

Prudhoe Bay was one of a series of oilfields spread along the northern coast of Alaska: the North Slope, as the locals call it. The complex of facilities stretched for about two hundred kilometres along the shore. There were scores of drilling pads, marching off across the land. In each pad you could see the central rig facility, a gaunt dinosaur-skeleton of rusted iron surrounded by small boxy buildings. The ground between the pads was cut through by straight-line roads, now disused, the tarmac crumbling and coated with mud. It was a very strange sight from the air, an alien forest of iron and tarmac.

I was stunned by the scale of it. Once, I knew, this had been the largest single industrial facility on Earth. The rigs had sucked up oil from kilometres down, and as in those days the sea coast had been ice-bound for most of the year the oil had been sent south through the Trans-Alaska Pipeline, across more than a thousand kilometres. It was a complicated irony that the Warming, by causing the final retreat of the sea ice, had opened up the north Alaska ports all year round; if only the Warming had come a little earlier they wouldn't have had to go to the trouble of building that thousand-kilometre pipeline – but of course the oil shipped through that immense pipe had itself contributed to the Warming.

Now the rigs were obsolescent, but the rumps of the old oil companies still owned these facilities, and were loath to abandon decades of infrastructural investment. And so the area had become a kind of adventure playground for large-scale industrial experimentation: that was why the EI engineers had chosen to come here for their trials. Plus it was American soil, which made a big difference in permissions, administrative support and other bureaucracy. Makaay told me it was a *lot* easier to attract visitors to American territory than abroad, even to a place as remote as this.

I was landed at an airstrip outside a small town called, unpromisingly, Deadhorse.

My automated cab from the airport gave me a profoundly irritating commentary, as if it imagined it was a tourist bus in Manhattan. Once, the cab told me, the hotel I was heading for had been the only accommodation available to visitors. But now that the oil industry had imploded there was plenty of accommodation to be had on the old drilling pads. There were even theme parks, where you could play at being a rigger, with grubby jeans and a hard hat.

Outside the town, the ground was churned-up mud where nothing grew. Once this area had been a vast swathe of tundra, like Siberia. But as the permafrost melted, the delicate tundra ecosystem had melted away too, and just as in Siberia the people had gone, the subsistence-hunter types who had endured here for millennia.

Deadhorse turned out to be barely a town at all; grim, functional, it was like an industrial yard. Many of the buildings were abandoned altogether, their roofs collapsed, concrete walls cracked. As we drove in through this decay and abandonment along a thin strip of silvertop, the light was failing, the day ending. It felt as if the walls of the world were closing in around me.

The hotel was basic, just a series of two-storey blocks. There were long corridors that stretched on and on, like a prison, and the flat heavy light of the fluorescent strips embedded in the ceilings washed out any colour, any vitality. The automated reception facility told me a fault had developed with the systems in my room, where an oversensitive chemical toilet had developed a habit of spitting unwelcome waste back out at its unlucky user. An animist had been summoned from Fairbanks to administer therapy, but wouldn't be here until the morning. In the meantime I could take a chance with the angst-ridden toilet, or switch to a room with a shared bathroom.

The hell with it. I took the switch.

My room was just a box. It looked clean and was reasonably bright, with a little alcove where you could make coffee. But everything was old, the pipes rusted, the plaster and skirting boards crudely repaired, and dirt and grease had accumulated in cracks in the walls.

I threw my clothes into the small cupboard, and headed down the corridor to find the shared john. The toilet was none too clean, the shower just a nozzle over a stained bath. The water looked clear, but smelled suspiciously of chlorine.

Back in my room, I used the very basic VR facilities to contact my party.

Everybody was here in Alaska, Tom and Sonia, Ruud Makaay and his people, Shelley and some of her colleagues, even Vander Guthrie. I was too tired to do any business that evening, but would have enjoyed company, I guess. I longed to see Tom again, a deep cell-level impulse. But he knew I'd been with Rosa 'telling ghost stories', as he put it, and he was pissed with me, and I didn't feel up to any more rows. Meanwhile Shelley was finalising details for the demonstration due the next day. Everybody else was working, or had crashed out. A bit wistfully, we promised to meet up in the morning.

I rolled into bed and watched some news. There was actually a relevant item: more instances of localised hydrate release around the Arctic Circle, more water spouts and clouds of lethal gases. I guessed it was local interest up here.

I was dog tired, my eyes felt like they were coated with sand, but I found it hard to rest. My muscles ached from the long hours of sitting around on planes, and I felt tense, full of energy that needed burning off. The light that leaked around the edge of my curtains was bright, not quite like daylight, enough to throw off my body clock. Though it was close to midnight the sun was still up; this was Arctic midsummer.

I lay still, eyes closed. I tried to talk myself into sleeping. I felt myself drift inward, away from the poky reality of that dismal Alaskan hotel. But as my conscious mind receded I only seemed to uncover a deeper layer of anxiety, like a beach exposed by a low tide.

I needed the john.

I pushed my way out of bed, and fumbled my way in the dark to the door. The light in the corridor was briefly dazzling.

I stumbled along one wall. The only sound was the padding of my feet. There was an odd quality about the light. It was a dead and colourless glow, lacking any of the photosynthetic goodness of sunlight. Barefoot, shambling along alone, I felt like a convict.

The corridor seemed to stretch on, longer than I remembered. I wondered if I had come the wrong way, if I was somehow getting lost. But I kept on, figuring I had to get somewhere eventually.

At last I came to the bathroom. I pushed my way inside, used the facility, came back out. Again the corridor stretched away to either side of me, infinitely long, identical whichever way you looked. For a second I had to think which way I had come. My thinking seemed stuck in my head like glue in a pipe. I turned right. I figured that was the way. I began stumbling back down the corridor.

Then I saw her.

She was a slim figure, far off down the corridor. I heard her voice. She was speaking rapidly, just as she had at the Reef. But the thick-painted walls jumbled up her voice into whispers and echoes.

I ran, of course. I felt absurd running in my bare feet, with my pyjama pants flapping around my legs, my belly heaving under my vest. But I ran anyhow, as I had run before, as I knew I always would run after her.

I kept my eyes fixed on Morag. I had the feeling she wanted me to reach her. She was just standing there. But though I ran as hard as I could, I didn't get any closer. I felt no fear: none of that awful sucking banal cold of evil that Rosa had described. She was there *for* me. But I couldn't reach her, no matter how hard I struggled to run down that endless corridor. She looked helpless, her hands spread.

She turned away from me and stepped into a room.

I tried to count, to remember which door she had chosen. Twenty, twenty-five down? I counted off the doors as I passed.

But a wall loomed before me.

I had to stop. I stood there panting, staring at the wall blankly. It was just a hotel wall; it had small arrowed signs pointing me to reception, and to a fire exit. It had seemed to come out of nowhere, materialising like a VR and cutting off the corridor.

I turned and looked back. The corridor didn't seem so long now. I could even see the bathroom door I'd left open.

I knew I wouldn't see Morag again that night. I stumbled back down the corridor, looking for my room.

I longed to call Tom, but I knew I must not.

In the morning I was up early. I checked at the hotel reception for any records of last night. There were a few surveillance cameras dotted around the building, but none in the rooms, and only one to cover that corridor.

After some electronic arm-twisting I persuaded the hotel's sentience to show me images. I saw myself stumbling, running, staggering down that corridor. I had been half-asleep; I looked almost drunk. But there was no clear image of Morag. The cameras' fields of view never quite stretched far enough, and the sound pickups were overwhelmed by noisy air-conditioning fans. Perhaps there was a shadow – a fleeting shape, a glimpse of ankle, a trace of voice on the audio recording. That was all.

Once again Morag had come and gone leaving scarcely a trace.

Chapter 37

The day after Alia landed on Earth, Leropa arranged to meet her in a township built inside the ruins of a Conurbation that she referred to by an old number, '11729'. It was apparently a place of great historical significance. Alia knew nothing of this, and didn't ask. Buried at the heart of the solar system, she was beginning to choke on age and mystery.

When morning came, Alia flew alone in Reath's shuttle. The little craft confidently skimmed north, and circular-plan cities fled endlessly beneath the shuttle's prow. The sky was a washed-out blue, and in the day no stars were visible. There was no Moon in the sky either. Alia wasn't sure if the Moon, so familiar from her viewings of Michael Poole's time, had ever been visible in the daytime. And now, of course, the Moon was gone, detached as an accident of mankind's endless wars. She wondered if Michael Poole could have got used to a sky without a Moon.

At last something altogether more grand began to loom over the horizon.

It was a framework, an open skeletal structure. It was pyramidal – no, tetrahedral, Alia saw, with three mighty legs plunging towards the ground. It was coloured blue-grey, though its true shade may have been masked by the mist of distance. Streaks of cloud curled languidly around the apex of that immense tripod, but its base was still hidden by the horizon – the whole must have been kilometres tall.

As the shuttle swept closer this structure loomed ever taller in Alia's sky, until at last her shuttle was flying through the vast open space cradled by the framework. At the heart of the triangular floor over which the tetrahedron loomed was a city: Conurbation 11729 itself. This city retained some of the ancient domed architecture, but the overlapping domes had been worn by time, cut through and patched up, over and over.

The shuttle descended. On the ground Leropa was waiting to meet her.

'So,' Leropa said, 'you are the young Elect who has caused so much trouble.'

'I'm sorry,' Alia stammered. 'I didn't mean to.'

'Of course you didn't.'

'And I'm grateful that you, the Transcendence, is giving me time.'

'Oh, you don't need to be grateful. The Transcendence can't help but devote its attention to you. Don't you understand that? Perhaps your tuition hasn't been as thorough as I imagined. Child, you are already part of the Transcendence. So your doubts and questions are *its* doubts. Do you see?'

'I think so—'

'And so the Transcendence *must* deal with you, to set its own mind at ease.' Leropa closed her eyes, and nodded as Alia had seen Reath bow his head when naming the Transcendence.

Leropa's face was very strange, small, round, her nose and cheekbones so shallow she was all but featureless, like a crater eroded to smoothness by great age. Her lips seemed without a drop of blood, and her eyes were grey orbs as dry as stones. Alia wondered *how old* this person was – if she could still be called a person at all. In Leropa's presence Alia felt transient, transparent.

Leropa smiled at her; it was a cold grimace, inflicted on the muscles of her face by an act of will.

Together they walked through the vast circular courtyards of the domes. From the ground the domes were peculiarly dull to look at: they were simply too big to be taken in, for Alia could only see to a dome's horizon, and could make out nothing of its true scope. But over it all the struts of the tripod, from here a vivid electric blue, swept up until they penetrated the sky.

Alia grew increasingly uncomfortable in Earth's heavy gravity. She kept trying to break into a run, forgetting the economy of walking – and besides her body, no longer truly bipedal, was not designed for walking. After a time she settled on a compromise, taking some of her weight on her curled fists as she loped along.

Leropa watched without comment as Alia knuckle-walked through the ruins of Earth.

Leropa spoke, in a voice like dry leaves rustling. The tetrahedron was a ruin too, of a sort, she said. It dated from the time after the fall of the Coalition. A religious group called *Wignerians* or *Friends*, having arisen illegally in the military colonies at the centre of the Galaxy, had emerged as a unifying force in the aftermath of political collapse. In its glory days it returned here, to Earth, where it had erected the mightiest of all cathedrals over the ruined capital of the Coalition that had once banned it.

In the end the Friends' creed had become the most powerful and magnificent of all mankind's religions. It converted a Galaxy, and explored the depths of humanity's soul. Now it was quite vanished.

Leropa said, 'At the heart of the religion of the Wignerians was a belief that all of history is contingent – that all possible world lines will be gathered together at the end of time, where history will be resolved in favour of the good, and all pain wiped away.'

'A Redemption,' Alia said.

'Yes. The Wignerians' vision of entelechy has perhaps influenced the thinking of the Transcendence.' She looked up at the cathedral's skeleton, squinting in the light. 'But everything passes, Alia. Once this was the capital of a government which ruled the Galaxy. Eventually nothing remained of the Coalition but the religion it had tried to ban, and in the end nothing remained of *that* but this one idea, a dream of entelechy. That and a few ruins.'

This was an appropriate place for the undying to gather, Leropa said. In time the cathedral had been looted, its walls crumbled – but not this central framework which, made of something called exotic matter, defied entropy itself. 'The undying have contempt for mere stone, which in time rots in your hand. *This* deserves respect.'

Alia, faintly repelled, said nothing.

Then, in the shadows of the broken domes, they came on the undying.

There were few of them to be seen. They moved slowly, cautiously, each rounded figure surrounded by a cloud of servitor machines. But each walked alone. They had empty faces, blank expressions. They didn't even speak, though some of them seemed to be mumbling to themselves. Just as she had glimpsed on that other Transcendent world in the Galaxy Core, the undying were weighed down by the huge burden of the past, each locked into a separate world.

It struck Alia how Leropa was different. Of all this shuffling crowd of ancients, it was only she who even seemed aware of Alia's presence.

'What are you thinking, Alia?'

'All I see is what's missing. There is *nothing here*. No art. No music—'

Leropa grimaced. 'Can you imagine a single piece of art that wouldn't appal you after too many viewings, a piece of music or verse of poetry that, after a thousand years of listening, wouldn't sicken you with boredom? The very abstract endures longest, I suppose. Cold, voiceless music; pale inhuman art. But in time *everything wears away*, Alia. Everything visible turns to dust – and so you turn to what remains, the invisible.'

'What's inside you.'

'Yes. The present is just a surface of sensation surrounding a great bubble of memory. You forget how to see, to hear; you forget how to talk to people. You forget other people even *exist*. You sink inwards into yourself, thinking about the past. Living on and on, without end.'

'And yet you do live on.'

'Oh, yes.'

These ancient figures, and the wisdom they had accreted, were the treasures of mankind, in a sense, and the foundation of the Transcendence. And so they were cherished. But not envied.

Leropa said, 'I understand this repels you. I have seen such a reaction many times before – an instinctive loathing, the rejection all young feel for all old. It is the natural order of things. But you will come round. The alternative to living on and on is, after all, death. And we do have some value, you know.'

Leropa reached out and, without warning, touched Alia's forehead. Her touch was cold.

And suddenly Alia was standing on top of a mountain, drenched in cold air that dragged at her lungs. She stumbled and wrapped her arms around her body.

Leropa watched her dispassionately. 'You'll be fine,' she said.

Alia's systems, suffused by Mist, adjusted to the shock. The feeling of cold, of vertigo went away. She stood straight, composing herself.

She was on a plateau no more than a hundred paces across, smoothly cut from the summit of this steep-sided mountain. Walls of granite fell away to valleys far below, and more mountains loomed on all sides. The rock was slippery underfoot; there might be no ice left at Earth's poles, but there was ice up here.

An immense barrel of some cold blue metal pointed up out of the rock of this summit, straight up at the sky. Monumental, many times her own height, it was obviously a weapon.

'Where am I?'

'Does it matter?' Leropa's thin lips pulled back into a smile. 'Ah, but you have Witnessed the career of Michael Poole, haven't you? In his day these mountains were known as the Pyrenees.'

'Did we Skim here?'

'Everybody Skims everywhere, on Earth. The people burn up the planet's energy store as if it were inexhaustible. You must have seen the floating buildings, the way the whole planet glows from space. Earth has always stayed strong, you know. Even when the Coalition fell it was the capital of the strongest of the successor states. And through all the wars and vicissitudes since, it stayed safe, unharmed. We ensured it did.'

'We?' But Alia knew who she meant. *The undying.*

Leropa said, 'And by staying strong, its people naturally became rich – even if the planet was bled of its own substance in the process. Those who have inherited the Earth live exotic lives, Alia. More exotic, more fantastic, more *rich* than a ship-born waif like you can imagine.'

Alia resented that. 'Maybe. But if they have such rich lives how come they needed to come look at me?'

Leropa laughed, a dry, eerie sound, quite without humanity. 'Perhaps you're right. They caper on the wealth of ages. But they are bored; they are too ignorant not to be. And they are spoiled rotten.'

Alia looked up at the barrel of the weapon. 'And what is this?'

'A weapon of war,' Leropa said. 'In fact an ancient star-breaker cannon. It is at least three hundred thousand years old, but fully functional. It will probably last as long again.'

'What's it doing here? Defence?'

'In a sense. Its sentience is programmed to seek out and destroy any impactors – asteroids, comets – that might threaten the planet.'

Alia frowned. 'Is that likely? This system's asteroid belts are depleted.'

'True. An atmosphere-penetrating impact sufficient to cause significant damage is likely only once every million years: in Poole's time it would have been once a century. And there are more defence perimeters in space.' Leropa glanced up at the weapon. 'But this guardian is here even so. Of course the worst case would be a strike that took out this defender, and a second strike that would, undefended, do even more harm.'

'Surely that sort of multiple accident is almost vanishingly unlikely.'

'But a real risk nonetheless,' Leropa said. 'And so I like to check this installation over, from time to time. This is why I showed it to you; *this* is the protection we undying offer to the people of Earth. You understand, don't you?'

'I think so...'

It was an elementary insight for a student of the Implication of Indefinite Longevity. The biggest difference in the perception of an undying was time itself. If you were an undying, you could expect to live so long that risks statistically negligible on the timescale of a normal human lifetime became significant. So a once-a-megayear risk of an asteroid strike in this cleaned-out, heavily defended system became worth thinking about, planning for.

If the species were to survive into the very far future, of course, such thinking was necessary. Mankind *needed* the undying, or at least their instincts for very long timescales. But it was a deadening, fearful perspective.

'And you feed this caution into the Transcendence,' Alia said.

'The undying founded the Transcendence. The undying have always shaped it. How could it be otherwise?'

'But you old ones bring other baggage, don't you?'

Leropa smiled. 'Baggage? Ah, you mean regret – the driver behind the Redemption. At last we are getting to the point. You have doubts about the Redemption, don't you, child? You think it is perhaps unhealthy. Obsessive. And you suspect there is more to it than mere Witnessing, don't you?'

Alia felt weak before the force of personality of this ancient creature. But she gathered her courage. 'I think there must be. *Because Witnessing isn't enough for atonement.*'

Leropa nodded approvingly. 'Your intuition is sound. Witnessing is in fact only the First Level of Redemption, as defined by the Colleges. And, no, it isn't thought to be sufficient. How could it be? Witnessing is for children.'

'What is the Second Level?'

'It is called *Hypostatic Union*,' Leropa said. 'A union of substances, of essences. Do you know what that means?'

'No.'

'Then learn.' She reached out and once more, with a fingertip that was colder than the mountain-top ice, touched Alia's forehead.

Alia fell into a bloody dark.

Chapter 38

In the morning we gathered outside the hotel's main entrance, ready to be taken to Makaay's demonstration. The weather was cold but clear, the sky a pale blue. Tom was here with Sonia, and Shelley and her people, Makaay, and a number of EI workers, most of whom I hadn't met before. Vander Guthrie was here. His blue hair, sticking out from under his fur cap, looked frankly ridiculous. We huddled together, wrapped up in heavy fake-fur coats and Russian-style hats provided for us by EI. 'We all look like bears,' Shelley joked, although there had been no bears in this area, polar or otherwise, for decades.

Awkwardly Tom and I embraced, father and son reunited in this industrial wasteland. Tom didn't have much to say to me. I was still in the doghouse for daring to speak to Aunt Rosa, and I refrained from telling him about my nocturnal pursuit of his mother's ghost. Business as usual. I got a kiss on the cheek from Sonia, however.

A pod bus came to collect us. At the coast we piled out into a chill wind that swept in off the sea and cut right through our clothing. We looked around.

The core of our hydrate-stabilisation plant had been built into the hulk of an offshore oil rig. We could see the rig from here, a blocky monochrome shape that loomed maybe a couple of kilometres from the shore. On a scrap of low, badly eroded cliff, a marquee had been set up, a brightly lit dome of some transparent fabric with a good view of the offshore rig. Here we would witness the ceremonial start-up of the facility. And then, assuming the whole thing didn't blow itself sky high, we would be flown out by chopper in small groups for a hands-on inspection. It was all good showmanship.

We pushed into the marquee through a kind of airlock,

past the scrutiny of massive EI security guards. We dumped our coats; I was grateful to get into the warmth. A hovering bot offered me alcohol or hot drinks. I accepted a nip of Scotch, and a big mug of steaming latte. I wandered away from the rest, taking in the scene.

Maybe fifty people milled in that marquee, most of them EI employees or colleagues of Shelley's. The accountants and other administrative types wore crumpled suits, but the engineers tended to be more casual, in jackets and jeans. The place was surveillance-rich, with football-sized drones that floated in the air, and a finer mist of micro-drones, a glittering dust that you only noticed if you focused closely.

'An impressive set-up. And all for my benefit.' The liquid female voice was very familiar.

I turned to see Edith Barnette standing at my side, with Ruud Makaay at her elbow, beaming proudly. Barnette wore a mid-length black dress; her legs were thin and pale, her feet clad in heavy-looking shoes. She was surprisingly tall, and her face was big-boned, her jaw heavy. Her skin, deeply wrinkled, was tanned pale gold, and her hair, sprayed into a dense helmet, was an uncompromising white. But she stood straight, her eyes were bright and alert, and when she spoke her voice was as mellow as it had always been.

At the side of today's sole VIP, Makaay was in his element. His blond hair shone sleek in the bright lights. 'Not entirely for your benefit, Madame Vice-President, though of course you are more than welcome.' He outlined his plans, and his intention that today was a rehearsal before we came up against more unforgiving audiences.

Barnette said, 'Then I will be sure to give you plenty of constructive criticism.'

'I'll welcome it. Forgive me, I'm due on stage.' He ducked out, bowing.

'So, Mr Poole,' Barnette said to me. 'All this was your idea, the stabilisation project?'

'I guess so. It was me who asked the right questions. But it was in the air, the community I work with. Sooner or later somebody would have seen the need to—'

'Oh, don't whiffle, man, I've no time for that.' She fixed

me with a pointed finger, slightly crooked. 'Your brainchild. Yes or no?'

'Yes.'

'It seems we will all owe you a debt of gratitude.'

I felt uncomfortable. Like Barnette the world tended to have a simple view of such projects; the media always looked for the chief engineer, the unsung double dome behind it all. But it wasn't a role I was going to be comfortable playing, even if the project went well.

'I guess so,' I said. 'If it works.'

'If?'

'We can't be sure. We think we've modelled all the consequences.'

'You consulted Gea, didn't you?'

'Gea has supported us from the start... You know her?'

'Never met it. Her? But I was responsible for major tranches of her development funding.'

I nodded, impressed. 'But even with Gea on board, all we have are theoretical models. We can't be *sure* what will happen.'

'Because we are dealing with the biosphere, correct? I'm told some scientists believe the biosphere may be *algorithmically incompressible*. Is that the right phrase? It literally *can't* be modelled, for its intrinsic complexity is simply too great. The biosphere is its own unfolding story.'

She surprised me with her understanding. 'I've heard that too.'

'Do you believe it?'

I shrugged. 'I don't think it makes a difference. The biosphere is bigger than we can manage confidently right now, so it doesn't matter *how* big it is, ultimately.'

She smiled. 'Spoken like an engineer. I always liked engineers, you know, though I was a philosophy major. You are pragmatists! Though I suspect many of you couldn't even spell the word. Despite the unfathomable complexity of the world, we must pragmatically tinker with it because of this hydrate-destabilisation business, mustn't we?'

'I believe so.'

'Well, I hope you're right. About everything.'

She was interrupted by a soft chiming. Ruud Makaay

had mounted a low stage and in his customary fashion was gently tapping a glass with a pen.

'Madam Vice President, everyone, thank you for joining us here on this exciting day. Of course most of you are paid to be here, and mostly by me, but thanks even so...' Expert delivery, laughter easily evoked. 'We're here to witness the first full-scale end-to-end integrated trial of the hydrate-stabilisation system prototype,' he said, to a few whoops from his engineers. 'But I think we should begin with some context.'

Makaay snapped his fingers, and a screen appeared in the air behind him. To my surprise it showed an image of what looked like an oasis in the desert, a splash of green against pale yellow, with a clear blue pool at its centre. 'The polar hydrate deposits, a massive store of greenhouse gases, are unstable. But they are not the Earth's only instability...'

The images he showed us were of the Sahara desert. As everybody in the marquee knew, one twist to the general global pattern of climate change was that the Sahara was greening. It had happened before, Makaay said. Five thousand years ago an extended drought had caused an environment of woodland and marshes full of crocodiles to flip over to a parched plain with only a few scattered oases, with crocodile bones left under the drifting sands for palaeobiologists to puzzle over. The Sahara appeared to be on a permanent knife edge, flipping between dry desert and wet woodland. It was thought such astounding transformations could take just twenty years – maybe less. This fundamental instability was why it had been possible for EI to hurry the process in selected parts of the desert, with its immense artificial lakes back-filled with Mediterranean water.

This was one example, Makaay said, of a common feature of Earth's climatic evolution. If you forced it, for instance by injecting greenhouse gases in the air, it tended not to respond smoothly, like rubber deforming under pressure. Instead it tended to snap, like the Sahara, switching abruptly from one stable state to another. The world was full of systems which, if pushed too far, might undergo 'abrupt and irreversible change', as Makaay put it: he listed the possible failure of the Gulf Stream, and the creation of a permanent El Nino storm which might dry out rainforests and create deserts across the tropics.

'We know we have to stabilise the hydrate deposits,' Makaay said. 'But this will not be the last time we will have to intervene on a massive, indeed global scale, if we are to ensure that the Earth's systems do not transition into a condition that makes the planet uninhabitable for us. We must learn to manage the Earth, our home, even while we cherish it...'

Edith Barnette leaned down to whisper to me, 'Nice presentation. I enjoyed the focus on the green Sahara – nothing wrong with an unexpectedly positive image. But now he sounds like an EI corporate report. I suggest in future he cuts to the chase.'

Now Makaay showed us blown-up images of our new baby, a glistening, complacent-looking mole. The moles had been trialled individually, but today was the first integrated trial of the system as a whole. A dozen moles would be dropped down defunct oil boreholes to begin the construction of an interconnected network, spreading out through hydrate strata, chattering to each other through sonar and other comms channels, and closing the complex loops around which the liquid nitrogen would flow.

For now the condensation plant and liquefaction gear would be based on the central oil platform. But that was only a stopgap design for this proof-of-concept pilot; in the future, working out 'in the wild', as Makaay put it, submersibles would install liquefaction and condensation gear on the seabed, to link up with the moles' tunnels beneath. And so the network would grow, spreading across the ocean floor, until the pole was encircled.

We were shown live images of the old oil rig a couple of kilometres offshore where our nitrogen liquefaction plant had been installed. Big liquid-nitrogen tanks glistened in the sun, frost sparkling on their surfaces.

A countdown clock appeared in the corner of our image and started to tick away the seconds before the insertion of the first moles. A hush fell over the room, as the show took on the feel of a space launch, a fond memory of my childhood. Makaay was never one to miss a trick, I thought respectfully.

There were about five minutes to go on the clock when Morag appeared to me again.

I could see her through the translucent wall of the marquee, out on the cold, dead ground: that slim, tall figure, the unmistakable shock of strawberry-blonde hair.

I left the Vice President for dead and ran for the exit. Behind me, ignored, Ruud Makaay was still talking. Heads turned as I passed, concerned.

Tom caught up with me before the doorway. 'Dad. What the hell are you doing?'

I pointed. 'Can't you see her?'

'I see – something. A woman out there. So what?'

'*You know who it is*. Come on, Tom. I just have to deal with this.'

'You mean *I* have to.'

I felt cold, determined. 'Yes. You have to. Because if you see her, she's haunting you too.'

At the exit I found myself facing an EI security guard, a slab of muscle. The guard looked confused, but her job was to keep people out, not shut them in, and she stood aside. I pushed through the airlock, and into the fresh air outside, dressed in nothing but my flimsy suit. It was bloody cold. There were drops of rain in the air, or maybe it was salt spray off the sea.

I glanced around, getting my bearings. To get to where Morag had been standing I would have to cut around the base of the marquee, to my right. I ran that way, not bothering to check if Tom was following. I had to jump over ropes and skirt blocks of equipment, generators, VR projectors and heaters. More security guards watched me go by, and I saw them speak into the air, reporting my progress, but I wasn't impeded.

Around the limb of the marquee I stumbled to a halt. Tom came up beside me, breathing hard.

There she was: Morag, standing in an open area beside the wall of the marquee, looking back at me. She was dressed in a plain blue smock, her favourite colour, the colour that

340

brought out her eyes, she always said. She didn't seem cold, despite the Arctic breeze. She was no more than fifty metres from me, just fifty paces. She had never been so close. *And she wasn't running away*, not drifting mysteriously down corridors, or disappearing into dust or mist. She just stood there. She was smiling at me. Her hands were open, as if to show me she meant me no harm.

For a heartbeat I drank in every detail of her, the hair that flopped over her brow in the breeze, the way the dress clung to her slim figure like a flag draped around a pole.

'It's her,' said Tom. 'It really is.'

'You do see her,' I breathed.

'Yes. Dad – what do we do?'

'I don't know. It's never been like this before.'

I spread my hands, mirroring her gesture. I took a step towards her, then another, cautiously. I was like a police officer approaching a suicide bomber, I thought. Still she didn't recede from me, as in all those nightmare pursuits of the past. She just watched me approach, smiling. A part of me was aware of glowing motes that danced before my eyes. We were saturated by surveillance by EI's security systems. There could be no doubt that there would be a record of this encounter, full and clear.

And there was no doubt in my mind that Morag was allowing this to happen, that this was her choice, to break through whatever barriers there were between us. I wondered why she was doing this now, here. Was she here because of the hydrate project? Was Rosa right, that Morag was somehow an angel from the future, drawn to significance?

I was so close I could see details, the tiny flaws in her skin, the beauty spot on her cheek, the small scar on her forehead. She was just as I had remembered her before her pregnancy, the labour that had killed her. It had been seventeen years since her death, but she hadn't aged a day. Oddly it might have seemed stranger to me, at that moment, if she had aged. She seemed full of mass, somehow, dense with matter and light; she stood out of the background, as if patched into a faded photograph. And still she didn't go away.

Ten paces from her I stopped. I feared what might happen

if I pushed this too far. If I got too close, if I tried to touch her, would she pop like a bubble?

'Morag. Can't you speak to me? What do you want?'

She smiled, encouraging. Then she spoke. It was *her* voice, undoubtedly, light, airy, salted with a trace of her Irish background. But her words were a rapid gabble, just as they had been on the Reef, in the hotel corridor. Her tone was wistful, her eyes bright, her gaze fixed on me. I couldn't bear to look away. But as the moment stretched, and as her only words were that strange compressed pseudo-speech, a kind of anxious sadness filled me.

A siren clamoured, echoing across the flat sea. It was coming from the oil rig, out on the ocean. Distracted, I looked that way, and saw vapour venting into the air. I knew that the siren had been the signal for the start of the trial – and cheering from inside the dome, slightly muffled, told me it had been a success, that the moles had been launched and were doing their job. At that moment I couldn't have cared less. I turned back to Morag.

And she was gone, gone, in that instant. Perhaps there was a trace of her, a profile of her figure in dancing dust, hanging in the air, sparkling; but even that dispersed on the wind. I was oppressed by guilt, as if it had been my fault that she had gone, as if I had broken the rules by looking away.

There was a soft whirring at my feet, a crackle of friction sparks. I looked down. The little Gea-robot rolled back and forth on the concrete at my feet.

'Gea, did you see that? Did you see *her*?'

'I recorded everything, Michael,' the robot said. 'But for now I think you should consider your son.'

Tom. I had forgotten him. I whirled around. Tom was hunched over on the ground. His whole body heaved as he wept. I ran towards him, but Sonia Dameyer got there first, and wrapped him in her arms.

And in that vignette you have the whole story of our two lives.

Chapter 39

Alia was immersed in some deep, dark, viscous ocean. She tried to struggle – but she could not, there was nothing to fight *with*. She tried to concentrate on her fingers, to move her toes, but there was no sensation. She felt no pain, nothing but a cushioning, cradling warmth.

She couldn't even feel herself breathe, she realised suddenly. She panicked. She looked deep inside herself, but she had no sense of her own pulse, the rhythms of her body. Even her sense of her body, her arms and legs, her torso and head, was dissipating. She cowered, even more terrified.

She had no idea what had happened to her, where she was – if she was *anywhere* in any meaningful sense. Of course it was all something to do with Leropa, and her strange projects. Was this another hideous Skimming – or something stranger still? And what could it have to do with Redemption?

But a kind of acceptance began to steal over her. Bereft of choice, she floated, without her body, a mote adrift in this strange sea. Was this mood of resignation itself part of the process? Without a bloodstream fizzing with adrenalin, perhaps it was impossible for her to *feel* fear: perhaps there was too little left of her even to be afraid. And if she had no body, did she have a self any more?

She felt herself spreading out. If the edges of her body had been erased, now so was the boundary of her mind, her very self. She was merging with this wider sea, she thought, like a drop of colouring in a bottle of water, growing more and more dilute. It wasn't uncomfortable, this subtle dissolving. It was like falling asleep.

Or it was like joining the Transcendence, she thought, like being immersed in that vast panoply of linked minds. But the Transcendence was something higher than mind. This bloody ocean was different; it was something *lower* than the body, lower than biology itself. Still she tried to fight it, to reflect back on herself.

It was her last conscious thought. After that, for an unmeasured time, there was only an endless, formless, oceanic dreaming.

And then something new.

Separateness.

There was no detail, nothing to be said about *this* which was separated from *that*. There was only the separateness itself, a relation between abstracts, beyond analysis or understanding. But that was something to cling to, a source of a deep formless pleasure – an exultance that *I am*.

Then something more. A kind of growing. Splitting, budding, a complexifying of the *I*, of whatever it was that had separated out of the rest. The growth was geometrical: two, four, eight, sixteen, a doubling every time, rapidly exponentiating away to large numbers, astronomical numbers. *Cells*: they were the units of the dividing, specks of biological matter each with their walls and nuclei and complicated chemical machinery.

The cluster that was growing out of the doubling cells was an embryo.

But that was a wrong thought, an inappropriate thought. It was not something the *I* should understand, not now, not yet. And that realisation of wrongness was *itself* wrong. A recursion set in, a feedback loop that multiplied that awareness of wrong.

Here was another separating, a distancing. Within the *I* – or around it, or beside it – was another point of view, separated from the I by an awareness that could never be part of the I itself. The viewpoint was a witness to this growing thing, this budding coalescing entity. It felt everything the I felt; it was as close to it in every sense as it was possible to be. And yet it was not *it*.

The separated viewpoint was Alia. She knew herself, who she was. She even had a dim, abstract awareness of her other life, like a half-remembered dream.

And meanwhile the *I*, the subject of her inspection, continued to grow.

That relentless budding was not random. In the final body there would be hundreds of different kinds of cells, specialised for different purposes. Already an organisation was emerging in this growing city of cells. Over *there* was a complicated cluster that might become a nervous system, with terminations flowering into what might become fingers, eyes, a brain. And over *there* were simpler blocks that might become kidneys and liver and heart.

This was a wondrous process, for there was nothing here to tell the cells *how* to organise themselves in this manner. As the cells split and grew and split again, they communicated with their neighbours through salts, sugars, amino acids passed from one cell's cytoplasm to another's. In this way the cells formed collectives, each dedicated to developing a special function – to become an eardrum or a heart valve – and, through a clustering of the collectives themselves at a higher level, to ensure that ears and hearts, arms and legs, developed in the right place. Out of this mesh of interaction and feedback the organisation of a human body developed.

The whole process was an emergence of complexity, an expression of a deep principle of the universe. Even the *I*, the wispy unformed mind that was lodged in this expanding, complexifying cluster, was itself an emergent property of the growing network of cells. And yet already there was consciousness here, and a deep, brimming, joyful awareness of growth, of increasing potential, of being.

Now, strangely, death came to the differentiating cluster of cells. Succumbing to subtle pressures from their neighbours, cells in the shapeless hands and feet began to die, in waves and bands. It *hurt*, surprisingly, shockingly. But there was purpose to this dying; the scalpel of cellular death was finely shaping those tiny hands and feet, cleaving one finger from another.

The growing child lifted its new hand before its face. Not *its*, Alia thought – *his*. Already the processes of development had proceeded that far. His fingers were mere nerveless stumps yet, and could not be moved; and in this bloody dark nothing could be seen, even if the child had eyes to see. And yet he strained to see even so, motivated by a faint curiosity.

His curiosity, not Alia's.

This union was not like Witnessing. She was embedded deeply in the machinery of the child's shaping body; she felt everything he did, shared every dim thought, every sensation. But she was somehow, subtly, separated from him, and always would be. She was a monitor, a watcher; she shared everything the child lived through – and would throughout his whole life – but not his will, his choice.

And there was something wrong, a note out of place in this great symphony of manufacture and assembly. There was something not quite right with the heart, she saw, a place where the mindless self-organisation had gone awry. Nothing was perfect; this was not the only flaw in the growing body. Perhaps it would not matter.

As his body and nervous system developed, the child's mind continued to evolve.

At first there had been no sense of time, or space. There were only abstractions like separateness, one thing from another, and only events, disconnected, acausal. Time gradually emerged as a sense of events in sequence: first the hands, then the cellular die-back, then the separating fingers, one after another. Space came after that, as the body itself grew in extent and emerged from formlessness into a tool that he could, in a limited fashion, use to explore the space around him. It was a passive exploration at first, not much more than a dim realisation that the universe had to be at least big enough to encompass his body. But then he had fingers to stretch out, legs to kick with. Soon he could feel the sac that contained him, could kick against its walls, and he began to get the sense that even beyond this sac was a wider universe, perhaps including beings more or less like himself.

That sense deepened when sight arrived. He could make out a dim ruddy glow, that waxed and waned. Sometimes, when the light was at its brightest, he could even make out the pale fish-like shape that was his own body, the rope that anchored him to the walls around him.

But the light would dim and return, dim and return, and a

new sense of time imposed itself on him: not a time dictated by the events of his own body, but a cycle that came from a wider world outside him. There were processes that went on independently of him, then; he was not the whole universe – even though it still *felt* like it.

Then there were sharper sensations, brought to him in a rich stream of blood. The nourishment he received could be rich or thin, familiar or strange. Sometimes it was even intoxicating, mildly, so that he thrashed uncomfortably in his tank of flesh. This came from the mother, he knew on some deep level.

For the child in the womb, here was still another lesson to learn. Not only was there a universe outside this womb of his, but there were creatures out there who imposed their will on him: even his mother, who lived her own life, while cradling his. It was a gathering awareness of separateness that presaged the child's ultimate ejection from this crimson comfort into the harsher, much less sympathetic world beyond the walls of the womb.

But now came the pain.

It was extraordinary. It flooded the child's still-developing nervous system as if hot mercury had been injected into it. The walls of the womb flexed, pressing at the helpless body, overwhelming his struggles. There was a new taste on his soft pink tongue, a taste he could not recognise, was not supposed to know, not yet. But Alia recognised its iron tang. It was blood.

Something was badly wrong.

The pain passed. The child relaxed, exhausted. Groping in the dark he pushed one tiny thumb into his mouth and sucked. Alia, floating with him, longed to comfort him. But the memory of the pain clung deep, and nothing was quite as it had been before, or ever could be.

Now there was another intrusion into this amniotic refuge. It was something *sharp*, and it was *cold*, unbelievably so in this little universe of soft, cushioning flesh. A probe, Alia thought, pushed in from outside. Was it possible somebody out there was trying to help this damaged child? But if so, how crude a way to do it! The child thrashed, distressed down to the core of his being. The probe sucked away some of the child's flesh and withdrew. The child folded over on itself, scrabbling at its small face with its hands. Again peace returned, like an echo of the endless tranquillity from which the child had been separated at its conception. But it did not last long.

And when the pain came back, Alia knew that there would be no respite. Again the child shrieked silently, but there was nobody to hear him; again the womb walls flexed helplessly, as if trying to crush the child out of existence.

There was another sharp intrusion from outside, but this was much more drastic than the earlier probing. A blade slashed uncompromisingly through the wall of the womb, and light poured in. The child thrashed and grasped; it was as shocking as if the sky itself had cracked open. Huge forms descended and something smooth and cold closed around his torso – hands, gloved perhaps? And now, in the ultimate horror, he was lifted up, pulled *away* from the womb into a sharp coldness, a new realm of bitter light. But he could feel the cord in his belly tugging him back to the womb.

Amidst all this unimaginable horror the pain returned again. It was even worse now. It seemed to emanate from the core of his being, his chest and belly, and flooded out through his limbs to his tiny fingers, the thumb he had sucked. It was as if some immense hard object was slamming against his chest, over and over.

He was aware of motion, a smooth surface under him; he had been laid down. Then came a sharp pain at his belly as the cord was cut. Immense objects, perhaps fingers, dug into his mouth. He could see only a blur, only light, smeared with a crimson film of blood and amniotic fluid. But objects floated through that blur, looming down. They were faces, human faces. Even as the terrible pain continued, the child struggled to make out the faces – a first reflex of his nervous system, Alia knew. He looked for smiles, for welcoming. But there were no smiles here. And one of those faces, even though it was just a moonscape of patches and blurs, looked oddly familiar to Alia.

It was Michael Poole.

But now the faces receded, and darkness washed over

the child's vision. That pounding pain continued, and he thrashed feebly, even now fighting. But he was tiring quickly. There was a kind of question in his mind, Alia realised, an expression of a deep longing. This new darkness – was it the womb? Was he being returned to the place he belonged?

Alia could not answer him. She was only an observer. And yet she replied: *Yes. There is nothing to fear. Lie still.*

The darkness rose up around him now; the faces had gone, vanished for ever. The miracle of biological self-organisation and emergent awareness was dissipating, crumbling, and so was his mind.

At least the pain stopped.

Chapter 40

The day after that first integrated test was launched, Edith Barnette returned to her home in DC.

She took with her good wishes from our confused little crew. It meant a lot that such a grand old lady had hauled ass all the way to Alaska to see us, for she had demonstrated concretely that there was support for our work out there, if only we could tap into it. We were a somewhat fragile alliance of partners, with both Shelley's concerns and EI always having their eye on the need to make a profit some day. Barnette's endorsement would help keep their boards and shareholders happy – or at least nobody was talking about pulling out yet.

In the days that followed, we dug into the work once more.

What Barnette had witnessed was only the beginning of the integration trials, the first tentative burrowings of our moles into shallow sea-bottom sediments. It had mostly gone well. Around ten per cent of the Higgs-field power packs had suffered glitches of one sort or another, but as Higgs was the one really novel technological element, you had to expect unpleasant surprises..

Most of the smart moles had behaved much as expected, but the network they had begun constructing hadn't been quite of the quality we'd hoped for. Small-world networking: a useful, robust network should be designed around a number of key nodes with plenty of links between them, so you can get from one point to another with very few steps, and yet with the whole thing resilient in the face of failure. As we wanted our refrigerant network to be working from the moment we put it in the ground, we were seeking a kind of rolling optimum, with it being as good as it could be at every stage of its extension. In those first few hours of work, what we built was good, but not quite as good as that. Some of the moles seemed to have forgotten the wider goal, and had gone burrowing off according to their own agenda. We speculated that maybe the unusual environment of the moles led to a kind of mechanical solipsism, as if each mole was tempted to believe that it was alone, the centre of a cramped, dark universe of cold and sediment. We were going to have to pull some of the moles back for therapy, we decided. This was twenty-first-century engineering, where you wielded TLC rather than a spanner.

The plan beyond that was for the moles' drillings to extend out to about a kilometre from the central rig. Then an array of condenser stations would be established across the sea floor to complete the logical closure of our refrigeration loops. After that the first liquid nitrogen would be pumped through our lined tunnels, and we should begin to achieve actual cooling over a significant chunk of the seafloor, and deep beneath its surface. All this, Ruud Makaay hoped, would be achievable in a few more months.

It was at that point, when we were able to demonstrate significant temperature reductions, and we were sure about the heat flows and efficiencies and other parameters of the whole process, that we would go public.

It would be a sales pitch, and would have to be carefully choreographed. We hoped to be able to use Edith Barnette as a lever to bring us some attention from the world's decision makers. Gea's projections of how well our refrigerant technology would work, and the difference it would make to the state of the planet, were also going to be crucially authoritative. Then, so the best-case scenario went, with endorsement from the Stewardship, the US federal government, and various other agencies of governance, we would begin the roll-out of the technology around both poles of the planet, tweaking the design and learning all the way. This might be as little as a year from now.

And at that point, the business analysts suggested, serious money would start to roll into the coffers of EI and the other private agencies involved. Even I would be getting a consultancy fee, I was assured. Capitalism would save the world, but only so long as it showed a profit.

That was the plan. To achieve it there was still a hell of a lot of work to do, for all of us. Even Tom and Sonia had carved out a role as a kind of watching brief on the project, which was turning out to be surprisingly useful. They couldn't contribute much technically, but they had a good sense of the impact our project was going to have on the high-latitude communities on which its infrastructure was going to be 'imposed', in Tom's word. They added a degree of cultural sensitivity which our little engineering community perhaps lacked.

And while all this was going on we had to deal with the fall-out from the Poole family circus show.

On the day itself, Ruud Makaay explained away the Morag incident to Edith Barnette as a personal issue for me and Tom. She clearly didn't buy this, but her only comment was that it was a good thing there had been no press here to see it. After all the centre of the incident was *me*, who everybody knew was the originator of the whole project in the first place; it couldn't have been more high profile.

As for everybody else, Deadhorse was a pretty desolate and uninspiring place, and I was suddenly a valued source of scuttlebutt. Makaay was irritated at the way his people were distracted by 'this stupid sideshow', as he called it; it was 'getting in the way' when there was already too much work to do. Shelley was more circumspect. She didn't say much, and I knew she would support me in trying to resolve this knot of strangeness in my life. But I think she, too, wished it would all just go away.

As for Tom, he avoided me for days.

I took Shelley's advice not to push him. He had a lot to absorb, after all: this was the first time *he* had been haunted too. And besides, as Sonia confided in a discreet moment, his pride had been hurt. Whatever the cause, fifty people had seen him crushed and weeping on the frozen ground. So I tried to give him space.

But I had to follow it up myself. I parcelled up the records of that day and beamed them over by high-bandwidth link to Rosa, my wizened, black-clad aunt in Seville, to see what she made of them.

352

A week after that strange day, Rosa called me back.

Ruud Makaay, bowing to the inevitable, gave us one of his conference rooms to take Rosa's call. Tom and Sonia were there – though I gathered that Sonia had had to twist Tom's arm. I could understand his reluctance, but my son was no coward, and I knew he would face up to all this strangeness in the end. However I asked Shelley Magwood to attend too. I had often observed that we Pooles behaved better towards each other when outsiders were present. Or maybe I just felt I needed an ally. Gea, my strange artificial companion, was there too.

So we sat around a simple circular table, Gea's little toy-robot avatar rolling back and forth on the table-top.

And Rosa materialised among us, a dark, brooding presence in her black priest's garb. The VR facilities were functional rather than corporate-luxurious, and you could see a ghostly second surface where the projection of Rosa's table was overlaid on ours.

'So,' Rosa smiled at us. 'Who's first?'

It was actually Gea who started us off. She had been analysing the surveillance records of the day. She conjured up a snippet of the visitation, played out by manikins on the table-top, ten-centimetre-high models of me, Morag, Tom and Sonia. The resolution was good, far better than Rosa's image of the Reef; the whole area around the marquee and the offshore rig had been drenched with sensors. And the data went beyond human senses. Gea was able to show us an X-ray image of Morag, for instance; we saw bones, a regular-looking skeleton, the ghostly images of internal organs – a brain, a heart.

'Whatever this creature is,' Gea said, 'the body of "Morag Poole" responds to our sensors, every one of them. It has mass, volume, an internal structure. It is in our universe. It is no hallucination, and no ghost, in the sense of the word as I understand it. *It is really there.*'

But who *was* this? Gea snipped out a little volume around Morag's head and blew it up until it was life-size, a disembodied head with a serene, somewhat vacant expression. Gea overlaid this with an X-ray image of the skull within, and she compared it to images of Morag from her medical records and my own personal archive. Rapidly we were taken through a point-to-point matching of facial structures, of the deeper bones, even of her teeth. All this was completed in seconds. The implication was clear: any forensic scientist would have concluded that the face in our image was indeed Morag.

'But,' Gea said, 'there are anomalies.'

The Morag creature was dense, massive, in fact about twice my weight. Gea had been able to measure that by studying seismic echoes of her footsteps. The sense I'd sometimes had that Morag was somehow more *real* than me and the rest of my world seemed to be borne out. But Gea's sensors had detected only flesh and blood and bone, and it wasn't clear what form her invisible mass took.

For all her intense reality, the sensors had no clear record of where Morag had come from, or where she had gone to. It was as if the myriad artificial eyes just looked away, and she was gone.

As Gea went through this, Rosa watched Tom carefully. She seemed fascinated by his reaction, his emotional state. Tom was expressionless, but even that was eloquent, I thought.

Rosa said at last, 'Whatever we are to make of all this, one thing is clear. The visitations are now part of our consensual reality. Michael may indeed be crazy, but we can't explain away his experiences that way any more.'

'Thanks,' I said warmly.

'Well, personally I'm awed,' Sonia said. 'Scared.'

'Me too,' Shelley said. 'It's a ghost story suddenly coming true.' But she didn't sound scared, or particularly awed, and neither did Sonia; they sounded curious. I was impressed by the resilience of their minds, the minds of a soldier and an engineer. It wasn't just their professions that gave them such strength, I suspected, but a deeper robustness of the human psyche. I said, 'There's no reason to be afraid. If strangeness spooked us we'd still be competing for gazelle bones with the hyenas out on the savannah. We'll deal with this—'

Tom turned on me. 'That's typical of your bullshit, Dad. What we're trying to deal with here is *my mother*. Or rather, that thing that looks like my mother. And all you can come up with is some fucking pep-talk about walking out of Africa.' His voice was controlled but brittle.

Rosa said evenly, 'We all need ways of coping with this, Tom. You must find your own path, as your father is finding his. This is a reality Michael has accepted for some time, I think. But now suddenly this is real for *you*. You were even able to approach your mother—'

'It wasn't my mother,' he snapped.

Rosa nodded. 'Very well. You were able to approach *the visitor* closely, to inspect her, as I hadn't been able to in Seville. What did you feel?'

Tom wouldn't reply. He shot me a resentful, pitying glance.

As for me, I truly believed that this visitor *was*, on some level, Morag, it really was her. I had always believed that. So how was I supposed to feel? I had never known that, not since my first visitations as a child. My reaction was to figure it out, try to make sense of it. But maybe I was the weak one; maybe the true, strong reaction was actually Tom's, his devastated weeping on the plain; maybe he felt the reality of this return, its strangeness, in ways I was incapable of.

Shelley's hand crept over mine.

Rosa had been concentrating her own studies on Morag's speech. She played us a sample. Once again a disembodied head floated over our table-top; once again I saw that beautiful face, those full lips. But Morag spoke strangely and quickly, a string of syllables too rapid to distinguish, her tongue flicking between her lips.

Rosa froze the image. 'There is no known human language detectable in this signal. And yet we can detect structure...' She told us, somewhat to my surprise, that there was a flourishing discipline in the study of non-human languages.

It had originated in questions about animal communication. The songs of whales and whistles of dolphins were obvious case studies, but so were the hoots and screeches of chimps and monkeys, the stamping of elephants – even the dull chemical calling of one plant to another. But how much information was contained in these messages? Even if you couldn't translate the language, even if you didn't know what the whales sang about, were there ways of determining if there was any information in there at all – and if so, how much, how dense? This was a discipline that in latter years had been useful in helping us figure out the sometimes cryptic utterances of our more enigmatic artificial intelligences – and, I thought, it might be useful some day if we ever encountered extraterrestrial intelligences.

Rosa waved a hand, and the air filled with graphs. It was all to do with information theory, she said, the mathematics of sequences of symbols – binary digits, DNA bases, letters, phonemes. 'The first thing is to see if there is any information in your signal. And to do that you construct a Zipf graph...' This was named after a Harvard linguist of the 1940s. You broke up your signal into its elements – bases, letters, words – and then made a bar graph of their frequency of use. She showed us examples based on the English alphabet, presenting us with a kind of staircase, with the usage of the most commonly used letters – *e*, *t*, *s* – to the left, and lesser usages represented by more bars descending to the right. 'That downward slope is a giveaway that information-rich structure is present. Think about it. If you have meaningless noise, a random sequence of letters, each one is liable to come up as often as any other.'

'So the graph would be flat,' Sonia said.

'Yes. On the other hand if you had a signal with structure but no information content – say just a long sequence of *e, e, e*, like a pure tone – you'd have a vertical line. Signals containing meaningful information come somewhere between those two extremes. And you can tell something about the degree of information contained by the slope of the graph.'

Sonia asked, 'What about the dolphins?' She glanced apologetically at Tom. 'I know it's nothing to do with your mother. I'd just like to know.'

Rosa smiled. 'Actually the analysis is a little trickier in that case. With human languages, it's easy to see the breakdown into natural units, letters, words, sentences: you can see what you must count. With non-human languages, like dolphin whistles, it's harder to see the breaks between linguistic units. But you can use trial and error. Even dolphin whistles have gaps, so that's a place to start, and then you can expand the way you decompose your signal, looking for other trial break markers, until you find the breakdown that gives you the strongest Zipf result.'

Sonia asked, 'And the answer?'

Rosa waved a hand, like a magician. A new line on the graph appeared, below the first and parallel to it. 'Dolphin whistles, and whale songs and a number of other animal signals, contain information – in fact they all show signs of optimal coding. Of course knowing there is information in there isn't the same as having a translation. We know the dolphins are talking, but we still don't know what they are talking about.'

'We may never know,' Gea said. 'Now that the oceans are empty.' She rolled back and forth, friction sparks flying. You wouldn't think a tin robot could look so judgemental.

Rosa said brightly, 'As far as Morag is concerned we aren't done yet. There is a second stage of analysis which allows us to squeeze even more data out of these signals.'

As I'd half-expected, she began to talk about entropy. The Zipf analysis showed us whether a signal contained information at all, Rosa said. The entropy analysis she presented now was going to show us how complex that information was. It makes sense that information theoreticians talk about entropy, if you think about it. Entropy comes from thermodynamics, the science of molecular motion, and is a measure of disorder – precise, quantified. So it is a kind of inverse measure of information.

Rosa showed us a new series of graphs, which plotted 'Shannon entropy value' against 'entropy order'. It took me a while to figure this out. The zero-order-entropy number was easiest to understand; that was just a count of the number of elements in your system, the diversity of your repertoire – in written English, that could be the twenty-six letters of the alphabet plus a few punctuation marks. First-order entropy measured how often each element came up in the language – how many times you used *e* versus *t* or *s*. Second-order and higher entropies were trickier. They were to do with correlations between the elements of your signal.

Rosa said, 'If I give you a letter, what's your chance of predicting the next in the signal? *Q* is usually followed by *u*, for instance. That's second-order entropy. Third-order means, if I give you two letters, what are your chances of predicting the third? And so on. The longer the chain of entropy values, the more structure there is in your signal.'

The most primitive communications we knew of were chemical signalling between plants. Here you couldn't go beyond first-order Shannon entropy: given a signal, you couldn't guess what the next would be. Human languages showed eighth- or ninth-order entropy.

We talked around the meaning of this. The Shannon entropy order has something to do with the complexity of the language. There is a limit to how far you can spin out a paragraph, or even an individual sentence, if you want to keep it comprehensible – though a more advanced mind could presumably unravel a lot more complexity.

Sonia asked, 'And the dolphins?'

Sadly, the dolphins' whistles showed no more than third or fourth-order Shannon entropy. They beat most primates, but not by much.

'I guess they were too busy having fun,' Sonia said wistfully.

Tom had glowered all the way through this. Now he asked, 'And the signal from the mother-thing? What does your analysis tell us about that?'

'It passes the Zipf test,' Rosa said. 'And as for entropy—'

She laid a new line on her graphical display of plant, chimp, dolphin, human languages. Sloping shallowly, it tailed away into the distance of the graph's right hand side, far beyond the human.

'The analysis is uncertain,' Rosa said. 'As you can imagine we've never actually encountered a signal like this before. Human languages, remember, reach Shannon order eight or nine. This signal, Morag's speech, appears to be at least order thirty. We have to accept, I think, that Morag's speech does contain information, of a sort. But it is couched in a fantastically abstruse form. As if it contains layers of nested clauses, overlapping tense changes, double, triple, quadruple negatives, all crammed into each sentence—'

'Jeez,' Shelley said. 'No wonder we can't figure it out.' She sounded daunted, even humbled.

It wasn't a comfortable thought for me either. The bright new artificial minds, such as Gea, would surely have scored more highly than us on a scale like this – but at least we *made* them. This was different; this was outside humanity's scope altogether. Suddenly we were going to have to get used to sharing the universe with a different order of intelligence than us.

'And,' I said, wondering, 'it's coming out of the mouth of my dead wife.'

Again my words sparked Tom off. He stood up, pushing back his chair. 'No,' he shouted. '*It's not her.* That's the point – can't you see? Whatever is animating that fake shell, whatever is producing these alien words, *it is not her.*' And he stormed out of the room, without looking back.

Sonia hurried after him, with a mouthed 'Sorry' to me.

The meeting broke up. I was left with the patient VR image of Rosa, and the graphs that scrolled in the air around her.

I apologised for Tom.

'Give him time,' Rosa said. 'After all it is a strange business. His mother is trying to talk to you.'

'If it is Morag.'

'*You* believe it is, don't you? But we face this odd mixture of emotional power – she is your wife, after all, and Tom's mother, there can hardly be stronger emotional bonds – coupled with this strange symbolic over-complexity. She has something she needs to tell us, that seems clear, but she doesn't seem to know how to do it.'

I had no answer. I just sat there, my head and limbs heavy; I felt simply overwhelmed.

Rosa watched me carefully. 'Are you all right?'

'I think so.' I rubbed my temples. 'So much is going on, so fucking much. I'm trying to push forward the hydrate project. I'm trying to deal with Tom, and John, and everybody else. Even Shelley. Even *you*. And I have this business of Morag, which only seems to get stranger and stranger. I don't want to hurt anybody, Rosa. Especially not Tom.'

'I know that,' Rosa said gently. 'You think you are weak. Don't you, Michael?'

I shrugged. 'What else should I think?'

'You are buffeted. You are surrounded by epochal events in our history; you are at the centre of a storm. And at the same time you are being subjected to these extraordinary manipulations and messages.'

I forced a smile. 'Messages from beyond the grave?'

'From somewhere else, certainly. We may yet learn there is some connection between all these different sorts of strangeness in your life, and things will get more complicated still.'

Just as her brother George had hinted, I thought uneasily. But I had enough conspiracy theories in my life.

Rosa said, 'But at the eye of the storm *you keep going*, Michael. You keep trying to do your best for everybody. You know, you remind me of Saint Christopher.'

I tried to remember my Catholic lore. 'The patron of travellers?'

'Yes. The story is he offered to carry the Christ child across a river. But the child got heavier and heavier. The child told Christopher it was because he was carrying the weight of the whole world on his shoulders. And yet Christopher kept on going, one foot after another, until he completed the crossing. That is exactly what you are doing, Michael, and you will continue to walk forward, until you reach the far bank.' She smiled. 'I don't think you are weak at all.'

There was a soft chime. Evidently Rosa heard it too, for she was disturbed in her sanctum in Seville, as I was.

The call was from John. Uncle George, Rosa's brother, was dying.

Chapter 41

After Alia emerged from her Hypostatic Union, Reath lifted her out of the claustrophobic antiquity of Earth and restored her to the comparatively familiar confines of his ship. The six of them, Alia, Drea, Reath and the Campocs, sat in a huddle in Alia's cabin, as she tried to describe her experience.

'How fascinating,' Reath said. 'You begin even without a sense of self. Then comes a feeling for events, disconnected in your awareness. You have to *learn* sequence, order, separation. How remarkable that time comes before space! Does phylogeny recapitulate cosmology?'

Drea had her arm around her sister. 'Reath, can't you shut *up*? Alia, you say you saw Michael Poole's face?'

Alia sighed. 'I think so. But I was looking out from inside a prematurely born baby's head. A *dying* baby.'

Reath said, 'In Poole's era even very young babies were innately programmed to respond to human faces. An evolutionary relic of obvious utility. It's not impossible you really did make out his face.'

'I knew the event,' Alia whispered. 'The birth. I've seen it many times, in the tank. I even Witnessed it again after I came out, to check.'

'The child was Poole's,' Drea prompted.

'His second son. Killed by a heart defect. The mother died too – Morag. It was an incident that shaped Poole's whole life, subsequently. I've seen it many times.'

'But never from the inside,' Reath said grimly.

'No. Not that way.'

Alia understood now. She had lived out the child's life, its whole life from conception to death. She *felt* as if she had been away for eight months – though only eight hours had passed for the others. If Witnessing was the First Level of the Redemption, this was the Second. You didn't just watch a life from the outside, unlike the conceptual simplicity of Witnessing; you saw it from the *inside*. You lived it through heartbeat by heartbeat from the moment of conception to the finality of death, and you shared every scrap of sensation, every feeling, every thought. All you didn't have was will.

'It wasn't much of a life,' Alia said. 'Less than eight months – not that time meant much at first. But I lived through it all.'

Drea shook her head. 'What's the point of going through all that pain? It's so *morbid*.'

'I think I can see the theory,' Reath said. 'At the heart of the Redemption is a desire for atonement, bringing the past into oneself. Perhaps that can be achieved through a reconciliation, a unification of oneself with a figure from the past. Witnessing was a first step. But by going to this Second Level, by suffering *with* that figure, by living through such a life, the anguish of the past can be –' he waved a hand '– internalised sufficiently.'

Bale said sceptically, 'Sufficiently for what?'

'To make this strange superhuman guilt go away.'

Seer laughed. 'So is that the truth behind our glorious Transcendence, our superhuman future? It's all just a grim nostalgia for the womb?'

'I still say it's morbid,' Drea said.

After a day in orbit Alia descended to Earth. She met Leropa once more in the attenuated shadows of the ruined cathedral.

'Reath speaks of atonement,' Alia said. 'He says that perhaps by joining with a figure from the past you can expiate its pain.'

'Reath is a wise man,' Leropa said.

'So I was united with Poole's lost son.'

'Yes. The Second Level is a Hypostatic Union with the past, a union of substances beneath external differences, beyond the trivialities of locations in space and time. You felt that poor child's small joy, his pain. And you will never forget, will you?'

'No,' Alia said fervently. 'And this is the redeeming?'

'It is the beginning,' Leropa said.

Alia frowned. 'I have to do this again?'

Leropa seemed surprised by the question. 'Of course.'

'I have to live through a whole human life, *again*?'

'It isn't so bad,' Leropa said. 'Subjective time, the time of the hypostasis, passes more rapidly than externally. To join with Michael Poole himself, for example, a life spanning nearly a hundred years, would take only a few days.'

'But a hundred years,' Alia said, 'for *me*. A hundred years of being trapped, helpless, in some tormented body of the past. How could I survive that?'

'Oh, but you would. You're strong, I can see that. And then of course—'

Alia saw it immediately. 'I would have to do it again. Another life to be endured. And again and again.' But the present was a surface surrounding a great ocean of past; the dead far outnumbered the living. 'How many lives must I live through, Leropa?'

Leropa frowned. 'If you have to ask that, as I told you, you don't understand the nature of the Transcendence.'

'*How many*?'

'All of them,' the undying said simply.

It was the ultimate logic of Redemption. The purpose was atonement, not just for *some* of the past, for *some* of the human suffering it contained, but for *all* of it. And how could that be achieved piecemeal? So Alia, like every Witness, would have to live through *every* human life that had preceded hers: Michael Poole, his second son, his family, his ancestors, and *their* ancestors all the way back to the point where humanity first emerged, perhaps a hundred billion of them – and, looking forward, all his descendants, to the mighty Galaxy-spanning Exultant generation and beyond. And in the future, all those watchers would themselves have to be watched – and then there would be watchers to watch the watchers – on and on, a recursive chain of watchers upon watchers.

The ultimate logic was that *every* human being, undying, should live through the lives, and absorb the pain, of *every* other.

'No doubt the process will be made more efficient,' Leropa

said, unperturbed. 'But the number of encounters is always finite. And finitude withers to nothing in the face of infinity.'

Alia remembered Reath's grave, sad voice: *To understand the Transcendence, you must understand infinity, Alia.* 'But all that pain, multiplied over and over, combinatorially, *for ever.*'

Leropa spread her hands. 'This is atonement. Atonement must *hurt*. To a creature of infinite capacity like the Transcendence, what can serve as atonement but to pay an infinite price?'

Alia backed away. *This is insane,* she thought, but she dared not say it. 'I don't want this.'

Leropa's frown deepened. 'You choose death over life? Smallness over infinity? Are you sure?'

'I'm not ready.'

Leropa bowed her head. 'Take all the time you need. But I will be here, waiting for you. *For ever.* And remember,' she called. 'Redemption has more Levels you've yet to glimpse...'

Alia turned and ran for the shuttle.

It was a huge relief once more to get back to orbit. But Drea had news from the *Nord* – bad news.

Chapter 42

We got together to discuss what to do: George's surviving family, John, Tom, my mother, me, even Rosa, all huddling like VR witches behind George's back.

We'd been told that none of us was to fly to England. George made it abundantly clear that any fuss and expense would embarrass him. He didn't even want VR visitors, he said. We all had our own lives to lead, et cetera, et cetera. I don't think it fooled anybody. But then the guy was eighty-seven and he was dying; I guess he had a right to a little muddle.

We had to see him, of course, virtually at least. John agreed to dig into his pockets once more. But we decided we weren't going to go over in a mob, VR or not, like a presaging of the funeral the doctors were saying wouldn't be more than a year away. We would visit one at a time, or in pairs. Tom went first, with Sonia. George would surely want to meet Tom's partner, but he had his pride; we knew he would feel happier about facing her while he was still able to put on a show.

While Tom visited I carried on with my work in Alaska, on the hydrate project. Rosa and Gea continued to analyse the visitations, but for a while I spent no more time on Morag. My Morag problem had always tended to make us fight, me against John, Tom against me; it drove us apart. At such a time as this it all seemed trivial, a sideshow, whatever its astounding implications.

Then, a week after Tom's visit, I VR-travelled to England myself.

George was glad to see me. That was obvious, gratifying, painful.

He wanted to take another walk, which surprised me. So we stepped out of his house, trailed once more by his Gea-robot care assistant. George guided me away from the maintained silvertop roads, and I soon found myself walking down the greened centre lane of one half of an immense dual carriageway, as they call them in England.

It was the middle of the night for my body in Alaska, and I felt dislocated, faintly jet lagged. The experience of that fresh English day, the quality of the virtual sunlight on my virtual cheeks, was enough to make my body respond, to wake me up.

The road was a mighty ribbon that curled between banks of houses, shops and factories. Traffic lights and road signs, the clutter of the roadside, mostly survived, but the paint of the signs had long faded to illegibility. The tarmac itself was giving way to green. For long stretches it was broken up by weeds, grasses and a few bright wild flowers nuzzling into pores in the road surface – 'pioneer species', George said. It was strange to see that carpet of green unrolling before me like a long, thin stretch of parkland, empty of people save for ourselves.

George was in a nostalgic mood. 'Sometimes I miss the traffic,' he said. 'When I was a kid – why, when *you* were a kid – the towns and cities were full of cars day and night, and there was this dull, continual roar. I used to think about the roads, how they joined up the country. You could drive your car out from your own garage, and then expect to be able to roll all the way to wherever you wanted to get to, from Cornwall to Scotland, without your tyres ever leaving the tarmac. It was as if some great volcanic eruption had flooded the whole country with asphalt.

'And then it went away, just like that. Christ, Spaghetti Junction is a world heritage site now. All that *noise* went away, the roar of the rushing cars, the honking of horns, the sirens, brakes squealing, music blasting. I miss the noise, I think. I miss it the way I miss the smell of the stale cigarette smoke my parents would leave around the house; you know it's bad for you, but it still reminds you of home. If you'd told me as a kid that in my lifetime people would give up the car I'd have laughed at you, it would have seemed much more fantastic than going to Mars…'

Green kilometres slowly piled up behind us. George seemed to have plenty of energy, but he walked stiffly, in an ungraceful, asymmetric way. Walking had become an awkward, mechanical action he had to think about.

There was a tumour in his belly 'the size of a tennis ball', he said.

It might have been caught earlier if George had allowed the medics to insert the appropriate implants and nano-monitors. Like many people his age, though, he had a deep distrust of having such gadgetry inside his body; he had lived through an era in which technology had betrayed as much as it had delivered. So he lived, and died, with the consequences of his choices. 'But at least they were *my* choices.'

He had been gratified by Tom's VR visit, and he had been glad to meet Sonia. 'She'll be good for Tom. We need some-body to inject a little sanity in our lives, we Pooles… Speaking of which, how's this business of Morag coming along?'

He knew about the language analysis, as far as it had got.

'We're still trying to break down the encoding of Morag's signal,' I said. '*We* meaning Gea and Rosa. It's a scary thought that the combined resources of the top biosphere-modelling software suite and one of our most ancient religions are being devoted to figuring out my little ghost story.'

'And do you still think it's just a ghost story?'

I thought it over. 'No. I don't think I ever did. Not even from the beginning.'

'What beginning?'

So, walking along the empty road, I told him about the prehistory of my haunting, back to when I was a kid in Florida. I think he felt hurt I'd never shared this with him at the time. But then I'd never told anybody about it at all before confiding in Shelley, only a few weeks ago.

'George, I believe that in some way this is Morag, it really is. Of course I fully accept she died, all those years ago. So something is going on here which isn't normal, rational. It's acausal for one thing. But I don't believe she's a ghost, with all the connotations of that word. There is no quality of—' I hesitated, unwilling to finish the sentence.

'Evil?' George asked softly.

'None of that, no. And it *is* Morag. Does that make sense?'

'No. But then, rainbows would make no sense if you had never seen one. If she's not a ghost, then what is she, do you think? That language is obviously not human – or at least, not twenty-first-century human.'

'No.'

'Then what? Some kind of alien?'

'I suppose it's possible. It seems a strange way for them to communicate, though.'

He shrugged. 'What's a good way? I've speculated about this stuff over the years. Look at it this way. I still cut my lawn.' It was just a scrap, overgrown by clover and weeds, but George seemed to like it that way, and he said he didn't trust nano-gardeners he couldn't even see. 'Now, my evolutionary divergence from the grass is, what, half a billion years deep, more? And yet we communicate. I ask it if it wants to grow, by feeding it phosphates in the autumn and nitrogen in the spring. It answers by growing, or not. It asks me if I want it to grow over five centimetres, or start colonising the verges. It tells me this by actually doing it, you see. I say no, with my mower and my strimmer. So we communicate – not in symbols, but with the primal elements of all life forms, space to grow, food, life, death.'

'And you think it might be that way with intelligent aliens?'

'If there is no possibility of symbolic communication, maybe. But if they have the capability to reach us then they will be the ones with the lawnmower...'

'I don't think aliens have anything to do with this,' I said firmly. 'It feels too human for that.'

'Then there seems only one possibility left,' he said.

We both knew what he meant: that my Morag, with her high-density speech, was a visitation, not from the past, and not from some alien world, but from the future – our human future. In some ways I found that the most terrifying prospect of all, because it was the least comprehensible.

'Rosa guessed this,' I admitted. 'Even before we recorded and analysed Morag's speech.'

'Well, she is a Poole.'

We could only speculate; we didn't know enough. George changed the subject. He asked me if I still flew Frisbees.

When I was a kid, growing up on the Florida coast, I became fascinated with Frisbees. Everybody played with them. But try as I might I couldn't find anybody, any book, to explain to me convincingly how the damn things actually flew – and especially how come they were so hard to fly right, why they dipped and flapped the way they did.

So, aged about ten, I started buying up old Frisbees to experiment with them. At first it was just kiddie stuff, painting them or adding spectacular, useless fins. But then I tried a more deliberate series of modifications. I cut chunks out, or added strips of plastic to the rim to change the weight distribution, or scored the flat surfaces with new patterns of grooves to change the flow of air. I didn't really know what I was doing, of course, but I was instinctively systematic. I kept logs and even made little cell-phone movies of how my Frisbees flew, before and after the modification. It didn't last long – kid fads never do – but when George had visited in those days he had always shown an interest.

'But what you don't know,' I said to him now, 'is that playing with Frisbees got me one of my first career breaks.'

In my final year at college I happened to look up Frisbees on the net. I found to my surprise that still nobody had figured out how a Frisbee flew, not really. Not only that, there would be practical applications of such knowledge, for planetary probes targeted at airy worlds like Mars and Venus and Titan would be spun for stability – they were high-tech, hugely expensive Frisbees sailing into unfamiliar atmospheres, sent to their fates on the basis of a scarily shallow knowledge of how they actually flew.

'So I dug out some of my ten-year-old hobby,' I said to George. 'And I looked up the theory, such as it was. A Frisbee gets its lift like a wing, but the front of the disc tends to get more lift than the back, which makes it unstable. But unlike an aeroplane wing it's spinning, so that uneven lift is like a finger prodding a spinning gyroscope; it deflects a Frisbee's course rather than makes it flip completely. But I found that nobody had got beyond rough rules of thumb.

'Anyhow I started trying to figure out how a Frisbee really flies,' I said. 'I went beyond what I could do as a kid. I scrounged some parts from my college lab, and gave a Frisbee a black box recorder.' I had installed a small accelerometer to measure the forces on the disc, and a magnetometer and light sensor so I could track its position compared to the sun and the Earth's magnetic field, and a computer chip. Soon I was able to record all the essentials of a flight, and reproduce it at leisure in a simple VR environment. Later, when my professors got interested in what I was doing, I went further, such as by coating a Frisbee's upper surface with sensors to measure the pressure and air flow in detail.

'I quickly figured out the gross aerodynamic coefficients,' I said. 'To optimise your flight you have to match your spin rate to your forward speed and angle of attack. But more important, I started to get an understanding of how pressure was distributed over the surface of the spinning disc, and was able to model ways how you might control this optimally, for instance with small flaps and holes to direct the airflow. NASA was doing the same sort of study, of course, but using spinning models in wind tunnels. I was able to get better results far more cheaply, just by smothering a Frisbee in sensors and flying it outdoors.' In the end the study turned from a hobby into a term paper, which NASA took up and sponsored. It was a great line on my CV when it came time for me to look for a job.

'I didn't know all that,' George said. He grinned. 'So you managed to combine career advancement with throwing Frisbees all day. I'm even more impressed.'

I shrugged. 'You have to enjoy yourself.'

'Absolutely.'

I knew what I had to say next, even though it was difficult for both of us. 'George – you always took an interest in my stuff, a proper interest, back when I was ten or eleven.'

We both knew what I meant. My dad was always faintly bemused by such stunts as experimenting with Frisbees. He would throw a Frisbee or two with me. But he always spoke to me as a kid, if you know what I mean, which wasn't necessarily the right thing to do, even if I was a kid. George spoke to me as a junior engineer; he took me seriously.

'It made a difference. To my whole life.'

George just nodded; he knew this had to be said. He clapped me on the shoulder. 'I guess you were never going to be a Steve Zodiac. But you would have made a good Matthew Matic.'

'Who?'

'*Fireball XL5*... Something else that will disappear from the world with me. Never mind.'

George started to tire, so I called for a pod bus, and we found a bench and sat. Sitting there, breathing hard, I thought he looked ill for the first time during the visit. I could see the skull under his flesh, I thought, the skin tight beneath his cheekbones, his mouth drawn in, his eyes perhaps creased in pain. A row of blank-walled modern houses, eyeless without windows, loomed before us, uncaring.

To my surprise George said he was thinking of selling up and moving away from England altogether.

'I'm going back to Amalfi,' he said. A small town on the Sorrento coast of Italy. 'I went there after Rome, you know, after I went in search of Rosa. Once I found her I needed some time to recover, to get myself together again. The weather is still better there than here. I know it will be hard to sell up. Hell, it will be awful having to fly again. But I think I will be able to rest there, you know? That's the way I've always thought of Amalfi, a place I could rest.'

Maybe that was true. Or maybe he simply wanted to be that bit nearer to Rosa, the sister he had lost for so long.

The pod bus arrived, sighing smoothly over the silvertop, its tiny noise a ghost of the roar of the monstrous torrents of traffic that had once poured this way.

When I emerged from the VR it was early morning, Alaskan time. I napped, showered, ate, worked for a few hours.

Then I put in a call to John. We had got into the habit of talking more regularly, after the George situation landed on us. It seemed the right thing to do.

John predictably thought a move to Amalfi was a bad idea. 'It will kill him,' he said bluntly. 'What's the point? It's a waste of time and money.'

'He's dying anyway, John! Now he's got this idea in his

head, he has an ambition, a plan. It gives him things to do, arrangements to make. What else is he supposed to do with his time, dig his own grave? And as for the money, he'll have more than enough when he sells the house. He isn't asking anything from us, John. Let him do what he wants.'

John, a massive-shouldered VR looming in my Deadhorse hotel room, shrugged. 'OK. I doubt if we could stop him anyhow.'

As so often, John was subtly off-key in his dealing with George's illness, to my ears anyhow. I appreciated his emptying his pockets to reunite us all in glorious VR immersive detail, but he also had a habit of reminding us constantly that he was doing it. He always *lacked* something in these situations, as if he didn't quite feel what the rest of us were feeling. I didn't want to say any of this to him, but he saw some of it in my face, I think. Sour, deflated, I didn't need a fight. 'I said I would go back tomorrow. That is, tonight. I think there's something else he wants to talk over.'

'Fine. I'll alert the service provider.'

I stood up, meaning to break the connection. But John still sat there, on a crudely sketched upright chair, watching me.

I sat down again. 'Is there something else?'

He glowered at me. 'I'm wondering if you've done any more thinking about the other business.' By which he meant, of course, Morag.

'Gea and Rosa are progressing it. I guess I'll get back to it later.'

'I still think you should give it up.' His face was always more massive, more obviously strong than mine; his expression had never looked so intense, I thought. Suddenly it was obvious that he cared a lot more about the business of Morag than George's illness.

'John, why?'

'We've been over why. It's bad for you. It's bad for Tom. It's bad for all of us. I don't know what's going on, the meaning of those strange recordings. But it's morbid, Michael. You must see that. It's like a hole you're digging yourself into, deeper and deeper. *Morag is dead*. Whatever is happening with these images isn't going to change that.'

I stared at him, trying to figure him out. I remembered what Rosa had had to say, that John seemed to have his own agenda in this – that he was hiding something. '*Images*. What images? This visitor, whatever she is, is real, John. She left footprints in the dirt! She's real, and we have to deal with her.'

'Whatever she is, she's not Morag.'

'Now, how would you know that? Why are you so concerned, John? Why do you want me to keep away from this?' Fishing, I said at random, 'What are you scared of?'

That got a reaction. He stood up, knocking back his chair, which disappeared once it wasn't in contact with his body. 'I'm scared of nothing.'

'Then tell me what's on your mind.'

For a moment he hesitated, as if on the verge of spilling something. Then he drove a fist into his palm. 'Damn it, I wish I hadn't sent you over to Rosa. That old witch is responsible for all this.'

'That makes no sense.'

'Just drop it,' he said.

I said coldly, 'Why should I do what you tell me? And if you think you can somehow pull the plug by cutting off the money, it won't make a difference. Other people are involved now. Gea is funding the studies from her own resources. Rosa too. It's out of your control, John.' I stood and took a step towards his image, deliberately trying to provoke him. 'It can't be stopped, no matter what either of us wants. Is that a problem for you, John? *What are you afraid of?*'

'You really are full of it, Michael,' he said with disgust. 'You've blighted my entire life, do you know that? Are you going to keep this up until one of us is in the grave? Ah, to hell with you.' He waved a hand, cut the connection, disappeared.

He left me alone in my room, staring at empty space, shaking with anger, utterly baffled.

I have come to stay in Amalfi. I can't face going back to Britain – not yet – and to be here is a great relief after the swarming strangeness I encountered in Rome.

I've taken a room in a house on the Piazza Spirito Santo. There is a small bar downstairs, where I sit in the shade of vine leaves and drink Coca Light, or sometimes the local lemon liqueur, which tastes like the sherbet-lemon boiled sweets I used to buy as a kid in Manchester, ground up and mixed with vodka. The crusty old barman doesn't have a word of English. It's hard to tell his age. The flower-bowls on the outdoor tables are filled with little bundles of twigs which look suspiciously like fasces to me, but I'm too polite to ask . . .

'You don't have to read it if you don't want to,' George said.

We were sitting in his living room, my VR presence expensively projected so my ass seemed to nestle gratefully into one of George's slightly over-stuffed armchairs. The room had some mementoes, photos and ornaments. Maybe that kind of clutter is inevitable when you get older, as the years pile up. But the equipment, the softscreens and the like, was modern, the furniture not too decrepit. There was little of the old man about the room.

George had given me a manuscript, a heap of six, seven hundred pages of word-processed text, dog-eared, bound together by bits of string. I couldn't touch it, of course, or turn its pages. George said he had already sent me a data file with its contents, but he wanted me to see the manuscript itself. After I was gone he'd throw it in the fire.

'I wrote this out in Amalfi. One reason I stayed there so long. I wanted to get it all off my chest, to tell the story, even if it was only into the memory of a computer.'

'It's the story of how you tracked down Rosa, to Rome.'

'Yes. And what I found there.'

'You've never shown this to anybody?'

'No. Who was there to show it to? But I don't want it to disappear into the dark.' He shrugged, his shoulders like bony wings under a loose woollen sweater. 'Do with it as you will.'

I could tell this meant a lot more to him than his casual tone implied. 'George – what did you find, in Rome?'

'It's all in here,' he said.

'I know. But I want to hear what you felt about it. You tracked down Rosa to the Order, I know that much . . .'

He had found his way to Rosa, who had taken him into the

headquarters of the Puissant Order of Holy Mary Queen of Virgins. The Order ran a vast subterranean complex, located beneath the Catacombs, the ancient underground Christian tombs on the outskirts of Rome. 'It was nuclear bunker and Vatican crypt rolled into one,' George said darkly. It was in this environment that Rosa had been brought up. 'They called themselves sisters.'

'Like nuns?'

'No. *Sisters.*' The Order had been like one vast family, he said. They were mostly women in there, very few men. 'Everybody was everybody else's sister or cousin, aunt or niece.'

'Or mother or daughter,' I said.

'Oh, everybody was a daughter. But there were very few mothers. I called them the queens. Not that that was the language *they* used. *Matres* – that was the word.'

There are advantages in having read too much old science fiction. I saw it immediately. 'Shit,' I said. 'You're saying that the Order was a hive mind.'

'There wasn't much *mind* about it,' he said. 'I don't know what the hell it was. I'm no sociobiologist. But I can tell you this. *It wasn't a human community.*' He tapped his manuscript again. 'It's all in there. And you know what? It was all an off-shoot of our family, from a deep root that seems to go back to the time of ancient Rome itself. *Our* family. That's how Rosa got drawn into it. That's how I did, I guess.'

No wonder Rosa had been intrigued by the strange collective organisation of the Reef, I thought. I forced a grin. 'You do always say we Pooles are a funny lot.'

'And so we are.' His face was dark. 'And how it's happening again.'

'What is?'

'I once had a friend who helped me figure this stuff out. It's in here.' He leafed through the manuscript, looking for a passage towards the end. 'Here it is. "*The great events of the past – the fall of Rome, say, or the Second World War – cast long shadows, influencing generations to come. But is it possible that the future has echoes in the present too?*" ... I thought I saw the future of mankind in that hole in the ground in Rome, Michael. Or *a* future. I can't say I liked what I saw. And maybe now it's happening again, with you and Morag. Echoes of the future in the present.'

'But why now? Why us?' I didn't quite want to say, *why me*?

'Maybe because we seem to be at a dangerous time in our history, Michael.' He looked at the back of his hand, poked at skin stained brown by age. 'You know, when I was a kid I think I never believed I would grow old, like this. I was never interested in gardening, because I thought I would never live to see a tree grow tall. You know why? The threat of nuclear war, of extinction in a flash. It hung over my whole childhood like a black cloud. But the hard rain never fell, and eventually the cloud went away.

'Now a new cloud has gathered over us, every bit as threatening as before. We're at another tipping point in human history. And who is here trying to show us how to keep our balance? *You are*, Michael. A Poole. Who else?'

'And you think that's why I'm getting these visitations?'

He reached out to touch my hand, but my VR presence made that impossible, and he pulled back. 'Think about it. If you're right about this hydrate threat – and if you manage to lead the programme to stop it wiping us out – then you will be remembered as one of the most important humans who ever lived. Now, if I was a time traveller from the future, this would be *exactly* the kind of era I would be drawn to, and you would be *exactly* the kind of person I'd long to meet.'

'Shit.' I remembered that Gea had said something similar, so had Rosa – so had George himself, when he talked about the strange circumstances of my birth, the coincidence of the discovery of the Kuiper Anomaly. Suddenly I felt extraordinarily self-conscious, as if a corridor a thousand centuries long had opened up before me, and a million eyes were fixed greedily on my every move.

'George, if this is true, what should I do about it?'

He shrugged. 'Accept it. I mean, it makes no difference. You just have to do your best even so, don't you?'

'I guess.'

We just sat for a while. Then I said, 'It's morning in Alaska. I ought to go to work.' I stood. 'Can I come visit tomorrow?'

'Of course.' As my VR broke up, as his room turned transparent around me, I saw him in his chair, smiling, waving a gaunt hand, his fingers bent over and stiff.

As it happened the next day we hit a problem with the Higgs-field power plant of the moles, and I was kept too busy to get away. The following day was worse. By the third day I was putting off going to see George; I didn't want to get immersed in all that difficulty again. Tomorrow, I told myself. Or the day after that.

I never saw him again. A week after that last visit, John called to tell me George was dead.

Chapter 43

Even at full speed the journey back to the *Nord* took two full days.

The sisters spent their time alone, shut away from the Campocs and from Reath. Alia didn't want to talk to anybody else but Drea. She didn't want Bale, she couldn't bear the thought of him touching her, and she certainly didn't want to join in the Campocs' group consciousness, that pale echo of the Transcendence. She didn't even want Poole, in his Witnessing tank.

To get through this, she felt, she had to retreat into herself, become again the woman she had once been. She had to be *Alia*. So the sisters sat together, limbs entwined, as they used to when they were small.

But her feelings were complicated.

Alia found herself thinking that if Drea had not been here, then her sister would surely have been on the *Nord* and shared the still unknown fate of her parents. And if that had happened, Alia might have been left alone. Then she was racked by guilt that she seemed to spend so much time thinking of herself, rather than about those who had been hurt. If she was so shallow, so self-obsessed, then how could she possibly imagine she could deal with a Transcendence?

It made it worse that they had no real news. The fragmentary reports from *Nord* were little more than a cry for help. As the long hours wore on, that uncertainty was impossible to bear.

Drea thought Alia could ask the Transcendence.

'You could talk to the Campocs,' Drea whispered. 'They might be able to contact Leropa. Or Reath might have a way to contact another Transcendent community, nearer to the

378

Nord. For all I know there might even be a Transcendent or two *on* the *Nord*...'

Alia knew that was too simple. Drea still thought of the Transcendence as a kind of comms network, as if the Transcendents themselves were nothing but monitoring stations, their eyes cameras. But the Transcendence was more than that. The Transcendence was literally beyond human imagination. The only way to understand the Transcendence, she thought sadly, was to be part of it, as she had been, and even if she never went back to it again there would always be a gulf between herself and her sister.

But, she felt instinctively, the Transcendence was not a place to seek help at a time of human crisis.

At last Reath alerted them that their journey was over.

The ailing *Nord* was surrounded by a multitude of craft, compact and slender, robust and delicate. The crowding visitors had come to give aid, Reath assured the sisters. 'Your *Nord* has many friends.'

'But at least one enemy,' Drea said bleakly.

As they approached, cautiously picking their way through the crowd of ships and darting shuttles, their view became clearer. And even from a distance, Alia could see that the *Nord* had been grievously harmed. The squat cylinder that was the core of the *Nord*'s architecture had survived – it would take the outright demolition of the ship to destroy that – but huge energies had been splashed against the hull, leaving blackened scars and deep notches cut into the *Nord*'s blunt symmetry. Away from the ancient core the superstructure of habs, antennae, sensors and manipulators was tangled, as if a great wind had torn through that fragile artificial forest.

Some of the *Nord*'s ports were still functioning, at least. The semi-sentient machinery of the dock interfaced with the shuttle routinely, but a bit hesitantly, Alia thought. Perhaps machines could suffer shock too.

The shuttle wouldn't let them out until they donned face masks and gloves. Inside the *Nord* there were stretches of vacuum, and even where there was air it was likely full of toxins. With dread Alia pulled on her mask, the mask she had once worn to go into a Coalescence; it was terribly hard to have to don protective gear to enter your own home.

At last the hatches and locks slid open. A smell of burning washed over them, unfiltered by their face masks. And in the corridors, people in masks and gloves swarmed everywhere, cutting, patching, moving bits of equipment. The place was unrecognisable. The sisters clutched each other. Alia had been determined to be brave, but even in that first moment her strength seemed to drain away. Drea was wide-eyed, unnaturally still, not even trembling – in shock, Alia thought.

There was no welcome for Alia and Drea: no message, no news, no words of reassurance, or confirmation of their fears. It was as if this damaged place had forgotten they even existed.

Reath tried to keep them focused. 'It doesn't mean anything,' he said. 'The *Nord*'s in chaos. It's only three days since the disaster. People are just too busy... Don't worry. I know the way. Follow me.' As he made his way out of the shuttle he stumbled and drifted until he got hold of a rail: his body plan was designed for planet-living, not for this microgravity scramble. But he gamely got his orientation, beckoned to the sisters, and began to make his way through the corridors.

Alia followed. Drea moved mechanically.

The damage inflicted on the *Nord* had been internal as well as external. Corridor walls had been sliced through and rooms had burst open, their contents scorched and smashed. Alia saw with a sense of outrage that vast clumsy energies had been poured out into this fragile human place. And if it was distressing now, it must have been a lot worse before, she saw from the ripped-open walls, the splashes of blood on the floor: those first few hours must have been dreadful indeed.

But she was being selfish again, she thought with a stab of shame, thinking only of herself, and how she had been spared the worst of it. If she had been *here*, where she was supposed to be, perhaps more lives could have been saved.

They clambered up through the *Nord*'s levels, heading for their home. Activity throbbed through the ship as partitions were patched, debris removed, fresh goods brought in. The ship, itself badly hurt, was already recovering. But in emergency hospitals the wounded were arrayed in stacks, through which medic machines and human nurses drifted, and in makeshift mortuaries there were more arrays of bodies, ominously still.

Reath murmured, 'I admit this is beyond me. I'm planet-born, an earthworm. Even on a planet the odd catastrophe strikes – an asteroid impact, a volcanic eruption, a quake. But at least the *world* survives; you can rely on that. Here, though, on this fragile ship, even while you were trying to save those around you, and cope with your own injuries, you had to try to stop the very fabric of your environment from unravelling around you. For if you failed...'

If they had failed, Alia thought bleakly, the *Nord* might have cracked open altogether, and tens of thousands of humans would have been spilled into the vacuum.

'You can see the patterns,' Drea said suddenly.

'What patterns?'

Drea pointed to an irruption through the roof of this corridor, a hole surrounded by smashed and distorted panels, and a matching hole at the angle of floor and wall. Peering down Alia thought she could make out the green of the Farm, even the hulking machinery of the Engine Room, far below. If you looked into one of those mighty gashes you could see how a crude tunnel had been cut through deck after deck, in a rough straight line.

Drea said, 'They just came blasting through here, right through the fabric of the ship.'

Reath said, 'The *Nord* must be riddled with these wounds. The scars of energy weapons, perhaps?'

'No,' said Alia. 'Oh, weapons were surely used. But these tunnels are too wide.' Any ship-born would have recognised such signs.

'The Shipbuilders,' Drea whispered.

For ship-born children across the Galaxy, the Shipbuilders were bedtime monsters. But they had at last come here. And in their voracious machines they had eaten their way through the soft body of the ship.

Reath watched this exchange, excluded from their tradition, his eyes narrow.

At last they arrived at the upper level, just beneath the

hull, where their home had been. The delicate superstructure of the *Nord* had taken even more of a battering than its robust interior. Alia and Drea picked their way through a tangle of melted and snapped struts, fragments of smashed dome, bits of broken furniture and machinery. Debris floated about, unrestrained in the absence of artificial gravity, contained by an emergency force shield that shimmered over everything like a huge soap bubble. People picked their way through the rubble, searching, inspecting. The regular light globes had failed, and the few emergency lanterns cast long shadows everywhere, making the place even more of a visual jumble.

When the sisters reached their home, their worst fears were confirmed.

The ship's hull had been smashed open here, leaving only a few drifting bits of translucent ceramic. The sisters pulled themselves through the wreckage, searching. Alia felt fragile, edgy. The conjunction of this wreckage with shards of the familiar, with bits of stuff, fragments of furniture she thought she recognised, made this whole experience seem unreal. On one section of floor she found a splash of dried blood, not yet cleaned up. It looked exactly as if a sack of the sticky stuff had been dropped and splashed open here. A sack about the size of a baby.

Her stomach clenched. Suddenly she was vomiting. She got her face mask out of the way just in time to keep it clear of the bile that spewed out of her mouth.

'Alia...' She looked around wildly.

It was her father. He was waiting for her outside the broken hull. Drea was already with him, her face buried on his shoulder. Alia launched herself up through the murky air. Surrounded by the floating wreckage of their home, the three of them drifted together.

Gently Alia disengaged herself. 'My mother—'

'She's dead,' Drea said. 'Bel is *dead.*' Her voice was raw with weeping.

Suddenly all Alia could see was her mother's face, its fading beauty, sometimes weak, always full of helpless love. 'And the baby?'

'Gone too,' said Ansec. 'It happened so quickly.'

More conflicting emotions swirled in Alia. *You drove me away so you could have this kid. And now you've lost him anyhow.* It was a hard, savage thought that shocked her. *What kind of monster am I?* But as she stared at her sister and her father, the complex muddle of these emotions washed away, leaving only regret, and an elemental anguish.

Reath touched her face. 'Are you going to be all right?'

'I'll cry later,' she said. It was true. She clung to thoughts of Michael Poole, whose family had been ripped apart by a similar tragedy. Not for the first time in her life, she sought comfort from his endurance.

Reath said grimly, 'I think you'd better tell me what you know about these Shipbuilders.'

The Shipbuilders, like Alia's own people, were relics of the deepest past.

In those early days, even after the discovery of the earliest faster-than-light drives, generation starships had been a common way to reach for the stars. Sailing on into the dark, travelling much slower than light, these ships were worlds closed over on themselves, with whole generations living out their lives between launch and landfall. Alia knew this lore well, for it was the heritage of her own people.

But it wasn't a reliable way to travel. Most generation ships failed en route – or so it was believed, for many of them simply vanished into the dark. It wasn't hard to see why. Since most generation ships had been launched at a time when mankind was still better at taking ecologies apart rather than building and managing them, it wasn't a surprise that so many ships expired long before their intended journeys were complete.

There were other hazards. Alia's own ship had been overtaken by a friendly bunch of FTL travellers, and reconnected to the worlds of mankind. Other ships were not so lucky. Fat, helpless, resource-rich, they had fallen foul of pirates and bandits; there had been terrible tragedies, massacres in the silence between the stars.

But there were other sorts of survivor.

Sometimes, by accident or design, a ship would simply plough on into the dark, never making landfall. Things might go well for centuries, even after the deaths of the original crew, when nobody was left alive who could remember the point of the mission. Much longer than that, though, and things started to drift.

Over millennia languages changed, ethnic compositions drifted. Those few ships that lasted so long became like monasteries, with cowed, constrained crews labouring endlessly over tasks they barely understood, seeking to preserve a purpose set down by unimaginably remote ancestors, all for the benefit of descendants who would not be born for millennia more.

And some ships went on even longer.

Given enough time natural selection cut and shaped the ships' hapless crews, as always working to make its subject populations fit for their environment. And in the closed spaces of a generation starship there was always one common sacrifice, cut away by that pitiless scalpel: mind.

After all, on such a ship, what did you need a mind *for*? The ship would manage itself, more or less, or it wouldn't have made it so far anyhow. With mind, the crew would only get restless, start to wonder what was beyond the walls – or, worse, start to tinker with the plumbing. In the first generation such activity would be against ship's rules. In the hundredth it would be a sin, a taboo. By the thousandth generation it would be a selection pressure.

This was the origin of the Shipbuilders. Their ships had sailed on, even though the descendants of the first crew had long lost the intelligence that had enabled the ship to be launched in the first place. They maintained their ships' essential systems, if only by rote. They even grew inventive over such fripperies as external superstructure. Their ships became gaudy, impossibly impractical creations, their purpose being to attract other such crews – and to mate.

And they remembered how to make weapons, for piracy – or rather, since piracy implies a conscious purpose, parasitism. It was necessary. No closed ecology was perfect; any starship required some replenishment. The Shipbuilders simply took what they needed.

'They are brutal,' Alia said to Reath, 'because they are mindless. They launch themselves on missiles that rip through the fabric of their targets, scooping up stuff indiscriminately.'

'And so they shot up your *Nord*,' Reath said.

Alia said, 'The Shipbuilders are the stuff of nightmares to us.'

'Because they might come out of the dark to attack you at any time. An arbitrary horror.'

'Not just that. The Shipbuilders come from the same place as us. We could have fallen, as they did. *They are like us.*'

Unexpectedly Reath folded Alia in his arms. 'No,' he said. 'They are not like you. Never think that.'

For a heartbeat she was rigid with shock. Then she softened against his musty robe, and the tears came at last.

She spent the night with Drea, in a small compartment in Reath's shuttle, orbiting the wreck of the *Nord*. They shared a bunk. Sometimes they held each other, and sometimes they just lay together, back to back, or nestling.

Alia wasn't sure if she slept at all. Her head was full of pain, of inchoate longing and guilt and regret. She was still working through her muddled feelings about her mother and brother, her guilt over not being able to resolve their final argument. Underlying it all, though, was the simple flesh-and-blood reality of the loss. A family was never a fixed thing, she thought, but a process. Now that process had been cut short, leaving nothing but a bloody splash on the floor. It wasn't just her mother who had died, not just a brother, but her family too.

It seemed strange that such things could happen in a Galaxy governed by a superior form of consciousness. And while the Transcendence agonised over the loss of *all* the ancestors of mankind, here she was trying to grieve over her own mother. Perhaps, in her anguish and muddled pain, she felt some ghost of the higher, more exquisite regret that had impelled the Transcendence to attempt the Redemption.

And of course, she thought reluctantly, the Transcendence must be cognisant of the disaster, as it was of all of the past. The Transcendence must already, in principle, be seeking to redeem the suffering inflicted on her, as it did every scrap of pain and anguish right back to the dawn of human consciousness.

If she wished, Alia could Witness the *Nord*'s disaster. She could even, through Hypostatic Union, live through it. She could ride around inside her own mother's head and experience her death. But this was her family, her own mother. Even the idea of delving into the Transcendence and using its superhuman powers to *inspect* their suffering made her recoil.

And it wouldn't be enough, she saw immediately. It could never be a true atonement for her, no matter how many times she lived through her mother's life. *For her mother's suffering would still exist*, no matter how minutely Alia inspected it.

This must be the heart of the Transcendence's dilemma over Redemption, she realised. But if it was not enough to watch the past, not even to live it out through Hypostatic Union, not even if that process were driven to infinity – *then something more must be sought*. And the Transcendence must know it too. But what more could there be? Curiosity burned in her, and a vast longing for a relief from her own pain.

Drea stirred in her half-sleep. Shame laced through Alia. In her Transcendental scheming she had once again forgotten her simple humanity. She held her sister, until Drea was still.

At the start of the next day the six of them – the three Campocs, Reath, Alia and Drea, gathered in Reath's shuttle, and shared hot drinks. 'Just like old times,' Seer ventured. Nobody responded.

They talked desultorily of the menace of the Shipbuilders.

'It's hard even to resent them, hard to hate them,' Alia said dully. 'Because they have no minds, no purpose. This is just what they do. But the menace is getting worse.'

'It is?'

'This is a time of peace, Reath. Once the Galaxy was full of warships; in those days the Shipbuilders were kept in their place. But now there aren't so many weapons around.'

'They will have to be dealt with,' Bale said.

Drea said coldly, 'Or welcomed into the family of mankind, to become a part of the awakening of the cosmos. Isn't that how your friend Leropa would put it, Alia?'

Alia studied her sister, shocked. Alia had never seen such a hard expression on her sister's face. 'What's wrong with you?'

Drea stared at the Campocs; they avoided her eyes. Drea said, 'I've been doing some thinking. Alia, doesn't it strike you as *strange* that just as you swim off into the Transcendence, this horror should be inflicted on the *Nord*?'

'I don't understand—'

'I don't believe in coincidences,' Drea said.

Bale put down his drink and leaned forward. 'Drea, you'd better say what you have to say. Are you accusing us of something?'

'You bet I am,' Drea said fervently. 'You set up Alia's election to the Transcendence so you could use her as a tool to study the Redemption. Then you kidnapped *me* and threatened my life, to force her to go on. And now she wanted to come home; you knew she was thinking about abandoning the whole cosmic mess. So you acted again, in your clumsy, vicious way—'

Alia put her hand on her sister's arm. 'Drea, please.'

Drea turned to her. 'Don't you see? The Redemption is about regret, about loss. So the Campocs have engineered this whole incident. They wanted to inflict loss on you, Alia. They wanted to give *you* something to regret. They took away your mother and your brother, to make you go back into the Redemption.'

Alia felt bewildered. 'But how—'

'*The Campocs led the Shipbuilders to the* Nord.'

It seemed unbelievable. Alia looked to Reath for support, but his face was expressionless. If it were true—

Rage exploded in Alia. She stood and loomed over Bale, her fists bunching. 'Is she right? Lethe, I made love to you. If you have done this for your own twisted purposes, the truth is the least you owe me.'

Bale met her gaze calmly. She thought he seemed calculating, but his thoughts were seamlessly closed to her. 'Maybe we did, maybe not. You'll never know, will you? If I tell you it's true, you might think I'm just trying to manipulate you. And if I deny it, you won't believe me.'

Alia turned to Reath. 'Do *you* think they did it? Did they lead the Shipbuilders here?'

'I don't know,' Reath said reluctantly. 'But whether they did or not, they seem to have worked out they can use it against you, haven't they?'

She remembered her own musings of the night before, her own deep hunger to know what might be found at the higher levels of the Redemption. She had seen its ultimate logic, the madness of infinity: if Bale was concerned that the Redemption would waste the resources of mankind, he was right to doubt. She doubted too. But now, after her own loss, she was driven by a hunger to know *if the Redemption was possible after all* – if the wound in her own small life could be healed. And so she knew that she would do as Bale wished. And she hated him for it, whether he had set up the disaster or not.

'You are monsters,' Drea said to the Campocs.

Seer actually grinned. 'Ah, but we're charming monsters. Don't you think?'

Alia glared at Bale. 'Very well. If the Transcendence is what you want, let's call it now.' With a strength fuelled by anger she grabbed his shoulders, hauled him to his feet, and slammed her awareness into his mind. He cried out, but he could not escape. Her force of will poured along the interconnections to his relations' consciousnesses, and they screamed and writhed. Peripherally she was aware of Reath and Drea pulling away, shocked.

With the minds of the Campocs wrapped around her own like a cloak, she called for Leropa. 'Take me back. I need you now. Oh, take me back!'

Chapter 44

A month after George's funeral, Ruud Makaay announced that he believed that the trial hydrate-stabilisation project off Prudhoe Bay was 'mature' enough to be presented to the world's decision-makers. A day was set.

It would be a key moment for us. After weeks of construction and development we now had a properly interconnected prototype network, dug out by the moles and extensively tested. All that remained was to start pumping liquid nitrogen through the veins we had burrowed into the methane-laden sediments of the seafloor: all we had to do, in other words, was switch on, and we ought to be able to reduce the temperature of Arctic seafloor strata across a rough circle kilometres across. 'Serious chilling,' as Shelley Magwood said.

And we were going to do it in the full glare of media attention, and in the presence of every key agency of governance from the state government of Alaska up to the Stewardship itself. I tried to be confident. I'd pored over EI's test results, analyses and modelling. I saw no reason why anything serious should screw up.

I was optimistic; I usually am. I expect people to behave rationally and for the common good. John always said I was an idealist, and he meant it as an insult. For sure I was wrong to be confident in my fellow man, that particular day.

In a way, it all started to go wrong the moment I saw Morag.

On the morning of Makaay's sales pitch I was late rising. Still staying in that dreadful sanatorium-like hotel in Deadhorse – and now plagued by visitations – I hadn't slept well. Alone, I took a pod bus from the hotel, and rode in silence to the coast.

The layout at Prudhoe Bay was much as it had been before, when Makaay had tentatively launched the project's integration stage before a crowd of engineers, employees, and one former Vice President. You had the rig out at sea, clearly visible under a very pale, very cold blue sky, and on the shore EI had once more set up a marquee for the visitors. But the marquee was much larger and grander than the tent they had put up the last time. This marquee was actually several stories tall, like a transparent apartment block, its walls so clear you could barely see them except when the wind off the sea made them ripple.

When I stepped inside into dry air-conditioned warmth, I was immediately immersed in a pleasant buzz of noise, of crowds. Somewhere music discreetly played, a warm bath of sound. There was a fine view of our rig, and of the other old oil facilities that littered this part of the coast. The floor was carpeted wall to wall with a pale green-brown weave, colours sympathetic to the tundra shades of the North Slope. Above my head flags hung, a Stars and Stripes, the UN flag, banners bearing the EI logo and the cradled-child symbol of the Stewardship. All very classy: the EI folk had a lot of experience of this sort of event, and they knew how to impress without overwhelming.

We had attracted quite a crowd. Throughout the marquee expensively dressed people mingled confidently, and there was a hubbub of loud conversation as acquaintances were made and renewed, and, no doubt, deals were done, few of which would have anything to do with our hydrate project. Serving bots hovered in the air, bearing trays of drinks and exotic-looking snack foods. Here and there I saw subtle imaging imperfections: expensively shod feet suspended mysteriously a centimetre or so above the carpet, a gown billowing in a non-existent breeze, a shadow across a beautiful face cast by an invisible light source. I imagined only ten per cent or so of these movers and shakers were here in person.

Here was the other side of the vast collapse in transportation infrastructure which Edith Barnette had, in part, overseen. Few governmental agencies, corporations or other organisations actually 'existed' anywhere meaningfully, except in cyberspace; and few crowds were ever as populous as they seemed. Well, on this occasion it was probably just as well that people projected rather than travelled. If so many VIPs had descended on Prudhoe Bay in the flesh, that dismal hotel in Deadhorse would have been overwhelmed, temperamental en suite bathrooms and all.

However, somewhere in that crowd, Edith Barnette was here in person once more. And so was my brother John, and Tom and Sonia, and Shelley, and Vander Guthrie – all the core team who had driven the project, in their different ways, from the beginning. I walked through the crowd, trying to pick out familiar faces, and to hold my nerve.

There were cameras, microphones and other sensors everywhere, and as I walked big drones descended on me, and an animated cloud of electronic dust swirled around. Given there were plenty of VIPs present, it was faintly disturbing such a large chunk of that electronic attention was turned on me. I tried not to think about George's speculations that I might be under even more intense scrutiny by a curious future.

That was when I saw Morag.

I saw her out of the corner of my eye. She was moving through the crowd, some distance from me. I helplessly turned to her, as I always did. I thought she was turning towards me, I thought she smiled, but before I was even sure it was her, I lost her behind a knot of gabbling VIPs.

I didn't want this to be happening. In the last few days I had suffered this kind of visitation over and over – and *suffered* is the word. There had been no repeat of that close encounter out on the tundra I had had before, when she had smiled, and let us take her picture, and record her words, even if we couldn't understand what she had to say. I was back in a world of glimpses, a flash of strawberry blonde hair in my peripheral vision, a soft voice. And there were more of these visitations than ever before, many more of them, sometimes more than one a day. I didn't want to deal with her, not this way, not if I was going to be so tantalised, and certainly not on a day like today.

But then I saw her again, on the far side of the marquee this time. And when I looked away, there she was again, this time close to the small podium at the front of the marquee. It was as if she was teleporting around the place.

I grabbed a vodka and tonic off a floating bot's tray and downed it quickly.

John approached me, a tumbler of whisky in his hand. A small, dark, intense figure was at his side: Jack Joy, I recognised after a moment, the Lethe Swimmer. John seemed uncomfortable to be tailed by the guy. But he had got Jack involved in the first place, and since the Swimmers had put money into the project Jack had a perfect right to be there.

Jack Joy held out a hand, but his unreal fingers just brushed my sleeve; he grinned apologetically. 'Sorry I couldn't haul my ass here in all its glory. Commitments, pressures – you know. Actually I really am sorry not to be here. Look around, the sky is full of free booze!...'

Distracted by the glimpses of Morag, I wasn't interested in anything the man had to say. I looked at John. It was the first time we had been together in person for weeks. I felt that usual complicated emotional tug towards my brother, a mix of rivalry and helpless love. 'So here we are,' I said.

John shrugged. 'We're a strange family. We gather in person for a function like this, but we send VR projections to a funeral.'

I shrugged. 'George always said, "*We Pooles are a funny lot*".'

'If you say so. Anyhow you're the Poole, I'm a Bazalget, remember.' He stared at me hard, and I thought I knew what was on his mind: *Morag*, the whole phenomenon which had become such an issue between the two of us. But we couldn't talk now, not with Jack Joy there.

Jack said to me, 'I was just saying to your brother, don't you think it's an impressive place? Prudhoe Bay, the whole oil complex. I mean, look around. For the United States it was a historic achievement to be able to establish an oil industry up here, in a place of Arctic dark and cold, and thousands of kilometres from civilisation. You may as well have had to develop an oil industry on the Moon. In fact it might have been *easier* on the Moon, because here you have this fucking tundra all around. You know, you make a wheel track on that stuff and it's there *for ever...*' His tone was clipped, his speech rapid, and he kept flashing nervous grins. He was sweating, a small virtual incongruity in the air-conditioned comfort of the marquee.

I said, 'So you don't approve of eco-protection, Jack.'

'Approve, disapprove, it was the flavour of the times. It still is.' He bunched a fist. 'In this day and age, a person who wants to achieve something is hedged around by bleats about don't hurt this, don't disturb that. I always say, if God hadn't wanted us to dig up the planet He wouldn't have given us the mechanical excavator.' He nodded, as if trying to convince himself. 'And in the end it's all bullshit.'

'It is?'

'Of course! Look at the precious tundra that those rough-necks weren't allowed to take a piss on. When the permafrost melted it turned into a swamp! So what difference did all that effort to preserve it make? None. It just got in the way of getting the job done, is all.'

I turned to John. 'So is this the way all Swimmers think?'

He looked increasingly uncomfortable. *This guy isn't with me.* 'The Swimmers are a broad church, Michael. We live in complex times, with challenging, interconnected problems that may demand out-of-the-box thinking. You have to have a forum where radical opinions can be expressed.' But all this sounded like a party line; he didn't sound as if he believed it himself.

Jack Joy said, 'I didn't mean to disturb you, Mike. I see some people I know. I'll catch you later. This is your day, enjoy it, I wish you success, et cetera et cetera.' Sweating and grinning, he sidled away from us.

John eyed me. 'I'm sorry if that guy upset you.'

'He didn't.' I found Jack Joy faintly disturbing, I guess, but I didn't take him seriously. How wrong I was.

'You look like shit.'

'Oh, thanks.'

'You haven't been sleeping.' He stepped closer to me, and said more quietly, 'You've been seeing Morag, haven't you?'

I glanced around, at the hovering dust drones, the crowd-ing VR VIPs. 'Keep your voice down, John. All right. Yes,

I see her. I *keep* seeing her. It's driving me crazy. Even if I fall asleep, I hear her voice, smell her breath, she's *there*, but when I wake she's gone, and I can't sleep again.'

'But she isn't speaking to you,' he said. 'Not like that one time.' He stared at me intensely, hungry. In that moment I was struck by how he had aged – the thickened neck and jaw, the burly body, the flesh of his face slowly crumpling, the marks of a man in middle age. But there was a passion in his eyes I had rarely seen before. My brother didn't do passion.

'This really matters to you, doesn't it? The whole business with Morag. *Why*, John?' And I made another leap of intuition. '*Do you think you know what she's trying to tell me*? Is that it?'

I expected him to deny this, but he just stared at me, that strange, vulnerable mix of anger and longing on his face. He said grimly, 'We have to get this resolved.'

'Fine,' I said, scared, bewildered.

I think we were both relieved when we heard a soft chiming, much amplified; it was Ruud Makaay rapping a pen against an empty glass, calling us to attention.

Barnette and Makaay stood alone on a plain stage, with a view of the offshore rig framed in the big clear wall behind them. Technicians, clearly visible, performed last checks on the big nitrogen-liquefaction plant we'd installed on the rig. And, more importantly, we saw maps of the network of tunnels the moles had already dug out through cubic kilometres of the fragile seabed strata. Now the wall began to fill up with images from the project. We saw a mole's eye view of a tunnel being dug into the undersea rock. 'Although actually,' Shelley had pointed out to me, 'since the tunnel is being constructed *behind* the mole as it burrows along, that's actually a mole's-asshole view...'

Makaay said, 'We call this project *"The Refrigerator"*. It isn't a fancy name, but then I'm not a fancy guy, just an engineer who likes to get the job done – and I've never worked on a job of more significance than this. I'm very proud of what we've achieved so far, and I hope to persuade you to support us in the future, as we seek to extend our technology through all the threatened hydrate strata around both the north and south poles...'

As Makaay spoke, John and I drifted through the crowd towards the podium. Here we found Shelley, with Vander Guthrie, Tom and Sonia, other project people.

There was no seating plan, no front row – in fact there were only a few seats of any kind. Ruud Makaay, an expert at crowd manipulation, didn't like obviously stage-managed events. He believed in what he called 'choreographed informality'. He was aiming for a human warmth that would belie the usual accusations of arrogance that stuck to projects like this. There would come a point when I, like the other key players on the project, would be invited to come forward to be presented to Barnette, like the winner of some VR-soap award. But, happily, I wouldn't be called on to make any kind of speech.

'Of course we can give you as much technical detail as you want,' Makaay was saying. 'Our analysis of the network in terms of connectivity and robustness has assured us that every functional parameter has been addressed, all local geological conditions accommodated – and all this put together by our moles, working solo and in cooperation. Those little critters have done a good job.' Behind him a blown-up image showed a mole pushing its whirling snout up out of the ground, and it waggled this way and that, as if seeking our approval. It was a shameless bit of anthropomorphism, but it worked, and won Makaay a smattering of laughter and applause.

The crowd, evidently enjoying the show, were sympathetic for now – though whether they would be when they went back to their offices, and we started to ask for serious funding for the roll-out, was another matter. We project types were all tense, agitated, sipping drinks and grinning nervously at each other. Even Tom grasped Sonia's hand so hard his knuckles were white. John seemed distracted, though. I thought he looked at me as much as at the presentation. Even now, at this crucial moment, the Morag business was obviously on his mind.

To a little more applause, Makaay yielded the floor. Edith Barnette stepped forward, utterly at ease, wearing her years well.

'I'm not qualified to talk to you about the majestic engineering we're here to witness today,' she said. 'I'm not even qualified to talk about methane hydrate reservoirs, which are causing such concern to those who monitor our climate for us, friendly minds both human and artificial. But I can, I think, grasp the wider implications of what is happening here. For I understand heroism.' Her voice was soft, but it carried to every corner of that big marquee, and the faces of our guests, important or self-important, intelligent or merely self-obsessed, were locked on her. 'A new kind of heroism,' she said. 'A heroism that seeks to save, not merely oneself, not just one's friends or family, not even one's nation or creed. It is a heroism that seeks to save the planet itself, and its fragile cargo of living things. It is a heroism that seeks to save the very future...'

Standing there with the vodka coursing through my blood, her words took me back to the hopeful days when President Amin had woken us all up from our nightmare of oil dependency. Amin's own story was a mixture of meritocracy and openness. She was the child of Iraqi refugees, and her journey, if not quite log cabin to White House, was pretty much the twenty-first-century equivalent. Amin had had a simple vision, comprehensible to all, and by asserting it she managed a national, indeed global transformation.

Of course the demons fought back. Amin's assassination had been a great punctuation mark. And then had come 2033, the Happy Anniversary bomb. It had been a HANE, as the counter-terrorists called it, a high-altitude nuclear explosion, a bomb not much bigger than the Hiroshima device lofted a couple of hundred kilometres high aboard a small tourist spaceplane. X-rays cooked all but the most hardened low-Earth-orbit satellites, while gamma rays battered the upper atmosphere, releasing high-energy electrons that disabled any sensitive electronics in line of sight, and charged particles made the Earth's magnetic field oscillate so that electric surges ruined cables and circuits. And a blood-red aurora had spread across the skies of a hemisphere, a sight you would never forget. The developed world was paralysed for eight days.

It was one hell of a strike. But even now, fourteen years

later, nobody knew for sure who had delivered it. An anonymous message called the 'Happy Anniversary' note was sent to the FBI. It was thought perhaps it referred to the two-thousandth anniversary of Jesus's crucifixion. Perhaps anti-Christians were responsible, then – or they may have been a Christian splinter sect – or perhaps it was just mischief-making by terrorists determined to stir up as much trouble as possible.

There were plenty of people who had problems with the Stewardship. Abroad, there were many who resented the sudden about-turn of America from the world's worst polluter to a new conscience of the planet. And at home, many groused at our new engagement with the world: America was 'a giant submitting to flea bites', as one opponent put it. For sure there had been plenty of people who wanted to lash out in inchoate rage, at somebody or something. It could have been anybody. But the US and the world had recovered. The bombing was treated as a wake-up call. The years of national introversion were over, and America began to take a lead in the wider programme Amin had always envisaged.

Barnette now spoke of how the Stewardship drew on deeper traditions of American environmentalism, dating back to Henry David Thoreau and John Muir, and landmark pieces of environmental-protection legislation like the Endangered Species Act. Speaking quietly and calmly, she seemed to summon the ghost of Amin with every word.

'I hear much talk of despair, these days. We are in a Bottleneck, a time of maximum danger. Well, perhaps that's so. But I don't counsel despair. For all the ages to come will stand in the shadow of what we do today, and their people will look back on our generation, and they will say, *they* were heroes. And they will envy us...'

I was distracted. I thought I saw Morag again, out of the corner of my eye, sliding through the group of VIPs as silent as a fish in deep water.

And then everything started to unravel.

As Barnette kept talking Gea appeared at my feet, a little robot rolling quietly on the green carpet. 'Do not be alarmed.

Nobody can see me but the project team. We have a problem on the rig.'

'What kind of problem?'

She conjured up a VR image. It appeared in a glowing cube at our feet, a box of light like an aquarium. A young man stood on a metal platform. His image, ten centimetres high, was finely detailed; I could see the rivets in the plates beneath his feet, like pin-heads. He was holding a cylinder from which wires protruded. He was no more than a kid, I realised, younger even than Tom, and he was nervous; you could see his sweat.

We stood around in a circle and peered down at this thing, me, Shelley, John, Tom, Sonia, Vander. Others were distracted by our behaviour. Jack Joy came sidling up from nowhere and joined our group. He was watching us suspiciously, but I was confident he couldn't see the fish-tank VR. Barnette kept talking, in bold, bright colours, and kept most people's attention focused on herself; perhaps she too had heard what was going on, and was doing her part in keeping everything together.

Tom whispered, 'I don't get it. What's that he's holding?'

'It's a mole,' I said. 'Partially disassembled. It's lacking its nose cone, the spiral bit.'

Sonia was glaring down, her eyes sharp. 'I don't know anything about the technology, but the set-up's obvious. I've had to deal with it a dozen times. You can see it in his posture, his body language. He's a suicide bomber.'

I think we all knew it, on some deep level. But having Sonia say it out loud in her precise soldier's tones was something else.

Shelley whispered, 'He's one of our technicians. I suppose we weren't hard to infiltrate. And you can see how he's made his bomb. That mole might be lacking its nose, but it still has its Higgs-energy heart.'

I stared at her. 'The Higgs pod?' I had been intimately involved in the design of the pods; they were intrinsically safe anyhow, and were laden with security factors. 'I can't imagine how he's rigged it.'

'Then he's more imaginative than you, Michael. Say goodbye to innocence.'

Tom asked, 'What happens if it goes up?'

'Like a small nuke,' Shelley said.

Sonia glanced around. 'How close are we?... Too close, I guess. We ought to think about evacuation.'

'It's already in hand,' Gea said quietly. And, looking around, I saw that people were quietly being led out of the back of the marquee. Gea said, 'The worst may not happen. There are measures in place.'

Sonia didn't say anything, but she looked dubious.

I felt bemused, battered. I was aware of my heart beating slowly, steadily. It was all happening too quickly for me to take in. I didn't even seem to be concerned that my son was standing with me here at ground zero. I just stood there, waiting to see what happened next.

John tugged my sleeve, and drew me aside. 'You saw her again, didn't you?' he hissed.

'What?'

'Morag. *You saw her.* Just before Gea showed up. Listen, Michael.' He glanced back at Tom, to make sure he couldn't hear. He was conflicted, I saw, bursting with whatever he had to say, but still hesitant. 'There's something I have to tell you.'

I almost laughed. 'Now? Can't it wait?'

'It's to do with Morag,' he said heavily, painfully. 'Michael, if we don't get through this – or if Morag shows up again, and she tells you herself – Lethe, I can't believe I'm talking about a fucking *ghost*—'

His intensity broke through my numbed detachment. 'Tell me *what*, John?'

He took a breath. 'About me. Morag and me. Something you never knew. We meant to tell you – we didn't want to hurt you – but we always waited, waited, and then she died, and I couldn't bear to hurt you again.'

'You had an affair.' Suddenly I saw it. Of course she had been a friend of John's first. Even after our marriage they had worked together, she and John, the bioprospector and the environmental-compensation lawyer, immersed in complex and urgent twenty-first-century issues. 'All those times I was working, when travel was just impossible and I had to stay away, when Morag and Tom stayed with you –' In my head the events of those years shivered into fragments, whirled like kaleidoscope pieces, and came down in a different pattern.

'We didn't mean it to happen,' John said, more defensive now. 'All right? It wasn't *deliberate*. But we were thrown together, and you weren't there. *You weren't there*, Michael. And then the baby...'

'The baby who died,' I said stupidly. 'The baby whose birth killed my wife. What about the baby?'

But of course I knew the answer. The baby had never been mine.

Tom was looking at us both through the crowd. His face was empty of expression. He knew something was wrong between us, but he didn't know what.

'I knew I had to tell you sometime,' John said desolately. 'I never had the guts. And then Morag showed up. What if that's why she's come back, Michael? That's what I keep asking myself. *What if she's come back to tell you what we did*, me and her?'

I don't remember throwing the punch.

Suddenly John was on the floor, blood streaming from his mouth, and my fist felt as if I had slammed it against a wall. People scattered around us, shocked.

Shelley Magwood grabbed my arm and dragged me away. 'I don't know what the hell's going on with you two, but we've got enough trouble.'

Around us the flow of VIPs out the back of the marquee was becoming noticeable. Barnette was still talking, but her message was now one of reassurance, admonitions to keep calm. And in the little fish tank, the tiny figure of the bomber was gesticulating, shouting tinnily at unseen negotiators.

John slowly got to his feet. He wouldn't look me in the eye.

I said, 'All right. I'm calm. Are they getting anywhere with the nut?'

'He's a suicide bomber,' Shelley said, her voice full of anger and despair. 'What do you think?'

'Can't we just disable his trigger?'

'Not remotely. He's got it figured out pretty well. And he

has a dead man's switch.' She laughed, hollow. 'The kid's a good engineer. Our only hope is to talk him down. But we can't even figure out what he wants.'

'He probably wants many things.' Jack Joy stood beside me, sweating harder than ever. 'But we all act for many reasons, don't we?'

I stared at him, trying to figure him out. 'What do *you* want?... Can you see this VR? How?'

He tapped his ear. 'I have my own channels.'

Shelley glared at him. 'Who are you? Have you got something to do with this?'

He wouldn't answer. He said mournfully, 'It isn't personal. Please believe that. I as an individual in fact sympathise with your goals, on this specific project; the hydrates are clearly a menace. But it's what you represent, you see. The movement of which you have become a part. The philosophy behind your actions. The futile attempt to resist a change in the world's natural order, when we should be relishing the opportunities opened up to us. The curtailing of our liberties in the process. The accruing of power by unelectable and unaccountable organisations and individuals.'

This dreary listing was a type of argument I had heard many times before. But this wasn't the time for bullshit. I tried to grab his collar, but he was a VR; my hand passed harmlessly through his shirt, scattering flesh-coloured pixels. 'If you've got information, spill it.'

'I apologise,' he said almost formally. 'Sincerely. I like you, Mike. I do, really!' He winked out of existence.

And, two kilometres out to sea, the bomber pressed his trigger.

Chapter 45

Adrift in dark corridors of mind, Alia explored the Transcendence.

'Awareness is the core of the Transcendence,' Leropa said to Alia. 'Think of it as an awakening. In sleep you are aware only of yourself, your dreams and hopes and fears. It is consciousness of a sort, an awareness of self. But as you awake from sleep, you become more aware of yourself, and of a wider universe beyond your own head – and of other consciousnesses like your own, your parents, your siblings. It is essential. You must see the universe through their eyes, understand how they feel, before you can *care*.'

'It is more than care,' Alia said. 'It is love.'

'Love, yes! Love is the full apprehension of another soul, and the cherishing of her. And through love you awaken to a new level, a full awareness of others, so your own consciousness expands further. This is a deep root of our very humanity,' Leropa said: 'It is believed that consciousness evolved as a way to deal with *other* consciousnesses. So full self-awareness is not possible in isolation, but only through an engagement with other minds. And the deepest such engagement is through love.

'Thus the Transcendence is built on awareness. On love as you have experienced it. But it is more than that, for the Transcendence is more than human.

'The Transcendence reaches across all of space. Each new soul drawn into the Transcendence, like yourself, enriches the whole. And each new form of humanity, each with its own unique sensorium, deepens and widens our apprehension of the universe. All of this is brought into the centre and shared among all. It is no coincidence that the Transcendence's political presence is called the *Commonwealth*, for this merged awareness is the true common wealth of mankind.

'And there is more still. By reaching around the curve of time *the Transcendence is awakening to the past too*, awakening to the rich experience of every human who ever lived. This is an extension of the Commonwealth in time as well as space, to kinds of people who once existed, as well as those who exist now. In the end the universe will be like a jewel held in the palm of the hand, its every facet and glimmering refraction – yes, and every flaw – fully known and understood. This is the ultimate prize.

'Why must the Transcendence aspire to this? Because it is essential if we are to survive. Alia, the more awake you become, the more control over your destiny you acquire. We must escape from our long dreaming if we want to live!

'And then there is our greater fate. Beyond the walls of time there are greater minds still, Alia. We call them *monads*. Our universe might not have been; there were other possibilities. Why our universe? *Because of us* – because of our potential to grow into a full apprehension of the cosmos, an expression of the objective cosmos in subjective awareness. So you see, Alia, we humans, through the Transcendence, will become the consciousness of the universe itself – and we will, we *must*, fulfil the great project of the monads.

'And all of this is built on love!'

Once more Leropa had met Alia on Earth, beneath the ruin of the ancient Wignerian cathedral. It was dismaying to return to the drab, subdued community of undying. Even Leropa was like a shadow. The undying aspired to something higher, but it was as if they had forgotten what it was to be human, Alia thought.

But after the intensity of emotions on the *Nord* it was almost a relief to plunge once more into the abstract mysteries of Transcendence. As they floated through this sky of consciousness she could see its immense trans-human ideas like vast clouds, its thoughts crackling like lightning between those clouds. And in every direction she could see the awareness of the Transcendence elaborating, multiplying, exponentiating, its vast intellect growing as she watched.

Leropa was not literally a guide for Alia, her words not

a literal whisper in Alia's ear. *This was the Transcendence*; Alia and Leropa were both parts of a greater whole, and yet expressions of it, as Alia's own consciousness might briefly be focused on a bruised finger. But the mote that had been Alia found it helpful to cling to the metaphor of novice and guide.

And now, here in the dark, Alia had come to learn the truth about Redemption, and she listened to Leropa speak of love.

'The Transcendence loves you. The Transcendence loves *every* human. It must, for love is the full apprehension of another, and so of oneself. Love is the foundation of everything, Alia. Can you see that? And it is love, the cherishing even of the unhappy past, that has led to the Redemption.

'For the Transcendence to become complete we must redeem the suffering of the past – we *must* – or the Transcendence will always be flawed. And we can only save the past by apprehending it, loving it.

'First there is the Witnessing – a trillion tiny viewpoints like yours, Alia, each studying some corner of the past, some lost life, and integrating it into a greater awareness of the whole. The next level of awareness is the Hypostatic Union, in which your consciousness is *merged* with your subject in the past – and you express your love for her by sharing every particle of joy in her life, absorbing every morsel of pain. A full Hypostatic Union of every soul in past and future with every other, the ultimate logic, would require an infinite effort. But the Transcendence will be/is infinite and eternal; for such an entity an infinite recursion is possible, and so it will/*must* come to pass. You understand that now.

'But all of this, even the fully realised Hypostatic Union, is a mere viewing. And even when viewed the suffering will still exist out there in the past.'

'Yes,' Alia said. She was on the verge of understanding – almost thrilled by the intoxicating ideas. 'Even Hypostatic Union is not enough. We must do more.'

'Yes,' Leropa said. 'And *we can do more.*

'It is as if, up to now, we have viewed the past as a magnificent tapestry. We follow every thread, every life, as it weaves its unique way through the tremendous patterns of the whole. But we have seen the past as a fixed thing, frozen; we have never allowed ourselves to *tamper* with it, to change the slightest detail in the weave – not even to repair the most obvious flaws, or to amend the most grotesque suffering.'

Suddenly Alia saw what the next level of Redemption must be – what the Transcendence had done. 'We have touched the past,' she whispered.

'Yes.'

Leropa showed her Michael Poole in a glittering crowd of people, and an explosion out to sea frozen in time like a deadly flower.

'Watch now,'Leropa said.

Chapter 46

The flash came first. The curtain-wall of the marquee turned black, saving my eyesight. For a fraction of a second we all stood there in the dark.

Then the shock wave hit us. *Bam.*

The marquee was whipped away in the wind. Under the sudden sky the whole world was full of immense energies that roared over me, oblivious to my presence. Around me VIPs fell like skittles, or went whirling away into the air. It was like being overwhelmed by some immense wave.

When the shock passed I found myself on my back, all the air smashed out of my lungs, staring up at a racing sky. I struggled to sit up.

Over the sea, a mushroom cloud was gathering. Small, perfect, symmetrical, it was a return of a twentieth-century nightmare. Around its base great streamers of fire gushed up out of the water. I guessed we had managed to destabilise some of the very hydrate deposits we were supposed to secure, that the flames came from the ignition of some of the released methane. Now a wind began to rush the other way, at my back, as the huge blast of heat over the ocean began to push the air skywards, and suck colder air in from the land.

I was surrounded by wreckage, scattered people. I couldn't see Tom, or John, or Shelley, or any of the others. I had no idea what had become of Makaay and Barnette. There wasn't a trace left of the low stage where they'd been standing.

A camera drone hovered before my face, not five centimetres from my nose, a spinning sphere the size of my thumb. A tiny portal dilated open and a jewel-like lens glinted down at me. I stared back, bemused.

I didn't seem to be functioning. I was having trouble breathing, as if iron bands had been clamped around my chest. I couldn't seem to feel anything, not even the hard ground under my back, or the Arctic chill, and I could hear nothing but a vague, dull roar. It was almost comforting to sit there, while running people, spinning drones, bits of ripped-apart marquee flapped around me.

And Morag was beside me.

She sat on the ground, not a hair out of place despite the wind. But her face was creased with anxiety. 'Are you OK?'

I could hear her, but I couldn't hear any other damn thing. I flexed an arm, testing the joints. 'I think so.'

And then the meaning of our mundane exchange hit me. She was here. I could even make out her words. I stared at her. 'Shit. *Morag*.'

'I know,' she said. 'It's a heck of a thing, isn't it?'

We sat there. Then I reached up, and suddenly she was in my arms, warm and real.

I think I blacked out.

Three

Chapter 47

Sonia loomed over me. She was covered in mud and bleeding from a wound in her forehead, and she held her right arm clamped against her belly. She yelled, 'Can you hear me, Michael? Can you move?'

I pushed myself upright. For a second the world greyed. Sonia reached down with her good arm to help me up, but she winced. I stood, unsteady. I don't think I had ever felt so old, so drained of strength.

I leaned on Morag. I leaned on her!

She had always been strong, but now she felt very solid, like a stone pillar. She was wearing a simple white coverall, the kind of practical gear she had always preferred. But her coverall was mud-streaked and splashed by a spray of blood, somebody else's blood, and her strawberry hair was mussed by the breeze. She was embedded in the world now. Somehow she had come back: not a ghost this time, not an elusive vision glimpsed from the corner of my eye, but *here*.

'You're real,' I said.

She looked down at herself. 'Real?'

'You're back in the world.' I touched a mud splash on her sleeve. 'You weren't before. You are now.'

'It looks that way, doesn't it? How strange.'

Suddenly I had a head full of questions, and things I had waited seventeen years to say to her. But even at that moment, behind my eyes was a single sharp memory of what John had said to me about their affair, a grain of pain.

I became aware of the others, Shelley, John, Tom. They all looked battered and muddy, but had no obvious serious injuries – none save Sonia herself, who was shepherding us, despite her damaged arm. She seemed to be the only one of us thinking clearly. I guessed her military training had kicked in, and I was grateful for it.

The crowd was actually thicker than it had been before the blast, I thought. Engineers and VIPs, covered in mud and blood, wandered around or sat in the dirt. The VR guests had been untouched by the blast, of course. They walked like glittering ghosts through the battlefield that our event had become; some of them even had drinks in their hands. I wondered if we had a few visitors who hadn't been here before the blast. It was a phenomenon of our catastrophe-plagued time: Bottleneckers, they were called, disaster tourists.

Everybody was staring at Morag.

Tom's mud-streaked face was a mask of hurt and bewilderment. 'Dad—'

I felt a stab of regret that I hadn't been able to save him from this profound shock. 'Later. We'll deal with this.'

Something of his dry cynicism returned. 'Well, we'll have a lot to talk about, won't we?'

Sonia tapped her ear; maybe she was getting information through her service-issue implants. 'OK. EI security are getting a hold of things. Makaay and Barnette are dead. Many casualties on the rig. The EI people are doing a good job, but they are concerned about follow-up attacks. And they hope to get the VR facilities shut down so we can lose these Bottleneckers.'

'What about the police, the authorities?'

'See for yourself.' She pointed.

Outside the footprint of the wrecked marquee, cops and military types swarmed, and as my hearing recovered I heard the roar of vehicle engines, the flap of chopper blades. They must have been on hand to provide cover for this VIP-heavy event anyhow, but they had been unobtrusive, and now they seemed to just melt out of the tundra.

Sonia began to herd us away from the marquee. 'The Alaska State Troopers are taking charge of the incident for now. They want to get us out of here, the five of us—'

'Six,' I said. I got hold of Morag's arm. Whatever happened, I wasn't going to be separated from her.

'Six, then. The marquee area and the rig will be closed

down as a crime scene. We'll be flown out to a hospital. But we'll be in military custody.'

Shelley said, 'So we're suspects?'

We had all grown up with terrorism, and we knew the mantra: everyone is on the front line, everyone is a suspect. But it was depressing to be caught up in its dreary processing.

John said, 'We'll be held as witnesses at the minimum. I'll make sure we get proper legal representation. I have contacts…' He tailed off. He had struck his usual blustering competent-man-taking-charge pose, and it was briefly impressive despite the mud streaked across his face, his torn shirt. But Morag stood here, impossibly alive, watching him without expression. He crumbled, his words drying up, his personality imploding.

Sonia led us towards a site that was being marked out by troopers as a landing area. A chopper descended towards us, a big old Chinook in camouflage colours.

I asked, 'Where are they taking us?'

'Fairbanks.'

'Fairbanks?' That was in the interior of Alaska, six, seven hundred kilometres from Prudhoe Bay.

Sonia shrugged. 'Not my decision. It has a good hospital, I'm told. And we can be made secure there. You need to remember that the military's response to situations like this is always to establish control. Dispersing key components isn't a bad way to do it.'

Shelley forced a grin. 'So I'm a *key component*. Gets you right there, doesn't it?'

Tom, freaked out, said, 'Shut up, shut *up*.'

The chopper landed heavily, and a trooper waved at us. Sonia ran towards the chopper, holding Tom's hand. They ducked to avoid the still-turning blades. Shelley and John followed, and then me and Morag.

I clung to Morag's hand firmly. 'I always did want a ride in a Chinook, ever since I was a kid.'

'I know,' she said. 'On any other day this would be a thrill, wouldn't it?'

I glanced at her. Was she joking? But that was how Morag would have reacted, with dry humour. 'Come on, that trooper is starting to look pissed at us.'

We sat strapped into canvas slingback seats bolted crudely to the floor. Battered, bruised, bloodied, we looked like refugees from a war zone – as we were, I guess. Six troopers rode with us. Their faces hidden by faceplates like spacesuit visors, they watched us, calm and alert, cradling massive weapons.

We took off with an unceremonious lurch. It was true that I had always wanted to fly in a Chinook. It was a design so good it had been flying since before I was born, and was still in operation now, all over the world. But the interior of that old bird was hideously uncomfortable, a roar of noise.

We saw the rig through the open door of the Chinook's cargo bay. From the air it was spectacular. The rig's heart had been torn out by the Higgs-field suicide bomb, leaving a hollow tangle of rusted metal that stood precariously on bent stilts. Whatever was left to burn was doing so, fitfully. Choppers, planes and drones buzzed around the rig like flies, and launches skirted it nervously. Away from the rig the sea seemed to be boiling, with immense slow-moving bubbles of gas breaking the surface. The gas was methane, of course, escaping from the hydrate deposits we had meant to stabilise, but had only succeeding in breaking apart. But at least the flares that had ignited in the first moments after the detonation seemed to have burned themselves out.

The chopper slid away from the coast and swept south, heading inland towards Fairbanks, and I could see no more.

Sonia seemed to have run out of the adrenalin that had brought her so far. She was bent over her damaged arm, grimacing with pain. I wondered if one of the troopers could give her a morphine shot or somesuch, but Sonia was capable of asking for that herself if she wanted it. Tom, John and I were locked in a tense silence. We avoided each other's eyes. John just sat there with his hands clasped, staring at the floor.

Morag herself sat, eyes wide, mouth a small bud, her expression unreadable. I wondered if she was going through some kind of shock too. After all what greater trauma could there be than to be reincarnated?

As for me I felt utterly dislocated, battered by the blast we had lived through, and now suspended in midair in this antique military vehicle, with my dead wife at my side. I couldn't have guessed even an hour before that the logic of my life would bring me to this situation, here and now, with everything turned upside down.

Shelley said at last, 'I wonder what happened to our moles.'

I imagined all those moles burrowing in the dark, plaintively listening for each other with their fine acoustic, electromagnetic and seismometric senses. Mostly they would have survived; they were surely far enough away from the detonation. 'They are probably fine,' I said. 'They'll find each other. They'll know something has gone wrong, and will go dormant.'

'Yes. But they'll be frightened.'

John raised his eyebrows. But Shelley wasn't being anthropomorphic; this was the nature of the job. I said, 'We'll get them back.'

Sonia said, 'So we did more harm than good in the end.'

'We'll fix it,' I said. I surprised myself by my firmness. 'We have to. The issue of the hydrates hasn't gone away, no matter what happened today.'

Shelley said, 'But Ruud Makaay is dead. So is Barnette.'

'We'll just have to fill Ruud's shoes,' I said. 'And, to be blunt, maybe we can leverage Barnette's death to help us.'

'You think that will work?'

'I bet it's what she would have wanted.'

John raised his head. After all we had been through, even a bomb blast, his mouth, where I had hit him, was still leaking blood. 'That doesn't sound like you, Michael.'

'Maybe I'm not the same person I was a couple of hours ago,' I snapped back at him. 'Things sure don't feel the same to me. How about you?'

He risked a glance at Morag. 'I don't know how we're supposed to deal with this situation.'

'Then shut the fuck up,' I said.

He dropped his head again.

One of the troopers took a message from the Chinook's pilot. The mass distribution was wrong, she told us; the pilot was actually worried we might have a stowaway. So we were all searched, and the troopers combed the hold. It turned out to be Morag. Her actual mass far outweighed the Chinook's systems' estimates, which were based on her external appearance. The troopers looked at Morag, and at each other, and shrugged. We flew on.

We landed at Fairbanks International Airport. We clambered out of the Chinook while more choppers, military, police and coastguard, swooped out of the sky, and ambulances and military vehicles bustled on the ground.

Our trooper escort tried to hustle us into a military lorry, a heavy-duty armoured job that stank of gasoline; the military had held onto the raw power of gas. Tom made a fuss about Sonia's damaged arm, and demanded an ambulance. But Sonia herself brushed that aside, and we all got in the back of the lorry.

Under escort, we were whisked away from the airport, and raced along a straight drag called Airport Way. We turned off before we reached Fairbanks's downtown, such as it was, and pulled into the Memorial Hospital, where still more troops had gathered to meet us. I had to admire the speed with which all these resources had been mobilised.

Inside the hospital a serious young Army officer told us we were to be treated for our injuries, and then interrogated about what had happened out at Prudhoe. He didn't say anything about our legal status or our rights. John made some noises about legal representation, and he gave the officer some contacts he wanted called. But I already had the sense of being trapped in a vast, inhuman process that wouldn't let up until I was spat out the other end, drained of any useful information – and hopefully cleared of suspicion.

We were to be separated, we were told, to be examined individually. But I wasn't going to let Morag go. It wasn't just my personal feelings; the situation seemed far too strange to allow it. At first the Army officer wasn't having any of it. But I pulled rank. I was a senior figure on the Refrigerator project, after all, and John weighed in.

So while the others were taken away individually Morag and I were allowed to stay together, although our guard complement was doubled.

We were led to an examination room, where we were attended by a bewildered-looking local doctor, a couple of nurses, another Army officer, and a black-suited FBI agent from the local field office in Fairbanks. The doctor briskly put us through medical checks. I was treated for cuts, bruises, a bang on the back of the head. My breathing had taken a battering, my chest crushed and my lungs filled with smoke; they made me suck down pure oxygen for a while. Otherwise I was unharmed. Then I was put through more checks that had little to do with my health. My blood and DNA were sampled; I was X-rayed; my implants were interrogated; I was even put through a full body scanner. I expected it all and endured it.

In parallel, the medics investigated Morag. She gave up blood when they stuck a needle in her, her cheek swabs offered up DNA, the X-rays showed she had bones and organs in the proportions you'd expect. But that business of her excess weight clearly baffled them. And the scanning machines were puzzled when she showed none of the implants you'd expect in somebody her age, no spinal interface, no sonic chips in the bones of her skull, no medical monitors swimming around her bloodstream.

It wasn't impossible to find people free of such gadgets. There were those who had religious or other moral objections to interfacing so directly with technology, and in many parts of the world such facilities weren't available anyhow. Older folk especially resisted having electronics stuffed deep inside their bodies; I don't think Uncle George had a single implant his whole life. But for most citizens of the advanced societies of the west the implants were so obviously convenient, and such a key interface to services and products, that you just absorbed them without thinking, the way earlier generations had bought cell-phones and transistor radios. Anyhow, Morag was bare.

And when her detailed lab results came back the Army officer and FBI agent started to look at her very quizzically. I could understand why. Even if nothing else had turned out to be odd about her, she had given them the DNA of a woman seventeen years dead.

When they had done with their examinations, the medics insisted we get a little rest before the authority types started in on their interrogations. The FBI guy and the Army officer agreed to leave us alone for a couple of hours. We weren't going anywhere, the search through the debris at Prudhoe Bay by fingertip, sniffer dog and microscopic robot was only just beginning – and I was sure our private room would be saturated by surveillance technology, our every word and gesture monitored, recorded and analysed. Odd how you start to think like a criminal in situations like that.

Anyhow they left us. And for the first time since her return, I was alone with Morag.

We lay side by side on cots in our room, holding hands. As we calmed down, out of the rush of events, I had time to think, to feel. And I tentatively began to explore, in my head, the possibility that all this might be real.

'I wonder what they're making of me,' she said. 'Not only should I be dead, that's bad enough. I should be seventeen years older than I am. I'm probably freaking them out.'

'Maybe they think you're a clone,' I said. 'There are simpler explanations than—'

'Than the truth?' She turned on her side and looked at me; her strawberry-blonde hair fell across her face. 'And what about you? Is the truth freaking you out too, Michael?'

'What truth?'

She had no answer.

'I don't know how I feel,' I said. 'I feel like I'm waking up. You know? That it's just sinking in.'

'I know. I don't know what to say. We'll have to give it time.' Her voice had that light lilt that was a legacy of her childhood, and her tone just the right frisson of humour. She was exactly as I remembered her, and more; she had even brought back things I had forgotten about her, things that had once been so precious.

For seventeen years I had been storing up all I had longed to say to her, all I had longed to tell her I felt, after I thought I'd lost the opportunity for good. But somehow, with her there beside me, none of that stuff mattered. It was as if the intervening seventeen years had never existed. I was taken back to the immediacy of her death, how I had felt in the first days and weeks, and the wound was as raw as it had ever been. It made no sense, emotionally. But then the situation we were in made no sense. My heart wasn't programmed for this, I thought.

Morag was watching me. 'You've been through a lot,' she said.

That made me laugh. '*I've* been through a lot... You know, I think the doctors' tests have started to make it more real for me. I mean, ghosts don't have DNA, do they?'

'I'm not a ghost,' she said faintly.

'OK. But I think you've been haunting me all my life.'

'All your life?' She sounded genuinely puzzled.

'Since I was a kid.' I'd never told her this before she had died. Now, though, I hesitantly ran through the strange story for her.

She blew out her cheeks. 'On any other day that would be a hell of a story.'

'Do you remember any of this? Like those times on the beach, when I was nine or ten—'

She said, frowning, 'I feel like there are gaps. I don't *know*, Michael.'

I asked her the basic question bluntly. 'How did you get here?'

'I don't know.'

'Why has it happened? Why are you here?'

She had nothing to say.

I propped myself on one elbow and looked at her. Now that I had started asking questions, more occurred, as if my brain was starting to work again. 'Why should you be the age you are?' As far as I could tell from what the doctor had hinted, she was precisely the age she had been on the day of her death.

'I don't know,' she said. 'It just is.'

'And how come you weren't fazed to find out what date it is – seventeen years in your future?' I rubbed my own jowly jaw. 'How come you weren't horrified to find I'd turned into the oldest man in the universe?'

'I just seemed to know where I was. *When* I was. The way you know such things without thinking about it.'

'But that must mean you were set up, somehow. Prepared for your return.'

'Rebooted? Is that the word you're looking for?' There was fear in her voice, but there was an edge of humour too. 'You were always such a tech-head, Michael. Believe me, I want to know too. But I think you're skirting around the big questions.' She shook her head. 'Seventeen years and you haven't changed a bit.'

She was right. Only a couple of hours after her reincarnation, metaphysics just didn't matter. I sat up, swinging my legs over the edge of my bed, and faced her. 'All right, let's get to it. There's no sign of the pregnancy, is there? Or of the labour, the birth?'

'So that doctor said.'

'But you remember it.'

She frowned. 'I went into labour too early. It hurt like hell. You rushed me to hospital with Tom, in the car.' I remembered; what a ride that was. 'I was taken in for a C-section. I was drugged to the eyeballs, but the pain – I knew something was going wrong—' Suddenly she was weeping, even as she spoke; her shoulders shook, and she wiped angrily at her eyes. 'Damn it, Michael, for me this only just happened.'

My heart was being ripped apart. I longed to hold her, to comfort her. But a spasm of anger stopped me. 'What else happened in between? A tunnel of white light, a guy with a beard and a big book at a pearly gate?'

'I don't know.' She hid her eyes with her arm, a gesture I suddenly remembered so well. 'Something... I can't say. It's not even like a memory. I didn't ask for any of this, Michael.' Then she lowered her arm and faced me. 'Just as I didn't ask to have a relationship with John. You must know about that by now.'

'How do you expect me to feel about that?'

'*It just happened*,' she said. 'It wasn't anybody's fault. You were away so much... John and I worked together a lot. We sort of fell into it. And then the pregnancy.'

She had chosen not to terminate, she told me, even though the baby was obviously John's, even though she knew how much hurt it would cause everybody – and even though the doctors had advised her to abort for the sake of her own health, I learned now – because she couldn't bear to lose it.

420

'So you let me think it was mine.'

'We didn't know how to handle it, John and me. We didn't know what to do for the best.'

'Did you love him?'

'Yes,' she said bravely. 'But I loved you more, Michael. I always did. So did John. Neither of us wanted to hurt you. And then there was Tom to think about. I never planned to leave you, you know, to go to John. Our relationship was just a – a *thing*, and then we got caught out. We didn't know what to do. I'm not expecting you to sympathise, Michael, but we were both in a hell of a state.'

It was hard to imagine John, my competent older brother, having got himself into such a mess.

'We put off telling you,' she said. 'We decided I'd wait until I had the baby – as much as we decided anything. Once it was born, once it existed—'

'He,' I said. 'The baby was a boy.'

She took that in, and nodded carefully. 'OK. Once he was there, it would all *feel* different. You remember how we were before Tom was born, frightened and elated at the same time? But then once he was born things sort of clarified.'

'I remember.'

'So when the new baby came, when it was real, a person, we would see how we all felt. And then—'

'And then you'd tell me that this wonderful bundle of joy was not mine but my older brother's?'

Anger flared in her eyes. 'Is that all you think about, that it's John's child? If it had been some stranger's, would you feel better? You've suddenly gotten so old your face looks like it's melted. But you're still a little kid inside, still competing with your brother...'

Maybe she was right. After all my fist still hurt from where I had punched John in the mouth. But I wanted to be careful not to think that way, not to go down that road, because I didn't want to draw the conclusion, on any emotional level, that my brother had killed my wife. How could I live with such a thought in my head?

We seemed to run down. We sat there facing each other.

'I can't believe it,' I said. 'We've only been together a couple of hours. You've been returned to me from the dead, for God's sake, like fucking Lazarus. And we're yelling in each other's faces.'

'You started it,' she snapped back.

'No, I didn't. You slept with my brother.'

We stared each other out. Then we laughed, and fell together. I held her in my arms, and pressed her face to my neck. Her skin was smooth, astonishingly soft. It was young skin, I thought, young compared to mine anyhow.

'What about Tom?' she asked, whispering into my shoulder. 'It's going to be hard for him.'

'I told him we'd get through this together.' I squeezed her hand. 'And John. We'll get through it somehow.'

'Yes. But what a mess. A funny lot, you Pooles.'

I pulled back and looked at her. I wondered if she knew George was dead. 'How are you feeling now?'

'I just came back from the dead,' she said. 'I don't know how I'm supposed to feel.'

I was scared to ask it, but I had to. 'Do you remember dying?'

'No. I remember the table, the anaesthetic, the pain. I remember a feeling that things were going wrong. It was like losing control, like a car going off the road.' That wasn't a simile that anybody would use nowadays. She pulled back a bit and looked at her own hand, flexing her fingers. 'I feel as if I've had a close shave. As if I *nearly* got caught by the ocean current, or *nearly* fell off the cliff. My heart is thumping. You know? I feel as if I *nearly* died.' She stared at me, helpless, looking for guidance. 'But I did die, didn't I?'

And we were both weeping.

But there was doubt in my heart. At first none of this had seemed real. Then, as we floated into the hospital here through the equally unreal experience of a Chinook flight, I guess I had just accepted the whole thing as a happy miracle. Now, though, as my head started to work again, the glow seemed to be fading, and questions continued to press me.

The fact was, whatever mechanism had brought her back and whatever reason it had for doing so, since her death seventeen years of life had gone by for me, a life I had lived without her, which she had never shared. So there was a barrier between us seventeen years deep. That thought made me cry even more.

We stayed that way, crying and hugging, until the FBI agent came to ask us hard questions about the events at Prudhoe Bay.

Chapter 48

Drea came to Earth to offer Alia some support. They met in a small hut near the centre of the Transcendents' community beneath the cathedral. The cabin's walls were translucent, and if Alia looked up she could see the monumental tetrahedral arching scraping at the sky.

Leropa sat with them, a chill, motionless presence.

They had to sit on pallets; there were no chairs in this little room, and its floor was just a woven carpet thrown over the dirt. Somehow this was typical of the Transcendence, Alia thought, its grandiose ambition rooted in shabbiness. She wondered now if the drabness of the worlds she had seen, the Rustball and the Dirtball, even Earth itself, had something to do with the stupendous distraction of the Transcendence: unhealthily introverted, obsessed with the past, it was not sufficiently engaged with the present – and it neglected the impoverished environments of its human subjects.

Through the hut walls she could see others of the community, other Transcendents. They were just a bunch of very old people, making their slow and cautious way through the ancient rubble of the cathedral, trailed by their serving bots and a few human attendants. Today the Transcendents' movements were disturbed, edgy, as if something was troubling them.

It is doubt, Alia thought uneasily. A vast doubt embedded in the cosmic mind, folding down into the fragile bodies of these Transcendents. That is why they seem so disturbed. And perhaps *I* am the source of that doubt.

Drea was watching the undying too. Boldly she asked Leropa, 'Why aren't you like *them*?'

Leropa looked out of the hut at her peers. She sat on the

floor with her legs crossed, in no apparent discomfort. 'One reason, perhaps. I never had children.'

Alia sat forward. It was the first time Leropa had told her anything of her own past. 'You didn't? Why not?'

'Because I am undying. If I had had children, even if they bred true and were undying themselves, accident statistics dictate that at least some would have gone before me. We humans haven't evolved to outlive our children. Could I not be spared that?'

Drea said, 'But they would have had children of their own.'

'Yes, and then what? You feel a bond with your great-grandchildren, I'm told, or even a generation or two later. But after that the genes are diluted by a muddy tide of the semen and oestrus of strangers. Occasionally in the great crowd of your descendants a chance gathering of features will remind you of *you*, or your children, of what once was. But mostly, whatever there was that defined you is simply washed away, like everything else in this transient universe of ours.

'And still they breed, your descendants, on and on. Soon they are so remote they don't feel as if they have anything to do with you at all. After a thousand years their belief systems will have changed utterly. Chances are they will not even speak the same language. And your genetic contribution dilutes further, diffusing through the population like a disease, until everybody is a part of you, and nobody is. Given enough time, *nothing* is preserved, Alia, nothing you build, nothing you pass on, not even your genetic legacy, save only in a cold biochemical sense. How crushing that is, how desolating, how isolating! And of course, it's all quite irrelevant.'

'Irrelevant to what?'

'To the great project of immortality – of personal survival. Alia, if you choose not to die then you are doing it for *you*, not your descendants – because you are choosing not to clear the stage for *them*.'

'So you compete with your own children.'

'You must. That is why only individuals muddled by sentimentality and doubt would choose to have children; it is contradictory to the basic goal of longevity.'

And even the impulses of the genes were served, in a sense, Alia thought. The genes strove for their own biochemical survival. If they could not be passed on to the young, then their only means of survival was in the body of their undying host. This was the final logic of immortality: an immortal must displace her own children. If we were animals, Alia thought, we would eat our young.

She said, 'And you have no regret?'

Leropa looked at her scornfully. 'Have you not listened? There is nothing to regret. Better to be alone than to be abandoned. No wonder all those out there are flattened by time! This is a choice you will soon have to make for yourself, Alia. To have a child is to open the door to death, for it means the dissolution of self.'

How cold, Alia thought, how selfish. So much for the love of the Transcendence. They sat in the shabby hut while outside the undying shuffled in the dirt.

Chapter 49

We were all held for a week, in the secure but smothering confines of the hospital at Fairbanks. We weren't allowed out to attend the funerals of Makaay and the others – not even the state funeral of Edith Barnette, a Vice President assassinated like the President she had once served.

Morag was an unresolvable problem for the authorities.

As far as they were concerned she had just appeared out of nowhere. In their endless stocktaking of orderly births and deaths her sudden appearance was as jarring an event as a disappearance would have been, the mirror-image of a murder or an abduction. Immigration also needed an explanation for her presence on American soil. And they needed to understand how it could be that she had the DNA of an American citizen seventeen years in the grave.

Shelley muttered darkly about the limitations of the bureaucratic mind. 'They're bothered about a few anomalies in records of births and deaths. But Morag appeared out of nowhere. What about the conservation of mass? Shouldn't we all be arrested for breaking that little law?'

There was certainly nothing Morag herself could tell them. She didn't try to hide anything. What point would there be in lying? On the other hand she didn't answer any questions she wasn't asked.

She seemed to have a reasonably complete set of memories up to the moment of her death, seventeen years before. Past that point she seemed to have some partial information – impressions, not memories. On some deep level of her mind she seemed to know that seventeen years had worn away, but it wasn't something she could articulate. The doctors speculated about parallels with amnesiac cases. I doubted that was going to lead them anywhere. The FBI seemed eventually to settle on a hypothesis that she was an illegal clone of some kind. I was happy for them to lose themselves in that fantasy; I knew there was nothing else to find.

Her legal status remained a puzzle, however. She certainly wasn't Morag Poole, the person who had died so long ago, not in the eyes of the law. So she was assigned an open 'Jane Doe' file – 'like a faceless corpse fished out of the river', as she said herself. Morag wasn't given her full freedom, not for now. She was released into my custody, but even that deal took some swinging, as the authorities had decided I was somewhat flaky myself. What saved the day was a surprise intervention from Aunt Rosa, who used the authority of the Church to back me up.

Anyhow after that week, we were released – all, to my astonishment, save John. He was sent to a more secure FBI facility down at Anchorage. There were 'connections' the G-men wanted to investigate further. His legal status was dubious, but I wasn't too concerned. If anybody could look after himself in a situation like that it was John. And anyhow, I had enough spite in me to be glad that the Feds were giving him a hard time; I knew it was ignoble, but I felt he deserved it.

The rest of us were asked not to leave Alaska for the time being. We all went back to Prudhoe Bay, a strange, confused crew.

Shelley and I threw ourselves back into work. I was guiltily glad to have a distraction from the strangeness of Morag. Tom and Sonia agreed to come back to the project too. Tom said he didn't want to see the bombers win, as he had seen for himself the damage the destabilisation of the undersea hydrates could do. It pleased me deeply that we were going to continue working together, even though I knew the return of Morag was bound to put us under extraordinary strain.

The rebuilding of the Refrigerator itself had already begun, even before Shelley and I got back to the coast. Many of the techs working on the project were very young – just like the suicide bomber, a technician himself – and a good number of them had been killed. But the deaths seemed to have welded the survivors together; there was a determination that 'the bad guys' would not win, that we who remained would see this thing through as a memorial to those we had lost. Maybe that was a predictable reaction: we had all grown up sharing a world with terrorists, with the dreary knowledge that with every step forward there was somebody waiting to drag you back. But it was moving even so.

The work proceeded quickly. The network of tunnels we had already built, burrowed through cubic kilometres of the seabed, was intact save for the area beneath the rig itself. Shelley needn't have worried about our moles; most of them still functioned, as I had hoped. When the command signals stopped coming they just sat patiently in their tunnels, waiting for we contrary humans to figure out what we wanted to do next.

The oil rig we had used as the base of the project was wrecked beyond usefulness, however. A whole new project to dismantle it safely was soon underway, an enormous undertaking in itself. A new nitrogen liquefaction plant would be set up on a platform not far from the site of the rig, anchored to the seabed. Once that was in place and attached to our network we would start everything up again and finish the analysis of our prototype system, work we had barely begun on the fatal day of the explosion.

And after that, with our proof of concept in place, we would go cap in hand to the authorities for backing for a wider roll-out. The loss of Barnette had been a huge shock, but the whole incident had raised the profile of the project, and we had every reason to hope that in the end the bombing would do us more harm than good.

So we began to move forward again. We were all helping each other recover – and we were, maybe, saving the world in the process. It was deeply satisfying and thoroughly absorbing.

In the middle of all this, I found Morag a distraction. Can you believe that?

We ate, walked, slept together.

It was a joy, of course, to hold her, to immerse myself in her scent, her warmth, the way her hair curled against my chest – sensations my mind had forgotten but my body remembered. It was as if I was suddenly made whole again.

We didn't have sex, though. I wasn't sure why. My body responded to her closeness, and I thought hers did too. But somehow it didn't feel right. Maybe it was something to do with the strangeness of her new body, a density I could feel when I touched her. But the truth may have been simpler. I was seventeen years older since the last time, though she hadn't aged at all; maybe I didn't want to disappoint her.

Morag wasn't freaked. 'Give it time,' she said. 'It's not as if either of us is supposed to know how to handle this. I mean, how many support groups are there for husbands whose dead wives have come back to life? We'll find our way through...'

Just as I'd said to Tom. But soon I wasn't sure I believed it myself.

When we talked we did fine, so long as we talked about the past, the years we had in common. She was interested in my work, because she was interested in me.

But if we talked about the wider world she quickly grew confused, and even, I feared, bored. She had been out of the loop for seventeen years, after all. She had no memories of 2033, for instance; she was like a coma victim who had slept through the whole thing, and the transformation of global society wrought by the Stewardship and the Happy Anniversary strike was something she was learning about, not something she had lived through, as I had.

I was ripped up by guilt to feel this way, as if I somehow wasn't deserving of the strange miracle of her return. But being with Morag was – a dislocation. I really was relieved to get away from her, to get back to work, to normality.

She continued to be subjected to examinations by more or less baffled federal-agency scientists and doctors. I think they might have left her alone if not for that strange anomaly of her weight. Rosa, too, or anyhow her VR presence, was a frequent companion for Morag, and so was Gea, manifested in the form of her little rolling robot. Charmingly, Morag remembered the toy that had gathered dust on Uncle George's shelf for decades. They would sit with Morag, hour after hour, the bent-over little old woman in black and the absurd robot, gently interrogating her. I was happy about this; I suspected they had a better chance of figuring out some aspect of the truth behind Morag's reincarnation than any number of government doctors.

I was also keen for Tom to spend some time with his mother. He was very reluctant at first. He surely didn't want to get hurt again. Or maybe some deeper instinct was operating, some aspect of Tom's humanity blocking her out, because *this couldn't be her*. But he accepted he had to deal with the situation. I knew this contact wasn't making him happy, though.

After a couple of weeks we got a call from John in Anchorage. The FBI had reconstructed the story of the bombing – and he was to be released at last. So Tom and I flew down to Anchorage to collect him, and to learn the truth.

Sitting in the Anchorage FBI field office John looked healthy enough. He was clean-shaven; he had even managed to get his hair cut. But you could tell he had been living in the same set of clothes for weeks, even though they had been laundered and repaired; there were faint traces of bloodstains on one jacket sleeve.

And there was a hunted look in his eyes, almost indefinable, but there. After all he had spent twenty days in custody at the whim of a vast system, without charges, without information on the process he was being put through. 'Did me good to see the other side of the bars for once,' he told me when we met up. But I could see that was just a front, that he was never going to sleep so easily again. My stab of unholy glee when I first heard he was going to be detained now made me ashamed.

But I knew that Morag had spent some time with John, as a VR projection from our base at Prudhoe Bay. When I turned up in Anchorage I had no idea how those sessions had gone. All John had said was how awkward she seemed with the VR technology, which had moved on hugely since she had disappeared from the world.

John, Tom and I studied VR images of our bomber. His name was Ben Cushman. He had been twenty-three years old. I hadn't known him personally, but his personnel file described him as one of EI's best and brightest young talents. Not only that, I was shocked to learn, he was married. He even had a kid, a three-year-old girl, a cute little button. His young wife, a college sweetheart in her pretty newlyweds' house in Scranton, was now a widow, and that little girl would probably not even remember her father.

Tom said, 'My God, he was younger than me. And he seems so normal. I thought he'd be some kind of zealot, or so stupid he was easily manipulated, or else he'd just be crazy. But he was none of those things, was he?'

No, he wasn't. Cushman was intelligent, from a reasonably secure background, successful in his own career. There were none of the usual risk factors of suicide in his background: no mood disorders or schizophrenia, no substance abuse, no history of previous attempts on his own life.

'And he had a kid,' I said. 'Who kills himself if he has a three-year-old daughter? That's what I can't figure out.'

John said grimly, 'But you don't need to be crazy, or ignorant, or desperately poor, or blinded by ideology, or in any way disturbed to become a suicide bomber. They are just like you and me – like Ben Cushman, here. Over the decades the feds have had to figure it out. And in the last few weeks I've learned more about it than I ever wanted to know...'

There had been suicide bombers throughout history, he said, all the way back to Jewish Zealots who had attacked the imperial Romans in the first century, and the Islamic Assassins in the Middle East in the eleventh century, even the Japanese kamikaze pilots of the Second World War. The modern wave of suicide attacks had begun with a truck-bomb attack on the US embassy in Beirut in the 1980s. Since then the psychologists and anthropologists and others had had sixty years of experience in figuring out the patterns of such attacks, and the individuals behind them.

'Except it's not usually the individuals that count,' John said. 'It's the organisation.'

Tom leaned forward. 'What organisation?'

Cushman, it turned out, had been a member of a radical anti-conservation group who called themselves the Multipliers. John showed us a VR clip of Cushman himself, speaking brightly, standing to attention, a smile on his face. *'Be fertile and multiply. Fill the Earth, and instil fear and terror into all the animals of the Earth and birds of the sky...'*

'This is from his "suicide note",' John said.

'Biblical,' Tom said.

'Yes. God's mandate to Noah.'

The Multipliers were an extreme group who embraced the changes the world was going through. Let the climate collapse, they said, let the Die-back finish off the animals and plants and birds and fishes. After all there was no likely scenario in which *people* would go extinct. We should follow Noah's mandate to be fertile and multiply – even if the end result was that we would finish heaped up in vast domed arcologies surrounded by fields of soya. And so they opposed organisations like EI with their vast ambitions to change the course of events, to save things.

It was hard to understand how a kid like Ben Cushman had got involved with a bunch like the Multipliers. But when you looked a bit closer, Cushman's background was more complicated than it appeared. His father, and the Cushmans for a few generations back, had worked in the steel industry that had imploded when America gave up on the automobile. A deep sense of failure, of abandonment and betrayal, had lodged itself in Ben's head at a very young age.

He was a bright kid, of course. He had gone away to college; in fact he had won a scholarship from EI. With one part of his head he was attracted to the scale and ambition of EI programmes. But there was a contradiction, for EI was a product of the world that had grown up after the collapse of the industries that had provided income and self-respect for Cushman's family. There must have been a level on which he felt deeply uncomfortable with what he was doing.

'Like the child of a peacenik going to work on weapons systems,' Tom speculated. 'The work might be fascinating. But you know it's wrong.'

So there was a deep conflict in Cushman, so far below the surface nobody was aware of it, not his family or employers – maybe not even himself.

'But the Multipliers spotted it,' John said sourly. 'It seems they have become expert at rooting out people like

Ben Cushman. They are predators, the Feds say, feeding on emotional vulnerability.'

Tom said, 'I still don't understand what made him blow himself up.'

'I told you it was the organisation,' John said. 'The Multipliers. Suicide terrorism is an organisational phenomenon, not an individual one. It's as simple as that.'

If the authorities had decades of experience in dealing with suicide bombers, so organisations like the Multipliers had decades of expertise to draw on in turning a confused kid like Ben Cushman into somebody prepared to kill himself for a cause he probably hadn't heard of a year before.

John said, 'They draw you in gradually. They present their case as a noble cause on behalf of a community – in this case, all those disenfranchised and impoverished by the Stewardship and other global projects. They argue you step by step into more extreme positions. They show you martyrs – nothing breeds a suicide bomber like previous bombers – who are made into heroes you would want to emulate. And they praise *you*, they make you part of the group, and get you to aspire to a certain kind of heroism.

'And *then* you make a public statement, on record.' Gloomily we watched as the tiny VR Cushman, smiling confidently, mouthed his selective quotations from the Bible. 'This was really the moment Cushman killed himself,' John said. 'Because once he had recorded this statement of intent there was no way he could back down. It was actually easier for him to die rather than suffer the loss of face of not following through.'

I said, 'And he did all this while working on the project he was planning to destroy.'

John shrugged. 'VR links make it possible to be with your brothers, your teachers inside the sect, right under the nose of your enemy. Odd how advancing technology only makes it easier for us to hurt each other.'

'OK,' I said. 'But whatever this kid's motivation, he still needed back-up.'

As I had suspected it wasn't easy to turn a Higgs energy pod into a devastating bomb. Cushman used a tailored virus to break through the pod's layers of protective sentience, and

434

even then he had needed an elaborate triggering device to make the thing go bang. Cushman had been one of our best engineers, a bright kid, but there was no way he could have put this stuff together himself; he must have had support.

John wasn't meeting my eyes. Tom looked from one to the other of us, uncertain.

I said, 'And that's where you come in. Isn't it, John?'

He waved his hand. Cushman disappeared, and new VR images coalesced. 'They found traces of DNA on bits of the bomb-making gear left behind in Cushman's room, up in Prudhoe.' We saw faces in the display on the table-top, faces extrapolated from the DNA traces: an embryo, a baby, a young child, a boy, growing to adulthood.

I wondered if this technology was something else that would startle Morag after her seventeen-year absence. It was now possible to take a DNA sample and compute how that genome would have expressed itself as a fully grown adult – or indeed any age you cared to choose. Thus the criminologists had been given the ability to recreate the faces of the victims or perpetrators of crimes from the slightest human trace, a fleck of spittle, a flake of skin under a fingernail.

I recognised who it was long before the reconstruction was finished: those broad features, the deep, eager eyes, the prominent teeth.

'I know him,' Tom said. 'I saw him at the launch event.'

So had I. The image was of Jack Joy.

'You were his first contact,' John said to me defensively. 'After he met you on the plane. He looked you up, found out what you were doing, decided it was something his destructive little band might be interested in. It's the way they work. Opportunistic, probing, looking for a way in.'

'I didn't know he was in the Multipliers,' I said, 'or anything like them. Obviously. He told me he was in the Lethe River Swimming Club.'

Tom asked, 'So how did he get through to the project?'

John sighed. 'He got in through me. I'm a Swimmer too.'

Tom just gaped.

'Jack cross-checked the Swimmer membership with EI and the hydrate project, and out popped my name, as neat as you like. Couldn't have been easier for him. Opportunism, you see. And that was the in he needed. He called me to introduce him to the project; he was talking about the Swimmers backing it financially. I couldn't see any harm. It was only when he actually showed up, as a VR anyhow, that I started to feel uneasy.'

'I don't get it,' Tom said. 'If this guy wanted to destroy the project, why would he put money into it?'

'As a way in,' John said. 'If you invest, you're inside; the more you invest the closer to the centre you get. And once he was inside it wasn't hard for him to find Ben Cushman, who was already being groomed by the Multipliers.

'I couldn't see any harm in the Swimmers,' John said miserably. 'There is a whole spectrum of us, Michael. There's a lot of humour in there, you know – black, but it makes life a bit more bearable...'

I wondered if he knew about the Last Hunters, another group in his 'spectrum', and what he would think of their expression of black humour. 'And because of this stupid indulgence of yours a suicide bomber got through to the heart of my project. Because of you, we nearly all got killed.'

'The FBI cleared me,' John said, still defensive.

'But the moral guilt is all yours,' I said heavily.

He looked at me for a heartbeat, as if he was going to fight back. But then he hung his head, beaten.

Tom touched my arm. 'For God's sake, Dad. Take it easy on him.'

I didn't really want Tom to see me in this black mood. 'I've got a lot I have to forgive John for right now, Tom. I guess I'm not big enough to do it.'

Tom sat back. 'You're talking about Mom.'

And there it was, the issue that divided and united us, out in the open.

John raised his head, and I saw true misery in his eyes. 'Michael, if you want to know, if it helps you at all, I'm ripped up inside too. And at least I told you what happened between us before—'

'Before her ghost came back to life to tell me herself? Do you think that makes it OK, what you did?'

'You have to see, Michael, that we, Morag and I, had

436

reached a kind of settlement between us. We had decided what to do. She would have the baby, we would see how we all felt after that, and then we'd talk to you. It was going to be OK; we would fix everything.'

A settlement, I thought: a verbal contract, a lawyer's way of rationalising away pain.

'But she died,' John said. 'Death came down on us like a blade. After that everything changed, all the threads of our life cut short.

'And in all the time since then, I've had to deal with this in my head. Michael, once Morag was dead, *nobody* knew the truth about that pregnancy, nobody but me. I knew how much you had been hurt – and how much more you would be hurt if you knew what I had done, you and Tom – and I couldn't tell you. And, with time, we settled down to a new way of being in each other's lives, you and me. That was my way of coming to peace with myself.'

'Some peace,' I snapped. 'You found Inge, you had two kids. And she left you, didn't she? Maybe you were just as haunted by Morag as I was.'

His eyes blazed angrily. 'I didn't choose any of this, Michael. But I had to cope with it. But now Morag has returned, she hasn't lived through any of this, she can't understand it—'

Tom blurted, 'I've spoken to her too. Mom.' His voice was strained. He was sitting with his legs crossed at the knee, hands neatly folded on his lap.

I hated to see him like that, to think how I and John had put him in this position – how we'd failed to protect him.

He said, 'With me it's the kid, the damn kid. My little brother who killed my mom.'

I said, 'I know—'

'I always felt second best to a foetus. To the *ghost* of a foetus. I grew up feeling that way. I always imagined she must have loved it more than me. Because she let it take her life, right?'

'And you talked about this to Morag?'

'She doesn't listen. Or she *can't*. To her it's yesterday,' he said. 'All that stuff when the baby was born. There's some-thing inside her that knows I grew up, I think, that knows all that time has passed, something deep down that recognises me. But she doesn't know how to talk to me. She remembers me as a happy kid of eight. She asks me about my life, about Sonia, like I was still a kid at grade school. She doesn't know anything about how I spent seventeen years trying to cope with all this. I don't want to hurt her. It isn't *her* fault. And she's my mom. But at the same time she isn't. Do you know what I mean? My mom coming back hasn't helped,' he said emphatically. 'I'm sorry, Dad. That's the way I feel.'

He was right, I thought. It was strange: a year ago, the fondest wish you could have granted me was to have Morag back in my life. And now she *was* back – and it was making nobody happy. It was as if Morag was a bomb that had been dropped into the middle of our tangled, multi-layered relationships. 'Look at us, the three of us. What a mess.' I stood up. 'Come on. Let's get out of here. Now you've got your implants reprogrammed you can buy us both a beer, John.'

John stood, rapped on the door, and we were let out into the town.

Chapter 50

Drifting through the mind of the Transcendence, Alia and Leropa explored the Redemption, and how it had touched Michael Poole's life.

'This is the Third Level of Redemption,' Leropa said. 'It is called *Restoration*. It is the beginning of a new age, in which the Transcendence will assume full responsibility for the past. If you have the power of a god, you have a responsibility to use it.'

To touch the past was easy for the Transcendence, Alia could see now, for it had a mastery of the finitude of the universe. If you could see the chains of causality wrapping around the curve of the universe, you only had to make the slightest adjustment and your touch would cause ripples that would wash out to the furthest future – and then around the arc of time to the deepest past, and up through the long prehistory of humanity, ripples at last focussing on one woman and her unborn child. A flawed gene which might have expressed itself *this* way no longer did so – and a child was born safely, a mother survived to a healthy long life. That was all that was needed.

And Morag Poole, her death averted, could walk through the walls of reality and back into the life of her astonished, still-grieving husband. Suddenly this part of Michael Poole's life, embedded in the past and viewed many times through the lens of Alia's Witnessing tank, was not as it had been. It was a magnificent vision, Alia thought, as all of history, past and future, shifted and waved like a curtain in a breeze.

'We gave Michael Poole his Morag,' Leropa said. 'Not a copy – she *was* Morag! Restored, identical in every way philosophy can identify. Morag was selected for the sake of Michael Poole. *And for you, Alia ...*'

But Alia had learned that nothing the Transcendence did was for her, but only ever for itself. And she knew that if you wanted to understand the Transcendence, you had to think things through, to think like the Transcendence itself.

'History was changed,' she said.

'A defect in the tapestry of the past was repaired,' Leropa replied. 'Think of it that way.'

'But Poole *knew* Morag had been restored to him. It is not as if her death was eliminated from reality. He remembered her dying.'

'Of course. This is not some mere toying with reality strands. This is Redemption, Alia. Its purpose is atonement. And there can be no atonement for Poole's loss if he isn't *aware* of that loss. Morag was saved from death, and given back to him, who remembers that death.'

But that wasn't the end of it. 'In saving Morag you saved her child. So that child will now live out a life that should have been, *was*, terminated at a premature birth.'

'Yes. That life too will be redeemed in the fullness of the Restoration.'

'But there's a second-order effect. That child will now go on to father children of his own, children who would never have existed. And those children in turn will bear more children, the actualising of more lost possibilities...' A wave of shifting, of change, would wash down the river of history, as a new population of never-weres attained a life, a reality that had been denied them. All rising out of this one change, the restoring of Morag.

And even that wasn't the end of it. Think it through, Alia, think it through to the end, to the fulfilment of the Transcendence's infinite ambition. *If this goes on...*

Some hundred billion humans had lived and died before the birth of Michael Poole, and most of those lives had been miserable and short. If you added infants who had died in the womb or at childbirth you might multiply that number by ten or twenty. If the Restoration was carried through, then *all* of those lost billions would be restored to time. And the descendants of those restored ones would in turn be actualised from a universe of lost possibilities.

It wasn't as if the Transcendence were meddling with alternate histories, spinning off different realities branching from decision points, from the life or death of an individual like Morag Poole. It was as if *every* possibility was being generated in some meta-reality, every human who might *ever* have lived under *any* contingency was to be born – and all these possibilities folded down, regardless of logic, into a single timeline.

'History will be meaningless,' Alia murmured. 'The world will be a hall of mirrors, crowded out by the shining Restored...'

'All wrongs righted,' Leropa declaimed. 'All injuries averted. All deaths eliminated. Every human potentiality actualised, the realisation of entelechy!'

Even cushioned by the Transcendence, Alia felt bewildered. For a start it would be the ultimate in overpopulation. How could all those crowding Restored be fed, even find room to stand on Earth or the human planets of the future? But such problems were trivial for the Transcendence. The number of the Restored would be huge but finite – and any finite problem was trivial to a power of infinite capability. It could be done.

There was a deeper objection, however. This transfinite miracle wasn't working. *Getting Morag back wasn't making Michael Poole happy.*

That one hard fact cut through her chain of thought. Suddenly the bewildering madness of it all overwhelmed Alia. She was aware of her body, a distant scrap of flesh in the shadow of a ruined cathedral, that thrashed and curled over on itself.

Chapter 51

I startled awake, spooked.

Morag was sitting up in bed, a baggy T-shirt draped over her body. She rocked back and forth, her eyes closed, her face lifted up. I could see her quite clearly, the smooth lines of her arms, the oval of her uplifted face, even though the only light in that poky Deadhorse hotel room was the dial of a small alarm clock. It was as if she was bathed with light from some source I couldn't see, a warmth like the glow from a hearth. A glow that *came from her*.

Her lips moved and her tongue flickered. She started muttering, a kind of high-pitched gabbling. It was her strange high-speed 'speech', full of mysterious, unfathomable complexity.

'Light,' I snapped. The room filled with the washed-out glow of fluorescents.

Morag stopped her rocking. In the flat bright light she just looked like a woman, like Morag, unreasonably sexy in my baggy T-shirt. But I could see the way the mattress was compressed under her weight. She smiled at me. 'Are you OK?'

'No,' I said. 'You know how that stuff freaks me out. Shit, Morag.' I sat up, pulling the duvet over my chest protectively. 'Don't you ever sleep?'

'Not much,' she said. 'We've been through this.' She rocked gently, bathed in that light from nowhere that the fluorescents did nothing to banish. She was quite relaxed, her voice almost dreamy. 'I'm happy just to sit here. I like to watch you sleep.'

'Well, it bothers me.' It was true; it stopped me sleeping. I was always aware of her watching me, no matter how silent and still she was.

442

She teased me. 'We used to stay awake all night. You didn't complain then. Remember that time in Edinburgh?' I did remember; as guests of a nuclear energy facility on the coast of the Firth of Forth we'd gotten to stay in Holyrood House, the seat of the old royals. She said, 'You, me, a couple of bottles of champagne—'

The memory of it, the way she spoke, turned me on immediately. 'OK,' I said. 'It's as if I can smell the baby oil. But—'

But there was something wrong. She *was* Morag – I felt that deeply. But it was as if there was another presence in the room with us, another identity embedded in Morag. I had no idea how to express this. I wasn't sure if the feelings were even clear to me. And besides, at that moment I felt like shit, my eyes gritty, my throat dry, my head heavy with that overfull feeling you get when you haven't given sleep a chance to clear it out. 'I'm getting too old for this,' I said feebly.

'Then go back to sleep.' She closed her eyes, rocking gently.

I lay back and closed my own eyes. In my head I sought the elusive rhythms of sleep, tried to dig up fragments of the dream state I'd been in before I woke. But I couldn't ignore that heavy rocking, back and forth, back and forth, as the bed tipped this way and that, creaking. I looked at her again. She had turned her face away, looking to the ceiling, as if seeking something I couldn't see.

'I can hear them all the time, you know,' she said softly.

'What?'

'Voices ... It's like a river running, but just out of my sight, beyond a screen of trees, maybe. It's always there in the background, and if I let myself hear it, it sort of washes through me. I sometimes think that if I could just push through that barrier, step through the last trees to the river—'

'What? What would you see?'

She closed her eyes again, concentrating, peering inward. 'I don't know. Sometimes I feel I can almost understand. Like when you are at school, and you're struggling to grasp some concept. You see it in outline, you grasp a few steps of the chain of logic. But then you drop it all, like juggling too many balls, and it goes away. Or maybe it's like a download.'

'A download? What are you talking about, Morag? Who is trying to download into your head?'

'I don't *know*.' She smiled faintly. 'Maybe the answer is in the download itself, and I'm too dumb to see it. Do you think that's possible?'

'I really have no idea.'

She faced me. She held out her hands; she was relaxed, but I could feel the strength in her fingers, the strange density of her warm flesh. 'But the trouble we have has nothing to do with my dream-talking. Has it, Michael? Or even me keeping you awake.'

'It doesn't help,' I said sincerely.

'I know.' She rubbed the backs of my hands with her thumbs. 'There's a barrier between us. Something that's stopping us connecting the way we used to.'

'Of course there is,' I said. 'You were *dead*. I saw you die. You were dead for *seventeen years*. That can't just be erased.' I was speaking more harshly than we had spoken before. But at that moment, under the cold hospital-like light of that dismal room, I felt too tired to care.

'We'll get there,' she said now, unfazed. 'We'll talk through this. We have to confront the truth, that's all. We just need time.' But as she spoke she seemed distracted again. She lifted her face to the ceiling, her eyes half-closed. And her lips began to work, her tongue to flicker like a tiny pink snake in her mouth, as she started her strange speaking-in-tongues once more.

I felt excluded, even repelled. 'Christ.' I tried to snatch my hands back.

But I startled her, and she clenched her fingers. I heard the bones in my hands snap, and was screaming before the pain hit me.

The Deadhorse clinic was basic, but the work they needed to do on me was simple. The doctor numbed me, set the broken bones in the back of my hands, injected nanomachines to help promote the bones' knitting together, and treated the bruising.

After that I sat in the out-patients area, my hands in blow-up casts like boxer's gloves, waiting for Tom to come pick me up and take me back to the hotel. A clock on the wall told me it was still only five in the morning. 'Shit,' I said.

'Indeed,' said Rosa. Her voice appeared before she did, her compact body gathering out of the air. In the bright antiseptic light of the hospital she looked totally out of place. She eyed the bench beside me. 'If you don't mind I'll stand,' she said. 'The VR facilities at this hospital are limited. I wouldn't want to alarm anybody by slipping through the chair to the floor.'

'You didn't bring any grapes,' I said sourly.

She bent to inspect my boxing-glove hands. 'Oh, dear. You have been in the wars.'

'It was fucking painful.'

'I'm sure it was.'

'She didn't mean to do it,' I said. 'Morag. It's just she's so *strong*. Her new body, whatever. She hasn't got used to it yet. I've taken a few bruises before. We're learning together, I guess. This is the first time she's broken a bone, though.'

Rosa nodded. 'The simplest test shows her strength is off the scale, for a person of her height and size. Like her mass, there is, um, more of her than there should be.'

I looked at her reluctantly. 'Do you think she's even human?'

'I don't know,' Rosa said. 'I believe that inside *she* thinks she's human, and perhaps that's what's most important in the end. But her body is something more than human.'

Gea and Rosa's studies were bearing fruit, she said. 'Gea will give you the physics. When we draw Morag's blood, we find human DNA. Her molecules are made of atoms, of protons and neutrons and electrons every bit as mundane as yours and mine. And yet there is the mystery of this extra mass. Her weight is measurable, so the mass is responsive to gravity, yet it is invisible to our eyes, all our senses. Gea tells me that there are many forms of invisible matter in the universe. Perhaps Morag's visible body is like the bright swirl of a galaxy, cradled in a wider pool of dark matter.'

'And what do you think?'

She folded her hands neatly in her sleeves. 'There are

older ideas which may help. Theologians have a long history of distinguishing between the form of an object and its substance, its true nature. It's an analysis that goes back to Aristotle, of course. The Church subsumed his philosophy to find a way to think about the Eucharist.'

'The Holy Communion.'

'Yes, the host that is at once a piece of bread, and at the same time the flesh of Christ. Morag's remarkable new body may have something of the qualities of Christ's resurrected body – indeed, the bodies promised to us all on resurrection. It is a body, but something more. The resurrected body is *impassible*, beyond pain, *agile*, so that you move as you like, and it has *subtility*, so it is totally subject to the desires of the soul. And in its glory, it shines like the sun.'

'Oh, hell, Rosa. Do you *believe* any of this stuff?'

'Not everybody who lived before the age of enlightenment was a fool, you know. Whatever is going on here, whatever her origin – what if Morag is *not* the first manifestation of her kind? If there have been earlier Morags in history, the thinkers of the day will have tried to explain her away in the language of the time, in concepts alien to us. But their analyses may record some imperfectly understood aspect of the truth.'

Exhausted, still in pain, I shook my head.

Rosa was watching me. 'I don't think it's the nature of Morag's transmogrified body that is troubling you, though. Is it, Michael? You have her back,' she said gently. 'And it isn't as you imagined.'

It was hard for me to answer this, for I hadn't yet admitted it to myself, and Morag and I had come nowhere near talking it through. But she was right. 'We can't talk,' I said.

'She was taken out of the world, but the world kept turning. And the more the years have passed, the more has happened that she simply did not see, did not share with you.'

'The dead get deader,' I said sombrely. 'I feel ashamed that I can't—'

'That you can't love her? Don't be ashamed, Michael. You didn't ask for this situation; you may be in a situation nobody has *ever* had to face before. No wonder your emotions are all over the place. But you're doing your best, for everybody, including Morag. Just as you always do. I have faith in you, you know.'

'Thank you.'

Rosa watched me carefully. 'What about your work, Michael? Is all this getting in the way?'

Of course it was. I glanced at the clock. Not yet five thirty, but I knew I had a breakfast appointment at seven a.m.

I was working hard, because I believed in it all. Since the bombing, as I had immersed myself in the hydrate project, I had thought harder than I had ever before about the context of my life, the meaning of my work. I had discovered conviction in myself, for the first time since I was a kid, before cynicism knocked it all out of me. We had to do this; it was as simple as that. And I was central.

'Gea keeps telling me she believes I am a fulcrum of history,' I said. '*Me*. And you've said the same sort of thing. Even George said it. Now I've started to believe it, to believe my own myth. Is that crazy?'

'Not necessarily. But Morag is getting in your way.'

'I guess so.'

'The restoration of a lost wife is a fantasy of redemption. I daresay it was *your* fantasy. But has it made you happier?'

I thought that over. 'Even if you give me Morag back, you can't wash it all away. The memories of her death. All that suffering, all that pain. It's as if it still exists, out there somewhere, beyond reach... Does that make sense?'

'And what do you fear most?'

'That I will come to hate her,' I said honestly. 'I don't think I could bear that.'

She straightened up, purposeful. 'We don't know how she got here. We don't know the meaning behind your visitations, this strange reincarnation. We don't know who is meddling with your life in this way, or why. But we must take control of the situation, so that, with or without Morag, you can move on. I think it's time we bring it to a head.'

'Bring it to a head? How?'

I would never in a thousand years have guessed the word she used next.

'Exorcism.'

Chapter 52

They sat in their translucent-walled hut, beneath the towering cathedral.

'I still have doubts about the Redemption, Leropa.'

'I know. The Transcendence knows. You have become something of a focus, Alia, for internal debate.'

'If you're going to say that I'm not fit to question the wisdom of an infinite entity – a being that is to me as I am to an individual cell of my body—'

'I wouldn't dream of saying any such thing,' Leropa murmured. 'Your humanity is the point of the exercise, Alia. The Transcendence loves you as you are. And the Transcendence's love for you means that it knows you – *it shares your doubts*. You are far more important than you know.'

'You already said the Transcendence loves me,' Alia said dully. 'Several times.' It seemed to mean nothing. Perhaps the Transcendence was too large to know what love truly was. Perhaps the finitude of humanity was part of what made love work; perhaps the need to devote such a large fraction of your own limited life to others made love precious in the first place. Or, she thought guiltily, perhaps the Transcendence was simply immature, emotionally. Powerful it might be, but it was very *young*. And if the Transcendence didn't understand love, could it ever achieve the Redemption it sought?

'Even the Restoration isn't enough,' whispered Alia. 'How can it be? Just to be made alive again – it's such a crude, mechanical, *imposed* solution – it simply isn't enough. Leropa, can't you see that? Michael Poole loved Morag. *His* Morag, who died. And his love for his Morag, in the end, encompassed her death. His loss deepened his love, enriched it. That is the nature of life in a universe of mortals. If you crudely reverse her death, simply bring her back, then you are taking her out of her context of history. How did Michael Poole put it?'

'*The dead get deader,*' Drea said bleakly.

'And you can never put that right.' Alia took a deep breath; this was the heart of it, though she scarcely knew how to express it. '*The Restoration is futile,* as futile as all the watching was, the Witnessing, even the Hypostatic Union. Because even if you allow Morag Poole to survive the suffering of her childbirth, that particle of suffering *still exists,* out there in a wider universe of possibility.'

Leropa stared at Alia for long heartbeats. For the first time Alia detected hostility in her gaze. 'You reject the Restoration,' Leropa said. 'But I wonder how you would feel if those *you* have lost were Restored to you.'

A shadow moved on the wall of the hut – a human form, dimly seen, perhaps a woman with an infant in her arms. She walked uncertainly, as if lost. Drea's eyes widened, and she clutched at Alia.

Alia snapped, 'Leropa. Don't do this.'

Leropa smiled thinly. 'Think about your own mother, your baby brother. They died in pain, pain beyond your imagination. At least your brother, an infant, didn't know what was happening. But your mother knew. In those last heartbeats an awareness of her approaching death, the loss of the rest of her life – the loss of *you* – deepened her anguish, exponentiated it far beyond the physical. But it needn't be that way.'

Alia glared at Leropa. 'You call it love, to inflict this horror upon us?'

Leropa actually seemed puzzled by her choice of words. '*Inflict?*'

Drea buried her head on her sister's shoulder. 'Make her stop, Alia. I can't bear it.'

That shadowy woman seemed to spot the hut. She walked slowly towards it, clutching her child. She seemed confused and exhausted, as if she had been through a great trial. But through the misty translucence of the hut's walls her features were gradually becoming clearer.

Leropa said, 'Don't you even want to say goodbye to her? Don't you even want to say *sorry?*'

'Leropa, I'm begging you.'

The woman hesitated again. She paused for a moment, looking around. She seemed to be murmuring comforting words to the child in her arms. Then she turned away and walked off, her figure diminishing and blurring, until she was gone, as if she had never existed at all.

Drea glared at Leropa through tear-streaked eyes. 'You know what the trouble is? You Transcendents, with your obsession with the past, don't listen to *people*. I've had enough of being *used*. Leropa, if you Transcendents want to use the people of the past as a dumping ground for your guilt, then you ought to ask them first. You should have asked Michael Poole if he wanted his wife back!'

Leropa sighed. 'What if we asked *you*? Alia, would you choose never to have even the possibility of seeing your mother again? You might refuse now – but how can you be sure how you will feel in ten years, or fifty, or a thousand? *You will be an undying*, Alia; you would have a long time to regret such a choice.

'And even if you did make the choice for yourself, would you make it on behalf of others? Your father, for example? And what about those you have never even met – the whole of the rest of humanity? You are arrogant, Alia – and that's not necessarily a bad thing – but I don't think even you are arrogant enough for that. So what do we do?' She laughed, a strange, dry sound. 'Shall we take a vote?'

'Appoint a representative,' Alia said impulsively.

Leropa glared at her.

Alia quailed, but stuck to her ground. 'I think my sister's right. The Redemption is for the benefit of the Transcendence, not us. And in its quest for Redemption the Transcendence has lost sight of simple human morality.' *Am I really lecturing a near-god?* 'Appoint a representative to speak on behalf of the rest.'

Leropa said loftily, 'Impossible. A mere human could not bargain with the Transcendence. She, he couldn't possibly comprehend the meaning of the choice, let alone make a valid decision.'

Drea snapped, 'You aren't *better* than me, Leropa, you wizened old—'

'But she's right,' Alia said quickly. 'Drea, this isn't about rivalry, about one bunch of humans lording it over the rest. *We're dealing with the Transcendence.* It genuinely is a higher life form, a higher consciousness. You could no more debate with it than a blade of grass could argue with you.'

Drea said, '*You* could.'

Alia smiled, feeling tired. 'Actually I'd be in a worse position than you. I am part of the Transcendence itself – it's true, Drea, already, even though my Election isn't complete. I am like one neuron among the billions in your head.'

Leropa said, 'A mortal creature cannot negotiate with its god. Only a Transcendence can negotiate with a Transcendence.' But she looked into Alia's eyes.

Alia saw the answer there. 'Then,' she said, 'we must make the representative equivalent to the Transcendence. Just for one day.'

'Just for one day,' Leropa said slowly. 'Well. Quite an ambition. But who will speak for all mankind?' She smiled coldly. 'Michael Poole, perhaps?'

Oddly, that made sense to Alia. After all, Poole had been the recipient, or the victim, of Morag's Restoration. He knew what was being offered; he had lived through it.

And then there was Poole himself. After a lifetime of Witnessing Alia knew Poole as well as she knew anybody of her own time. Michael Poole was flawed but decent, a loving and courageous man who tried to cope. He was everything that had been best about the humanity of his era, she thought. 'Yes. Michael Poole.'

Leropa looked surprised, as if a bluff had been called. 'Then you must prepare him, Alia,' she said.

'Very well.'

Drea stared from one to the other. Alia saw she shivered with fear – of *her*, of her sister, as much as of the strange old Undying, Leropa.

Chapter 53

A couple of days after my talk with Rosa, we gathered in a function room of the Deadhorse hotel, which we'd reserved for our purposes: me, my reincarnated wife, Tom and Sonia, John, Rosa, Gea. Gea had saturated our environs with counter-surveillance technology. We most assuredly did not want stories of what we were attempting that evening to leak out to the press.

We drew upright chairs into a horseshoe, and we all took our places. John's lips were pursed, his arm folded, his opinions obvious. Sonia was wide-eyed. I couldn't tell what she was thinking – maybe, *What the hell kind of family am I attaching myself to here*? The little Gea toy robot rolled backwards and forwards on the floor, somehow reassuring in her absurdity. Rosa sat in her chair, or appeared to; she had a stack of leather-bound books in her lap, and she wore a surplice and a purple stole.

At the head of the horseshoe, the focus of the group, Morag just sat there, head up, eyes wide open, watching us, expressionless. She was wearing a simple dress, open at the neck, her favourite blue colour. Her hair was brushed back, her beautiful young face lifted to the light. When she moved, the chair creaked under her weight. It might have been funny if it wasn't so strange.

Tom gazed around the room. 'I cannot believe we're doing this. Dad, do *we* have to be here?'

'An exorcist doesn't usually work alone,' Rosa said. 'Usually I would be accompanied by a younger priest. Someone who could take over if I die, or am possessed. There would be a doctor, to provide medications if necessary. And there would be a family member – somebody strong, in case things get, um, interesting.'

'You've done this before?' Sonia asked, amazed.

Rosa inclined her head.

'This is all quackery,' John said sternly. 'Mumbo jumbo.'

'It's an ancient ritual,' Rosa said, admonishing him. 'It derives from the New Testament. Christ Himself drove out demons: "My name is legion."'

'I remember that line,' I said. 'Lots of pigs got drowned, didn't they?'

'The word *exorcise* actually comes from a Greek root meaning to swear. You bind the demon to a higher authority – Christ – so that you can control it, and command it against its will.'

Sonia asked, curious, 'And is that what's written down in your little books?'

Rosa held up one battered-looking volume. 'This is the *Rituale Romanum*, a priest's manual of services. This contains the formal exorcism rite sanctioned by the Church. Dates back to 1614. I don't think we have to be too formal today, however.'

John was mocking. 'What, no bell, book and candle? I'm disappointed.'

'But I am wearing the required uniform,' she said, smiling. 'And I took confession before coming here. I'm absolved of my sins; there's nothing a demon could use against me during the ritual.'

'Quackery,' John said again. 'After all, what was "demonic possession" but the symptom of some illness – hysteria, multiple personality, schizophrenia, paranoia, some other neurosis – even just a chemical imbalance in the brain? I wonder how many hundreds, thousands of mentally ill people had to endure the cruelty of rites like this.'

Rosa said, 'Maybe a little humility is in order. We can already foresee a time when diagnoses of "hysteria" and "schizophrenia" will seem just as foolish, ignorant and superstition-laden as talk of demons. Besides, John, belief isn't necessary for your participation. A funeral doesn't change the fact of death, but you wouldn't refuse to attend one, would you? And having attended you would feel better, for through our rituals we feel we have some control over such an extraordinary and powerful part of our lives, even death.

This rite is merely a way of managing the ineffable.'

'So is that what you're trying to do today? Make us all feel better?'

Rosa replied, 'No. This isn't just cosmetic. What we have here is a ritual of proven power. And it's the only way I can think of to break through the barriers inside Morag – to communicate with whatever she truly is, or whoever sent her here. If nothing else this will surely make it clear that we want this state of affairs to change: maybe just the fact of our desire will get through, our sincerity.'

'Get through to *where*?' John demanded. 'To *what*?'

'I don't know,' Rosa snapped. 'If I did, perhaps we wouldn't need to do this. But if you have a better idea I'll gladly hear it.'

He had no reply, but I felt he was covering a deeper fear. As he sat there, arms folded, face knotted into a scowl, I felt a surge of helpless, protective love for him; after all, whatever he had done, he was my brother.

Morag, expressionless, said now, 'Maybe if we push at the door, we may find there's somebody pulling from the other side as well. Let's do it.' Her voice was clear, calm, strong.

We all stared at her.

Rosa said, 'Michael, do you have the props?'

I had a small bag under my seat; I brought it out and opened it. 'Props? Is that the right word?'

'Just hand them over,' Rosa said, sounding grumpy herself.

I produced a small bag of salt, which I set on the floor to one side of Morag's chair. There was a vial of wine, blood-red, which I put down on the other side.

Tom asked, 'So what's with the salt and the wine?'

'Salt represents purity,' I told him. 'The wine the blood of Christ.'

John said, 'Shame we haven't a few relics to hand. A bit of the True Cross. A saint's toe-bone.' He laughed, but it was hollow, and nobody laughed with him.

I reached into the bag again, and drew out a crucifix. It was a small silver pendant, in fact a legacy from my grandfather Poole, a Manchester Catholic, who died when I was ten. It was only the size of a quarter, with a little Christ like a toy soldier. But it was an extraordinary moment when I held up the crucifix before Morag, and I was aware of everybody staring at the little medallion, the way it caught the light.

I passed the crucifix to Morag and leaned over her. 'I'm sorry,' I whispered. 'I can't believe I'm putting you through this.'

She took the pendant and smiled. Her face was only centimetres from mine, and I could smell the sweetness of her breath. 'Everything is going to be fine. You'll see.'

I pulled away and sat down.

Rosa turned to her book. 'Let's begin.' She began to read, rapidly, in a low voice.

John listened for a minute. 'Is that Latin?'

'Prayers,' I said. 'The Lord's Prayer, or perhaps the fifty-fourth psalm, are customary. Latin is thought to be more effective.'

John threw his hands in the air. 'Who am I to argue?'

Rosa's quiet voice murmured on, the only noise in the room. We sat in our horseshoe. Morag just sat, her gaze downcast, her hands folded in her lap, the crucifix glinting between her fingers. She seemed calm, so still I couldn't even see the rise and fall of her breathing. It struck me that it must have been many years since I was in an environment so empty, so denuded of electronic gadgetry, the rich and colourful texture of modern life. Here we were in this room with nothing but a row of chairs, a handful of people, a woman in black muttering prayers in a language none of us could understand. But it was extraordinary how the tension built.

Suddenly Rosa stood up. We all flinched. Rosa pointed at Morag. 'Who are you? Abandon your pretence. Tell me your true name. *Who are you?*'

Morag gazed up at Rosa. Then she rubbed the little crucifix and smiled at me. She didn't seem at all afraid. She mouthed, *I'm sorry*.

I was too shocked to react.

And then Morag began to change.

Her body seemed to shrivel inside her clothes, the skin of her face to crumple. Some kind of fur was gathering on her skin, long, pale brown hairs, not sprouting but coalescing in place over her face and arms, like a morphing VR. She continued to implode inside her clothes, so her dress was collapsing like a tent with its ropes cut. But soon her arms were protruding out of her sleeves, as if they were growing longer. With an impatient spasm she kicked off her shoes, revealing feet with long toes, as long as a child's fingers. She stood up. She had become so slim that her blue dress fell away around her. Wisps of underwear, a bra and pants, still clung to her, but she pulled them away, handling them curiously.

All this took just seconds.

Naked, she was only about a metre and a half tall. Her body was coated with the orange-red fur. She was slim, but she had breasts with hard, prominent nipples. Her arms were long, about as long as her legs. Her all-but-human face, with a long nose and prominent chin, was covered by that soft fur, as was her small skull. I wondered what had become of Morag's beautiful hair.

Her eyes were human – pale grey, soft. She smiled at me, showing a row of perfectly white teeth. She held up her arm, with muscles like knotted rope beneath the fur. She was still holding the crucifix.

I risked a glance at the others. They sat in their chairs, staring. Tom was grasping Sonia's hand so hard his knuckles were white. The Gea robot just watched, its plastic eyes bright.

Rosa was smiling.

John said, 'What – the fuck – is that? Some kind of ape?'

Rosa asked again: 'Who are you?'

The Morag-thing spoke, but it was a burst of that rapid-fire speech. Somehow it didn't seem so strange coming from her mouth.

Rosa cut her off. 'We can't understand.'

The creature was still looking at me. She hesitated, then spoke more carefully. 'Sorry,' she said. She pronounced every part of the word with exaggerated care: '*Shh-oo-rrh-yy*.'

I said, 'Tell us who you are.'

'My name,' she said, 'is Alia.'

Chapter 54

Alia, the ape-thing that had been Morag, turned around slowly, those human eyes bright. Carefully she put the little silver crucifix down on her seat. Then she bent down – she was very limber – and inspected the tumbler of salt and the vial of wine beside her chair. She made no comment; maybe she thought that having salt, wine and crucifixes around was normal for us.

Alia was more upright than any chimp, although her body was undeniably ape-like, with a high chest, and arms as long as her legs. There was something odd about her hips too, narrow with an odd geometry. Maybe she was like our remote ancestors, I thought, the australopithecines, the early sort not long after they split off from the chimps.

She straightened up, and studied us again.

We all just stared. John looked the most horrified, but then he had a lot to be horrified about. John's world had always been a very orderly place; he'd had enough trouble getting used to the idea of ghosts and reincarnated dead wives. And now *this*. But even Rosa, who I had thought would never be fazed by anything, was clutching her prayer books.

And Alia stared at me, as if she was as stupefied to see me in the flesh as I was her.

Suddenly Alia ran a few steps towards Sonia. We all flinched, and Tom and Sonia clutched each other. Alia stumbled after a couple of paces and stopped. 'Sorry,' she said, in that elaborate, slowed-down manner. 'High gravity. Better to walk. Forgot.' She took a more cautious step, two, not very gracefully; I got the impression walking was not what she was used to.

She stood before Tom and Sonia. I was proud of them that they just stared back. She said, 'Sonia Dameyer.'

Sonia was rigid.

Then she turned to Tom. 'Thomas George Poole. Tom. I have seen you grow up. Variant pigmentation.' She reached out again and, to my horror, ran a fingertip down Tom's cheek.

Tom slapped her hand away. 'Back off, Planet of the Apes.'

Alia's mouth dropped open. She looked shocked – suddenly her face looked very human, under that mask of fur. 'Have I given offence? I apologise. I am sure it will not be the last time I get something wrong.'

Sonia said, 'What's the problem, don't they have white people where you come from?'

Alia thought about that. 'Before the First Expansion of Mankind the homogenisation of culture on Earth had eliminated the already minor differences between human racial groups. Skin pigment is one of the most heritable of human genetic features, and differences diluted quickly.' Her voice was getting better, I thought, her grammar a bit more precise, her tone more controlled. But this stuff about skin pigment sounded stilted, as if she was accessing some data store. She smiled brightly at Sonia, and pulled at the fur on her own face. 'Some of us don't have skin pigment at all!'

Tom asked, 'What's the "First Expansion"?'

'The future,' John hissed. 'She's talking about the future. I think.'

Perhaps he was right. But, I thought, if there had been a 'First Expansion of Mankind' there must have been a second, at least, maybe a third. In that one phrase I glimpsed a towering history.

Alia moved on from Sonia. When she got to the Gea robot she bent down, reached out – and picked her up. She turned the robot over and over, while Gea's tiny wheels whirred. I was stunned. Alia had shown she was 'real', as real as Morag had been, by handling the exorcism objects, by touching Tom's cheek. But she seemed to be just as 'real' in Gea's VR world. Maybe they had different categories of reality, wherever she came from.

Alia put the robot down, squatted and faced it. 'You are Gea. An artificial mind.'

Gea rolled back and forth experimentally, as if checking her wheels still worked. 'You already know all about me.' Somehow Gea's pompous B-movie-robot voice fit the situation.

'Yes, I do.'

'May we scan you?'

'Of course,' Alia said cheerfully. 'In fact you're already doing so.' She patted Gea on the head. 'You are so well crafted. We will talk later.'

Well crafted? This was one of the planet's most advanced artificial sentiences. Alia sounded like a patronising museum-goer admiring the artistry of a Neolithic flint hand-axe.

Alia walked past John, who recoiled.

And now, at last, she came to me. She was a creature the size of a ten-year-old child, her fur shining where it lay in layers over her flesh. I could hardly read the expression in her squashed-up face, she was too alien for that. But I thought I saw warmth in her eyes.

I said, 'I suppose you're wondering why I asked you here today.'

John snorted. 'Christ, Michael. How can you joke?'

'I like your humour, Michael Poole,' Alia said. 'Not that I always understood it.'

'You did?' My head was spinning; I tried to make sense of this. 'You've, uh, studied me?'

'We say *Witnessing*,' she said. 'I've Witnessed you, Michael Poole, all of your life. All of *my* life.'

'Then you really are from the future,' Tom said. There was an edge to his voice. 'My father is dead to you, isn't he? He's a fossil you dug up. You can read his whole life the way you can read a book. From birth to death. *We are all dead to you—*'

Sonia touched his arm. 'Tom, take it easy.'

'It isn't like that,' Alia said. 'Thomas George Poole, to Witness isn't just to watch. It is to appreciate. To share. Michael Poole, I have shared your life, your triumphs, your woes. And now I meet you at last. It is more than an honour. It is – fulfilment.'

Rosa pursed her lips and nodded. That I was being watched by the future was one of the possibilities she had guessed at.

She looked almost satisfied, the puzzle resolved.

But I felt deeply uneasy. It was more than self-consciousness. I was a bug trapped beneath a microscope slide, my whole life splayed open for inspection. 'And what about Morag?'

Alia's smile faded. 'I stand before you, and you ask for Morag?' I couldn't believe it. She sounded hurt.

Rosa spoke, for the first time since this new apparition had come to us. 'Tom is right, isn't he? That you are from the future?'

Alia turned to her. Her small face was creased, comically quizzical. 'It depends what you mean. Can you rephrase the question?'

Tom asked cautiously, 'Were you born on Earth?...' His nerve seemed to fail him. 'Oh, hell. I can't believe I even asked a question like that! This is like something from that old stuff you used to read, Dad, it's a cliché—'

I cut in, 'This is difficult for all of us. Just try, Tom.'

Tom took a breath, and tried again. 'OK. So *were* you born on Earth?'

Alia snorted. 'Do I *look* like I was born on Earth?... Sorry. I was born on a ship, called the *Nord*.' She hesitated. At times it seemed to take her a while to find the right word, as if she was accessing some nested data store. 'Um, a starship.'

'Ah,' said Rosa.

John turned on her. 'What do you mean, *ah*?'

'That explains the long arms, the high chest. Like our primate ancestors, Alia is evolved for climbing – or for low gravity.' She smiled. 'Our ancestors were apes, and so will our descendants be. Bishop Wilberforce must be turning in his grave.'

'Descendants?' That was too big a leap for me. 'Alia – are you human?'

'Of course I'm human.'

Again she seemed hurt, upset I'd even asked. Oddly, at times she seemed very young, even adolescent, and easily rebuffed, especially by me. I decided I was going to have to be very tactful. Or as tactful as you can be with an ape-girl from the future. What a mess, I thought.

Alia went on, 'But in my time it's different. Humans have spread out. We have become a family.'

'Across the stars?' Gea asked.

'Across the Galaxy.'

'This is the Expansion you mentioned,' I said. 'Or *Expansions*.'

'There are lots of different sorts of humans. Just as there are in your time.' She frowned. 'Or not. Are there? I'm sorry, I should know.'

Rosa said gently, 'It's some thirty thousand years since the last non-human hominid died. *Homo sapiens sapiens* is alone on Earth.'

'Thirty thousand years? Oh, well.' Alia said this in a flip way, as if thirty thousand years was *nothing*, her mistake forgivable. Her manner was playful, almost coquettish. But there was a bleak, chilling perspective behind her words, a vastness of empty time.

I said, 'All right. Then you are from the future. What *date* are you from?'

'I can't say.'

'What date were you born?'

'I can't say!' She flapped her hands, agitated. 'These are slippery concepts. I want to give you answers, but you have to ask the right questions.'

Gea said, 'Of course she can't answer questions about dates.'

John growled, 'What are you getting at?'

'Relativity.'

It is a strange consequence of Einstein's special relativity that time is fragmented. Information cannot travel faster than light, and that finiteness makes it impossible to establish true simultaneity, a universal 'now'. And so there is a sort of uncertainty in time, which increases the further you travel. If Alia was born halfway across the Galaxy, that uncertainty could be significant indeed.

'How strange,' Rosa said, 'to live in a geography so expansive that such effects become important.'

'Oh, for Christ's sake,' John snapped.

Gea said to Alia, 'Suppose your ancestors had stayed on Earth.'

'Yes?'

'That would eliminate relativity ambiguities. In that case, how long would have elapsed, on Earth, between Michael Poole's birth and your own? Do you know that?'

Alia said, 'Round numbers?'

'That will do.'

'Half a million years.'

There was another stunned moment, a shocked silence. The human race in my day, as I now had to think of it – was only, *only*, maybe a hundred thousand years old. Alia was remote from me indeed, the species itself many times older than in my era. It was hard to take in such a perspective.

Tom said, 'So how did you get here? Did you travel in time?'

Alia cocked her head. 'I hate to be boring. Here we go again! Can you rephrase the question?'

'"Rephrase the question"?' Tom laughed, an explosive giggle. 'Sorry,' he said. 'Every so often I just lose it. I mean, it's just –' he waved a hand, '– you're asking me to accept that *this* is a superhuman being from the far future. This *ape*. Where's the disembodied brain in a jar? I mean, what can *she* do but swing on tyres?'

I think we all knew how he felt. It was a difficult dialogue. We were the ignorant talking to the uneducated. I got the impression Alia really didn't know much about many things, and cared less – as a modern teenager wouldn't know anything about the implants in her body, as long as they worked. And we knew too little to make much sense of what she said; we had to translate it into terms we understood, interpret the information she gave us in terms of our own modern theories, which might have been as partial, falsely based or just plain wrong as notions of planet-bearing crystal spheres. And every so often, as we worked our way through these miasmas of interpretation and guesswork, we were confronted by vast conceptual gulfs.

Still, with Gea giving us the lead, we managed to extract a little more.

Alia was a projection across time, in a way – but, oddly, a projection into her own future, not the past. The universe was finite. It was folded over on itself in spatial dimensions

– modern cosmologists knew that much – *but also in time*, so that the future somehow merged with the past. So to get to the past all you had to do was travel far enough into the future – just as Columbus had once tried to find a new route to the east by travelling far enough *west* around the curve of the Earth.

I was struck by a resonance with something I'd read in Uncle George's manuscript: *If time is circular, if future is joined to past, is it possible that messages, or even influences, could be passed around its great orbit? By reaching into the furthest future, would you at last touch the past?*. . . George, or anyhow his strange friends, had intuited something of the truth, perhaps.

'Our time must be strange to you,' Rosa said. 'If you were born on a ship, among the stars. The way we live must seem very alien.'

'Oh, but I prepared,' Alia said. 'In the course of my Witnessing. You don't have to visit Earth to know what it must have been like!'

'I don't understand,' Tom said.

Alia spread her arms wide, and her long hairs dangled like curtains. 'There are things about me that have got nothing to do with being born on a ship. I like open spaces, long prospects. I don't like enclosed spaces or running water, or rats or spiders, or blood. I grew up in zero gravity, but I can be scared of heights! All these are responses ingrained deep into my system, and the systems of my ancestors, long before they left Earth. So, you see, even if I knew nothing of Earth, I could reconstruct it just from my own responses. In fact, that has been done a number of times, by cultures cut off from their origins – people who forgot where they came from. Even they can deduce something of Earth.'

'Astounding,' Rosa said. 'You left Earth behind half a million years ago. You travelled across the stars. And yet you took the savannah with you, didn't you?'

Sonia said, 'You mentioned rats. Are there animals where you came from?'

'Animals? There are rats everywhere. They don't all sing. There are bugs and birds.' Birds flocked on her starship, she said; I couldn't think of a more exotic, charming image. 'Earth's biosphere shows more diversity than any other human world in the Galaxy, however. That's one reason we know it really is Earth, the original.'

'Like Africa,' Rosa said. 'There is more genetic variation there, too. As Africa is for us, the home of mankind, so Earth is for these future people.'

Sonia prompted, 'And there are still animals on Earth?'

'Birds. Snakes. Insects. Bugs. That's all, really.'

'They are the supertaxa,' Gea said. 'Taxa have different evolutionary rates. Some speciate more rapidly than others; some lineages last longer than others; and some taxa – the birds, snakes, rats and mice, various weeds – have both a high speciation rate and a high longevity. And so when an extinction event strikes, the supertaxa provide the great survivors. What Alia describes is exactly what I would have expected to find on an Earth of the future, after our extinction event is done. Snakes and rats and birds.'

'But no big animals?' Sonia asked.

Gea said, 'I want to show you something.' She produced a VR image of a lumpy-looking animal: a rhino, but covered in shaggy brown fur.

Alia gaped. 'Megafauna!'

Tom said, 'That's a Sumatran rhino, isn't it?'

'Yes,' Gea said. 'An unusual form, adapted for living in hilly rainforests. It went extinct, earlier this year. The last of them died in a zoo in Germany.'

'I've never seen anything like it.' Alia sounded as if this creature was as exotic as a dinosaur, to her. She glanced at me. 'Michael, have you?'

'I'm not a wildlife buff,' I said. 'If you followed me around all my life you'll know that.'

Gea said, 'The Sumatran rhino was a living fossil. It is the least changed of all large-mammal lineages since the Oligocene, thirty million years ago, half way back to the dinosaurs. We live in extraordinary times. That species endured for thirty million years. Even the people in this room had the opportunity to meet it, to touch it, just months ago. And now it has vanished, a geological instant after its encounter with humanity. Just like that. As all the megafauna which survived the Ice Age have gone, one by one.'

Sonia said wistfully, 'And they never came back, according to Alia. You'd think they could have been brought back from the DNA.'

'Perhaps there was never room,' Rosa said. 'Not if the world remained owned by humans. For we would not allow anything bigger and hungrier than us to survive.'

'Besides, evolution goes forward, not backward,' Gea said. 'The mega-mammals, once gone, will never return.'

Alia was watching us. 'You all sound so guilty!'

Tom said, 'Do people in the future look back on our time?'

'Oh, yes.'

'And do they judge us?'

'Judge you?' Alia laughed, a strange whooping sound, but then bit it off. 'I'm sorry. I know this concerns you, in this age. If not you wouldn't even be attempting the hydrate-stabilisation project.'

'You know about that?' I asked.

'Of course. I Witness you, Michael Poole. But why should you be judged? Look – if one species of bird out-competes another, are you going to talk about morals? Of course not. It's just a question of competition for space in an ecology.'

'And is that how you see us?' John asked bitterly. 'Are we just animals in an ecology to you?'

Alia seemed genuinely puzzled. 'How else would you want to be thought of?'

I said, 'There is much debate about geoengineering projects. You must know that. We aren't sure if we have the right to meddle on a planetary scale.'

Again Alia seemed baffled by this. 'But you are already, um, meddling.' She paused, as if accessing more data. 'Consider the Earth. Twenty per cent of the land and a good proportion of the sea is covered by artificial ecosystems, each containing a small number of species, selected and bred for one consumer—'

'Farms,' Sonia said.

'Yes. You have changed the very geomorphology of the planet: you have carved vast chunks out of mountains and landscapes, you have built new lakes, and reclaimed other lands from the sea, and you have created entirely artificial land forms of a type never seen before.'

Gea interrupted, 'But all this must be trivial compared to the great transformation of your time, an age when mankind has covered a Galaxy.'

'Oh, of course. In the future we do it bigger and better. But planet-shaping, geoengineering, meddling, is what people do. Human history has always been a tangle of environmental changes, human responses to those changes, accidents... Human will is only one component. Just accept it!'

'There she goes again,' John groused. 'Talking about us as if we're nothing but animals. Like beavers, mindlessly building dams.'

I understood his resentment. But Alia was an advanced being. She was deliberately slowing her speech, speaking to us as if we were children. To her, I thought, maybe we really were as busy and mindless, as productive and destructive, as bower birds or beavers.

Sonia leaned forward, as fascinated as John was on edge. 'You must know the future.'

Alia said, 'In a way.'

'*What happens*? What happens to us? Do you know how we die?'

'Not all of you.' She said brightly, 'I know how Michael Poole dies. I have seen his life, the whole of it – like a book, complete from beginning to end.'

I snapped, 'I don't want to know.'

She bowed her head.

'But the future,' Sonia pressed. 'The bigger picture. Just the fact that you are here, you exist, says that we're not going to go extinct any time soon.'

'So mankind will make it through the Bottleneck,' John said.

Sonia asked, 'And then what?'

'And then, expansion,' Alia said brightly. 'Off the planet. To the stars!'

Sonia frowned. 'Yes, but what *happens*?...'

It soon became clear Alia knew little in detail about the unravelling of history beyond our present – indeed, beyond my own lifetime. But then, why should she? If I were dropped into the middle of the last Ice Age, what could I say to curious hunter-gatherers who asked about their future?

It will get warmer. A lot warmer. And then, expansion. Out of your refuges, all the way to the Moon!

And besides, she seemed to imply, the future wasn't as fixed as all that.

Rosa asked, 'And are there other cultures out there? Extraterrestrial aliens, civilisations among the stars?'

'Oh, yes,' Alia said. 'Or there used to be. Some of their biologies have merged with ours. And you can still find ruins.'

Sonia said, 'Ruins? What happened to them?'

'We did,' Tom said dryly. 'Ask the Sumatran rhino.'

There was a long silence.

Rosa leaned forward and faced Alia. 'I think it's time we got to the point. Don't you?'

'The point?'

'There is a reason you are here,' Rosa said. 'You have a purpose. And it is to do with Michael.' She turned to me.

I said, 'I have seen – apparitions – of Morag all my life. Morag, my wife. Since before I met her even, since I was a kid. You must know this. I want to know what that haunting meant. Was it to do with you, Alia? Your Witnessing?'

Again Alia looked oddly crestfallen, as much as I could read her small face, her ape-like body language – as if she was actually jealous of Morag. 'Yes,' she said. 'It was the Witnessing.'

As a Witness she had access to my whole life. She could dip into it at will, like a random-access file. She was naturally drawn to the key events of my life – and for her, that meant the times invested with the most emotion, the most joy, the most pain.

She said, 'We are so far apart in time we don't always communicate very well. Not in language, in symbols.' I thought of our failure to decode her speech; I knew that was true. 'But emotion comes through,' she said. 'Raw, powerful emotion can punch through species barriers, even through time. But Witnessing is always leaky...'

All that Witnessing had somehow worn holes in the fabric of my life.

'Like the pages of a much-loved book,' Rosa said. 'So worn

through by a tracing finger they become transparent, and you can read the next page.'

At an intensely Witnessed moment you could get leaks, Alia said, traces of events from other times in your life showing through. And since Morag had been associated with the most intensely joyful and painful moments of my life, it was those instants that had been rubbed through and linked up. It was as if all my life with Morag had been joined together in a single eternal moment.

Alia said, 'I'm sorry I can't explain it any better.'

John laughed. 'So even in the far future we are polluters! If you need a good compensation lawyer, Michael—'

'Shut up, John.'

Rosa nodded, as if satisfied. 'So Witnessing muddles future and past. I wonder if this rationalises away every ghost story – the few which were not simply delusional.'

Alia said to me, 'In fact Witnessing is *supposed* to be neutral. You aren't supposed to perturb your subject. Not many people know it has this kind of effect.'

'I thought I was seeing Morag. I always imagined she wanted to come back to me. I'm disappointed that it was all just some jerky time-traveller fuck-up from the future. I'm pissed that it was nothing but *you* all the time.' I spat the words at Alia. I wanted to hurt her.

Her face crumpled further. But she said earnestly, 'Michael, *she was there*, in the hauntings, the visitations. Yes, I was the Witness. But what you saw was *her*. And the revenant, the flesh-and-blood resurrection – that was Morag too, Michael, in every way that it could be her.'

'Ah, yes,' Rosa snapped. 'The revenant. And why was *she* brought back?' She used her sharp exorcist's voice again. 'You told me your name, but you have yet to tell me the full truth. What is your purpose, creature?'

Alia turned to me. 'You are special, Michael Poole,' she said. 'You must know that by now – it is true, whether you like it or not. You are truly a pivot of history in this age, and your name is known into the far future.'

'Here we go,' Tom said, and he linked his hands behind his head. 'The really nutty stuff.'

'His descendants too,' Alia said. '*Your* descendants, Tom.'

Tom wouldn't even look at her.

I turned away. I really, truly, did not want to hear this. Maybe every kid dreams that she is special, that her name will be known for ever. It's just a fantasy, an expression of adolescent yearning and uncertainty, something you grow out of. But now this Alia, this strange being from the future, was saying that for me, Michael Poole, *it was so*. It was as if every paranoid, grandiose dream I had ever had was folding down into this moment. But I did *not* want to be a fulcrum, famous for all time.

Gea said, 'To be clear, you believe that Michael's great contribution will be the hydrate project. The Refrigerator.'

'Yes. But there is more.'

'What else?'

'The restoration of Morag was part of it. I have more to ask of you, Michael Poole, a grave responsibility... You will see.' She glanced around at, our bewildered, angry faces. 'But this is not the time. I will return.'

'When?' Rosa asked.

But Alia would only speak to me. 'When you call me, Michael.' And she disappeared. There was nothing left but the chair where Morag had sat, with the little vials of wine and salt, and a small heap of crumpled, abandoned clothing.

We sat back. Tom blew out his cheeks. Sonia was wide-eyed, silent – shocked but delighted, I thought, full of wonder.

John seemed angry, resentful. 'I wish they had left us alone. These ape-people, whatever they are. This is the Bottleneck, for God's sake. Don't we have enough to do without dealing with the future as well?'

Rosa said, 'But we may not have a choice. It is precisely because this is a time of crisis that Alia has come here. It seems we are important enough to merit visitors from the future – or at any rate, Michael is.'

John said, 'I don't want to know about the future. I don't want to think of my life as just an archaeological trace, locked in stone. It's *my life*. It's all I have.'

'I understand. But it can't be helped.' Rosa stood. 'This has been a long session. I suggest we break, sleep, eat. We will talk tomorrow.' She eyed me. 'And then you will summon back your admirer from the future, Michael.'

'If I must,' I said.

'I think you do. For it appears you have a mission. How exciting,' she said dryly. And, with a flourish like a stage magician's, she vanished in a mist of pixels, just like Alia, if far more crudely.

Chapter 55

That night I lay down in my room, alone for the first time since the bombing. Morag was gone – if she had ever been there at all.

The exorcism and everything that had followed had been a roller-coaster ride for me. I was battered, bewildered, and resentful at everybody: Rosa for setting the whole thing up, Alia who had somehow engineered all this with her 'Witnessing' from the far future – and Morag for returning into my life in such an agonisingly incomplete way, and then leaving me again. None of which was fair, of course. Shit happens, I told myself, even such astounding shit as this.

Even Alia wasn't to blame. She might look like a stretched orang-utan, but I had seen in her eyes, in the way she looked at me, that she was a person, fully conscious, fully formed emotionally. She was no doubt a product of her times and her society, just as I was. And I had seen, inexplicable as it was, that she was fond of me. It was as if I had developed a crush on Wilma Flintstone. What a joke.

As I drifted towards sleep, exhausted, my thoughts softened. It was in just this sleeping-waking condition that I had had so many glimpses of Morag in the past. But I knew that this time she would not come to me.

The next day I woke feeling drained. When I ordered the curtains to open, they revealed a day that was harsh even by Alaskan standards, with a sky like a steel prison roof. I had a sudden, sharp memory of a contrasting morning in Florida, a winter's day full of bright cold sunshine, when I had gone out, age ten or so, to fly a kite or a Frisbee or a water rocket or some damn thing. I could hear the boom of Atlantic breakers kilometres out, smell the brine, feel the texture of the sand under my feet and on my skin. Every

471

sense open to the max, I was fully locked into the world, and I never felt so alive, so joyous. But I think I knew I wouldn't always feel this way. I would age, my eyes would glaze over, my hearing clog, my fingertips crust over with dead flesh, and my body would become like a spacesuit, insulating me from the world. I knew it even then, and I dreaded it. And in time it had come to pass: this was my reality, my own aching, ageing body, a face like old leather, a head stuffed with cotton wool.

When I thought back over the events of the day before – an exorcism, for God's sake, the strange appearance of Alia, all that allusive gabble about the future – it seemed foolish, an indulgence, like the memory of a dinner party where the talk got out of hand. It seemed to me that morning that Alia's future was a bright and shiny bubble that had somehow burst in my head overnight. And reality was responsibility: responsibility to my real work, the hydrate project.

So I went to work.

I grabbed some breakfast at Deadhorse's one and only coffee shop, and made my way to the offices EI had set up in a small three-storey block. I picked a cubicle, started up a softscreen with a tap of my fingernail, and put in a call to Shelley. While I waited for a reply I ran through my mail and other progress reports, trying to get a sense of where the project had gotten to while I had been absent in other realms.

Technically the project was going well. In a way the bombing had done us good; the lashed-up heart of our prototype set-up had been swept away, and Mark Two was proving to be a much sounder beast. We were beginning to look further afield too. We had started to talk to the Canadians about spreading our work out along their Arctic coast, and the Russian government had already given us permission to set up another pilot off the Siberian shore.

To obtain a mandate to roll out a global solution, it was the US government, the UN and the Stewardship agencies whose endorsement we really needed, of course. But once again poor, deluded Ben Cushman, our bomber, had probably done us long-term good. I thought that among the commentators and opinion formers a consensus was emerging that, regardless of the environmental arguments, to allow our project to fail now would be a betrayal of Barnette, and of the others who had died.

That was all fine, but we still needed to make the case. And so we were starting to work with Gea's sponsors towards a presentation to the UN. It would be made by Gea herself. Given the loss of Barnette, I couldn't think of a better spokesperson for the cause. But it would be the first time an artificial sentience had addressed the UN General Assembly: quite an occasion. I wondered what form Gea would choose to incarnate herself. Presumably not my Uncle George's toy robot.

'How about like Alia?' I said to Shelley, when she at last came on the line. I had downloaded a record of our exorcism to her. 'Perhaps an ape-like post-human form would be a fitting symbol. All our futures are in the balance, et cetera.'

'Yes. And if the crowd grows ugly she could climb a pillar and swing out the window.' Shelley seemed to be multitasking: as she spoke to me she kept glancing aside, and I thought somebody just out of sight was passing her bits of paper as we spoke.

Shelley had been at her desk since six. She had always had those enviable reserves of energy, but since the loss of Ruud Makaay a vast burden of responsibility had fallen on her, and the lines around her eyes were disturbingly dark. 'Hey, Michael,' she said, 'I don't want to hang up on you but we're kind of rapid-responding here. Is there anything else you need from me right now?'

'I called to see what I could do for you.'

She eyed me; for a moment I had her full attention. 'Look, Michael, we're trying to ramp up to a production facility. We're at a level of detail you can't much help with. There's always Gea's speech; you could work on that, if you're kicking your heels. But you have other stuff to sort out, don't you?'

'You know me too well,' I groused.

'Maybe. I know you're sometimes tempted to hide, just as you're trying to hide right now in work that you don't need to be doing. But this Alia came for *you*, didn't she? I think you're going to have to face that, and resolve it somehow, before you can move on.'

'I know.'

'Then get off the line and do it. Talk to you later, love you, g'bye.' She turned away. 'Now where the hell are the results of that last deconvolution –' The image blanked out.

There was a call from John, waiting for my reply.

Shelley was right, of course. I tapped the screen, took John's call, and immersed myself once more in strangeness.

John, Tom and I gathered in another small office. As drab as everything else seemed to be in Deadhorse, it was empty save for a small conference table and chairs, and a few softscreens on the wall. John and Tom looked as washed-out as I felt.

We were alone save for Gea, who trundled back and forth on the table-top, spitting toy-robot friction sparks. Gea was going to give us some preliminary results from her scanning of Alia's manifestation.

I spoke to John, who had called us together. 'I take it you didn't want Sonia here.'

'Tom agrees. This is a family thing, Michael. It's about us, about Morag. She was your wife, Tom's mother—'

'Your lover.'

His face hardened, but he didn't look away; for better or worse that awful truth was becoming embedded in the fabric of our relationship. 'I know the future is mixed up in all this. *Alia.*' He spoke the name like a curse. 'But it's about our lives, the three of us. So let's try to start from that basis.'

'And Rosa?'

Tom rolled his eyes. 'Let's keep it down to Earth, shall we?'

Maybe he was right. Three Pooles was probably enough craziness for any one room. I turned to Gea. 'So where do we start? What is Alia?'

Gea rolled complacently. 'First, she wasn't a VR. No doubt she was a projection of some sort. But equally she was real, as real as you are, Michael. Her body responded to our attempts to scan it, with X-rays, MRI, thermal imagers, other technologies. She shed strands of hair! With that we were even able to perform a genomic analysis.'

Gea said that Alia was human – almost.

As Rosa had guessed, that ape-like form appeared to be an adaptation to zero gravity. In an evolutionary sense a starship on a long-duration voyage was like an island on Earth, where, for instance, stranded animals routinely become dwarfs to spread out a limited food supply among more individuals. So the crew found their children growing smaller. And, in low or zero gravity, as the generations ticked by the children's forms had reverted to an ancient ape-like plan, with more of a balance of length between arms and legs – a design more suitable for climbing. Surprisingly, Gea said, the basic body-plan changes seemed to be the result of natural selection rather than deliberate engineering. I'm no evolutionary biologist, but it seems there are some changes the genes find 'easy' to make, such as relative growth rates, and faced with a challenging new environment selection reaches for the easy options first.

How strange, though, that these far-future people, projected into the unimaginable environment of space, had found their bodies reaching deep back in time for genetic memories of vanished African forest canopies.

John grunted. 'Next time you see her, throw her a banana and ask her to do some tricks.'

'Shut up,' I said mildly.

Gea talked us through more subtle changes, all of which pointed to an advancement over the *Homo sapiens* standard model circa the twenty-first century. The skeleton had been redesigned; Alia had more ribs than I did, perhaps to hold her organs in place more effectively, and so avoid hernias. Although she was designed for swinging around in weightlessness, Alia had thicker bones, vertebrae, discs in her back. She would be less prone to osteoporosis than I was, and would do a better job of functioning in high gravity, if she had to. Gea showed us images of a redesigned throat. Alia had no epiglottis, but there was a raised trachea, a kind of extension to her windpipe, so that food and drink could never get mixed up with the air she breathed; she was very unlikely to choke.

There were detailed modifications to her eyes too. The optic nerve seemed to be attached to the retina more firmly, so that there was less chance of suffering a detached retina, she had multiple eyelids, and there were rings of tiny muscles around Alia's pupils. 'She seems to have a zoom facility,' Gea said dryly.

And Gea talked about Alia's genome. Her existence was governed by DNA just as mine was, so we were both obviously products of the same lineage of life, both ultimately products of Earth. But Alia's DNA showed divergences.

'Some of these changes appear to be the result of genetic drift, of natural selection,' Gea said. 'But others appear to be engineered. We can only guess at the purpose of most of this. It may be she has a general regenerative ability, for instance. Cut off a finger, and another will grow in its place.'

John drew a softscreen towards him and made rapid notes. 'Somebody ought to patent this stuff,' he said. 'Just a thought.'

Tom sneered. 'Uncle, how crass to be thinking of commercial gain at a time like this.'

John was unperturbed; he had endured such insults all his life. 'Only doing my job. If there's profit to be made, why not by us?'

Gea moved on to still stranger aspects of Alia's anatomy. Much of what she had described so far had been extrapolations of the human. But there were signs of much more peculiar developments. Gea had imaged hard, impenetrable knots in Alia's bloodstream, motes that might have been technological, remote descendants of the nanomachines of our age, perhaps.

And there were even traces of other life forms in Alia's body. For instance there was a kind of sheathing around portions of her nervous system, its function unknown – perhaps it was there for protection from deep-space radiation. It seemed obviously alive, and was based on an amino acid chemistry, just as Alia was. But it did not share Alia's genome – indeed there was no trace of DNA to be found in it at all.

'Alien life,' I said slowly. 'Not from Earth, because not based on DNA. She has a kind of symbiosis with alien life forms.'

'So it seems.'

For long heartbeats we sat there, trying to digest this latest bit of news. I think I was the most imaginative of the three of us, the most open-minded. But even I was struggling with this. Here was not just a woman from the future, here was ET – and not sitting in a flying saucer looking back at me, but wrapped around the neurons of this remote descendant.

'All of this is evidence of advancement, in the broadest sense,' Gea said now. 'Many past developments of life's capabilities have depended on symbiosis, the cooperation of one kind of life form with another, or even the incorporation of one into the other.' Even complex cells were the result of one such merger, she said. Mitochondria, once independent creatures, were now used as miniature power plants within our own cells.

'And so what might come next,' I said, trying to follow her chain of thought, 'is more mergers. Of our bodies with machines, biology with technology. Or of our Earth-derived life forms with life from another biosphere altogether, alien life.'

'Just as we see with Alia,' Gea said.

John scowled at the little robot. 'I don't think I like you telling me I'm inferior to that monkey woman.'

Gea said, 'Then who would you like to tell you?'

Tom grinned, and I suppressed a laugh.

John leaned over the robot. 'And what about you, sparky? If humanity is progressing onward and upward, what's going to become of you?'

'I suspect we artificial types will play our part in your development,' Gea said, as unfazed as ever. 'We know that Alia is actually far more intelligent than any modern human being. With all respect. We have the evidence of her speech for that, her "true speech", the accelerated gabble we recorded from Morag. I strongly suspect that she is also more *conscious* than any human alive today, in the truest sense. She has a deeper mind, and surely a deeper sense of herself. Some humans fear that artificial minds will make humans obsolescent. But Alia shows us that humans will not become obsolescent, any time soon. So what has happened? Perhaps there has been a competition with the machines, a selection pressure to become smarter.'

John said, 'Or perhaps we absorbed you. Perhaps you're just another symbiote.'

'Perhaps. But we may have chosen not to participate in such a symbiosis. After all that is the great benefit of sentience – choice. And if that's so, who knows what our destiny may be?' And she rolled back and forth, a half-kilogramme of painted tin.

I spoke to Rosa later that day. She showed up in my hotel room, a small, dense, black figure. She listened patiently as I summarised what Gea had told us.

'Even what Alia told us of cosmology made sense,' I said. 'Or at least it didn't contradict what we know.'

I had been a cosmology fan all my life. I was encouraged by Uncle George, who said I was lucky to be alive at a time when cosmology was moving out of the realm of philosophy and into hard science. There had been the emergence of quantum gravity, and the great astrophysical satellite studies of the first part of the century that had mapped the relics of universal birth in fine detail, all of which had enabled us to put together a firm biography of the universe all the way back to the Big Bang. Of course being a fan of this stuff hadn't helped me spot the approaching Higgs revolution, which had developed from this.

But as part of the new understanding, we knew the universe was finite.

I said, 'We haven't mapped the topology of the universe yet – that is, its shape. But for sure, a finite, closed form of the kind Alia hinted at fits what we know.'

'Perhaps that finiteness is necessary for the development of life, of mind, in some way,' Rosa mused. 'If the universe were infinite, just dissipating into the dark, perhaps mind would simply fizzle out too. Perhaps everything is connected.'

'Maybe you should ask Alia about that.'

'It's you she's interested in, not me,' Rosa said. 'And what of the human future she sketched – these "Expansions" across the Galaxy?'

'That seems all too plausible too,' I said.

'Yes,' Rosa said. 'We humans seem to have been an unstable lot from the beginning. Unlike other animals, even our hominid forebears, we aren't content simply to find a role in the ecology. And in the future, it seems, that same restlessness will drive us on beyond the Earth. We will encounter others out there, and those others will go the way of the mammoth and the Neandertal, their last relics incorporated into the very bodies of their destroyers.'

'Um,' I said. 'Have you heard of the Fermi Paradox?' This was an old conundrum, dating back nearly a century. The universe is so old that there has been time for it to be colonised many times over, before humans even evolved – so if extraterrestrial aliens ever existed, why don't we see any sign of them? 'One candidate solution is that there is a killer species out there, a voracious predator that swoops down and assimilates any culture foolish enough to attract notice. It's a chastening thought that some day *we* may be the predators; we may be the instigator of a Fermi Paradox of our own.'

Rosa nodded. 'But does it have to be that way? The way we lived in the Order will always have its critics. But the Order was able to deliver very high population densities, very large numbers of human beings living orderly lives, and all without harming anybody else. So I have first-hand experience of how humans can get along with each other without needing to trash the Galaxy to do it.'

I guessed I knew far more about her Order than she could imagine. But I didn't want her to know about George's manuscript; he had made it clear he had never told her about it. I changed the subject. 'Rosa, you speculated about evolutionary purposes for ghosts, how maybe they evolved to help us through Bottlenecks of the past. Are you disappointed that the visitations are just –' I shrugged '– technological after all?'

She smiled. 'It is never a good idea to be disappointed by the truth. And besides, maybe I did hit on a deeper meaning. Perhaps the visitations, the Witnesses, *did* somehow aid us through those Bottleneck times, even if unwittingly. Perhaps humanity was able to survive, and grow to cover a Galaxy, precisely because the likes of Alia closed the time loops from past to future.'

'That sounds like a time paradox.'

'Alia is a traveller from the future. Her very presence here must be perturbing all our lives, already changing the future,

479

and yet she is here even so. What can be more paradoxical than that?'

'Maybe. But that doesn't help us much right now, does it?' I got up and paced around the room, my thinking muddy, unsatisfactory. 'The whole thing seems so old-fashioned. Welcome, O Visitor from the Incredible Year Five Hundred Thousand!... It's a 1940s dream.' I suppose I was thinking of George again, the heaps of decaying science fiction novels he had given me.

'Those dreams were a product of the age,' Rosa said. 'The twentieth century was a time of cheap energy, of techno-logical optimism. And so we dreamed expansive, progressive dreams. Now people turn inwards. The children are *taught* to do so – all those introspection classes in the schools! We live in a time of constraint, when one dare not dream that things might be different, for any other possibility seems even worse than what we have.

'But a deeper part of us knows that something is missing. We are a species that has lived through immense calamities in the past – vast climatic upheavals, huge natural disasters, plagues and famines, the rise and fall of empires. We have been shaped by such events. Even if we don't realise it, we yearn for the epic, the apocalyptic. And now the epic has found us. Or rather it has found you, Michael.' As always she spoke calmly, but her tone was warm.

'You think I should call her back?'

'Of course. What else is there to do? *You must resolve this*, Michael. But you must not be humble before her.'

'Humble?'

'She has come here for her own purposes, her own agenda. But we don't have to accept that agenda.

'Perhaps even Alia has limits. We know so much more now than I ever imagined we would learn, when I was a child in the 1960s. And Alia, with a half-million years' advantage over us, must know far more yet. But what of the deepest issues of all? Does *she* know why anything ex-ists at all, rather than nothing? Before such questions, the details of cosmological unfoldings seem rather trivial, don't you think? And if we can pose questions she can't answer, perhaps Alia's people are no smarter than we are, in spite of their redesigned rib cages and alien symbiotes.' Her eyes glittered, hard, knowing, sceptical.

That night, alone in my room, I called her. It felt absurd to be sitting on my bed, calling the name of a creature who wouldn't be born for half a million years until after my bones were dust, if she ever existed at all.

Yet she came. There were no special effects, no flashes or bangs or swirls of light. One instant she wasn't there, the next she was, a part of my reality as solid as the bed in my room, the table, the chairs. She looked out of place, though. With her slightly stooped stance and that long crimson fur hanging from her limbs, she still looked like an escaped ape. But she smiled at me.

She glanced around the room. She rubbed a cautious finger along the back of a chair, and tried sitting on it. But she wasn't comfortable, with her knees tucked up and her arms dangling to the ground. So with a lithe, graceful swing, she leapt up to the tabletop and sat in a kind of lotus position.

She said, 'I've Witnessed you all my life, but I don't know much about your social protocol. It is OK to sit on your table?'

I shrugged. 'It's not even my table.'

'You called me,' she said. The warmth in her voice was obvious.

'Did you think I wouldn't?'

'I wasn't sure.'

'Would you have come anyhow?'

'No,' she said firmly. 'You had to call. You have to want this.'

I wondered, *Want what*? 'Listen, Alia, if you're from the future, why don't you help us?'

'Help you? How?'

'We're struggling to get through this Bottleneck. Our hydrate-stabiliser scheme is a lash-up; you must see that. Why don't you give us some help – technology guidance, maybe?'

She eyed me, and I thought I could see the true answer in her expression. *Because it would be as useful as handing a laser rifle to an australopithecine.* She seemed to understand tact, however. She said, 'You don't need our help, Michael. Not in that way. You'll make it through without us. Isn't that better?'

Maybe. But I had had to ask. 'This means a lot to you, Alia. Your Witnessing of me, this visitation. I can see that.'

'Yes—'

'*I* mean a lot. Don't I?'

Her eyes, in that mask of fur, were bright as stars. 'I grew up with you. When I saw you, especially when you were unhappy—' She reached out a strong, long-fingered hand towards me, then drew it back. 'I wanted more. I wanted to touch you. Of course I could not.'

Shit, I thought. I found myself pitying her. But if I had to be Witnessed, maybe I was lucky to have happened on somebody who had affection for me. If I had found an enemy far down the corridors of time, the consequences could have been very different. Deep beneath these feelings of pity, though, I was angry, angry that my whole life had been fucked over by the carelessness of these future voyeurs.

And then Alia made it worse.

She leaned close to me. 'Michael, once I was joined with the child. Morag's second son. In Hypostatic Union, which—'

My son who died— no, John's son. I felt cold. 'You Witnessed *him*?'

'More than that. It was closer than Witnessing. I felt what he felt. I lived his life. He didn't suffer. He even knew joy, in his way.'

I moved sharply away from her. 'Christ. What gives you the *right*?'

She looked at me, shocked. 'I wanted to tell you about him, to help you.' Then she dropped her gaze, humbly. 'I'm sorry.'

'I... Oh, shit.' How was I supposed to cope with this stuff? 'Look, I don't mean to hurt you. I know this isn't your fault.'

'You always wanted Morag. And in the end she was returned to you.'

'Yes. But we weren't happy. Perhaps it was impossible we ever could have been.'

482

'I was sad for you,' she said. She sounded sincere and I believed her. 'But,' she said, 'it was *because* you couldn't be happy with Morag that I'm here now. And why I must ask you to help us.'

'Us? I don't understand, Alia.'

'There is much I must tell you,' she said. 'About the Transcendence. And Redemption...'

And as she spoke, a doorway to the ultimate destiny of mankind opened before me.

Chapter 56

When Rosa saw the virtual record of my latest conversation with Alia, she seemed electrified. She called us together. Once again the Pooles gathered in another Deadhorse hotel room: me, Tom, John, and Aunt Rosa projected from Seville.

This time Tom had wanted to bring Sonia, but she ducked out. Somewhat to my surprise, Gea dropped out as well this time. She gave the same excuse as Sonia: 'Family business.' But by 'family' Gea meant not just us Pooles but the human family. This was an issue for the species, and our artificial companions weren't going to be able to help us now. A deep instinct, though, prompted me as usual to bring in at least one independent mind, in Shelley Magwood. She griped about how busy she was, but she came anyway.

They had heard Alia's strange invitation to me, recorded by the hotel's security systems and by monitors Gea had left with me. We played it through again.

The record was hard for me to listen to over again, in that room, with us all sitting around a scuffed table-top, with cups of coffee and bottles of water and softscreens. 'I can't believe we're doing this. It's a cold Alaskan day. A *Monday*. This morning I ate Cheerios and drank coffee and watched football highlights. Out there people are taking their kids to school and putting in the laundry and going to work. And here we are talking about how we're going to deal with the far future of mankind. Are we all just crazy?'

John grunted. 'What do you mean, *we*? It's you who's being subpoenaed by the ape-people, as far as I can make out.'

Shelley was tapping at a softscreen on the table-top. She murmured, 'Nobody's crazy. I saw the records Gea has

484

been making, and her analysis of Alia, the chimp-thing. I don't know what the hell is happening here. But this is real.'

'OK,' said Tom. 'But even if you buy all that stuff, now we have to go one jump further. We have to believe that this – Transcendence, this mish-mash of super-brains – wants my dad to save them. *My dad*, sitting there like a barrel of goose fat, being summoned by the far future to save mankind.'

'Nicely put, son,' I said.

'It's another cliché, Dad. Like those old stories you used to read me as a kid. The decadent humans of the far future need our primitive vigour to save them.'

'You enjoyed that stuff at the time,' I said defensively.

'Yes, but as *stories*. Not as a career move.'

Rosa, dark, intense, solemn, said, 'Shelley is right. We all saw Morag – so did the world. And we Pooles saw Alia. Our best strategy is to assume that everything we have been told is real. Suppose, then, that Alia is telling the truth. Suppose that all of human history, folded back on itself, really is funnelling through this moment, into the conscience of one man, of Michael Poole. *Suppose it is true!* The question then is, what must we do about it?'

John surprised me by being constructive. 'In my business the key to success is to work out what the other guy really wants – your client, your legal opponent, the jury, even the judge. You may not be planning to give him what he wants, but if you know what it is you have a chance of manipulating him. So I think we have to consider what this "Transcendence" of Alia's, this vastly advanced composite entity, might *want*.'

Shelley was scanning through material on her softscreen. 'That's not so easy to answer. Since Michael asked me to join in with this, I've been digging up old references on how we thought far-future beings, or maybe advanced aliens, would behave, what they would do. And you know what? All we ever did, it seems to me, was to project ourselves up into the sky.

'Look at this stuff.' She displayed some table-top VRs for us. 'Here you have Dyson spheres, cultures taking apart worlds to enclose their suns and so trapping every bit of energy. And for what? Living space, uncountable trillions of square kilometres of elbow room. This *isn't* the future,' Shelley said, 'these are the concerns of the mid-twentieth century, about energy supplies, demographics, population explosions, painted over the sky. And all Dyson was talking about was the infrastructure of a civilisation. He didn't seem to have much to say about what an advanced culture would *do* with all this room.'

Tom nodded. 'Except to fill up the Galaxy with endless copies of its own kind. Just as we do.'

Rosa said, 'But there are other precedents in our intellectual history of attempts to analyse the motives of more-than-human minds.'

John pulled a face. 'I have a feeling you're going to get all theological again.'

Rosa smiled, aloof. 'Isn't that why I'm here? There can be no more superior intelligence than God's. What is Christian theology but a two-thousand-year-old quest to read His mind – what is our devotion but an effort to understand His desires and to act accordingly?

'Believe me, the universe Alia comes from, a universe that may soon be dominated by a superior consciousness, really isn't so different from the universe imagined by Christians. For example the old Fermi Paradox has much in parallel with the much more ancient conundrum of *silentum dei*. Bertrand Russell was once asked how he would respond to God if he were called to account for his atheism. Russell said he would ask God why He should have made the evidence for His own existence so poor.'

'And we want to break the silence,' Shelley said.

'Yes. We long to talk to the aliens, as we have always longed to talk to God.'

John glared at her. 'I can't make you out, Aunt Rosa. You're a priest, but you seem to put the subject matter of your own faith into the same box as wacko UFO stuff. I can't tell what you really believe.'

She wasn't fazed. 'I didn't have to check in my cerebral cortex at the door of the seminary, John. It's possible to have a mind, to be able to think, and to have faith. And even if the premises of my religion, of all our religions, have been wrong, perhaps our thinking about God has served a profound purpose if it has been a kind of vast practice run, to prepare us to deal with the *real* gods out there.'

'Even if they are our own future selves,' Shelley said, her voice small.

Rosa said now, 'I believe that everything about this strange situation is summed up in the two key words Alia used in her pitch to Michael: Redemption, and Transcendence.'

Transcendence: what could it possibly mean?

Rosa said, 'It's a word that has various definitions in philosophy. But Kant's notions have the ring of prophecy, I think. *Transcendent*: beyond the sphere of human knowledge or experience, above and independent of humanity, indeed independent of the material universe itself. From Alia's hints it certainly sounds as if the Transcendence will have many of the attributes we traditionally ascribe to our gods. But it is arising from humanity; it has embarked on a journey whose final end, perhaps, isn't clear even to it. And so it is an evolving god.'

She talked of a nineteenth-century German philosopher called Schelling, who had been responsible for the introduction into philosophy of 'evolutionary metaphysics'. What if God can grow, can change? And if so, what must He change *into*?

John said, 'I thought God is eternal, and hence unchanging, as measured by our petty notions of time. How can an eternal God evolve from anything into anything else?'

But old Schelling, it seemed, had had an answer to that. His God was the first and the last, the Alpha and the Omega, but the Omega state was in some sense contained within the Alpha. The only difference was in the expression of that potential. Rosa spoke of the unevolved God as *deus implicitus*, and His final state as *deus explicitus*; the two states were different expressions of the same identity.

'And Schelling imagined that the universe evolves along with its god. In its final state the cosmos will be fully realised, every potential fulfilled – and it will be at one with its god. It is as if God realises His own true potential through the vast self-expression of the universe. Perhaps these ideas foreshadow the entelechy of the Transcendence Alia described to Michael...'

I was starting to get rolling-eye signals from Shelley. 'I don't know if this is helping us any,' I said to Rosa.

She nodded. 'Then consider Pierre Teilhard de Chardin. Palaeontologist, theologian, Catholic mystic.'

John sighed. 'A regular Swiss army knife among wackos.'

Teilhard had imagined that the goal of mankind was to cover the Earth with a new layer of mind, of consciousness, which he called a noosphere. With time the coherence of the noosphere – the organisation of a kind of psychic energy – would grow, the 'planetisation' of mind would proceed, until at last a new plateau of integration would be reached.

'A singularity,' Tom said. 'The noosphere would emerge through a singularity.'

'He didn't use that language,' Rosa said. 'But, yes, that's the idea. So de Chardin spoke of earthbound humans becoming gods. And then there have been thinkers who have imagined a different sort of transcendence for mankind, a transcendence through an escape to the stars.'

She told us about a Russian tradition of thinking, dating back to another nineteenth-century thinker called Nikolai Fedorov. He had drawn on Marxist historical determinism, socialist utopianism and deeper wells of Slavic theology and nationalism to come up with a 'Cosmism' which preached an ultimate unity between man and the universe. Space travel was thus a necessary evolutionary step en route to our merging with the cosmos.

Fedorov's thinking had fed into the work of Konstantin Tsiolkovsky, the 'father of astronautics'. Tsiolkovsky had tried to turn Fedorov's cosmic theology into the precepts of an engineering programme: all the way to godhood with hydrogen-oxygen rocket motors. These strange, deep ideas had actually translated themselves into imperatives for the real-world Soviet space programme. To Americans space was a frontier, a place you went to explore, to colonise; to the Russians, space was a place you went to grow, as a spirit and a species.

Shelley started to argue with Rosa about some of the details.

There was something compelling in these old visions, I thought, these strange hybrids of theology and futurology and astronautics, of Christ and Marx and Darwin. Maybe they were products of their time, the struggles of thinkers born in an age dominated by religious thinking to cope with the great empirical shock of evolutionary theory, and the dreadful lesson of the geologists and astrophysicists that the universe was vast and indifferently old.

And maybe, just maybe, Rosa was right, that in all this muddled thinking done in the past we could discern, dimly, the patterns of the future. Alia's Transcendence sounded like nothing so much as a mixture of Teilhard's noosphere and Tsiolkovsky's *Homo cosmicus*, mankind projected into the stars, laced with a touch of Schelling's evolving deity.

John interrupted Rosa. 'All this antique fluff doesn't matter a damn,' he said. 'Let's cut to the chase. We're talking about what an advanced culture, an advanced super-human mind, might *want*. What does this Transcendence want with Michael?'

Rosa said, 'I believe that's where Alia's second key word comes in. *Redemption*.'

John said, 'Another oppressive old Christian concept.'

'It's an old idea, certainly,' Rosa said. 'But oppressive? That depends on the theologian you follow.'

In Christian theology mankind had become distanced from God by our primordial sin, the sin of Adam. 'And so we need redemption,' Rosa said. 'The goal of which is atonement – which means, literally, *to make as one*, to unite us once more with God. And that, some would say, was the purpose of the life of Jesus Christ.'

From the moment Christ died, it seems, His followers have been debating what exactly His death was for. *Why* did Christ have to die? If it was to achieve atonement with God, then how, exactly?

The earliest theories, dating from the first fathers of the Church, were crude. Perhaps Jesus was a sacrifice – and after all in His time Jewish temple rituals had been big on sacrifices. Maybe Jesus was a kind of bait to trap the devil, a triumphant moment in God's long war against Satan. Or maybe Christ was even a kind of ransom payment for our sins, paid not to God, but to the devil.

In the eleventh century Saint Anselm had come up with a more sophisticated idea. It was called 'substitutionary atonement', Rosa said. We still owed a ransom, but now the debt was to God, a 'satisfaction' for the great insult of our sins. But the trouble was we were too lowly even to be worthy to apologise. So God recast Himself into human form. Christ was a kind of ambassador for mankind – a 'substitute' for our lowly selves – and, being God Himself, He was able to deal with God as a kind of equal.

I think we all bristled. John said, 'It sounds feudal to me.'

'Plenty of people would agree with you,' Rosa said.

By the time we reached the Enlightenment in the eighteenth and nineteenth centuries, there was a new mood, a notion that humans could better themselves by our own efforts – and therefore we ought to live in a universe where that is possible. Now Jesus's sacrifice was not any kind of ransom or payment; it was an example of how we could grow closer to God, through love and self-sacrifice. 'Exemplary atonement', Rosa called this one.

'So we're no longer in debt,' Shelley groused. 'We're just too dumb to see what we ought to be doing.'

John asked, curious, 'And what do you believe, Rosa?'

She considered. 'I don't believe the purpose of Jesus's life was to be any sort of sacrificial lamb,' she said. 'The true legacy of His life is His message, His words. But historically the more sophisticated theories of atonement certainly completed Saint Paul's great project of turning the cross from a symbol of horror to an icon of love.'

'Quite a trick,' John murmured.

I said, 'And you think somewhere in this there is a lesson for us, for me, in dealing with Alia's Transcendence.'

'There may be,' Rosa said. She leaned forward, gazing at me, and I realised she was coming to what she had called us together to say. 'I have tried to interpret what Alia said to you, Michael. And I have come to believe that the network of linked minds she describes has not yet passed through its singularity. *It is on the cusp of Transcendence.* For now, they are still human, or as human as Alia is. But soon they must shed their humanity. And they know that with godhead will come remoteness.'

'Ah,' Shelley said. 'So we aren't falling away from God. God is receding from us.'

'So that's it,' Tom said. 'The Transcendence can't bear the coming separation from humanity.'

'Not with unfinished business hanging over it, no,' Rosa said. 'It is remorseful, perhaps. Regretful. Who knows?'

I said, 'I still don't see what is has to do with me.'

Rosa said patiently, 'The Transcendence wants redemption, Michael. In the Christian mythos, the redemption of mankind was achieved through the sacrifice of one man.'

'Oh,' I whispered. 'And this time it's me.'

Everybody started talking at once.

Rosa said to me, 'Think what this means, Michael. I listened carefully to the way Alia described all this to you. You would be a "representative" of mankind, in some way.'

Shelley said, 'That sounds like the feudal stuff. What did you call it?'

'Substitutionary atonement, yes. Michael will be our champion before the Transcendence, somehow able to deal with it as an equal, as Anselm imagined Christ negotiated with God over mankind's sins.'

'But what does it want me to do? Apologise?'

'Oh, I don't think you have to apologise for anything,' Rosa said. 'It is the Transcendence that is seeking redemption – not the other way around.'

'So *it* wants to apologise to *me*? For what?'

'You will have to find that out.' Her face was close to mine; she stared at me, intent, hungry. '*But this is why you must become elevated to the Transcendence yourself*, Michael, so that you will be worthy of absolving the Transcendence, as no mere human could be.'

My sense of unreality deepened. I whispered to Shelley, 'Why couldn't I just think I was Napoleon Bonaparte?'

Shelley grabbed my hand. 'Michael, I'm not about to let some posse of super-humans nail you to a metaphysical cross.'

'But there may be no choice,' Rosa said.

I said, 'This is insane, Rosa.'

'Yes,' she said urgently. 'That is precisely what it is. *Insane*. The Transcendence may be reaching for godhood, but it is somehow flawed, Michael. Otherwise, why would it put itself through such anguish, such contorted apologising? Yes, it is probably insane. But it is powerful, remember. We know it can reach around the curve of time. *We know it can bring the dead back to life.* An insane god is unimaginably dangerous. That is why we must find a way to deal with it.'

John stared at her, and burst out laughing.

'I understand how you feel,' Rosa said. 'Really I do. This is too big for us to imagine. But this strange responsibility has descended on us nevertheless.' Earnest excitement showed in her face. 'We find ourselves at the fulcrum of history, Michael. *You* do.

'I know you are full of doubt. I know you don't feel you are up to this challenge. You fear you may be carried away by megalomania; you don't even trust yourself. *But you will do this, Michael*. You will call Alia again. You will let her take you into the Transcendence itself. You will do it, won't you? I can see it in your eyes. It isn't in your heart, your soul, to turn away from this...'

I hated myself for it. I couldn't bear even to look at Tom, or John, or Shelley, those representatives of my common sense, my conscience. But Rosa was right. She knew me too well. Even if the ghost of Morag hadn't been involved, I would have gone diving in there.

Rosa said, 'Just remember the Transcendence isn't omnipotent.'

'It isn't?'

'We know that. The substitutionary atonement it is seeking proves that much: we surpassed that in the sophistication of our thinking centuries ago. We are small, slow, stupid, weak compared to the Transcendence. But there is at least one way in which *it is inferior to us*. Michael, you can deal with it.'

As we broke up, John had one more question for Rosa. 'Suppose all this is true. That the future folds over onto the present and the past, that our far-future descendants will become godlike. What chance will you Catholics have then? The game is up, isn't it?'

Rosa smiled thinly. 'The Christian Church survived the fall of Rome, and the science of Aristotle and Newton, Galileo and Copernicus and Einstein. Catholicism even survived Martin Luther. I think we will survive this.'

And she disappeared.

Tom came to me. He didn't bother even to ask whether I was going to do it. 'When,' he said. 'Tell me when, Dad.'

I shrugged. 'Why wait? I'm not getting any braver.' Not that I was sure if I needed courage; if something is so far beyond your imagination, it's hard even to fear it. 'You aren't going to call me an instrumentalist again, are you, Tom?'

'No. I can see you aren't doing this for yourself, not at any level. You're doing it for the same reason you went straight back to the hydrate project after the bombing. You're going to do it because you think you have to.'

'The Transcendence chose me...'

'I know.'

'But I'm sorry, Tom.'

'For what?'

'Because I'm going off and leaving you again. Same old story.'

'OK. But at least I have warning this time. Have you got any dinner plans?'

That took me off guard. 'I guess not. What are you thinking, a Last Supper?'

John and Shelley joined us. John said, 'A last beer may be a better idea.'

Shelley put her arm around my waist. 'Do you think it will make any difference if you have to go off and slay demons in the far future with a hangover?'

'It might actually help,' I said. 'OK, first round on me. What do you prefer, water or wine?'

Chapter 57

Leropa and Alia walked in the lengthening shadows of the cathedral's titanic ruin.

'So you visited Michael Poole.'

'It was – strange. Difficult. I believe Michael Poole will do what we ask of him.'

Leropa eyed her. 'And that pleases you?'

'Shouldn't it?'

'There is one corollary to our discussion I didn't want to raise in front of your sister,' Leropa said.

'*Corollary*,' Alia said dismissively. 'The Transcendence believes it is a creature of love. But its language is all logic.'

Leropa raised a hairless eyebrow. 'Let us talk of logic, then. You are not the first to have pointed out the ultimate logical flaw in the Redemption programme.'

'Yes,' Alia said. 'No matter what you do, even if you change history to eliminate every element of suffering, the suffering will still exist—'

'In a wider universe of possibilities. Yes.'

'So Redemption is impossible.'

'Not necessarily,' Leropa said. 'Your sister was right to intuit that the Redemption is not *for* those who suffered long ago; it is *for* the Transcendence itself. It is hoped – but it is only a hope – that somewhere in the Levels of Redemption might be found sufficient solace. At some point we might be able to say, even if the Redemption is not logically complete, *this is enough*. And it will be possible at last to look to the future – to look outward, not inward.'

Alia nodded. It was a valid hope. 'But if that point is never reached? If there is no solace to be found? What then?'

Leropa sighed. 'If suffering exists, no Redemption may be possible. But need it have been so? *What if humans had never existed at all*? What if the Earth had remained lifeless, like its lost Moon? Then there would have been no suffering to atone, no evil to redeem – no sin to expiate. Perhaps that would be a better state of affairs than to allow ineradicable suffering to exist, without the possibility of healing.'

Alia stopped in her tracks. 'Are you serious?'

'It is the final stage of Redemption, its ultimate logic. We call it *the Cleansing*. It is not that mankind will cease to exist,' said Leropa quietly. 'It never *will* have existed. And it could be arranged quite easily. Remember, the Transcendence can restore the dead to life, with a mere gesture. This final solution is almost elegant. Economical.'

A cold anger burned in Alia. 'Is this where logic has led the Transcendence – to love mankind so much that it must be eliminated?'

'This is only a possibility,' Leropa said. 'But in what is to come, you must always remember that this dark possibility is there – if Michael Poole fails.' She raised her hand, curling fragile fingers.

Alia imagined consequences flowing from that gesture, flowing out across space and time, to the far future and into the deepest past. Leropa was a small, hunched-over woman in a worn, shabby robe, shuffling through the debris of an immense ruin. And yet she held the fate of all mankind in her bony hand.

Chapter 58

Transcendence is—

I can't say. The words don't exist in my head. What is it *like*, then?

It is like stepping off a cliff. Or like suddenly plunging into a shocking new medium, like ice-cold water. Or like the instant your first child is born, and you hold him in your arms, and you know your life isn't your own any more, and never will be again.

It is like waking up. When I looked back on my entire life up to this point, it was as if I had been dreaming. I saw all my perceptions of the world, and even my experiences of my inner world, for the partial fantasies that they were. And I knew that if I ever got out of this strange state of new consciousness, it would be *this* that seemed like a dream.

I felt oddly confident, even though I knew I had come to a place beyond my comprehension. I could cope with this, I thought.

But where had I come to? If I had awoken from the dream of human existence, if I had opened my eyes for the first time – what did I see?

For now, nothing. It was not as if I had my eyes closed, but more as if I had my gaze averted, my head full of thoughts of other things. I couldn't see anything because I wasn't looking; it was a matter of will. I lifted my metaphoric head. I focused my metaphoric eyes. And I saw—

Light. It flooded into my mind, brilliant, searing hot. My mote of confidence was scorched, shrivelled, blasted. I tried to scream.

The light faded. I was back in my state of unseeing again.

'I know what you would have said if one of your students

at Cornell had gone plunging in like that.' The voice, gentle, dry, came out of nowhere, with no source. I wasn't hearing it, I couldn't turn my head towards it. Yet it was there even so, a voice in a dream.

'Morag?'

'Alia,' she said, a gentle regret shading her tone. 'I am Alia. I am here with you, to help you.'

'I'm glad,' I said fervently. 'So tell me what I'd have said.'

'You'd say, *Walk before you run.*'

'Quite right too.'

'I blame myself,' she said. 'When I was first immersed in the Transcendence, I had had months of training – of mental discipline, and of development of various faculties. Also I have half a million years' evolutionary advantage over you, Michael. No offence. And *I* found it overwhelming, that first time. For you it is all but impossible.'

'So teach me how to walk, Alia.'

'One step at a time.' I felt a gentle pressure, as if a hand had cupped my chin to lift my head, as if I were a child. Metaphor, metaphor. But metaphors are fine if they help you understand. 'Look now.'

I saw a black sky full of stars, all around me, above and below. It was as if I was a stranded astronaut taken far from Earth and left drifting in space. I had no sense of vertigo, though; perhaps that had been edited out. The stars were scattered deep through three dimensions, but they were a uniform colour, a kind of yellow-white. I began to make out patterns, groupings, tentative constellations.

'Stars. But they aren't stars, are they? Just another metaphor.'

'A metaphor for what?'

It was obvious. 'The Transcendents. The individuals who contribute to this group mind. Like us.'

'Like me,' Alia said. 'Not quite like you.'

'Am I not a star?' I felt unreasonably disappointed. 'Twinkle, twinkle.'

'Oh, yes,' she said. 'But a special sort of star.'

The stars began to drift around me. Now they were like fish in some vast dark aquarium. The patterns they made became clearer, swoops and whirls and sketches of light. And each of them was a mind, I marvelled. I knew the principle. The Transcendence was not a simple pooling of minds but a dynamic network, of which these stars were the nodes. The greater awareness of the Transcendence itself was an emergent property of the network, arising from the community of minds, yet not overwhelming them individually. It had something in common with an anthill, I thought – or even Uncle George's strange Coalescence.

'Everybody sees something like this,' Alia said. 'Nodes, networks...'

I wanted to see the Transcendence itself. I looked up.

I saw more stars, swarms of them flocking in patterns that elaborated scale upon scale, rising up as far as I could see. And at the very limit of my vision the shifting constellations seemed to merge into a mist, and then a bright point. That ultimate unity was the consciousness of the Transcendence itself, arising out of the interactions of the community of star-minds on which it was based.

When I looked around I could see the same point-like unity in every direction. An impossible geometry, of course, but a neat metaphor.

At Alia's subtle nudging, I widened my perceptual field still further. Moving through the flocks of stars were darker shapes, more elusive. Sometimes the stars would settle on their velvet surfaces, and I would make out the glimmer of an outline, a complex morphology. But then the stars would rise up again like startled birds, and the form would be lost.

'These are the structures of the mind of the Transcendence,' Alia said. 'Ideas. Beliefs. Understandings. And memories – many, many memories.'

I saw one form that was a little different from the rest – compact, almost glimmering, like a multi-faceted jewel, but of jet black. It was like a bit of polished coal. 'What's *that*?'

Alia sounded as if she was smiling. 'Take a look.'

I didn't know how to. But even as I framed the desire I felt myself falling towards the jewel-like knot of knowledge.

I felt a surge of new understanding – a moment of insight, like a breakthrough after years of study in some arcane subject, or the sudden clarification when the solution of a puzzle becomes obvious. This glimmering knot of understanding contained *all of physics*. In that moment I enjoyed a deep understanding of the fabric of the cosmos, from the minuscule symmetries of the fundamental objects from which space and time were ultimately constructed, all the way to the jewel-like geometry of the universe as a whole – although now I saw that those two poles of structure, large and small, were in fact one, as if all of reality were folded together on some more abstract scale.

But even as I wallowed in this joyous understanding, a part of me noticed features a physicist of the twenty-first century would have recognised – even an engineer like me. Our basic map of the universe's composition was here, the proportions of dark energy, dark matter, baryonic matter, as determined by our space telescopes; and I made out the familiar milestones of the universe's evolution out of the initial singularity, through stages of expansion and cooling, all the way to the matter-dominated age that had given rise to humans. Our theories were partial, just gropings in the dark, each tentative explanation like the light scattered from one facet of this ultimate jewel of understanding. And yet we got some of it right, I thought with a surge of pride, we primitives on our single, muddy, messed-up little world.

That sense of pride quickly dissipated when I saw that this jewel-like structure of knowledge, this 'ultimate truth', was *ancient*. The total understanding dreamed of by the physicists of my time, the limits of their imagination, had not only been achieved, but long ago – and it had been overshadowed by deeper mysteries yet.

Reluctantly I pulled away. I tried to remember, to hold onto some glimmering of this ultimate understanding, but already it was melting like a snowflake cupped in my hand, its beautiful symmetries and unity lost. Already I was forgetting.

But I wasn't here for physics, but to confront mysteries of the human heart – and the superhuman.

Alia said gently, 'Michael, I think you're ready.'

'Ready for what?'

'To meet the undying.'

Dread gathered in my heart. But you asked for this, Poole, I told myself. 'Let's get it over.'

'Hello, Michael Poole. I regret I was born too late to meet your most illustrious descendant...'

This was Leropa, then. The undying spoke as if from shadows. I didn't want to see her any more clearly.

'I don't understand how I'm talking to you,' I said. 'Or Alia, come to that. We're all part of the Transcendence – aren't we?'

'The Transcendence is a mind, Michael, but it is not a human mind. There is no reason why a mind must have a single pole of consciousness – as *your* pole of awareness feels like a mote lodged for ever behind your eyes.'

But, I thought uneasily, even in my time minds aren't so simple. Maybe we three are like multiple personalities screaming at each other inside the head of a schizophrenic.

'Or perhaps we are emblems,' Leropa said. 'We stand for certain traits of the Transcendence, as it tries to resolve the internal dilemma over the Redemption, which Alia so acutely identified.'

'In which case I might be no more real than a character in a Platonic dialogue? Charming. What traits?'

'I am the purpose of the Transcendence. Its will. And you, Michael, are its conscience. We are here to debate the Redemption.'

And to understand the Redemption, she said, I had to understand love. Again I felt feather-touch on a metaphorical chin, a ghostly finger directing my gaze to new horizons.

Through its closed cosmology the Transcendence was cognisant of the universe as a whole, of all of space and time, the whole of the human past. And now it showed me that past. I was dazzled by the great portrait; I longed to turn my metaphorical head away.

But I began to make out broad aspects. It all sprang from a deep root, the long prehistory of humankind on Earth, a root that emerged from down deep, rising through forms of hominid and ape and animal – not *lesser*, each of them was perfectly adapted for the environment it found itself in, but steadily acquiring an elusive quality of mind. That deep dark Earthbound taproot culminated in my own time, like a shoot bursting out of the soil. History after my day was a tangle of foliage that sprawled across the face of the Galaxy – knotted, fecund, vibrant, full of detail, from the rise and fall of empires and even species, down to the particular experience of a small child wandering along a beach by the light of a blue-white star a thousand light years from Earth. Again I longed to *remember*. Just the fact that humans would live so long and come so far would have been beyond the imaginations of most people alive in my own cramped and dangerous century.

But it was a saga full of tragedy. I saw the scars of war, and of mindless natural disasters, where trillions of human lives had been destroyed, as trivial as needles on a burning pine tree.

Leropa said, '*Look at it all*, Michael Poole. Look at these particles of humanity trapped in suffering. And the Transcendence loves every one of them. How can the Transcendence face the infinite possibilities of the future, when its past is knotted up with blood and pain?'

It was the paradox of a god born of human flesh and blood. To achieve full awareness the Transcendence had to absorb every human consciousness, even far into the past. And that meant it had to absorb all that pain.

'It will be born a wounded god,' I said. Just as Rosa had intuited. It was an unthinkable outcome.

Leropa said, her voice silky, 'One way or another the Redemption must be completed. And if atonement *cannot* be achieved then it would be better to make a simplifying choice.'

I knew what she meant. 'If you don't exist, you can never suffer.' The ultimate simplicity of extermination.

'The Cleansing is within our grasp, if we will it to be done.'

I was within the Transcendence, yet I *was* the Transcendence. For a brief moment I shared its huge ambitions, and its limitless fears – and I faced its dilemma. In that moment I fully accepted Leropa's logic. History must be cleansed, one way or another. And it must be done now...

But Alia whispered in my metaphoric ear. 'Michael. Wait. Think. *What would Morag say?*'

Morag? . . .

'You always were a berk, Michael Poole.'

I imagined I could see her, a kind of elusive shadow glimpsed from the corner of my eye.

'A berk? Charming.'

'You always have to meddle, meddle, meddle.'

'If you're going on about the hydrate project, I get enough of that from Tom.'

'Not that. I admit *that's* necessary. But it had to be *you* doing it, didn't it, Michael? It fit your personality like a glove, didn't it? An excuse to tinker. You were always mucking about at home too. All those pointless do-it-yourself projects you never finished.'

'Morag—'

'Your half-built conservatory, that you abandoned because you ran out of money. Or the way you changed half the windows in the house, then left the rest because you got bored. Or the way—'

'*Morag.* Is this going anywhere?'

'And now here you are fiddling with the whole of human history. You think it's a coincidence that this weird old woman picked *you*? Of course you're going to want to plunge your hands in up to the elbows. It's what you do. You're a meddler, Michael. An instrumentalist.'

I sighed. 'You always go over the top, don't you?'

'All right. Put it this way. You're childish. You're like a kid in an art show. You want to touch the paintings, scrape bits off, deface them, draw your own copies, put them in new frames. Because you're not mature enough yet just to sit back and enjoy the art without *fiddling* with it.'

I thought that over. 'But that's what we're like. Humans, I mean. We're a species who *do* things.'

'Not necessarily,' Alia said now. 'There are other ways to be.' And she widened my perspective yet again.

There was a spectrum of minds, here within the Transcendence itself, and yet more beyond its still-expanding walls. I sensed these different minds as if hearing voices at the ends of long corridors. All of them were human or post-human, and most were more or less like my own. But they incorporated other ways of thinking, other ways to live. The strange Coalescents in their vast hives, fecund, static, were one example; they were here.

And with Alia's gentle guidance I came on a people, a branch of mankind, who had long ago settled on a world in the Sagittarius Arm. It was a water-world, like an Earth drowned under an almost global ocean. The people here, post-people anyhow, had given up clothes and spaceships and even tools, and developed bodies like otters, and now spent all their lives in the endless calm of the water.

Alia said, 'They gave up their minds. They knew it was happening. What you don't use, you lose. But they didn't care...'

I didn't understand. 'They could do so much more. They once *did*. But they put it all aside. And they've left themselves vulnerable. A volcanic spasm, an asteroid strike—'

'They don't care! They have the present, they have each other, and that's enough.'

'So why bother getting smart in the first place?'

'Because there are circumstances where it is the only choice.'

Humanity's chimp-like ancestors had been kicked out of their ancestral forests by climate change. The savannah was a harsh environment, where you were exposed to extremes of temperature, easily spotted by predators, and where water and food sources were scattered far and wide. In order for humanity to survive, its intelligence had to mushroom.

'You need to be smart, if you're adrift in a hostile environment,' Alia said. 'But if you ever manage to stumble off the savannah and back into the forest again—'

'You can give up your mind,' I said.

Morag said, 'I think I understand. Birds give up flight whenever it's safe, if they happen to flap to an island without predators. Why not intelligence?'

Curiously I turned to the seal-folk flipping and gliding in their world-ocean. Their shining, shallow thoughts were contained within the Transcendence's awareness; cautiously I sampled them. I tasted contentment, as delicious and ephemeral as the salty flesh of a fish. Yes, for these post-people it was enough. Life had no goals, for them; life was a process, whose only purpose was to be relished.

Alia said, 'Michael Poole, are you seriously telling me *they* need to be redeemed? From *what*?'

'But I still don't understand,' I said. 'Intelligence isn't just a tool. Knowledge is worth having for its own sake... isn't it?'

Morag brought back the jewel-like knot of wisdom that represented the Transcendence's physics. 'Take another look.'

Again I peered into the mass of ancient wisdom. But this time, under the guidance of Alia and Morag, I looked deep into the heart of the jewel – and I discerned a tiny, crucial flaw. There were limits to understanding by any mind – human or post-human, even Transcendent. This was incompleteness: no mathematics, a logical construct of the human mind, could ever be made whole or completely consistent. Because of this, you could prove that there were limits to what any conceivable computer could do.

But a mind was at heart an information-processing system – so no mind, however vast, could ever be fully cognisant of itself. Not even the Transcendence.

'Ah,' Morag said, as if she was learning with me. '"What peculiar privilege has this little agitation of brain which we call thought, that we must thus make it a model of the whole Universe?"'

'Who's that?'

'David Hume. He wasn't an engineer so you won't have heard of him. Face it, Michael. No mind can ever be fully cognisant of itself – and mind is not the goal of the cosmos anyhow. The Transcendence can never achieve its ambitions. And the Redemption, this cack-handed do-it-yourself fix-up it means to inflict on human history, can only lead to disaster.'

Leropa had been silent for a long time. She said now, 'Flawed god the Transcendence may be, but it is capable of at least one great act. Perhaps we can never atone for the suffering of past ages. But we can at least wipe it away.'

Alia said, 'Leropa—'

'It is time for your decision, Michael Poole.'

The other voices, Alia, Morag, fell silent, and I was left alone.

I looked deep inside myself.

Could there be any possible ethical justification for the Cleansing? Could the elimination of suffering ever be worth the elimination of life itself? If the great cauterisation were done, then those unborn – *including myself* – would never have known it happened. It would not be felt, nor would the pain they might have suffered. But on the other hand, they would have no *chance* – no chance to be glad to be alive, however briefly.

'Life comes first,' I said. 'Everything else is secondary.' Yes, I thought as I framed the words; that was just.

'Then,' Leropa said, 'what of the Redemption?'

The Transcendence was like an immense parent, I thought, brooding over the lives of its children – the whole of humanity, in the future and the past. And the Transcendence longed to make its children safe and happy, for all time.

But I was a parent too. If I could somehow have *fixed* Tom's future at his birth, or even before he was conceived, so that his life would be lived out in safety – would I have done so? It seemed a monstrous arrogance to try to control events that might happen long after my death. How could I know what was best? And even if I did know, wouldn't I be taking away my son's choices, his ability to live out his own life as he wanted?

You had to let go, I thought. You had to let your children make their own mistakes. Anything else verged on insanity, not love.

I didn't have to say it. As I formulated these thoughts I glanced around the sky-mind of the Transcendence. There was a change, I thought. Those pinpoint awarenesses whirled in tight, angry knots, and giant reefs of wisdom loomed out of the dark like icebergs on a night-time ocean. I had troubled the Transcendence with my decision, then. Perhaps that meant it was the right one.

On some level, *the Transcendence must already have known*, I thought. I was just a lever it used to lift itself back to sanity. But that didn't mean it was happy about it. Or grateful.

Leropa hissed, 'Michael Poole. You know that if the Redemption is abandoned, you will lose Morag for ever, don't you?'

I recoiled from this personal attack. So much for the lofty goals of the Transcendence, I thought; so much for transhuman love. 'But I already lost her,' I said. 'Nothing the Transcendence can do will make any difference to that. I guess it's part of being human. And so is letting go.'

Leropa said, 'Letting go?'

'Of the past, the dead. Of the future, the fate of your children. Even an arch-instrumentalist like me knows that much.'

Leropa laughed. 'Are you *forgiving* the Transcendence, Michael Poole?'

'Isn't that why I was brought here?'

'Goodbye, Michael Poole,' Leropa said. 'We won't meet again.'

Suddenly, I knew, it was over. I searched for Morag. Perhaps there was a trace of her left. But she was receding from me, as if she was falling down a well, her face diminishing, her gaze still fixed on me.

And then the stars swirled viciously around me – for an instant I struggled, longing to stay – but I was engulfed in the pain of an unwelcome rebirth, and a great pressure expelled me.

Chapter 59

The six of them gathered in Conurbation 11729: Alia and Drea, Reath, and the three Campocs, Bale, Denh and Seer. Under the mighty electric-blue tetrahedral arch of the ancient cathedral, the undying walked their solitary paths. Some of them mumbled to themselves, continuing their lifelong monologues, but the very oldest did not speak at all.

Even now Alia was aware of the presence of the Transcendence, in her and around her. And she was aware of its turmoil, like a storm gathering, huge energies drawing up in a towering sky above her.

Campoc Bale drew Alia aside. She could still faintly sense the extended consciousness he shared with his family, like a limited Transcendence of its own. And about him there was still that exotic sense of the alien, the *different*, which had given their lovemaking so much spice.

He said carefully, 'We did not mean any harm to come to your ship, your family.'

'But you led the Shipbuilders to the *Nord*.'

'Yes.' It was the first time he'd admitted it explicitly. 'We were concerned that the Redemption would rip mankind apart. We were right to be concerned, weren't we?'

'And I was your tool, your weapon to use against the Transcendence.'

'You were more than that to me,' he said hotly.

'Your manipulation was gross. You threatened my sister, you endangered my family—'

'We would never have harmed Drea.' He looked up. 'I think on some level you always knew that, didn't you? And we did not mean the incident with the Shipbuilders to go so far.'

'*Incident.* My mother died, and my brother. Are you looking for forgiveness from me, Bale? Do you want redemption, after all that's happened?'

'Alia, please—'

She laughed at him. 'Go back to your Rustball and bury yourself in the empty heads of your brothers.'

His broad face was full of loss, and she felt a faint stab of regret. But she turned her back on him and walked away.

Reath walked with her. 'Weren't you a little hard on him?'

She glared at him, refusing to answer.

He sighed. 'It is a time of change for us all, I suppose.'

'What about you, Reath? What will you do now?'

'Oh, there will always be a role for me and my kind,' he said wryly. 'Many of the Commonwealth's great projects will continue whatever the Transcendence decides to do next: the political reunification of the scattered races of mankind is a worthwhile aim.'

'That's noble, Reath.'

They came to Drea, who was sitting, looking bored, on a block of eroded rubble.

Reath asked, 'And what of you two? Where will you go next?'

'Back to the *Nord*,' Drea said immediately. 'Where else? The *Nord* is home. Besides, I think my father needs us right now.' She reached up and took her sister's hand. 'Alia?'

But Alia did not reply. She found a decision formulated in her head, a decision she hadn't known she had made. 'Not the *Nord*,' she said. 'Oh, I'll miss my father – and you, Drea. I'll visit; I always will. But—' But she couldn't live there any more. She had seen too much. The *Nord* and its unending journey were no longer enough for her. 'I'll find a role for myself. Maybe I can work for the Commonwealth too... Some day I'll find a new home.' She pulled Drea to her feet and hugged her. 'Somewhere to have children of my own!'

Drea laughed, but there were tears in her eyes.

Reath watched them seriously. 'Alia.' His tone was grave, almost reprimanding; it was just as he had spoken to her when he had first met her.

She snapped, not unkindly, 'Oh, what is it *now*, you old relic?'

'If this is your true intention – just be careful.'

'Of what?'

'Of yourself.' He had seen it before, he said, Elect who had failed, or even mature Transcendents who, for reasons of health or injury, had been forced to withdraw from the great network of mind. 'You never forget the Transcendence. You *can't*. Not once you have experienced it, for it is an opening-up of your mind beyond the barriers of *you*. You may think you have put it aside, Alia, but it always lurks within you.'

'What are you saying?'

'If you are going to roam the stars, be sure it is yourself you are looking for – and not the Transcendence, for that is lost to you for ever.'

On impulse she took his hands; they were warm, leathery. 'You are a good friend, Reath. And if I am ever in trouble—'

'I am not hard to find,' Reath said, smiling.

'I know.'

Leropa emerged from the flock of the undying. She approached Alia, as enclosed and enigmatic as ever. The others stood back, uncertain – afraid, Alia saw.

Leropa said: 'The Transcendence is dying.'

Alia was shocked. Beside her Reath grunted, as if punched.

Leropa went on, 'Oh, don't be afraid. It's not going to implode, today or tomorrow.'

Alia said, 'But the grander aims, all that planning for infinity—'

'All that is lost. Perhaps the project was always flawed. We humans are a blighted sort. Too restless to be content, too limited to become gods: perhaps it was always inevitable it would end like this. The Redemption was our best and bravest attempt to mould a god from the clay of humanity. But we succeeded only in magnifying the worst of us along with the best, all our atavistic cravings. And so the Transcendence will die – but at least we tried!

'This is a key time in human history, Alia, the high tide mark of human ambition. We've been privileged to see it, I suppose. But now we must fall back.'

'And what about the undying? What will you do now?'

'Oh, we aren't going anywhere. We will get on with things in our own patient way. We still have our ambitions, our plans – on timescales that transcend even the Transcendence, in a sense. And even without the power of the Transcendence behind us, the issues of the future remain to be resolved.'

'Issues?'

Leropa's immobile face showed faint contempt. 'Alia, you and your antique companion Poole indulged in some wonderful chatter about the evolutionary future of mankind – the purpose of intelligence, all of that. Perhaps we can all find a safe place, where we can give up the intelligence we evolved to keep us alive out on the savannah, and subside comfortably back into non-sentience. Yes?'

'It happens. Like the seal-men of the water-world.'

'It's a bucolic dream. But unfortunately the universe cares little for our wishes, or our dreams.'

Mankind sprawled across the Galaxy it had conquered, speciating, variegating, gradually reunifying. But the wider universe was empty of mankind. And in those vast spaces beyond, enemies circled, ancient and implacable. Leropa said, 'We are still out on the savannah of stars. And there are ferocious beasts out there – beasts the Exultants drove out of the Galaxy altogether - *but they are still there*. And they are aware of us. Indeed they have a grudge.'

'They will come back,' Alia breathed.

'It's inevitable. It might take another million years, but they will come.'

'And you undying are planning for war...'

'Earth will endure, you know. One day even all this, even the traces of the Transcendence itself, will be nothing but another layer in Earth's stratified layer of rocks and fossils, just another incident in a long and mostly forgotten history. But *we* will still be here, taking care of things.' Her face was hard, set, her dry eyes like bits of stone. She had never seemed more alien to Alia.

And yet, Alia knew, this grim, relentless inhumanity might in the end be the saving of mankind. 'You frighten me, Leropa.'

Leropa grinned, open-mouthed, showing teeth as black as coal. 'I think you understand why we undying are necessary. Perhaps even *we* are an evolutionary recourse, do you think? But you aren't going to take your immortality pill, are you? You aren't going to join us.'

'No,' Alia said. She had no need of endless life. And she had no need of Transcendence. She would embrace her own humanity with two hands – that would be enough...

She staggered. The world pivoted around Alia, as if the wind had changed, or gravity had rippled.

Drea took her arm. 'Alia? Are you all right?'

Reath asked anxiously, 'Is it the Transcendence?'

Leropa said, 'It is nearly over.'

Drea grabbed Alia's hands. 'Then we must hurry. There is something I want to show you while I can. Come. Skim with me. Like when we were kids, before all *this*.'

'Drea, I don't think it's the time for—'

'Just do it!' Laughing, she Skimmed.

Alia had no choice but to follow. She found herself suspended over the head of Reath. His upturned face shone in the light, his mouth round with shock. Leropa had turned away, uninterested, already absorbed once more in her own long projects.

Drea was still laughing. 'Again!' she cried. 'Three, two, one—'

Clutching each other, the sisters Skimmed again, and again.

Alia found herself perched on a small platform, at the very apex of the cathedral's mighty tetrahedral skeleton. The three pylons of the frame swept away beneath her to touch the rust-red ground of Earth. Beneath the frame the undying community huddled in the ruined domes of Conurbation 11729.

The air was cold, and a stiff breeze blew. The platform's material shone brighter than daylight, and it underlit Drea's face as the sisters clutched at each other, exhilarated by the Skimming.

'Drea, what are we *doing* here?'

Drea stepped aside with a flourish to reveal a blocky

artefact. 'We're here for this,' she said. It was Alia's Witnessing tank, her most precious relic of childhood. 'Look.'

Within the tank Michael Poole, a figurine no taller than Alia's hand, sat quietly in a chair. From a window a warm light reflected from sun-dappled water poured into his room. Drea said, 'When the Transcendence shuts down the Witnessing tanks won't work any more.'

'I suppose they won't.'

'I thought you'd want to see him one last time.' Drea leaned over the tank. 'This is a time in his life *after* his encounter with the Transcendence. At this point in his lifeline, he remembers you, Alia.'

If he remembers anything at all, Alia thought uneasily, after his shattering self-sacrifice. 'The Witnessing worked, you know, in its own terms. I got to know Poole, and I became a better person for it. I think so anyhow.'

'You loved him, didn't you? Perhaps you still do.'

'But he never loved me, Drea. There was only ever Morag.'

Drea said earnestly, 'It's best this way, that it ends.' She trilled a few notes. 'Every song must end – and indeed an ending, if it is exquisite enough, is part of the beauty of the song itself.'

Alia felt huge forces gathering. She raised her face to the blue sky of Earth. Through the muddy daylight she thought she could see the Transcendence, the necklace-chains of minds, the drifting bergs of memory.

Drea clutched her hands. 'Alia?'

'It's going to happen soon.'

In a moment immense invisible muscles would flex. A wave of *difference* would wash around the arc of the universe, from the furthest future and seamlessly into the deepest past. And the powers the Transcendence had taken to itself, the power to meddle with the deepest past, would be put aside for ever.

The Transcendence churned around her, vast clouds of anguish and determination. Spacetime spasmed – she felt it, deep in the core of her being. And Drea gasped.

Alia looked down. The Witnessing tank was no longer clear; the image was broken, turbulent, like a pool of water stirred up with a stick. But in the last instant before the link collapsed for ever, Alia saw Michael Poole raise his head, look up out of the tank at her, and smile.

Chapter 60

I have come home to Florida. Although not to my mother's house, which is in increasing peril of slipping into the sea.

I live in a small apartment in Miami. I like having people around, the sound of voices. Sometimes I miss the roar of traffic, the sharp scrapings of planes across the sky, the sounds of my past. But the laughter of children makes up for that.

The water continues to rise. There is a lot of misery in Florida, as elsewhere, much displacement. I understand that. But I kind of like the water, the gentle disintegration of the state into an archipelago. The slow rise, different every day, every week, reminds me that nothing stays the same, that the future is coming whether we like it or not.

Alia told me stories of the far future, of her time. Her stories come back to me in dreams.

A half a million years from now, she said, children can Skim. It's like teleporting, I think, 'beaming', but you don't need equipment, fancy flashing lights and instrument panels and stern-jawed engineers. You just do it. You decide you don't want to be *here* any more, you would rather be over *there*, and there you are. Literally. Children are born this way. Babies learn to Skim before they can walk, or crawl, or climb. Teleporting babies: imagine that. Their parents have to chase them down with butterfly nets. And the problem of droppings is awesome. But nobody minds. On Alia's starship, people like having a sky full of babies. When you grow up, the ability to Skim atrophies. I got the feeling Alia was close to this age of transition, but she didn't want to think about it. All your life you have been flitting over the static crowds of lumpen adults. Now you are dragged down to join them, and you are going to be stuck in a spacetime suddenly as thick as glue, for ever. What a growing-up present, like all the trials of age hitting you at once.

Sometimes I dream of writing this up, of spinning fiction out of it. I could use the loss of Skimming as a metaphor for growing up. Or for the plight of the Transcendence, on the point of deity and yet unable to put aside its human past. I could add a title or two to George's ancient science fiction library. Nobody would ever know I had stolen it all.

I came out of my contact with the Transcendence shattered. Drained. It was like the bombing of the Refrigerator project, the very instant of the explosion, the world suddenly turned to chaos, the blast's tremendous punch in the chest. It was like that moment, but going on and on.

I don't remember much of the weeks that followed. Tom and Sonia looked after me during that time. I wasn't a basket-case. I was able to get dressed, take myself to the bathroom. I even kept working, after a fashion, on the hydrate project. I have notes that prove it, though now they read like they were written by somebody else. But I'd forget to eat, for instance. I'd forget what time it was and stay up through the night, and be startled by the dawn. That kind of thing.

It was a time when I needed my mother, I guess. But she died not long afterwards, not so long after her brother George. Ironic, one of life's little jokes. I miss her, of course.

I think there were rows between Tom and John about who should be responsible for me: 'You're his brother.' 'You're his son.' But they kept this away from me. I don't mind; if I'd been capable of it I'd have been rowing too. We were never again quite as close as we were during the crisis days. Maybe it's enough to know we were there for each other when we needed it. Funny lot, we Pooles.

From the beginning it was John's instinct to keep all this strangeness away from the authorities, and despite the fact that some oddities showed up on public records, not least Morag's incarnation, we succeeded, with some subtle help, I think, from Gea. Even the conspiracy theorists with their super-powered search engines and cross-correlation machines didn't get a sniff of me.

Astounding when you think about it. I saved humanity in past, present and future but nobody knows.

Even I'm not sure. What was it I *did*?

Trying to remember the Transcendence is like recalling a dream. The more you think about it, the more it eludes you. Or it is like my haunting by Morag: glimpses, remoteness, that you try to break through but never can. I feel as if I glimpsed a vast, rich landscape through a pinhole, just for a second. But as time passes, and the direct experience of the Transcendence recedes, I am left with memories of memories, like polished pebbles. In time, even the sense of frustration has passed away.

Gea's speech to the General Assembly of the United Nations went remarkably well.

She even put in a short plea on behalf of her fellow artificial sentiences, and herself. We humans weren't alone on the planet any more, she said. We had a duty of care for our children. After all, Gea said, an artificial like herself was not limited by human biology as we were. Potentially she could be immortal. But all that potential would be destroyed if the fabric of our culture fell apart, if the technological substrate on which she depended broke up.

You would think such an appeal would alarm us. The conventional wisdom has always been that humans won't share the future with anybody else. That even seems to have been the truth of the future I glimpsed through my contact with Alia. But according to the snap polls, the response to Gea's appeal was warm, sympathetic. This is an age when, conscious of the past, we feel guilty about it. Gea judged our mass psychology just right.

The Refrigerator won the backing of the Stewardship agencies, and was rushed through its final stages of technical validation. Now the roll-out has begun. Our pilot plant off Prudhoe Bay is the seed of what is still the largest single field, but other bases have started operating all around the Canadian Arctic, and across Siberia. Next year, Antarctica. Of course it's expensive. But the cost of *not* stabilising all those strata full of greenhouse cocktails would have been far more: potentially infinite, if the worst case had come about.

That isn't all EI are doing. Shelley Magwood is working on high-level concept designs of a whole range of ambitious new geoengineering projects.

The one that catches my eye is a direct challenge to the dreary modern paradigm of sea-level rise and flooding. At the end of the Ice Age, as the great ice sheets melted, swathes of landscape were drowned. There was 'Doggerland', which is now under the North Sea, and 'Beringia', which bridged between Alaska and Asia, and 'Sundaland', between Australia and South-East Asia, once the largest belt of tropical rainforest in the world. Now there are strong proposals to turn back the sea, to reclaim some of those vast stretches of lost terrain. It seems outrageous, but the geography of the seabed will allow it, in places. The new lands, opened up for refugees, will be farmed or given over to forest land, so sequestering some of our excess carbon out of the air. Shelley is in heaven with all of this. She's even becoming a media star. An engineer as modern hero: who'd have thought it?

The Stewardship authorities are already talking about a new model for the administration of the new provinces. There will be full local democracy and chains of accountability all the way up to the planetary level, but there will be no new 'nations' planted in Doggerland. We haven't always lived in nation-states, and they aren't always very constructive entities to share our world with. Maybe with the new territories as models of a different kind of governance, the old nations will at last wither away.

Of course there are still risks ahead, difficult times. We may have fixed the hydrate problem but there is plenty left to do. We'll just have to get through this damn Bottleneck one step at a time. But we're starting to believe we can achieve great things.

And after the Bottleneck, who knows? I'm starting to believe what Alia told me, that people of the future really will look back on our age as a time to admire, a time you'd wish you'd lived through.

John has a house not far away from me. But he is often off in New York, Washington or Geneva, pursuing his own projects, heroic in his own legalistic way. And he's at last writing his book on his new ethics-based economics paradigm, his new kind of money. I don't see much of his Happy kids. It doesn't feel like much of a loss.

Tom and Sonia are working on relief efforts in Siberia once more. Now that the Refrigerator project is rolling out there's a lot to be done. Sonia has resigned her Army commission to be with Tom. I keep a room in my apartment for them. They store some of their stuff there, so they have a permanent place in my life. I don't see as much of them as I'd like, however. I don't know what the future holds for them, but I think they'll be happy together.

I haven't seen Rosa for some time. She gave up her ministry in Seville, and has, well, disappeared, as if into a hole in the ground. Perhaps literally. The Coalescence was always a shadow behind her. Maybe it called her back – but from George's account that seems unlikely; *it* would have no use for her, a failed drone who did her job but got too smart for her own good. Maybe, on the other hand, she tracked it down, or some descendant of it after the great scattering in Rome. Maybe she's at least able to figure out what the meaning of it all was for her. I hope so.

Speaking of Uncle George, I made sure he got his gen-enged tree. It's growing in my garden, right outside the window. We are all getting rich, incidentally, we Pooles and Bazalgets.

John moved fast to patent as much as he could of the information derived from images and scans of Alia, and indeed Morag, in the name of EI and ourselves. The genomic studies seem likely to yield fruit quickly. Longevity treatments may be the first big payoff: EI even has a trademarked name for their soon-to-be-announced product range, *AntiSenescence*, or AS. They are paying us for licences to investigate the material, and in future we'll take a small but serious cut of the profits.

Shelley has expressed doubts about polluting the timeline. After all we are patenting genetic and other enhancements which have been fed to us from the future; we will be introducing them centuries, millennia, before they are 'due'. I don't worry about that, any more than about the nonexistence of the Kuiper Anomaly. I take my lead from Alia, who seemed to have a robust view of time paradoxes. The universe can take a few punches from us without disappearing up its own paradoxical fundament. Things will work out somehow – or maybe they already have. I don't have any qualms about profiting from my experiences, frankly. I suffered enough; I believe I've a right.

Anyhow when all this unravels the Pooles are going to be rich. Alia and Leropa hinted at the exploits of my descendants. We've always been engineers, we Pooles, we've always been meddlers, and now we will have money, and money means the power to do things. I guess my own race is run. But I wonder what the Pooles will do with all that power in the future.

Sometimes I think all our adventures, we Pooles, are to do with a quest for God. Rosa's Coalescence, if George's analysis was right, was certainly superhuman, but no god, nothing but a mindless multiplication. Alia hinted that at mankind's peak the Exultant generation went to war at the centre of the Galaxy, and what we found there was very strange, unimaginably ancient and powerful. So the Exultants found God, and used Him as a weapon. And in Alia's time the Transcendents looked for God in the last place He might be hiding – deep within ourselves. But He wasn't there either. I guess we'll just have to keep looking.

As for me, I've returned to my work on the interstellar-probe application of the Higgs technology. I love it. I feel like I'm a kid on the beach once more, ten years old, throwing Frisbees with Uncle George.

You'd think that my exposure to the future might have crushed my confidence in what we can achieve. Alia, after all, was *born* on a starship, a ship that had been cruising for half a million years. How can my trivial little unmanned probe, a one-shot water rocket, compare to that? But I don't feel like that at all. This is what *I* can build, this is what I can contribute. Anyhow, *they* wouldn't have been able to achieve anything without me.

Suddenly, though, the starship study has become a lot more urgent. NASA engineers have been poring over our results, and there is talk of some serious money being pumped our way. The motive is clear. The Kuiper Anomaly has vanished. That strange, tetrahedral object drifting among the dead comets and ice moons of the outer solar system, only discovered within my own lifetime, has suddenly disappeared. There's not a trace of its passage; it just went. And so people want to find a way to get out there, to find out what the hell is happening. It's ironic that the probe's disappearance has created more interest and alarm than its presence ever did. But then, while the Anomaly was evidence that there had once been other minds, its removal is proof that those minds *are still acting*.

I know, as very few others do, that the true purpose of the Kuiper Anomaly was to mediate the linking of the future with the past; it was the channel through which the Transcendent generation was able to reach us – reach *me*. When the Transcendence collapsed, its projects abandoned, the construction and launch of the probe in their future was aborted - and so it never reached our past.

I think reality has changed. I think the probe never existed, and I don't think any exploring astronauts are going to find any trace that anything was ever out there at all. Of course that begs the question of how come I remember the thing, how come there are libraries full of decades' worth of space-telescopic records of its presence. I try not to think about that.

I'm glad it's gone, though. The Kuiper Anomaly was a physical manifestation of the meddling of the Transcendents in our time. The more I think about the vast scope of their ambition, the more I resent their galling instrumentalism. Maybe I have more of Tom in me than I imagine.

But we have options. Think about it. *They* are up there in the far future, off in the highest branches of a huge tree. But we are at the tree's roots. And if we cut off the tree at the trunk, even the highest branch will come crashing to the ground. If nobody was to have another child ever again, for instance, then not one of the Transcendents could ever be born. There are no doubt less drastic ways to fight a war with the future.

I'm not advocating this, you understand. But perhaps we

should wargame options. If the future attacks us again, we should fight back.

Today is the first of January, 2048. The digital millennium has come and gone, and all those date registers in all those antique processors have absorbed the extra binary digit without so much as a squeak; there is no news of problems anywhere. Another disaster averted. Happy New Year.

Sometimes, however, I despair.

I look around at the world, I follow the news, and I count up what we've lost even in my own lifetime. And I know, from my contact with Alia, that Earth's ecology won't recover from the tremendous shock we have inflicted, not even in half a million years.

Once I tried to express all this to Gea. She told me to go outside, to the scrap of garden I share with the other tenants of this block, where George's tree grows, and to find an old piece of rotten log. I did as she asked. I found a chunk of crumbling wood, and turned it over. Roots and strands of fungi pulled apart, as if the ground didn't want to let it go, and a damp, cold, musty smell rose up from the thick dark earth that had been hidden beneath.

There was a whole shadowy world in there. A spider, her belly heavy with a white silk egg case, scuttled away to the shade. Millipedes coiled up into tight little spirals. A centipede squirted its slow way through a heap of bark fragments. But these naked-eye critters were the megafauna of Log-world. Following Gea's advice, I hacked off a chunk of the log with a knife, shook it out over a white handkerchief spread on the ground. I saw worms and mites and a dozen other sorts of creatures, wildly diverse in their body plans, all crawling around on my handkerchief. And even that wasn't the end of it. Gea showed me magnified images of droplets of water, each one swarming with billions of bacteria. The deeper you dig down the more tiny ecologies just keep popping up.

OK, we humans have made a mess of the biosphere we can see. But that's just a scraping of the planet's true cargo of life, and nothing we can ever do is going to make much of a dent in that crude mass. Such reflections are humbling. But they also comfort me. We shouldn't feel so bad about ourselves. Gea says she is trying to promote this kind of 'microaesthetic', to help us humans get a sense of perspective about ourselves. Vander was right; she does care about us.

Gea is a surprisingly good companion. She is smarter than me after all, and she will, with any luck, live for ever. Also the way she rolls about shooting sparks from her belly makes me laugh.

I sometimes think my collision with the Transcendence broke something inside me. Maybe I'm not who I was. But how would I know?

Here I am anyhow. I listen to the laughter of children, and I watch the sunlight dapple on drowned roads, and I dream of starships. Things could have turned out a lot worse, I guess.

But I'll always miss Morag.